PAM C

EARL FOR A SEASON

When Roderick Anhurst returns to England after a diplomatic posting in British North America, he finds himself heir to an unwelcome earldom. Not only that, an old flame is determined to reclaim her old beau — by fair means or foul! Unfortunately, the Earl of Selchurch is falling in love with lively, independent Julia, a lady as lacking in respect for wealth and high estate as he is himself. Meanwhile, the Dowager Countess of Selchurch is nursing a secret — a secret she calls a miracle. Will this miracle be the means by which Roderick will escape from his quandary?

BRENDA DOW

EARL FOR A SEASON

Complete and Unabridged

ULVERSCROFT
Leicester

First published in Canada in 2000

First Large Print Edition
published 2004

This is a work of fiction. Names, characters,
places and incidents are either the product of the
author's imagination or are used fictitiously, and any
resemblance to any person or persons, living or dead,
events or locales is entirely coincidental.

British Library CIP Data

Dow, Brenda
    Earl for a season.—Large print ed.—
Ulverscroft large print series: general fiction
1. Love stories
2. Large type books
I. Title
813.6 [F]

ISBN 1–84395–288–2

Published by
F. A. Thorpe (Publishing)
Anstey, Leicestershire

Set by Words & Graphics Ltd.
Anstey, Leicestershire
Printed and bound in Great Britain by
T. J. International Ltd., Padstow, Cornwall

This book is printed on acid-free paper

Prologue

Miss Stride brought the news to Mallow.

A wiry figure even in her shawl-draped pelisse, she jumped hurriedly from her father's old gig, pausing only to throw the travel rug over the steaming horse, and ran up to the rambling old house. Her impatience was such that after a spirited knock, she thrust open the front door and entered.

'Charlotte! What ever is the to-do?' A calm, musical voice spoke from the stairs. A tall, elegant young woman paused in her descent, one hand on the banister.

'Julia! Where is Ivor?'

'Probably shaving.' Julia Valliant looked at the unexpected visitor curiously. The face before her, attractive in a sharp-featured way, was glowing, either with excitement or from her long drive on that crisp February morning.

'Will he be down soon? I have awful news.'

Julia's humorous gray eyes were wide with astonishment. 'Tell me! Your papa has been made bishop and you must move to York — somewhere further?'

'Julia! This is no time for your jokes.'

1

Charlotte Stride brushed a frosting of snow off her half-boots. 'I bear the most terrible news! Oh, when will Ivor be down?'

'I am baffled. You come in here positively dancing with news, but then you call it terrible.'

'No, no!' exclaimed Charlotte in contrition. 'You mustn't think I am lacking in proper . . . respect. The news is truly dreadful. It's just that . . . well, sometimes good might come out of bad.'

Julia descended the last step. 'This confusion is not like you. Oh, my dear, you are all of a tremble. Unwrap and come into the drawing room. There's a good fire in there. You shall have some hot chocolate to warm you up.' Taking a moment to convey the appropriate request to the kitchen, she returned to help the visitor with her pelisse.

From upstairs, they heard a voice bellowing for Eli March to go out and look after Miss Stride's horse. Charlotte Stride glanced up the stairs expectantly. 'He knows I'm here, at least.'

Julia tucked her arm into that of the smaller woman and led her into the drawing room. 'If my brother is to be first recipient of your news, I will contain my curiosity. How is your papa?'

'Well enough!' There was a sarcastic smile.

'But not well enough for a bishop. His dyspepsia still bothers him.'

'I shall be down directly, Lottie,' continued the voice from on high. A few moments later, a heavy tread sounded in the hall and Sir Ivor Valliant's bulk filled the doorway.

'So the basilisk's dead, eh?'

Charlotte's eyes glinted. 'So you know!'

'Not till now! Heard he came a cropper, though. The news is all over the countryside. Didn't make it through the night, I trow!' He came forward in bluff concern at seeing her rubbing frozen hands. 'Come, sit closer to the fire, pickle! It's a cold day for a ten mile drive.'

'The Earl of Selchurch is dead?' Now serious, Julia looked from one to the other. 'An accident? What happened, Charlotte?'

'It is true, rest the poor man's soul. Sir Basil was putting a hunter at a barrier and the horse fell. It rolled on him. He could get to his feet, I'm told, but had to be carried home. A doctor was there within hours, but could do nothing. My father was ministering to him all night till he died in the small hours.'

'A little late for Basil Selchurch to find religion!'

His sister remonstrated mildly, 'Ivor! For heaven's sake! Consider Charlotte's position!'

Sir Ivor shrugged. 'If Lottie cares a scruple

about Selchurch, 'tis the first I've heard of it. The Countess — that's a different matter. We all know how devoted Lottie is to her.' He put his arm round Charlotte's shoulders and gave her a quick hug. 'Besides, she knows what I think of Basil, and wouldn't want me to be a hypocrite, would you, chuck?'

Charlotte pressed his hand. 'I can't spare long. I must get back to the Countess. Oh, to think! I should call her Dowager Countess now.' A thought struck her. 'Pray heaven her babe will be a boy.'

Julia looked interested. 'The Countess of Selchurch is increasing again? Then I add my wishes to yours, for otherwise her home will go to whomever succeeds to the earldom. Then where would she and all those girls of hers go?'

Charlotte seemed to have no answer for this. She was looking into Ivor's face with some intensity. Sir Ivor wore a thoughtful expression while scratching his hastily brushed poll. Though he was never at his best early in the morning, the news seemed to have had a stimulating effect on him.

Hiding a smile, Julia hastily made the excuse that she had business in the kitchen and left. This subterfuge lost credibility as she passed the housekeeper bustling in with hot chocolate.

An uneasy silence fell between the man and woman remaining in the drawing room. Charlotte studiously sipped her chocolate. Sir Ivor partook of a cup, and made a great thing of cooling his drink by blowing on it.

Eventually, he glanced across at her rather tentatively. 'Why don't you stay for the day? Your papa was up all night. He won't be needing the gig. Give the nag a rest! Julia has some new sheets of music sent up from London. You might like to give them a try.'

Charlotte rose and stamped her foot. 'Why are you talking about music? Can't you see what this means for us? The Countess will never stand in our way.'

Sir Ivor went a little red, but stood up to her manfully. 'There's where I'm ahead of you, dumpling.' A flash of anguish crossed the sharp little face looking up at him. 'I've already decided. I'll be calling on your papa first thing tomorrow.'

His reward was a transforming smile and a face raised to receive his kiss.

Julia had gone upstairs to her bedroom. She spent some time gazing out the window, not really seeing the bleak wintry scene.

Her own life must face repercussions from the death of the Earl of Selchurch. Well, life was prone to change, she told herself. She had lived with her brother and run his household since their mother had died, but now there would soon be a new mistress at Mallow. For several years, Sir Ivor had been conducting a semi-despairing, low key courtship of the daughter of the parson who had the living at Selchurch. However, an obstacle had lain between them because of a feud between Sir Ivor Valliant and the Earl of Selchurch. Rival magistrates, they had long differed over certain jurisdictional matters. The dead Earl had been a haughty and vengeful man, and Charlotte had refused to make a commitment for fear that her marriage to the Earl's enemy would prejudice her father's livelihood.

Julia had no doubt that Charlotte's friendship with the Countess would now remove that obstacle. A wedding would go forward. However, much as she enjoyed the occasional company of her brother's intended, she had a leaden feeling inside when she contemplated life at Mallow when Charlotte became Lady Valliant. She would naturally assume responsibility for running the house and Julia's position would become that of an unnecessary dependent. While she would never be made to feel less than welcome, the prospect did not suit her. Charlotte was honest, fair-minded and imbued with a satirical outlook that melded well with Julia's gentler humor. Julia appreciated Charlotte's many good qualities, but she knew that inevitably they would rub up against one another. Charlotte's straitlaced practicality would be at war with Julia's own preference for the relaxed, unhurried surroundings presently prevailing at Mallow. Charlotte would strip the ivy from the walls for she liked a modern look. The garden would be regimented into formality. Ivor would not mind. He had no great interest in the garden, nor the house, as long as the windows admitted no draughts and the chimneys were swept yearly. However, Julia loved the old place just as it was, and knew that Charlotte's tastes were far different from her own.

No, she would not stay long at Mallow. She would have her own home; but before that, she would indulge her ambition to travel. There was so much world to see! Her fortune was moderate, but with care would afford her sufficient means to visit a few foreign places. Later she would set up an establishment independent of her brother. Of course, Ivor would say it was out of the question for an unmarried gentlewoman to travel unless under the aegis of some respectable family. She did not know of any available respectable family, but did not despair of making some suitable arrangement. Ivor must realize that she would not stay at Mallow forever.

When she descended, she discovered not much to her surprise that Charlotte had already left, driven by a sense of duty to the family that had been her father's support.

'Where did you disappear to?' queried Ivor. 'I sent Lottie home with a fresh horse. I can make an exchange when I drive over to the Parsonage tomorrow.'

Julia had no need to enquire what business would take him to visit Mr. Stride on the following day. She put on a cheerful tone. 'Has Charlotte named a day?'

Her brother bent a knowing eye upon her. 'Well, as to that, we should let his lordship's bones chill for decency's sake. I'll not wait out a year, though. I've a fancy for a summer wedding trip to the continent now that we've seen the end of Boney.'

'Charlotte will enjoy that. When you get back, she will like to have the running of the house to herself. Then it will be my turn to travel.'

'Not that again, Ju! Dash it! You know my feelings. Papa would never have allowed it.'

'But, Ivor, you are not my papa!'

Julia gave him a peck on the cheek and left him to scowl in solitude.

1

The light gray traveling coach threaded its way through the busy London thoroughfare and eased to a halt in front of a hotel. A servant in maroon and silver livery sprang down and held open the door whilst his fellow started to pull baggage from the roof. Porters came scurrying out.

Roderick Anhurst cast an astonished eye over the façade of the bow-windowed building. 'The Pulteney? What maggot got in your respected papa's head, Cy? Pretty much for a lowly attaché!'

He grinned. 'Better than the reception I expected!'

His companion spoke with a low sultry voice. 'Are you still brooding about a few silly setbacks? You were not even in Montreal. The war is over now. No blame attaches to you, Roddie!'

'So you say. But they recalled the Governor General. It has been my observation that when a man goes down, his minions do not prosper.'

'Minions! For shame! I shall tell papa you are a hopeless case.'

9

'In truth, I enjoy my work. I liked the country. I would rather not be forced to relinquish my career.'

'You are too foolish. Papa has everything well in hand.'

'Even when he uses you as his courier?'

She chuckled. 'You are a prude, my dear. You always were.'

'And you are outrageous, and always will be.'

He gave her one last appreciative look as he thrust his portfolio under one arm and took hat in hand. The twilight served to mystify rather than to shadow her dark blue eyes, and long lashes spiked down over a delicately molded cheek. Smooth lips curved into provocative lines. The fates had been generous to Lady Cytherea FitzWarren, bestowing both wealth and beauty.

As he alighted from the coach, the new gas lighting, recently installed in Piccadilly, caught glints of gold in his fair unruly hair and threw his well-knit figure into relief. Any woman would consider his pleasant, well-bred countenance attractive.

Lady Cytherea moved across to the near window, putting her hand on his sleeve to detain him. 'You will think me a goose. In my vast excitement at seeing you again, I forgot! I am postman as well as courier.' She handed him a package. 'These letters were at papa's office awaiting your return.'

Roderick took the package, and touched his lips to the tips of her fingers, eyes looking up suspiciously at the innocent expression on her face.

As he watched the carriage proceed along Piccadilly, he was conscious of a feeling of relief. Why should he feel that way, he wondered?

It had been a very strange day! She must have boarded the frigate standing in the searoads off Deal from the pilot's galley. She had arrived in his quarters bearing a document urgently requesting his presence at the Colonial Office. However, since he was returning to England following the same orders delivered in Upper Canada, he was puzzled by the need for Lord FitzWarren to send his daughter on a courier's mission, and sans chaperon, at that! He suspected her of running some rig on her father, especially as she had just now 'remembered' to give this new package of correspondence.

She had flung herself into his arms and kissed him with all the passionate abandon he remembered so well. Three years ago, when he had stayed at Lord FitzWarren's country seat, he had become besotted with his daughter, and events had got out of control.

Yet, when passion and a sense of obligation spurred him to apply for permission to marry the fashionable Lady Cytherea FitzWarren, she had, in great despair, warned him that her father would have none of him. Although his career prospects were bright and he was, in addition, possessed of a moderate private income, his wealth would not be considered sufficient to win her hand. It had seemed no coincidence to him that within the week he had peremptorily been dispatched on assignment to Quebec — and that without having an actual interview with Lord FitzWarren. There had been a heart wrenching leave-taking between Lady Cytherea and himself in which neither had laid any obligation upon the other, and he had sailed across the Atlantic feeling that his heart would never be whole again. Thus he had learned the danger of going beyond the mark with an unmarried female of his own class.

He grieved for a year. Then, a lively widow in Montreal turned the direction of his thoughts. This affair had finished when the widow sailed out of his life to Paris. They had parted friends, this time undisturbed by any feelings of guilt on either part.

He had thought Lady Cytherea FitzWarren would be wed to some young lord by now. (It had been three years.) This speculation, when occasionally entertained, had given him no pangs at all! He smiled and shrugged as he turned towards the entrance.

The staff of the Pulteney were extraordinarily accommodating — 'my lord' this and 'your honor' that. He found himself suddenly homesick for the modest pension he had inhabited in Montreal.

He shrugged off his coat as soon as he was settled in his room, and sat at a desk. After opening the package of letters, he put aside one large, official-looking document and one other screw of paper with no writing on the outside, and slit open the wafer on a familiarly scented missive. His mother's letter, dated in March, dwelt humorously enough with her indifferent health and made spicy observations about the many valetudinarians resident near Harrogate Spa — Anne, his sister, was to marry a gentleman from Surrey in April, all the details to follow — Cousin Alicia wrote that she was expecting another little Basil, God help her if it were a little Alicia again.

Roderick grinned. The Earl of Selchurch was still intent on getting an heir. For his money he would have preferred Maurice, the brother next in line, in the upper house. There was a line squeezed along one edge of the paper, as a post script, obviously scrawled

13

in haste and tapering into illegibility. He could make out, 'Cousin Basil dead after fall from horse. You are new Earl of Selchurch.' Then there was something about Alicia that defied interpretation.

'Oh, God, no!' he said explosively. He didn't want that. He rose and took a quick turn around the room. Rubbish! His mother was too anxious on his behalf. She had misled herself. Just because she and Alicia were first cousins, there was little chance that he had inherited the title. Too many males stood in line between Basil, a distant kinsman, and himself.

His eye fell on the more imposing document left for his perusal. He tore it open with a sinking heart. This was a letter from a firm of solicitors informing him of his good fortune in succeeding to the title of seventh Earl of Selchurch.

He found he was not comprehending more than the bald fact that his life must undergo unwelcome change. Numbly, he put that letter aside and opened the screw of paper. Directed to him in his new estate, it put forward the claims of a Miss Sophie Kettle to be his dependent. This last was signed by a Mrs. Shackle, who by design or carelessness had given no address. He cast the latter aside, wondering if it might herald a variety of ramps designed to take advantage of his new station in life. After calling for a bottle of claret, he settled himself to assimilate the text of the solicitor's communication. As he smoothed the creases in the stiff paper, something struck him forcibly: Cytherea knew! Dash it all! Why had she not told him?

He found a competent hotel servant to work miracles on his clothing, creased and in need of cleaning after so many weeks at sea, so that the following morning he could present himself, if not in the first flight of fashion, at least with the appearance of a gentleman at the new Colonial Office now established on Downing Street. Lord FitzWarren being unavailable, he delivered his reports to the most senior official present. This official struck a fine balance between deference and authority as he pulled forward a chair for him, and proved more than ready to release him from immediate duties to attend to matters made necessary by his change of estate. Indeed, there seemed to be a general assumption that his presence in the office was a mere formality before he relinquished his post with the ministry. There was no mention of his old chief, the Governor General. As he rose to go he asked about that gentleman's well-being.

'Sir George Prevost!' exclaimed the official,

and gave a twisted smile. 'You have not heard? He died in January. A week before he was to face court martial.'

Roderick left the office in a shocked state. Death seemed to be besieging him. His mood was not greatly alleviated when later that day he received a brief ceremonial visit at his hotel from the senior partner and founder of Brundall and Durrant, Solicitors. The thin, distinguished looking octogenarian explained to him in ponderous detail exactly how he had succeeded to the title. Roderick had known of the death of the late earl's heir of a brain fever whilst at Eton, and was reminded of Selchurch's youngest brother also lost to fever whilst a midshipman in the Caribbean. He was appalled to learn of the loss of his friend Maurice and all his family aboard a ship that foundered in the Bay of Biscay. The solicitor described in detail how the previous Earl of Selchurch had died of a lung punctured by a rib broken in a riding accident. The animal had rolled on him.

'His last words were 'Shoot the beast!'' reported the old man with some relish.

'He would!' muttered Roderick, but on Brundall's look of inquiry, he said, 'My cousin Basil's wife? My mother writes that she is again in the family way.'

'Alas, the poor lady! She lost the child a

few days later — the horror of seeing her husband brought home on a hurdle.'

Roderick was silent for several heavy seconds, contemplating the untimely loss of so many of his family, distant though they might be. There had been no male heirs from intervening branches of the family he learned.

'Then there is no help for me!'

'Don't say that, my lord. Our firm will be at your service, I do thoroughly assure you.'

'Before you take leave, there is one matter you might shed light on.' He laid the screw of paper before the solicitor. 'This Mrs. Shackle got in touch with me directly. Why, I am not sure, and I don't wish to jump to any commonplace conclusions. Is this an affair of any delicacy?'

Putting on his spectacles, Mr. Brundall perused the letter, frowning over the many spelling errors and malformed hand without surprise. 'Ah, yes, the matter of Miss Sophie Kettle!'

'Is there any basis to this person's claim? I barely knew the late earl — he was, in fact, a second cousin. What little I saw of him left me an impression of conscious rectitude — too top-lofty to allow any tarnish on his own reputation.'

The lawyer allowed himself a thin smile. 'No blemish at all, my lord. Miss Kettle is no child of his get.'

'No bones rattling in the closet?'

'I wouldn't use those terms, sir.' The octogenarian coughed delicately. 'The child in question is the twelve-year-old daughter of Lady Patience, Sir Basil's sister.'

'That can't be!' Roderick cried out. He did hasty mental arithmetic. 'Patience died — too many years ago. It was my first term at Winchester College — all of fifteen years ago. Whoever this Miss Kettle might be, Patience was not her mother.'

Mr. Brundall apologized for divulging a family secret so abruptly. He continued, 'I fear the previous Earl of Selchurch misled both family and acquaintance by having it understood that his sister was dead — as dead she was to the family. She was cast off subsequent to an unsuitable match.'

Roderick frowned. 'Damn him! My family would not have cast her off. I'll go bail that my parents were left in the dark.'

'No doubt! But her brother regarded her actions as heinous.'

Roderick eyed him sharply. 'My cousin Basil might have been a lord, but he was a complete commoner as far as I am concerned. He had little love for his sister. She was — unusual — and didn't ever conform to his idea of what his sister should be — not fair enough, not compliant enough.

18

So she married to 'disoblige her family' as they say. Bravo, Patience! She escaped her family custody.'

Frosty eyebrows rose. 'You don't understand the egregious nature of her act, my lord. Lady Patience left her home in company with a member of the household staff.'

'Who was the man?'

The solicitor seemed to have difficulty mouthing the words. 'A footman.' He hurried on, 'A terrible blow for the Earl, you must admit, my lord. The fellow was newly taken on. A plausible rogue with cozening ways, I must suppose, to lead a foolish young woman to act against all that was due her family.'

Roderick looked incredulous. 'Then the fellow was an unusual footman, I promise you, Patience was never a stupid woman — nor such a young one, come to think of it.'

'Oh, as for that, I gather he was a bright enough fellow. He had been, I am told, on the stage. No doubt work within a household might fill in a dry spell, as it were.' The old man showed his teeth, as if he had uttered a mild joke.

Roderick regarded the solicitor thoughtfully, wondering if there was any core of sympathy for his cousin under that dry, professional exterior. 'Patience was, I am sorry to say, not well appreciated by her family. I hope she found happiness.'

'Only of a transitory nature, I fear, sir! There was a marriage. Of course, Lady Patience had some little money of her own, which would have made her a desirable bride for a man in good circumstances, so you may wager a common man would have jumped at the chance. Twelve years ago a child was born who was christened Sophie Psyche Kettle, and the birth was registered in the Parish of St. Mary-le-Bow, if I recall. Soon after, the father, Kettle, again without work, took up prizefighting and got into trouble with the law. He was sentenced to the death penalty, which was subsequently commuted to transportation.'

'Good Lord! What was his crime?'

'The family kept aloof, I assure you, sir. But I hear it was theft of prize money.'

'What happened to Patience — and her child? Did Basil do nothing for them?'

'I doubt if the lady would have wished to come back to her family in such undignified circumstances,' Brundall remarked sanctimoniously. 'Shame alone would forbid it.'

Roderick swallowed a sharp comment. Obviously the solicitor had been more in sympathy with the standards of his old client. However, quarreling with him would do nothing to mend the past.

'What of Lady Patience?'

'She died some three years ago. The child was taken by a sister of Kettle's.'

'And my esteemed cousin? Even then he had no interest in the child, I presume.'

'His sister was cast off. Her child would mean nothing to him. The child of a prizefighter, a convict — a play actor — the offspring of a servant!'

'This Mrs. Shackle is Kettle's sister, then?'

'I am unfamiliar with the name. Kettle's sister was a Mrs. Argyle. Possibly she remarried — or married for the first time, considering she was an actress.' He flicked the letter with a contemptuous finger. 'I would suggest that you do not see the woman, or, if she persists and causes you annoyance, refer her to me. It was obviously the wish of the late earl that this connection be severed for all time.'

Roderick's tones were of the driest. 'I will, of course, remember my cousin's wishes, but, if this lady should get in touch with you, be so kind as to send her to me. As I told you, I had a fondness for Lady Patience, and feel a duty towards her daughter.'

The next few days were full for Roderick, visiting his tailor for a needed update to his wardrobe and attending to melancholy correspondence necessitated by the recent deaths of his cousin Basil and of his late chief. He called at the Selchurch townhouse but learned that the Dowager Countess of Selchurch had retired to the country estate. He made no attempt to change his quarters to the townhouse as it was no part of the entail. He sought out an old chum from his school days, only to find Joseph Rayne away from home, and was obliged to leave his card with the name of his hotel scrawled on the reverse. A meeting at the ministry kept him in town until the Thursday, and after that he was free to post north to see his mother.

On the Friday, Roderick rose early, planning to pay a visit of condolence to the Countess at Bishop's Rise, some fifty miles from London and not too far out of his way on the long journey to Harrogate. He had barely finished a light repast of coffee and rolls when a porter of contemptuous mien brought a note to his door requesting that he receive Mrs. Shackle and Miss Kettle.

The woman who was conducted to his door was obviously not of a high order of society. Her clothes looked as if they had been seized at random from the racks of a traveling show; clothes of previous eras in satins and other unidentifiable materials in shades of dark red and crimson were mercifully disguised by a rusty black pelisse overtop. Her bizarre appearance was enhanced by a huge straw bonnet over a goffered cap. Her shoes were much run down at heel. She assumed a creditable air of confidence as she sailed forward into the room.

Her young companion hung back until Roderick invited her in with a gentle smile. Despite his benign exterior, he was by no means gullible, and he surveyed her critically as she edged in. He noticed with misgiving that she was carrying a rather battered bandbox. The child's stature was thin and gawky, but of an average height for a twelve-year-old.

A better effort had been made with her appearance. A plain blue woolen dress had once seen better days. It was neat and clean, but the skirt cleared the ground by a few more inches than was seemly, and the sleeves revealed an inch of white flesh over black gloves that showed signs of neatly stitched mending. Her clothing did not otherwise appear tight on the girl. Only in height was she outgrowing them. A plain bonnet, refurbished with narrow, striped ribbon framed a countenance that resembled Patience not at all. If anything, her face was more pleasing, her nose straighter, her eyebrows more arched. But then, Patience had never looked patrician. Miss Sophie Kettle, if this truly were she, must have got her looks from her father. However, there was a stubborn set about the mouth that reminded him of his old friend.

He saw Mrs. Shackle to a chair. After taking the bandbox from the younger lady, he set it down in a corner and pulled forward another chair. With a gesture almost of defiance, she moved over to the window and stared up at the chimney pots. As he saw her in profile, a gawky, slightly stooped figure, yet throwing her chin in the air, in that one awkward, defiant gesture he saw Patience, when he, as a much younger child, had first met her. Schooling his face into a noncommittal expression, he invited Mrs. Shackle to explain the nature of her business.

'My lord, you may well ask! To lay it out plain, this young girl, what has been left in my charge for six months, should more properly be wiv 'er own family. She was left wiv 'er aunt, Mrs. Argyle — you'd know 'er — a most talented star on the boards, and 'as been seen at Covent Garden Theatre time out of mind. 'Er mother, what was a sister of your cousin Lord Basil, died of lung sickness, and since then Mrs. Argyle and me looked arter 'er. Lissie — that's Mrs. Argyle — up and died on me, what was her dresser for twenty-two years, and now I'm out my employment. The money's run out, and I jus' can't keep Soikey no longer.'

Roderick turned towards the girl. 'Come and sit down, Miss Kettle, as this so particularly concerns you. Or may I call you Sukey?'

'My name is not Sukey!' The small defiant voice issued from the window recess.

Mrs. Shackle rolled her eyes heavenward. 'Oh, beg pardon, my dear, I'm sure. Soikey. That's what her papa called her. She never can abide it. Well Miss Sophie, then, what is to become of yer? Come sit down as the gentleman says! I can't afford the dressin' of 'er — great girl that she is! And what about the schoolin' of 'er? I can't afford to set 'er apprentice to some genteel occupation, and 'oo's goin' to want a lord's niece working as a maid? Besides 'er bein' so wild-like, running off to some fair or raree show, as soon as one turns one's back.'

'What news of her father? Is he alive?'

Mrs. Shackle sniffed loudly. 'We can forget 'im. 'E's not seen fit to come arter 'er.'

In the corner of his eye Roderick saw Sophie's head turn quickly, and caught a fierce look directed at Mrs. Shackle that seemed to give her the lie. 'What exactly is it that you expect of me, Mrs. Shackle?'

'Well, you're the new 'ead of the family, ain't yer? She's a good enough girl, but she's no kin 'o mine. I jus' lost — '

A discreet tap on the door interrupted her grievance. A lackey presented a salver bearing an embossed card with the inscription, The Honorable Joseph Rayne. Roderick picked it up, and slipped a coin to the lackey. 'Ask the gentleman to be sure to wait. I will be down in a trice.'

Roderick turned to Mrs. Shackle. 'It would be better if we had more help for this matter. Give me your direction, and I can make arrangements for us to meet at my cousin's solicitors later this month.'

'I started to tell yer, I jus' loss me 'ome, sir, so I can't do that nowise. I barely saved some of me furniture, an' that's gone by now. Besides, my Miss Lissie got nowhere with them lawyers, so I want nuffink to do with 'em.'

'Look, we'll sort this out in a little while. May I ring for refreshments for you? Coffee or a chocolate, perhaps, Mrs. Shackle? Miss Kettle?'

Mrs. Shackle looked tempted by this unlooked for attention from a nobleman, but resolutely refused. Sophie darted a quick look at him and shook her head.

'Obviously this discussion is not at an end. You must excuse me for a few moments. I am called to the lobby — a meeting I must not miss. I'll be back as soon as I may.'

It was an awkward situation to leave them alone in his room, but he did not intend to keep his old Winchester College friend kicking his heels in the lobby for ages. The present situation was not going to be resolved in ten minutes. He descended to the main floor, where he found Rayne studying *the Morning Chronicle* with puckered brow. His friend's face lit up as he approached.

'Ricky!'

'Hon Joe, in the flesh! Great to see you!' They shook hands enthusiastically. Joe punched Roderick in the chest, and he responded by clapping the other on the shoulder.

'How long has it been?'

'More than three years, and a total of two letters from you in that time, you dog. Come into the coffee room.' They ambled into that busy sanctuary and nabbed a table near a window.

'Up and shaved at this hour, Ricky? You didn't used to be up with the lark.'

'Stow it! You're talking to a working cove here. Actually, I'm posting north.'

'I expected to cadge a breakfast with you. Sorry I missed you the other day — I just got in from Newmarket.'

'How was your luck?'

'Comme çi, comme ça! Almost broke even!'

Roderick grinned. 'A matter for congratulation where you are concerned, I seem to recall. Look, Hon Joe, unfortunately I've breakfasted, and I can't ask you up to my rooms — business, and dashed inconvenient.'

Rayne cocked an cynical eye. 'Petticoat business?'

'Not what you're thinking. A family matter.'

'This earl thing not all it's cracked up to be?'

'Knowing as ever,' complained Roderick. 'Why don't you take breakfast here, and I'll expedite this matter — postpone it, if I can, and see you in a while.' As he spoke, a monstrous straw hat sailed by the elevated bow window of the coffee room. 'Wait a minute!' Springing to the window, he looked out just in time to see Mrs. Shackle clambering into a hackney. He craned his neck but could catch no sight of Sophie Kettle. 'Damn! I suspect my problem just got worse!'

Rayne had followed his lunge towards the window. 'Gad! Everyone has gruesome relations, but that one takes the laurels.'

'No relation, thank God. But she was only half my problem. I've got to leave you now.'

'Oh, no you won't! Don't cut me out of your problems, old chap. I'm good at advice.'

Roderick pulled a derisive face.

'No, really! M' parents wanted me to go into the church.'

'The church got a narrow escape! Come up with me, then!' As they climbed the stairs, he gave Rayne a brief outline of what had transpired, stressing his reliance on the other's discretion.

They found Miss Kettle still standing by the window. Her eyes rested fleetingly on the stranger accompanying Roderick. Breaking her rigid stance, she retrieved her bandbox, and walked to the door.

'You are leaving us?' asked Roderick warily. 'Where did Mrs. Shackle go?'

Sophie paused at the door. 'She must be going to her sister's. I don't know where, so there's no point in asking me. Out of the city, somewhere.' Her little, tight voice was low pitched.

'She has abandoned you, hasn't she?'

There was a quick nod. Her face was taut. 'She can't help me any more. I thought she'd go. I only stayed because — I thought maybe she'd come back — and I didn't want to be rude.'

'Rude? What would be rude?' Roderick was pleased to hear that her accents showed a refinement which owed nothing to the speech of Mrs. Shackle.

She looked surprised. 'Just to walk away. You are some sort of kin of mine, I suppose. I wouldn't have you think I'd no manners.'

'See here, girl — Miss Kettle, is it — what will you do?' demanded Rayne.

'Anything! I can do anything! The stage! I shall go on the stage.' Squaring her shoulders, she walked away, leaving two bemused gentlemen staring at each other.

Roderick broke the silence. 'My cousin, Patience, was a proud, bristly creature. This girl is my cousin's daughter, I truly believe, and she could be another such who would cut off her hand as soon as act in her own self-interest.'

'Your troubles seem to have disappeared for the moment.'

'You're supposed to be my conscience, here.'

'I'd be tempted to say 'why would you want her around,' but I suppose you've got a duty now you're the Earl and all.'

'She's a twelve-year-old girl. If she wanders off, abandoned or from some misplaced sense of pride, who knows where she'll end up! The landlady will likely put her in the Fleet for debt.'

'And that's not the worst that could happen.'

They caught up with the child at the entrance, where an overzealous hotel flunky

30

was physically ousting her from the hotel. His shrill voice disturbed the serenity of the elegant vestibule. 'Out you go, you drab! We don't want the likes o' you here.' The bandbox was about to follow precipitously out the door, as Rayne seized hold of it, drawing blood from the fellow's nose with a well placed elbow as he did so. 'Hotel staff should handle goods with greater care,' he drawled.

Roderick helped Sophie to her feet. She brushed her skirts and hurled a choice epithet at the discomfited attendant who was backing into the hotel lobby, trying to stop blood flowing onto his resplendent livery.

Rayne joined them on the flagway. 'Dashed embarrassing! If I were you, I wouldn't use this place again, Ricky — remove the patronage of the Earl of Selchurch and all.'

Roderick grinned. 'Consequence takes some getting used to. Look, Miss Kettle! It's not that I wouldn't conduct you back and insist on a proper apology, but it so happens I have a chaise ordered for ten o'clock. It must be ready by now. Let us go and find it. Mr. Rayne here will sit in it with you while I go and get my traps. Then we shall decide what should be done.'

'You don't have to do anything for me,' said Sophie.

'Yes, I do!' Roderick looked at her grimly,

wondering exactly what approach he should take with this proud child. 'Damme, you're as independent as Patience was.' He noticed a quick interest awakened by the mention of her mother. He continued with authority, 'Mrs. Shackle came to me because I am the head of your family. She behaved perfectly correctly. Therefore, you will enter my carriage and stay there till I get back.' His eye connected with Rayne's and that gentleman gave a gloomy nod.

Roderick paid his shot at the hotel, wondering what sort of shredded reputation he would leave in his wake. While he waited for his baggage to be strapped onto the back of the chaise, he thought furiously. It certainly was inappropriate for a bachelor to have charge of child on the brink of womanhood, but his acquaintance in London was neither large nor particularly close.

'Take her up to your mother,' suggested Rayne. 'You can't look after her.' He coughed. 'No chaperone and all that!'

Roderick shrugged. 'Too far! A trip like that would be no more eligible than putting the girl up here.'

Sophie showed signs of alarm. 'I'll not leave London!'

Rayne ignored this. 'I don't suppose — '

'Suppose what?'

'Your old friend, Lady Cytherea? She lives in London.'

'Why on earth would you — ? She's gone out of town.'

'Glad to hear it! Step carefully in that direction, Ricky.'

Roderick looked at his friend narrowly. 'In what way?'

'You know the ton. Always ready to make gossip. Don't poker up at me, old fellow! Here! Something to read on your way!' Rayne thrust the Morning Chronicle under his friend's arm. 'Compliments of the hotel.'

'Compliments, my foot! You purloined it, you reprobate!' He gave his friend a salute as the post chaise moved off. He had already decided that his only alternative might be to leave the girl at the Selchurch estate. He explained to Sophie that the Countess of Selchurch was a person of much kinder heart than her late husband.

'I don't want to go out of town. You can't make me go!'

Hearing panic in her voice, Roderick stared at her nonplused for a few moments. 'Believe me, you'd be better off with your family than on your own. Anything we do now is just temporary — until proper arrangements can be made for you. You will like the country. You're used to the city, I know, but you shouldn't be scared of something new.'

'I ain't scared of anything!' Her voice rose.

'No, Sophie, I'm sure you aren't.'

She peeked up at him swiftly. 'Why are you laughing, then?'

He continued to smile. 'So like your mother!'

'What do you mean?'

'Oh, I remember your mother. Patience was much older than I, but I like to believe that we were friends. She could be independent and cantankerous, just like you.'

'Cantankerous?'

'Yes, cantankerous! And I will not allow too great a degree of independence in my old friend's daughter. She would want me to make sure you were safe.'

She seemed a little mollified. 'She'd want me to stay in London.'

'I can't imagine why.'

Suddenly, big tears were welling in her eyes and threatening to fall. 'How else is my papa ever to find me?'

'Look, child, I will give you my word. When I return to London, I will find out all about your papa. There must be records to reveal his status. That is a solemn, solemn promise.'

While Sophie watched the city view yield to small villages and then open countryside, Roderick cast a cursory eye over *the Morning*

Chronicle before putting it aside. Leaning back, he half-closed his eyes, and was amused to watch Sophie craning her neck to read some of the closely printed paragraphs.

'You like to keep up with the news?' he asked, in a rallying fashion.

She straightened quickly. 'Oh, yes sir! But newspapers have not often come my way.' She looked a little chagrined to make this admission, and he felt ashamed to have teased her. It was not to be expected that a girl of her age, even one studying under the most exceptional of governesses, would have sufficient awareness of current affairs to enjoy a newspaper.

'How well do you read?'

'Very well!' she replied with dignity. 'My mother taught me. She had lots of books.'

Roderick had heard Patience referred to as a Bluestocking, and smiled at a vision of Patience running away from home, packing her baggage, not with clothes or jewels, but her faithful books. Numbered among them would have been a bible, standard fare for reading instruction for small children from his own experience.

'Mama gave me one book of my own — *Tales from Shakespeare*.'

Roderick nodded. 'By the Lambs. I've heard of it, though it's never come my way.'

'I've always kept it, though we had to sell the others. Then, when we went to live with Aunt Lissie, she would always have parts around, so I read grown-up plays, not just stories.'

He raised his eyebrows. Not so standard fare for a twelve-year-old, he thought.

She smiled beatifically. 'Oh yes. Lots of Shakespeare. And I've trod the boards, you know. I was Cobweb!'

'Were you indeed? Well, Sophie — may I call you Sophie? — we are cousins, even if a little distant. You'd better tell me more about yourself. Call it insurance against more surprises.'

She looked at him speculatively. 'You may call me Sophie. And what should I call you?'

A little startled, Roderick answered, 'How about Cousin Roderick? That would be appropriate.'

'Cousin Roderick!' She tried the syllables, making a great show of rolling the Rs. 'Your friend called you Ricky.'

He grimaced. Oh, to be put out of countenance by a twelve-year-old scrub of a girl! 'My friend has known me be a very long time,' he explained. 'He is entitled to do so. However, call me what is comfortable for you.'

Alert to a hint of frost in his voice, she said

36

cheerfully, 'Cousin Roderick it shall be, such a mouthful as it is!'

'Oh, read *the Chronicle*!' exclaimed Roderick in exasperation.

She grinned slyly, and picked up the newspaper while he closed his eyes for a while. For several moments she was immersed in sampling the various columns of political and society news, taking in those that piqued her interest or lay within her understanding of the adult world.

Suddenly, she said, 'What's 'marine' mean?'

'W'what?'

'Marine! What does it mean? I thought it was a soldier.'

'Oh! A marine is a soldier who serves from a ship as a base, but that word can mean anything to do with the sea.'

'On the marine scene! You were on the sea?'

Roderick sat up suddenly.

Her head turned down to the paper. 'It's talking about a ship ' . . . -da, -da -da - The new Earl of Selchurch was not among expected passengers disembarking at the Port of London last Monday. It was later learned that his lordship came ashore at Deal a day earlier.' Who is Lady C- F-?'

At that point, to her indignation, *the Chronicle* was ruthlessly snatched from her hand. In mounting fury, Roderick took in the rest of the item:

> It is further reported that a well-known ornament of London society, Lady C-F-, daughter of a highly placed Minister of the Crown, disembarked at Deal. Interestingly enough, this lady's name did not appear on the passenger list . . .

'Damn! Why couldn't she have been more — !' His jaw worked grimly. 'A lady whose name is not Discretion!' He moderated his tones. 'Never mind! It refers to a lady who was conducting some business on behalf of her father . . .'

'Oh!' The girl regarded him inscrutably.

They dined on the way, and it was already evening as they approached Bishop's Rise. With the sun low in the sky, they enjoyed a fine view of a glinting white classical structure built on a slight elevation, before the post chaise plunged into a twisting wooded drive to emerge on a gravel approach up to the Palladian entrance.

Not yet having furnished himself with cards embellished with his new style, Roderick presented one of his old stock to the butler. The man bowed deeply, obviously aware exactly who Mr. Roderick Anhurst was.

So, the Earl of Selchurch and Miss Kettle were ushered with all pomp into an unpretentious setting. Two ladies sat at a low table by the fire, poring over fashion plates.

The Dowager Countess of Selchurch rose to meet him. Her solemn curtsy, graceful for a tall women built on heroic proportions, reminded him that he was no longer a gentleman without degree. She was still a handsome woman, but her figure betrayed the depredations of producing several children.

'You take me by surprise, cousin! But you are most welcome.' Lady Selchurch gave a look of doubtful inquiry towards the young girl at his side. 'And this is Miss Kettle, I hear. Welcome to Bishop's Rise, my dear.' The name had brought no shade of recognition across the Dowager's face, and Roderick surmised that Lady Selchurch was unaware of her close relationship with the young girl. Was it possible she had never been told of Sophie's existence? This conjecture was in accordance with his experience of the late earl. While often behaving in a high-handed fashion, Selchurch had combined this trait with a secretive disposition.

Catching Roderick's meaningful glance, Sophie murmured awkward thanks.

After Roderick had expressed his condolences for the loss of her husband and said all that was proper, Lady Selchurch merely replied, 'I thank you. I have received your letter of sympathy. Until then I did not know you had returned to England.'

'I apologize that I am here on the heels of my letter. I should have given you better warning of my coming. Unfortunately a situation has arisen, the needs of which cause me to fall on your good nature. It is a rather long story.'

Lady Selchurch regarded Sophie for a moment. Noting that he made no immediate attempt to launch into that supposed long story, she said, 'Perhaps Miss Kettle, you might like to meet my daughters who are up in the schoolroom. I know Miss Stride will be delighted to take you up.' She turned to her companion who had stayed in the background. 'Would you be so kind, my dear?' To Roderick she complained, 'That tiresome Miss Randall is confined to bed with a sick-headache again today. Why I engaged so vaporish a governess, I don't know. Belle has been entertaining the younger ones, while Miss Stride and I were considering bride's clothes.'

Roderick vaguely remembered a pudgy infant named Arabelle from the last time he had visited the Rise. There had been another babe, he remembered. A pale boy who had even then been rather sickly. His death of a brain fever at Eton was only one of the chain of accidents that had landed Roderick in this drawing room at this moment.

Roderick smiled at Sophie and nodded encouragingly. Miss Stride had risen to her feet. As she took the girl's hand, it was to be seen they were somewhat of a height. Miss Stride was looking up at him quizzically, and he bowed slightly in her direction. A bold look for a companion, he thought as they left. Or did he recall the name of Stride? It had a familiar ring.

'Oh, and please, in due time, bring the children down for a visit.' Lady Selchurch turned to Roderick. 'You must know that it is our family practice to come together in the evening. Tonight, the children will especially enjoy making your acquaintance.' Tinkling a bell, Lady Selchurch sent for the tea tray, which arrived immediately. 'Sit down, Cousin Roderick.' She engaged him in commonplaces while she poured and offered macaroons. Was his voyage smooth? Had he heard from dear Mrs. Anhurst?

Eventually, Roderick broke in, 'You have been admirably discreet in restraining your curiosity about my young companion. I must thank you for not making close enquiries in the presence of your companion.'

41

'My companion — oh, Miss Stride! She is like a daughter to me. All honesty and responsibility. I can always rely upon her. We shall miss her. But I interrupt. Indeed, I am quite curious. A young relative on your mother's side, perhaps? I think I know all the Anhursts.'

Roderick drew a deep breath. 'Yes, a relative, but from your branch of the family more than mine. Will you be kind enough to care for her for a little while? She is Patience's daughter.'

Her surprise was genuine, her voice issued in something like a squawk, 'Aah! Tom Kettle! I had forgot his name. Kettle's daughter! They had a child?' Then in a shocked voice, 'Why have you brought her here?'

Carefully, Roderick allowed a few seconds to elapse before he spoke, and then did so deliberately. 'Because I had no option! She has nowhere else. Imagine the surprise I received on my return to England to find myself her guardian!' He narrated the events leading up to his depositing Sophie on her aunt's doorstep.

'But I never heard of her existence before this moment! Is this a take-in? Surely, if the solicitors — '

'There is no doubt she is a legitimate

family member.' There was a grim edge to Roderick's voice. 'The solicitors were well aware of her existence.'

'And by extension, my husband.' She fell silent, her lips compressed. Absently, she took a sip of tea, then, 'How like him! All too fond of his little secrets!'

'I need your help, Cousin Alicia.'

She moaned. 'But a footman's daughter.'

'Patience's daughter.'

'But Basil can't just have abandoned her! He may have cast Patience off, but she had money.' She looked at him. 'I remember hearing, she had six thousand of her own money.'

'Be sure I will find out what happened to that money,' declared Roderick, 'but in the meantime Sophie is destitute and in want of an upbringing.'

Lady Selchurch was quite affected. 'Poor little girl!'

'I am forced to put her on to you — for a few days at least. I am not asking forever. It falls to me to be responsible for her, but I am a bachelor — and living between hotels. How can I look after her? I know it is a lot to ask, particularly while you are in mourning. Please, Alicia, help me out for a little while.'

The Dowager spread her hands in rather bitter acceptance. 'Well, you are in the coach seat, Roderick. This house, this land — it all belongs to you. We are all, in effect, your pensioners.'

The young man reddened. 'As to that, I do not hold the child's care over your head. This house is your home for as long as you want it.'

'Foolish, Roderick! Your wife might disagree.'

He smiled. 'We need not cross that bridge yet.'

'We will try to make Miss Kettle welcome, though I don't know how she'll fit in after the life she must have led.'

'It is my intention to arrange education for her — maybe she should be sent away to school, but I need time to find a suitable place — any advice there would be helpful, Alicia — and, if necessary, arrange for caring guardians in the event that I am sent abroad again. I am not planning to resign my position with the colonial office.'

Lady Selchurch looked at him strangely and gave an enigmatic smile. 'By all means retain your post. A paid position should never be given up lightly.' She rang her bell again. 'I will have rooms made ready for you both.'

'I stay only one night, Cousin. I post north for Harrogate early tomorrow.'

At that point the younger members of the

schoolroom party erupted into the room. All the girls appeared to be small versions of their mother, golden roses cut from the same bush. Twin, bold-eyed viragoes of about fourteen years led the way, one dressed incongruously in breeches and ruffled shirt, followed by three more lively damsels ranging from about ten to six. A nursemaid followed, carrying a toddler.

One of the twins burst out, 'We're tired of *The Tempest*.'

Her sister added, 'We don't wish to play act anymore.'

Their mother admonished, 'Caroline! Katherine! Tell me all about it later. You must welcome your cousin Roderick, who is now Earl of Selchurch, you know. Come Linnet, Eve, Pauline — show your cousin how gracefully you can perform your curtsies.'

While these grave amenities were conducted, with reciprocal bows from their cousin, the eldest daughter entered the room. She was a budding beauty, with the large blue eyes of her mother and a wavy corn-colored mane that reached to the small of her back. Her chubbiness was a thing of the past.

Miss Stride followed close on her heels, with one arm round Sophie's thin shoulders. Sophie's face looked flushed and angry. After Lady Arabelle, the eldest daughter, had been

introduced, Miss Stride declared rather
ruefully, 'The Tempest raged a little too
realistically. You will find my talents as a fill-in
governess lacking, Lady Selchurch.'

Lady Selchurch waved her hand deprecat-
ingly. 'A minor squall, I'm sure, my dear. You
should have got them playing their instruments.' She turned to Roderick. 'You must
know that Miss Stride has taught the children
music over the years, and is a tremendous
favorite with them. She is particularly adept
at the harp, isn't that so, my dear?'

'The harp!' Roderick slapped his forehead
in self-disgust. 'Miss Stride — Miss Charlotte
Stride, of course! I apologize for a horrendous memory lapse. I should be drummed
out of the diplomatic service! I nearly
drowned you in the pond — a double injury
to forget about it. Even then you entertained
us on the harp. I remember. It was bigger
than you were.'

Miss Stride's lips bent into a mocking
smile. 'So many years ago it was.'

Lady Selchurch felt bound to affirm, 'Miss
Stride is our local Parson Stride's daughter.
Arabelle is to stand up with her at her
wedding at the end of July. I know we are in
mourning, but it will be quite a small local
ceremony. I thought it unexceptional to allow
her to participate, Charlotte being such an

old friend. Besides, Belle was set on it. There was no saying 'no.' The groom's sister, an excessively good-natured girl by all accounts, has made no objections, she being so much taller than Miss Stride.'

She drew the smaller children to her and had a few moments intimate talk with them. After dispensing wafers from the tea tray, she sent them up to bed, promising to come up to hear their prayers soon. At this point the butler brought his mistress the information that the parson's gig had arrived to take Miss Stride home.

Roderick had been making up for his earlier lapse by felicitating Charlotte Stride and learning that she was to wed a squire in the next county, Sir Ivor Valliant by name.

'I trust I shall have an opportunity of meeting your future husband, Miss Stride,' remarked Roderick, rising as she made her way towards the door.

Lady Selchurch spoke from her seat by the fireplace. 'In a few weeks, we will welcome both Sir Ivor and Miss Valliant to Bishop's Rise, I assure you, dear Charlotte. Come here, Sophie! Sit beside me! As you will be staying for a little while, I'd like to get to know you better. Try some refreshment! Our macaroons here at the Rise are quite special! After that we'll take you to your chamber. You must be tired after your journey.'

Prompted by her nervous glance, Roderick explained, 'You will be staying with Lady Selchurch for a little while. I know she will take good care of you. Tomorrow I must post on north to visit my mother. I shall be gone just a short while.'

'But why are you posting?' put in Lady Selchurch. 'Use Basil's carriage. Naturally, it is at your service.'

And so it was arranged. The following morning, Roderick paid off the postilion. The late earl's chaise was brought to the door with four horses harnessed up and a coachman placed at his disposal. Sophie maintained a stoical mien as she waved him farewell. That knot seems to hold, he thought to himself as the coach bowled away. Maybe he could extend his visit to a fortnight. Nothing untoward was likely to occur in the meantime.

2

The highway was unusually busy. Having twice been obliged to pull to one side, her wheels perilously close to the ditch, to allow the passage of a much faster vehicle, Miss Julia Valliant drove down into Beesley Dell with the intention of cutting over to a less traveled road. The cart track, which wound its way through the hollow, would eventually meet the byroad at the juncture of the lane leading up to Beesley's farm. She was bound on a visit to take some gammon and fresh eggs to a family beset by sickness some distance away. She had learned of its misfortune in the village earlier that day.

'You are the greatest slug in nature,' she scolded the aging carriage horse pulling the gig. With a supple wrist, she flicked the whip above the horse's head. He twitched his ear and broke into a brief trot but quickly reverted to a mincing amble.

She hoped she would not find the lane too muddy. A pleasant May had turned into an unsettled June and a quantity of rain had fallen over the last few days. A sharp wind had prompted her to don a snug close bonnet. Fortunately, she thought, in Beesley Dell the dashing Miss Valliant stood less chance of any acquaintance observing her dawdling along in this rickety old gig, which was all that was left in the stables after her brother's lightning depredations earlier that day.

According to Will, the old stable hand, Sir Ivor had led a hue and cry from Mallow, pressing into service any younger manservant or farmhand he could find, carrying away in his career: chaise, phaeton, his hunters and even Russet, Julia's own riding horse. Julia, walking back from the village, had seen the cortege erupting from the drive in a spattering of gravel. She thought she had caught a glimpse of the local constable in the gathering. Beyond wondering idly what signal event had galvanized the normally indolent squire into such concerted action, she had been more intent on taking immediate succor to Nell of the stricken family, who had once been a servant at Mallow.

Beyond warning the old nag of its danger of an imminent visit to the glue boiler (an idle threat) Julia resigned herself to the pace and let her thoughts drift. No doubt Ivor had been called out on some business connected with his role as magistrate. Civil disturbance seemed unlikely in their bucolic surroundings. The only possibility — even probability, she decided — was the setting of a prizefight in the vicinity. That might account for the number of sporting vehicles on the road. Ivor could not abide prizefighting, and with good reason. After a foolhardy encounter with a prizefighter, a friend of Ivor's youth, Philip Farlaine by name, had been reduced to a vegetative state that had lasted three years before mercifully death removed this burden from his parents. Julia sighed. Philip had been more than Ivor's friend. He had been her own intended husband, and during those years she had visited him many times, to sit with him and his mother. She had mourned him when he finally died, but nowadays scarcely thought about him any more. Her thoughts were on the future.

The lane through the dell was winding and narrow, but the grass and bracken by the cart track had been scythed recently. The dell ran roughly parallel to the busy road above it, and from time to time, the sound of carriages and hoofbeats filtered through to the sylvan trail.

The thud of a single horse trotting on the grass verge could be distinguished, and over to the side opposite the road she was conscious of a growing hubbub and even almost distinguishable shouting. The probability of some sporting event taking place in the farmer's field above was becoming a certainty. A gap in the trees showed a brambled wattle fence in a state of disrepair. It interspersed the hedgerow that protected livestock from straying over into the dell. The gap gave greater volume to the sounds.

A scrabbling sound drew her attention towards a youth slithering through the fence. There was a rattle of stones as the person tumbled down the scoop of the embankment and landed right in front of the gig. Wide, scared eyes looked up at the horse, but the nag stopped even before Julia could rein it in.

The youth stood up uncertainly. His face was scratched. His thin chest was heaving, and he was gasping for breath. A small hand clutched a tasseled cap over wispy hair. Julia thought he was on the point of running away.

'Are you hurt, boy?'

He controlled his breathing. 'No, miss, I — thank you!'

There were thrashing noises behind the fence above.

'Are you chased by Farmer Beesley's bull?'

There was a shake of the head.

' — or Farmer Beesley?'

Another small shake of the head but with less confidence.

The youth threw a panicky glance up the embankment, and moved to get out of the way of the gig. His leg gave way and he almost fell. As he took a further step he obviously could put no weight on his foot.

'Oh, you are hurt! What have you done to yourself?' Julia sprung down from the gig, and went to the youth.

He seemed almost angry. 'It is nothing! I'm forever turning over my ankle. It will be better presently.'

'Rubbish! You cannot walk on it.' She looked at him quizzically.

'Perhaps you'd rather wait here for whoever is chasing you.' She supposed him to have been up to some mischief. Filching barely ripe strawberries maybe. 'Show me your hands!'

The lad spread them wide before her, small, white hands with flat, curling thumbs — too delicate for the hands of a country lout. They showed no stain of juice.

'Climb up. I will take you — somewhere. Where do you live?'

The youth seemed unwilling to answer, but pulled himself awkwardly up to the seat of the gig and shifted over to make room for Julia. She didn't recognize him as belonging to any of the local families. It crossed her mind he might be a runaway.

'We'll carry on till we get to the road, and then you must direct me which way to take you.' She took whip in hand again, and urged the nag into a trot. 'You'll have to tell me. I can't hear thoughts.'

After some moments of silence, the lad said, 'I've not been stealing. I've not done anything wrong,' followed by another pause.

'Did I suggest you did? Well, maybe I inferred it. Should I apologize?'

She glanced at his profile. It was fine-featured with a straight nose and square chin. A bramble scratch ran down a cheekbone that was angular, but innocent of even a ghost of down. She guessed he could be no more than twelve or thirteen though his height might promise more. Her heart was moved by his scared expression. She found a handkerchief and offered it.

'Here! Your face is bleeding.'

He took it, muttering thanks.

There was a stir in the bushes ahead. The lad's small hand nipped Julia's sleeve. Suddenly, a man jumped out into the path of the gig. He was dressed in rough clothing, with a frieze coat, and loose kerchief around his neck. He presented a villainous appearance. This was no Farmer Beesley, nor any of his laborers that Julia remembered seeing. He raised one slab of a hand towards the gig.

Automatically Julia reined in, not wishing to run the fellow down. She scarcely needed to, the old horse was more than willing to stop. Afterwards, she thought she should have urged the nag on, but it probably had too much gumption to plough through such a roadblock, human or otherwise.

The man seized the bit. The horse snickered and tried to back away, causing the gig to pitch.

She was annoyed to find her mouth had gone dry. Obviously, this was the youth's pursuer, who had found an easier way down from the field above. She felt resentful that the boy had not been more forthcoming about the large nature of the threat against him. The youth shrank against her.

She patted his knee reassuringly.

'Why are you stopping me?' she demanded. 'Let me pass!'

'I want that young varmint sitting up there, so neat as you please.' He strode round to the side. 'Get you on down here!'

'Who are you, and what do you mean by stopping my carriage?'

The burly fellow looked at her appraisingly. She was dressed in a plain walking dress and that close, modest bonnet, but by the tones of her voice and authoritative manner he realized she was no simple country girl. He became a little more circumspect. He ducked round the horse and came to stand on her side. His tones became less demanding.

'This young 'prentice's running away on us.'

'A runaway apprentice! I don't believe that.' She took a sideways glance at the lad's clothing. Though muddied by the slide down the embankment, it was of excellent quality and well kept. She had a moment of doubt for his coat was not well-fitting: the shoulders were too broad so that the cuffs were over long. They could be hand-me-downs from an affluent family to a poorer one.

'The little devil's up to no good, d'you see, missee. 'E was in the guv'nor's things — ransacking 'em 'e was. I'll jus' take 'im back and let 'im give an account of 'imself.'

'So now he's a thief instead of an apprentice. And who is your 'guv'nor'? What is happening up there?' She lifted her chin contemptuously. She didn't like the cut of this man's jib. He reminded her forcibly of the kind of toughs and roustabouts she had seen hanging round traveling fairs.

'Just a little sporting event like.'

The thud of horse's hooves, which she had heard earlier, were coming closer. Her bonnet muffled her ears, and she was scarcely conscious of the sound. The ruffian's eyes shifted to the lane behind her for a moment.

'Now, miss. Give over. I'm taking the lad.' He started forward.

Julia stood up, her whip clutched in her hand. 'Stand away!' she ordered.

The noise of hooves ceased.

'Now, miss — you don't want to be obstructin' a man in what 'e 'as to do.'

'Obstructing justice, you mean? I think not. I can take this child to my brother who happens to be the local magistrate. You can take any complaints to him.' At the mention of a magistrate the man fell back a step, then, as if steeling his determination, came forward again. 'I ain't scared o' no magistrate. I'm not from around 'ere.' He made as if to reach for the youth.

Julia raised the whip, only too aware it was but a flimsy weapon, which would have little effect against the man's heavy coat. He sneered. 'That bitty piece 'o buskin string don't scare me.' He gained nerve. 'Put it in my reach and I'll pull you right off that high and mighty seat of yours.'

Julia's fighting spirit was up. She flourished her weapon menacingly. The ruffian stepped back suddenly, but his eyes were looking beyond her again. Hoofbeats thudded up the laneway.

Julia darted a look behind and half-turned toward a man riding a tall gray horse along the sodden grass verge. He came to a stop close to the youth. She got the impression of a man dressed with quiet propriety, though in town rather than country mode. She maintained her militant posture, a young Boadicea, standing at her full height, with strands of honey-colored hair straying from beneath her bonnet. She glared straight into his eyes.

The man, a complete stranger to her, appeared to be in his mid-twenties, and well favored. He sat back, regarding her. When he spoke, his voice had a pleasant, well modulated character. 'I beg you to sit down, ma'am. It is not wise to stand up in a vehicle.'

'Is that a threat?' Keyed up, she again flourished the whip.

'By no means. It is just that I would not have you take a tumble.' With some chagrin she saw his eyes were twinkling. Was she making a spectacle of herself?

The youth tugged at her. Color was returning to his cheeks, and he did not seem afraid of this second man. After hesitating, she plumped down on the seat and lowered the whip, maintaining a firm grip on it, however.

'You appeared to be in the middle of some altercation, but I perceive that my intervention was scarce needed. You were equal to the challenge.'

Confounded by his smooth tones, Julia glowered. Was he friend or foe? For a potential ally he seemed negligent of the threat offered by the large thug on her other side. That smile lurking at the corner of his mouth was ill-timed and downright unchivalrous. How dare he laugh at her!

The rough stood gnawing at his lip. He decided not to stand tamely by while his grievances were ignored. 'That's all well and good, but I still want that thieving brat.'

Julia said, 'The boy says he took nothing.'

'What is it that this — brat — has stolen from you?' interjected the stranger.

'The guv' found him rifling through his things. He sent me arter 'im. Why else would 'e be up there? Maybe 'e was arter the gate money.'

'I'm sure your guv' was not so careless as to leave the gate where it could be stolen, my man. I can hazard a guess why the boy was up there — and it was not to steal money.'

So there was a connection between the rider and the youth, thought Julia. She glanced at him. He still cowered beside her. The man on the gray continued, 'Make off with yourself, and tell your guv'nor that you failed to catch your quarry.'

'I've got me rights.'

'Have you, fellow? What I observed was you threatening a gentlewoman in a secluded lane.'

'Maybe it weren't me doin' all the threatening.'

'Be off with you! There's nothing for you here.'

The rough eyed the rider speculatively. His thoughts were transparent as he weighed the consequences of milling down a gentleman while controlling a screaming female, only to see his quarry take to his heels once more.

'You spurned your chance to go to the magistrate,' Julia reminded him gently.

That took the wind out of his sails. The clincher was a coin, which glinted as it spun through the air. The fellow caught it dexterously, and slunk away to the path leading back up out of the dell.

'You paid him off!' exclaimed Julia indignantly.

'Would you prefer I gave him a thrashing?'

'Much!'

'But can you be sure of the outcome?' asked the stranger mockingly. 'He's no mean weight. Much help I would be to you lying senseless in the ditch! You'd probably much rather watch the brawl than have the good sense to drive this whelp to safety out of this hollow.'

'Pooh! You were afraid.' She had the satisfaction to see his eyebrows come together. Her heart was beginning to slow to normal.

The stranger addressed the youth curtly, 'Up with you!'

The youth looked up at Julia hesitantly.

'Do you want to go with him? You do not have to.'

He nodded, then seeing the mistrust in her face said, 'He's a friend.'

'Come on!' The man said. 'The horse will carry us both.'

Coldly, Julia put in, 'You will have to help him up. He has hurt an ankle. It is not, I think, broken, but he cannot walk on it.'

'Which ankle? Can you stand?'

The youngster rose unsteadily, with a supporting hand from Julia.

'Good! Now cock your leg over here — no, behind me, lad!'

The boy's cheeks were suffused with color. Julia looked at him with astonishment. There was some awkwardness about his movements, but with a backwards arm scoop from the rider, he managed to install himself astride the horse's crupper.

Well, thought a puzzled Julia, if I expected some explanation of all this, it does not seem as if I shall receive one.

'Drive ahead!' instructed the rider. Then ameliorating his tones, he continued, 'Permit me to ensure your safe passage out to the road.'

'That is not necessary.'

'Please, indulge me! I am all admiration at so intrepid a female. However, I'll not leave you here in the woods where our truculent friend might return.'

Julia touched the nag's flank so sharply with the whip that the animal was goaded into unprecedented energy, and the trip to the end of the lane was accomplished with better speed than Julia anticipated. The gray with its double load followed some yards behind.

Soon, the little party drew out onto the busy road, less than a mile from the cottage to which Julia was bound. She pulled to a halt to allow a chaise to turn out of the lane to Beesley's farm. It was traveling so fast that she caught no more than a glimpse of its passenger. Definitely something of a sporting nature was going on up there, she conjectured. Turning, she stiffly thanked her shadow for his escort, and pointed out that it was no longer necessary.

'As you wish!'

Reminded of his manners, the youth offered her his thanks in a low stumbling voice. Apparently a nervous rider, he did not relinquish his grip on his deliverer's coat to doff his cap. The rider bowed and turned the horse back into the dell, leaving Julia much to ponder as she drove on.

Two hours later, having listened to Nell's woes over a dish of broth, heard about her husband's chronic sore back and helped minister to measles-stricken children, Julia returned home. Entering the side door leading from the stables, she heard voices coming from her brother's study. The tones, if not cordial, were not particularly confrontational. The door was open and she observed Sir Ivor perched on the edge of his desk, talking to the local constable and another man, who seemed on the point of quitting the room.

Such sights were not unusual to her. The constable, who was also the village saddler, frequently brought miscreants or those with civil complaints straight up to the house, there not being a more convenient venue.

'Then you'll not be detaining me? In truth, I can't see what grounds you might have for doing so.'

Her brother's voice replied something, which was not quite audible.

'It's been a pleasure. Sir Ivor. Constable.'

She stood aside and watched a tall, well-built gentleman bow himself out of the room. A striking head of silver hair arranged in such perfection that it almost looked like a wig framed a square, well-lined countenance.

His style was that of a well-to-do country-man. He was booted, and sported a well-cut coat of snuff-colored worsted over fawn breeches. Yet, the boots and clothing looked too new, not yet eased into the wear and tear of everyday living. Curiosity stayed her steps. He perceived Julia, and executed a deeper bow in her direction. Flashing an audacious smile he remarked back to the room he was leaving, 'But detain me if it is your wish, gentlemen. The amenities of your, er, stockade are not without their attractions, I assure you.'

Ivor's voice rumbled. 'Stockade, what stockade? Oh, we have nothing like that here, I assure you, sir. The lockup's in the village, y'know.' He caught sight of Julia. 'Oh, you're back, Ju. Wondered where you were!'

Julia raised an amused eyebrow, not in appreciation of the impudence of the unknown who was getting his congé, but that his impertinence had traveled over her brother's head.

Ivor continued, 'Dimmock, show the gentleman out, and then you can get back to your saddlery.' He looked narrowly at the silver-haired gentleman. 'We won't keep you longer, sir. But know that we don't tolerate these clandestine events in this neighbor-hood.'

'I entirely agree, sir, and are in mind with you about the evils of prizefighting. But don't mix up your villains here! We did agree, did we not, that I was not involved. And may I throw out a point to ponder? Where did the tip come from that sent you on the offensive.'

Sir Ivor growled, 'The tip took us in the wrong direction.'

The other shrugged. 'The venue was changed. An inconvenience both to you and to some of its patrons. I'll say no more.'

Constable Dimmock sidled out the study door, and conducted his self-assured guest towards the front of the house. 'Come along, sir. Your hat's this way.'

As they departed, Julia entered her brother's study. She rallied him, 'We have a better class of transgressor, these days. Front door clients.'

'Hm. Don't know that he is any sort of culprit, at that. Glib sort of fellow! A pretty warm man, if you take him at his word. He's looking round for a house and property, he says. Anyway, a delivery boy brought a note about an illegal prizefight. This fellow, Kestrel Barnard he calls himself, could have been the Johnny that sent it, according to the lad's description. The only thing was — it sent us to the wrong spot — wasted my time no end.'

'How provoking for you — and all the

horses and men you had taken, too.' His sister's tones were dry.

'It was, dash it! I'd like to know if 'twas him. Couldn't pin him down.'

'You could have held him and fetched up the delivery boy to identify him.'

'I'm not entirely sure about the boy. It might have been the butcher's lad or not. Urchins all look the same. Having wasted the dammed best part of my day, I'm not going to spend the afternoon chasing my tail. Besides, what could I charge him with if he was the man? His intention, however mistaken, might have been to do us a favor. He's seems dead against prizefighting. Fellow can make a mistake about where a mill's going to be. This county or that. They're forever changing the sites. They just do it to complicate things for the few honest magistrates who're willing to get after them.'

'So, your mission was unsuccessful?'

'Not completely. I put the Beesley boy in the roundhouse. I told Beesley it was either him or his son. Both were involved.'

'That hardly seems fair. Why the boy? The father must be the one responsible. It is his land.'

Sir Ivor looked at her keenly. 'Because someone has to run the farm, that's why. It would be too much of a hardship for the

66

family to have both men in gaol at this season.'

'Aha! A Daniel come to judgment. So Mr. Beesley will be forced to muck out his pigs instead of his son.'

Sir Ivor grinned. 'Or get one of his fancy dairymen to do it. What I want to know is — how did you know it was on Farmer Beesley's land?'

Julia pulled off her gloves and disposed herself in the chair beside the desk. 'I'm assuming there was a boxing meet. There seem to be all too many strangers in the area. Certainly something was going on there.'

'You were out that way?'

'In the lane below his big field, there.'

'What were you doing out in the first place? Didn't old Will tell you not to go out — and certainly not alone?'

'Well, he muttered something,' she admitted, not wanting to get the aging stableman into trouble. 'But I had little choice. Nell's husband is laid up, and two of her children ill. You know you wouldn't want me to desert them under those circumstances.'

'Argh! Will should have had more sense than to harness that old crock for you.' He shook his head, more in frustration than anger. 'She hasn't the legs to get you out of trouble. Besides, I don't like you exposed to that sort of thing.'

His sister smiled fondly. 'Silly! Sure it was a fight by the noise in the dell. But it does not concern me. I hardly ever think of Philip any more. I have finished with mourning. But you, I think, still remember. You can't abide those affairs.'

Sir Ivor grunted. 'Those bloody massacres seem more and more accepted. But they'll not happen around here, as long as I'm breathing.' She nodded in resignation. Her brother's intransigence on the topic of prizefights was the source of some bitterness among the local sporting squires and farmers, besides being the cause of the estrangement between him and the late Earl of Selchurch.

'Never mind that! I have something to tell you.' She related to him the events of the morning, complaining bitterly about the old horse, but giving a lively description of her encounter with the three strangers in the dell, and dwelling with humorous detail on her exploit with the whip and subsequent embarrassment. She ended up, 'Who can those people have been? Nobody saw fit to introduce themselves, including me. I was too mortified to tell anyone who I was — other than threatening them with you.'

Moving restlessly around the study, Sir Ivor adopted a thoughtful mien.

'They seem connected with the fight meet in some way — but the rider never got there, I believe.'

'No, he and the lad rode back through the dell. Although he seemed to know what the lad had been up to, he made no explanation to me.'

'Tush! The lad's boxing mad, probably. After some souvenir. Who knows?'

'He was of slight build, not at all a pugnacious type of boy. Besides, he seemed . . .'

'Seemed . . .?'

'Oh, nothing. Just my fancy! Who do you think the rider might be?'

'Describe him again!'

'Tallish. It's hard to tell when someone's on a horse. Fair hair from what I could see, but a brown complexion — not ruddy particularly, but used to the outdoors.'

'Yet a gentleman, he?'

'Of a sort!' responded Julia darkly. 'There was nothing in his appearance to put one off, anyway. His clothes, top-boots, all well kept. He was dressed with propriety, though his coat — well, I don't know much about male fashion, but I don't think it was what you would call 'up to the knocker.' He could be anybody . . . and he had such an irritating way about him! I'd swear he was laughing at me. I was so provoked, I became a real vixen.

I could have used that whip, I tell you. That would have been the end of his amusement.'

'He can't be so bad, Ju. He saw you safe to the end of the lane. Can't you find anything good to say about him?'

Julia thought about it. He had really been rather attractive, and she admitted to herself that she had hardly been on her best behavior. Well, she had been alarmed by the situation. She would not mind the opportunity to meet him again. She said, 'Beautiful big, gray horse, though, with a white blaze.'

'A gray with a white blaze, eh? Well, there are always new people around. Even the new earl.'

Julia looked interested. 'Has Basil's heir arrived at Bishop's Rise? Oh . . . Charlotte's letter. I recognized her hand.'

'Yes. Thank you for bringing it from the village. The new earl was in to see Lady Selchurch and off again next day. The countryside's all agog to see him. Nine day's wonder it'll be when he stays in one place so people can get a good look at him. No doubt he's keeping out of sight.'

'Why would he do that?'

'Be fair, Ju! The Johnny just got in from foreign parts. Probably hasn't had time to visit his tailor. He's got quite a position to live up to now. Won't show himself until he's fitted himself out in a proper style.'

'You make him sound quite elusive.' Her eyes danced. 'We must be on the lookout for strangers. Maybe he travels incognito. How about the mysterious Mr. Barnard? His clothes have not seen many day's wear.'

Sir Ivor showed a derisive face. 'His tailoring's nothing's special. An earl would go to a high-class London tailor.'

'Even for country wear? You don't, Ivor.'

'I ain't an earl,' he replied simply. 'Besides, the fellow's too old. Lottie once told me she met him years ago, and he's about her age. She didn't say he had a white mop of hair, so Barnard's out. Maybe it was your mysterious rider fellow.'

Julia considered this seriously. 'I won't allow he was anything out of the ordinary. Besides, he was by himself. He had no companions out looking for a missing youth, as far as I know. A powerful person like an earl would have plenty of servants on such an errand.'

'Well, he wasn't the earl, then. No boys at the Rise. There are just a brood of females there. It stands to reason. If there were any boys, they wouldn't need some remote cousin to be the new earl.'

'What did Charlotte say about him?'

'Nothing — just mentioned him in passing.

Begs pardon for not writing sooner.'

'She was probably waiting for a letter to answer,' said Julia in a damping fashion.

He ignored his sister's barb. 'My sweetie's head's full of marriage plans, as you can well imagine. Wants to know if she should write to her aunt in Wimbledon arranging to stay there on our way. Can't think why. The woman won't bestir herself to come to the wedding. I'd been thinking of something more in the center of things — the Farlaines place, maybe.'

'But, think, Ivor! The Farlaines will be at the wedding. They are to stay here with me for a day or two. You can hardly stay at their house if they are away.'

'Dash it all, I thought you were staying with them next week, Ju.'

'Perhaps they want to have a look at the new earl. Shall you invite him to the wedding?'

He pondered this. 'I don't think Lottie knows him that well. But we're hoping that Lady Selchurch will attend — now that Basil's underground. No, I don't think so . . . though it will be good to have new blood in the district. This may be a great opportunity for you, Ju.'

Julia knew exactly what he meant. 'To meet him and his wife and seven children, I have no doubt.'

'Now there you're wrong, m'dear. I have it on excellent intelligence that he is single and available.'

His sister rose to leave the study. 'I am not hanging out for a husband, Ivor, especially a peer. That would interfere with all my plans.'

Sir Ivor groaned. 'I know your plans. You just can't do that — a girl traipsing round like a gypsy — or setting up your own house.'

'At twenty-four I no longer consider myself a 'girl.''

'Pshaw! Look! Lottie and I are going to Brussels. Come with us and get your taste of travel.'

Julia gave what sounded suspiciously like a hoot. 'Pooh! I don't fancy sitting gooseberry with you and Charlotte on your wedding trip, let alone what Charlotte might think about that. Besides, we have it arranged that I shall look after Mallow while you are gone.'

3

The pair riding double atop the big gray stopped at the first decent looking hostelry to negotiate the hire of a light chaise. Luckily the house could accommodate their requirements. Roderick sketched the simple tale of a pony, which had thrown its rider before bolting for home, leaving a young boy nursing an injured ankle. If the landlord considered this a strange reason to hire a vehicle merely to carry a stripling with nothing but a twisted ankle a few miles, he accepted the explanation that the gentleman did not care to have his horse carry double any further than it already had. Fortunately, he seemed to have no great interest in the gray, giving Roderick to hope that the horse had not been recognized as belonging to the late earl. He had no wish for this escapade to figure in his introduction to the neighborhood. He prayed that the ostlers would be similarly unobservant.

Beyond casting a measuring eye upon them, the landlord seemed to accept their basic respectability, and invited them into the coffee room while he had his good wife bring a cold compress to place on the injury. He could also provide a late lunch if his honor could be satisfied with a morsel of beef and kidney pie with fresh asparagus on the side.

Momentarily put out by the honorific, Roderick decided that the form of address was intended no more than a show of flattery.

'A capital idea!' he approved. 'Lead the way! Come on, coz! I'll wager you're as sharp set as I am.' He gave a supporting arm to the youth as he hobbled into the inn. The landlord's wife clicked her tongue when she saw the swollen ankle, and hastened to bring a basin of water cold from the well, and bandages to wrap the injured member. The young gentleman was very quiet and pale, and she was solicitous as to whether he was in much pain, but was answered in monosyllables. Roderick filled the breach by maintaining a casual conversation about the attractions of the surrounding countryside and complimenting her on the pleasant aspect of the inn. As she appeared gratified by these comments, he hoped that she would attribute his companion's demeanor to shyness rather than surliness. He had warned his companion to say as little as possible. The woman finished her task deftly, gathered up her tools and, bobbing a curtsy, left. Then they had the coffee room to themselves, except for the maid laying the table. The silence was oppressive till the youth made as if to speak.

'You must wonder . . .'

Roderick made a warning gesture, and continued making inconsequential remarks about the countryside until the serving wench had left the room. Then he said, 'We will maintain this charade, if you please. News in the country travels like lightning, so be careful what you say. We'll try to get you back in girl's clothes without making a to-do if we can.'

'No one will guess,' muttered Sophie. 'That woman who swaddled me so fast didn't suspect anything.' She glared at her ankle. 'I didn't even want a bandage. It will get better without.'

'If it's too tight, we'll loosen it later. Look up at me.' Eyes flicked up from a lowered face, met his and then focused downwards again. 'I am not going to scold you. I'm not even going to blame you, for no doubt you think you have a uncommonly good reason for what you did. Did you not trust me to help?'

'But you weren't here — for ages.' The words burst out in tones almost of condemnation.

'A fortnight! Could you not have patience?'

His tones were matter-of-fact. 'I went north to see my mother whom I haven't seen for three years.' She continued to stare down. 'My mother's claims to see me might not stand against those of a father not seen for a decade, I grant you, but at least I knew where to find her.'

Her eyes came up searchingly, to see if he was laughing at her. He was. She flinched as if to acknowledge a hit. He had made a small breach in her armor of pride and the self-centeredness of the child in her. They were interrupted by the arrival of the luncheon, and Sophie lost no time in wading into a generous helping of steak and kidney pie. Roderick smiled.

She swallowed a mouthful and said conversationally, 'You heard my tummy grumbling.'

'Indeed I did! I was looking around for storm clouds. What time did you leave the Rise?'

'Before the maids were up. I climbed out a casement.'

'I know. You left it open. There was a hue and cry in the house, thinking some burglar had got in during the night. That was before you were missed. And you've had nothing to eat all day?'

'I saved some bread from last night.'

'Resourceful, I see. And how did you get to the fight?'

'I walked.'

'My compliments. It must be seven or eight miles.'

She shrugged.

'As far as I know, they have not yet missed the clothes.'

'Peter's old things? They won't miss them today. Riding day, so there'll be no *Tempest* doings.'

'You must be sorry to miss your lesson.'

She showed momentary offence. 'With the babies? How can you expect me to enjoy that? Even Linnet goes with the older girls, and she is two years younger than me.'

'But she's had years more in the saddle than you, my dear.' He cocked an quizzical eye at her. 'Those mulish looks leave my withers unwrung. Things may not be ideal, but do not be so foolish as to refuse what is offered to you.'

Sophie took this in. She selected a piece of fruit and took a bite. 'I was regularly flabbergasted to see you in the woods. How did you find me there?'

'Flabbergasted? As was I, to arrive back at the Rise this morning, in the midst of an extraordinary hubbub.'

'Just because I left a casement open?'

'Your Aunt Alicia realized who it was soon enough. You have made quite a reputation for wandering off on your own, young lady. However, she did not tell the servants.' Lady Selchurch had had a few more things to say about Miss Kettle, but he did not intend to go into them. 'How about your cousins? Have you made friends with them?'

'No.' Then, as if she considered her answer too bald, she carried on. 'Arabelle is pleasant enough, but she thinks of nothing but clothes, and being bridesmaid for Miss Stride — and — and, coming out!'

'And the younger ones?'

She said truculently, 'Just ignorant children — and the twins are tiresome — and so superior when they think they know something I don't. I know more than them about a whale of things.' She made an expansive gesture. 'It's just that — that they — think I'm making up tales.'

With deep misgivings Roderick asked, 'Such as?'

'Well, being on stage. You are looking at a person who has actually trod the boards.'

'I remember.'

'Just small parts — both boys and girls. But walk-ons are important.'

'I am sure.' It did not occur to him to doubt her word. In the unconventional way she had been raised, by an actress and then by a dresser, she undoubtedly had had many unusual experiences. However broad the education she had acquired in that environment, there must of necessity be grave gaps in those accomplishments forming an essential part of a young lady's education.

'Where do you go when you — wander off?'

'I like to be on my own. But sometimes I go to see Mrs. Bunting. She worked in the house years ago and was married to the gamekeeper. She remembers my papa, and tells me interesting things about him. He was very good-looking, you know, and had excellent address, she says.'

No doubt a smooth-tongued rogue, Roderick thought to himself. But he also remembered one of Lady Selchurch's complaints voiced to him that very morning — that the girl had a proclivity to hobnob with the servants. It had, in fact, been a major complaint, and a source of embarrassment to the family. However, a retired family retainer should be unexceptional. With a sense of fairness he realized how important it must be for Sophie to reach out to someone who knew her father.

'Where else?'

'I found the most splendid hidey-hole. You must not think I waste my time, for I go there to read and improve my mind. I can't tell you where it is.'

'If you mean the treehouse, Lady Selchurch has talked of it.' A comical expression of dismay crossed her face.

'Don't worry. I don't think she'd mind you using it — if you don't miss too many lessons. She is a good friend to you, Sophie.'

Roderick pushed his plate aside. 'We have to find a way to get you back into the house without causing attention. Maybe it's to the good you've made a reputation for wandering. No one will be terribly surprised when you return after several hours, though you may get a scold. You did not, I suppose, hide female clothes anywhere they can be retrieved before you go back? You were going back?'

She was annoyed at herself. 'Why didn't I think of that?'

'But you were going back?'

'Certainly!'

'Why on earth did you go to the prizefight? You could hardly expect to find your father there.'

She shook her head sadly. 'We would not recognize each other. I don't remember him at all.'

'You were searching someone's belongings there. What did you expect to find?'

She sniffed and dashed away a tear with the

back of her hand. 'There were some sketches of fighters — a whole pile of them. I thought I might find one of my papa — so I would know him when I found him.'

He regarded her thoughtfully. She could not have known she would find those pictures in advance. 'I repeat — what was your reason for going there — and to all those fairs that Mrs. Shackle talked about. What is this fascination for the seamy side of popular entertainment?'

She replied with dignity. 'There is a purpose to it all. I am looking for Mouche.'

'What in heaven's name is mouche?'

'It's a man.'

'Mouche is his name? Who is he and why are you looking for him?'

'You ask so many questions.'

'If you don't answer my questions, how can I help you?'

'Who is he? Just a man — he works with stones sometimes.'

'A jeweler?'

'No, big stones, in building.'

'A mason, perhaps.'

She nodded. 'He might know about my papa. He came to see us a year ago. He said we'd see my father soon. But Papa didn't come — Aunt Lissie died, and we had to move — and he wouldn't be able to find me

— and I just have to find Mouche.'

'What makes you think he frequents prizefights?'

'That's where he met my papa.'

Rod sighed. Obviously, championing this strange little cousin would lead him into strange places. Instinct told him that such places would be disreputable and insalubrious. Well, he had promised to help.

'We will see what can be done to find him. See if you can think of any clues as to where he frequents — besides prizefighting circles.' Thinking of the vast amount of building going on in the metropolis, he groaned. 'I'll be going back to London in a few days. I'll start enquiries there.'

Sophie beamed, and got up to make an exploratory hobble around the room. She said, 'But, you haven't told me how you found me?'

'And you haven't told me how you learned about the prizefight.'

'It's common talk in the servants' hall,' she replied airily.

'Spend a little less time under the servants' feet!' He rose. 'As for finding you — more or less luck! It so happens your Aunt Alicia cares more about you than you think. She was especially concerned that you had vanished without breakfast. Apparently you haven't done that before. She feared you had run away, and quite fell on my breast with relief when I walked in the door. Your disappearance did not astonish me, however. It so happens I put up at an inn not far from here last night. It would have been too late to arrive at the Rise without warning. The big argument in the tap was the actual whereabouts of a local prizefight. That, in conjunction with your truancy, seemed an interesting coincidence. I remembered Mrs. Shackle's complaints about your penchant for visiting fairs. It was not great leap from fairs to fights.'

'But you were right there . . . '

'In the woods. Well, a local directed me through the hollow as being a shortcut to the fight turf. By the way, I can only commend your discretion that you didn't turn up there in your petticoats. That would have been scandal indeed.'

Her mouth turned down sulkily. 'I'm not scared of scandal. Let people say what they want.'

He answered gently. 'But your Aunt Alicia might not like the scandal. She does not deserve that of you. Anyway, I see through the window that the chaise awaits our pleasure. We must be on our way. Later, when we reach the Rise, you shall tell me all about your adventures at the fight, and how you came to be rescued by the lady with the whip.'

The distance between the inn and the Rise was not above five miles, but on a sudden inspiration he took the more circuitous route through the village. His main preoccupation was to get Sophie back through the grounds and into the huge residence, creating as little attention as possible. Mindful of this he bade the girl sit as far back in the shade of the calash as she could to avoid being seen.

'Why are we going this way?' asked Sophie. 'We'll see more people through the village than if we'd taken the side road.'

'I believe I shall call on Miss Stride for help. It's a way out of our difficulties.'

Sophie looked a little daunted. 'But she's too severe to be a conspirator. I mean, she'd tell on us.'

'Years ago we got in lots of mischief together, she and I. I do not believe she has grown so stuffy she would turn her back on me.'

She perked up. 'By something she was saying, they are short of servants there. The cook has been given leave to visit an ailing sister. I heard Miss Stride telling Lady Arabelle that she might have to engage a housekeeper, especially as she will soon be gone from her father's house. All is in panic because of the nearness of the wedding. There is to be a tea party there in a few days. They think it's a good idea for me to attend.' She pulled a scornful face. 'You know she's getting married, don't you?' This last rather sternly.

'Acquit me! I offer no threat to her matrimonials.'

'That lady with the whip would make a good conspirator.' She peeped at him through the corners of her eyes.

'Hardly! All she saw was a scrubby school boy getting up to mischief in a farmer's field and being chased for his pains. It's a wonder she didn't hand you over to the ruffian straight away.'

'Well, she didn't. She's trusty as a Trojan 'cos she took my side. Don't you think she is very pretty?'

He considered this. 'I would not call her pretty.'

'Do you not think so?' She sounded indignant.

'Pretty is too weak a word. If I wished to compliment a lady, I would never say that she was 'pretty.' It suggests only a passing beauty.' He thought to himself that the woman certainly had more than a passing attraction. Prettiness was certainly not her style. Her features were interesting, well proportioned, her clear gray eyes well-spaced, direct and challenging, and in that moment of excitement, her cheeks had bloomed with a charming freshness of color. He wondered if she had a pleasant manner when her tongue was not sharpened by apprehension. No milk and water miss, that!

'That means you like her, doesn't it?'

'That means I like her,' he agreed. To himself he admitted that, despite her being a bit of a shrew, he liked her very well.

They were entering the village high street. He drew the horses back to a walk.

'What sort of trouble did you get into with Miss Stride?'

'Trouble?'

'You said you got into lots of mischief.'

'Oh that.' He looked down at her, and decided that she certainly ought to hear the story. 'That was so long ago, and we were very small. She used to come to play with the youngest Selchurch children — your mother's young sisters. Maybe you'll have a chance to meet them some day. Both are married and living many miles away.'

Sophie seemed uninterested in more Selchurch relatives. 'What about my mother?'

'It's a not a story I boast about. I took Charlotte out in a punt on the pond, or rather Charlotte took me, for it seems to me, as I think back, she was wielding the pole. It seemed a great lark at the time. There was a knoll in the center of the pond and we thought it would make a fine desert island, and made it our objective. It was nothing more than a glorified tussock, at that. We were not too expert on getting out of the punt. I got ashore safe enough, but Charlotte got a wetting and had to be pulled out. In the confusion, our boat drifted away. There we were stranded on our little island, and could not get home.'

'I've seen the pond. It is so shallow! How could you possibly be stranded?'

'I hadn't learned to swim at that time. Believe me, it looked deep to a six-year-old.'

'How old was Charlotte?'

'It's not for me to betray a lady's deep and dark secrets.'

'Of course — older than you.'

'Not that it matters, minx. Don't interrupt the story. I think you'll want to hear this. We were there for what seemed ages. Charlotte was wetter but we both were covered in mud and plaguily uncomfortable. It looked as if we would be there all night, for we had told no one where we were going. Evening came. We were getting scared and our desert island did not seem so exotic any more — just cold and damp.'

'How did you get off your little island?'

'Well, Sophie, who should come by but your mother. Lady Patience was the heroine who rescued us from our reedy perch.'

Sophie's eyes sparkled. 'She was looking for you? She came to rescue you?'

'Well, not exactly. She was carrying a fishing rod and was heading along the stream that fed the pond. Patience was in many ways an unusual person. She had her own ways. No! Through a series of misunderstandings, both my parents thought we were with the Strides and vice versa. We had not been missed. The horror of that fact translated to vehement anger when our bedraggled persons emerged from the woods, I assure you.'

'So my mother saved you.' This was said with a quiet satisfaction.

'She waded in and rescued pole and punt and retrieved us. I remember her saying not to worry too much about a scold — that it would be quite overshadowed by the tongue lashing she would receive when we got back. I didn't understand that, but you know she was right. I've always wondered about that. At the time I was astonished to learn that grown-ups could be given scolds.'

'But she was a heroine. You said so.'

'To the Anhursts and the Strides she was a heroine. But to the Selchurches, no! I was not too aware at the time, but she was often in trouble — going out at dusk to fish and without a servant at her heels would be typical. Her brothers could do it, but she, of course, was forbidden. It was just too unconventional for the stolid Selchurch family. My father was not approving of the way she was treated, and a certain coolness existed between our families from then on.'

'Then that is why you think Miss Stride will help? Because my mother saved her? In fact, she has obligations to Mama and me!'

Roderick gave her an amused look. 'Don't count on that. More likely she's blotted the whole episode from her mind. Embarrassing recollections frequently disappear into the mists of time, and we won't remind her of them — unless we have to. But, I have to tell you, Charlotte Stride was brave as a lioness throughout that whole escapade. I remember being scared that she would cry and there would be nothing I could do about it. But she didn't shed one tear. Yes, Charlotte will make a famous conspirator. This is the parsonage, I believe.'

Pulling the chaise up outside the long square building with a pleasant garden beside the churchyard, Roderick jumped down from the chaise. 'I will tie the horses to the gate post, so you need have no fears about them.

Stay here, and keep as far out of sight as you can. Yes, that's the ticket! Right back against the canopy.' So saying, he put the action to the words and less than a minute later was lifting the doorknocker.

Much to his gratification, the door was opened by Charlotte Stride herself. She looked surprised to see Roderick rather than one of her father's regular flock.

'Lord Selchurch! Please come in! You must be here to see my father . . .'

He forestalled her. 'No, no! Please don't disturb him. It is you I came to see, Charlotte. You don't mind me calling you Charlotte? We used to be Charlotte and Roderick twenty years ago.' He did not wait for her yea or nay. 'I have a delicate social problem that needs your discretion and cooperation to solve. You need not feel it will get you in trouble with Lady Selchurch. She will, I know, appreciate your help in avoiding undue notice of a, shall we say a prank, perpetrated by one of the children.'

Her eyes went past him to the chaise. 'Of course. One of the girls. I cannot, of course, venture a guess as to which one is in trouble. But to spare Lady Alicia I will naturally do my best. My discretion you can count on.'

'Good girl. I can always count on you. Oh! A change of clothing will be required.'

'Surely!' An ironic twist to the lips told him that he was presuming a lot on a friendship so distant that scarce a fortnight before he had not even recognized her.

'I will be in your debt, Charlotte.' He spotted beyond her shoulder a stand on which various pieces of outwear were hung. 'May I borrow that cloak?'

She moved aside to let him take an old cloak of her father's, which he would sometimes throw over his vestments when called upon late at night to minister to the sick or dying, and waited while he carried it to the chaise, returning to the house bearing Sophie swathed from head to toe in its heavy black folds.

'My father is immersed in his sermon. Come straight upstairs, quickly.'

She led the way up to the first floor and along a short passage to her own bedroom.

'My god, Charlotte. I hope no one hears me enter here. I'd hate to cast a cloud on the reputation of the parson's daughter.'

'Don't be silly. I am an engaged woman, and if I can't take a little latitude in an emergency . . . Besides, Papa is getting a trifle deaf. Just don't make the stair creak as you go down. You can wait downstairs in the front parlor. You'll find the door ajar.'

He deposited his bundle on the bed with

little ceremony. Sophie pulled herself into a more dignified sitting position. Then he left her to make whatever explanations seemed good to her.

Charlotte Stride did not seem anxious for explanations. She took one look at Sophie and set about planning how to put things to rights.

'Oh dear, Lady Selchurch must not see you in that suit. It belonged to her son, Peter.'

'But the girls use it . . . in the play.'

'Just the breeches, maybe. You didn't fancy wearing Ferdinand's doublet?'

Sophie pulled off the tasseled cap and gave a giggle. She pulled the pins from her hair and let it fall about her shoulders. 'Ferdinand's costume? It wouldn't look real!'

Charlotte thought for a moment. 'I have been working on a costume for Miranda. What an excellent excuse to go up to the Rise! I need to make sure of the fit.'

Quickly she pulled out some of her most modest garments, and selected a plain muslin, which seemed the most appropriate for a young girl. It fitted exceedingly well, their being of a size despite the difference in age between them.

She left Sophie to change and repaired to the front parlor where Roderick was waiting. Discovering that she had received no details of the day's happenings from Sophie, he furnished her with an outline of what had transpired. She did not seem greatly surprised, having been to the Rise only two days earlier and heard all about Miss Sophie Kettle's doings.

'We will pretend that she was walking nearby when she hurt her ankle. Her wandering habits are no secret. I will take her back up to the Rise myself.'

'Do you think that will do the trick?'

She smiled grimly. 'Far be it for a parson's daughter to prevaricate. I will be a little hazy about exactly how long she has been here. I'll get the boy's clothing back to the schoolroom lest it be missed. I'll put it in with some other clothes I will take over for use in the children's theatricals — old things of my mother's, long out of date. Lord Selchurch, you take the chaise back where you hired it and get your horse.'

'Thus we manage all,' said Roderick with a grin. He had a mental vision of a much younger Charlotte directing events as she marshaled him onto a leaky punt on a boggy pond many years ago. A managing female she could be, though levelheaded enough. Much later, at the Rise, he was recounting to Lady Selchurch the events of the day. Feeling some explanation was due as to why he would call on Miss Stride, he again recounted the episode on the pond. The dowager had heard something of the tale of the two children marooned in the center of the pond, but she had another morsel to add to the narration.

'I have heard about Patience's walk with a rod that night,' she declared. 'The poor girl would ever put her foot wrong. She went out in defiance of her family, who had arranged that very evening for her to meet a gentleman with whom they had great hopes of arranging an eligible connection. She found the thoughts of meeting this suitor so distasteful that she slipped out of the house rather than be presented to him. Irrational for her to take him in dislike without having more than a passing acquaintance with him. Pretty choosy for a plain girl. What happens after — she must needs throw everything away for a handsome face and fine physique.' She shook her head in disbelief and continued, 'The way I heard it was that the servants were, indeed, out beating the bushes, but not for two little stranded children. They were looking for the missing bride elect, who was not above angling for her own fish.' She held up one hand. 'Oh, before you go to change, Roderick — I received a letter from your mama the very day you left for Harrogate.'

He settled back in his chair watching her twisting fingers.

'Your mother writes that — I hate to be a gossip-monger here — that your name has been coupled with a certain young lady of my acquaintance. She had it from some confidant at the spa. We are talking, of course, about my friend FitzWarren's daughter.'

Roderick sighed. 'Yes, my mother mentioned it.' He thought it unnecessary to enlarge on the many arguments his mother had presented to him on the advantages of such a connection: that Lady Cytherea was of good family, well-connected, fashionable and had by common report an excellent dowry, and that now he was an earl, he owed it to the family to make a suitable match. On the other hand, his mother had been told the young lady was considered fast in some circles. Whatever her son thought was right for him, that would be good enough for her. He had even entertained these arguments himself. Cytherea had hinted at a softening of her father's stance towards him on the journey from Deal, but he had scouted such a suggestion, being at the time ignorant of his change in status. She had been provocative. He had been noncommittal. He had proposed once and been refused. There might it stand.

'Pray believe me, my dear cousin, that I have no immediate plans towards matrimony. You may rest quiet on that head.'

The Dowager was wreathed in smiles. 'That quite relieves my mind. I had other plans, you know. It's high time Lady Cytherea was wed, as I've often said to her papa.'

4

Relations between the Selchurches and the Valliants were to be mended. The late Earl of Selchurch and Sir Ivor Valliant, magistrates both, had rarely seen eye to eye, particularly on the matter of prizefighting, and in consequence had found avoidance the better part of friction, a convenient solution as their jurisdictions lay in different counties. The death of the Earl had provided an opportunity for reconciliation; indeed, his widow appeared anxious to amend relations. Thus it was that the Selchurches and the Valliants were coming together on the neutral turf of the parsonage to forge a stronger acquaintance.

Lady Selchurch would still be in black gloves for nine months, but the prospect of having a hand in Charlotte Stride's nuptials presented a welcome diversion. The wedding would, of course, be modest in nature, not only because of the mourning period but as both families involved were small. Mr. Stride's only other child was currently commanding one of His Majesty's vessels in the West Indies. Sir Ivor had but the one sister and few relatives.

Sir Ivor and his sister were waiting in the best parlor at the parsonage when they heard the party from the Rise arrive. Dressed soberly in gray in respect for the circumstances, Sir Ivor was fidgeting around, fingering ornaments on the mantelpiece that he'd seen fifty times before, and then pacing, arms behind his back. His cherubic countenance was flushed and slightly shiny.

Julia preferred to sit on a cushion in the window embrasure, calmly enjoying the beams of a fine summer day; she presented a charming picture as the sun glinted through her honey-brown hair.

The front parlor was sufficiently large to accommodate quite a number of persons. Besides her eldest daughter Lady Arabelle, Lady Selchurch had brought the twins, Caroline and Katherine, who she felt were of an age to take an interest in things bridal, and, after a battle of conscience, Miss Kettle. A little exposure among the minor gentry would be of benefit to the child, she thought. If the girl was to be cast upon the mercies of a private school for young ladies, it was necessary that she be armed with a modicum of social graces. Satisfied by her speech patterns, which reflected her mother's influence, Lady Selchurch had then taken care to furnish her with a wardrobe suitable for a young lady of gentle upbringing. Like the other girls, she was modestly clothed in white muslin, with a beribboned straw bonnet on her head.

Mr. Stride ushered the party in, and pressed forward to perform introductions. He was very different in appearance from his sylph-like daughter. Large in stature, with cheeks of high color, he filled the room with his joviality and pleasure at presiding at the long hoped for reconciliation of two old-established neighborhood families.

Julia had already met Lady Arabelle at the parsonage on one occasion. Her acquaintance with Lady Selchurch was limited to the extent that each knew who the other was. There had never been any cause for greater intimacy. The coolness between her brother and the late earl would have been no great obstacle to friendship had they been more thrown in each other's way, she believed, but circumstances had merely rendered pursuance of social intercourse inexpedient. Her ladyship was by common report a charming woman, generous in charitable works, and no more top-lofty than might be expected of someone of her station. Little as she knew her, Julia was hopeful that her character would match her reputation. Any doubts as to whether

Lady Selchurch would acknowledge any past acquaintance were banished by her warm salutation.

'What a pleasure to at last be able to cultivate a warmer acquaintance, Miss Valliant. I really look forward to making up for the loss of so many years' friendship.'

'How kind!' Murmuring a few more words of appreciation, a smiling Julia shook her hand, and then turned to exchange greetings with Arabelle, who showed composure beyond her years while not overstepping by so much as a hairsbreadth the modest behavior expected of one of her years.

The twins, eyes downcast one moment, the next peeking at each other in brimful mischief, gave the impression of over-strained propriety. Charlotte was eyeing them with distinct mistrust as they made their curtsies.

Miss Kettle was merely introduced as the niece of Lady Selchurch. Rumors had been flying round the countryside, and the Strides, at least, were well aware of her connection to the Selchurches. Miss Kettle's curtsy was a trifle rigid, and Julia noticed that she hung her head and averted her face from the company. The twins watched her introduction into society with derision, and encountered a forbidding frown from their mama. Did Miss Kettle suffer extreme shyness, Julia wondered, or was she perhaps just dazzled by the sunlight? As the company became seated, the child found herself a chair in the lee of a potted fern on a small table.

The conversation naturally focused on the wedding and the couple's proposed trip. The Countess addressed herself primarily to them. 'I understand you will visit the continent after your wedding. Two months, you'll be gone! But Brussels is a charming place, I hear — and I'm sure you will see other places . . . but how we all will miss your company, Miss Stride!' She turned her attention to Julia. 'Ah me! You will be left in charge, Miss Valliant. You will be quite tied to the estate.'

'There will be much to keep me busy. Don't see me a martyr, I beg you. I take my revenge in advance by seizing a visit to London shortly, abandoning my poor brother to oversee the painting and plastering he has taken in hand at Mallow — long overdue, I assure you.'

'Will you be remaining in the neighborhood after your brother's marriage, Miss Valliant?'

Considering the question intrusive, Julia answered simply, 'It is a matter undetermined, Lady Selchurch.'

'I am told you long to travel. Are you to be another Lady Hester Stanhope?' the Dowager continued, oblivious to Charlotte's blushes. The identity of her informant could hardly be a secret.

Sir Ivor looked as he would cut in, but Julia turned the matter aside lightly. 'I am all admiration of the lady's courage but I think I'd find the Syrian desert a little torrid for my blood. Neither am I, I hope, an eccentric. Europe would satisfy me, though I'd love to go even further afield. But, let us not send my brother into a gloom on the eve of his nuptials.'

'My father went on the Grand Tour in his day. How unfair that men can participate in such things, while we women are so trammeled by convention. I tread on sensitive ground, I apprehend,' said the Countess, somewhat complacently, and turned to Charlotte. 'Miss Stride, I heard you promise to show the children the contents of your bride's chest. We all know you to be a notable hand with a needle. May I beg that they be allowed to go up to your room.' It was a statement rather than a question.

Undismayed by the presumption of the request, Miss Stride jumped to her feet and shepherded the three younger girls from the parlor. Arabelle elected to join the upstairs party, comfortable in her role of bridal attendant.

Lady Selchurch returned to the subject of Julia's upcoming journey to London. 'Yet I collect you have made frequent visits to the metropolis over the last few years. Oh, we are putting you out of countenance, Miss Valliant. Perhaps it is a painful subject.'

Julia smiled perfunctorily. 'Not painful at this stage. I gather Miss Stride has told you something of my history. You will know my visits to the Farlaines in London were not passages of dissipation, but rather to visit one to whom I was affianced. Possibly you heard of his recent death.'

'Ah, yes! A severe loss, for which we extend our deep condolences — but a blessed release, it is our understanding. You are to be commended on your faithfulness to your betrothed.'

'Oh, no, I am not so deserving of praise. I have not been wearing any willow on Philip Farlaine's account, though I have often sat with him and read to him — been with him. I doubt he knew I was there. My visits served more to support his mother who was tireless in her devotion — ever convinced that he would one day be himself again. He could neither talk nor, I believe, understand anything that was said to him. Despite engaging the services of a full-time nurse, his mother spent a great deal of time with him, feeding him and doing all those special things that mattered, like putting fresh flowers in his room and making sure the fire was not smoking. He just seemed to shrivel away. His death in the end was not so much as a release for Mrs. Farlaine but a removal of her most important object in life.'

Sir Ivor interposed. 'A sad case — very sad! The reason I have been opposed to bare-knuckle bouts these many years. The silly young chub had no business getting involved in something like that. Oh, I know, Ju, you don't like to talk about it, but it was all for a silly bet, you know. A matter of honor!'

'I saw no honor in it,' flashed Julia. 'The things gentleman regard as matters of honor are beyond me.'

'Well, no honor maybe. Overmatched, and he wouldn't admit it. He'd been a pretty good fiddler with the gloves on, but . . . ' Recalling that prizefights had been his quarrel with Sir Basil, he broke off. 'That's not the same thing at all. Not the same!' He harrumphed. 'But you ladies don't want to listen to sporting talk. What a jackanapes I am! Not drawing room talk at all.'

By her sympathy and subsequent gracious

remarks, Miss Valliant conceded to herself that Lady Selchurch's inquiries, though seeming impertinent, were nevertheless kindly meant. They might even be intended to form a bond between them in view of her own recent loss. The Countess was saying vaguely that the Valliants should visit her at the Rise in no distant future.

'I look forward to meeting the new earl. Will he be taking up residence at his seat soon?' asked Sir Ivor.

Julia threw a reproving glance at her brother. She did not believe Sir Ivor intended to pay back Lady Selchurch in her own coin for her inquisitiveness — one sensitive issue for another. Basically a simple man, he could be tactless. Mentally she shrugged this off, and turned her head to Lady Selchurch for her answer. The whole neighborhood was interested in that information, after all.

'Whether the new incumbent at the Rise will be taking up residence soon, I cannot say.' There was an awkwardness in the Dowager's speech. It seemed as if she would say no more, but she continued, 'He is a young man with his head full of ambition. He seems unprepared to relinquish his interests with the Ministry, and I can only applaud his diligence.'

The return of Miss Stride, Arabelle and the

twins heralded the arrival of refreshments to the parlor. Miss Stride dispensed tea, assisted by a young, fresh-faced maid who offered around plates of delicacies.

Katherine and Caroline spoke admiringly of the beautiful phoenix fire-screen panel Charlotte was working. Lady Selchurch suggested that Miss Stride might be so kind as to design some similar project for them each to work on, which resulted in a mixed reaction from the twins. They seemed more interested in the strawberry tarts, albeit with a well-bred moderation.

Julia noticed, however, Miss Kettle was not tucking into anything at all. She was not there. No one else seemed to have marked her absence. Intrigued, Julia sensed a mystery. There had been something about the set of her shoulders . . . Wondering if the girl had stepped out into the garden, Julia glanced out of the window, which overlooked a pleasant prospect of mature flower beds, with summer blooms already creating a feast for the eyes. Old Jones, the verger, was staking perennials, and she saw him straighten and tip his hat to someone out of sight of the window.

On impulse she laid down her cup and saucer and slipped out of the room.

Making her way past the kitchen regions

she went out through the back of the house. A courtyard led out to a practical kitchen garden, which ended at a cedar hedge. Beside it lay the gravel beside the flower bed. The sun had gone from this side of the house.

Miss Valliant cut across the courtyard, pausing to exchange a few words with Jones. She spotted a glimpse of white fluttering beyond the cedar hedge. Casually, she strolled through the rambler-covered trellis arch, which led through the cedars to a grassy plot of land containing a few plum trees still in bloom. There she found Miss Kettle. She was standing examining the blossoms in evident admiration. She was securing her straw hat in the breeze with one small hand with a flat, curly thumb.

'So you enjoy the view, Miss Kettle!' she said as she stepped through the arch.

The young lady seemed startled, and the head only half-turned. 'Yes — yes, quite well.'

'And parties where you don't know everyone are a dead bore, aren't they?'

'Is this an orchard?'

Taken aback, Julia took a moment before she replied. 'You might call it that.'

'If there are only four trees, do you still call it an orchard?'

'I collect you grew up in London. Perhaps

four trees in London could most likely be an orchard.'

The little straw-hatted head tossed as if stung by this remark. 'Of course we have trees in London — parts of it. I just didn't know how many trees make an orchard.'

A gurgle of laughter escaped Julia's lips. 'If you think asking silly questions will chase me away, you are far off. Why don't you turn and face me, Miss Kettle? Don't you trust me?' There was a pause with no response. 'I believe you did once before.'

The head turned round slowly, and she found herself looking into wary hazel eyes in a pale, square face, the face she had seen last riding off with a man on a gray horse. The face broke into a reluctant grin. 'You recognized me?'

'I guessed. You know, I am not completely an idiot. It seemed to me that your quest for invisibility was directed to me rather than anyone else.'

Sophie cast her eyes down. 'You must think it strange in me — and I don't want you to think I'm ungrateful. You saved my life.'

Julia disclaimed. 'What high flight! I doubt if that man would have really harmed you. Your knight errant was hard on our heels, after all.'

'No, really. He would have come too late. I

would have been snatched away and utterly lost.'

'I am quite curious. What happened after I left you in the charge of your champion?'

Sophie seemed to hesitate. 'Nothing much. Miss Stride got me a change of clothes so I could go back to the Rise.'

'Miss Stride! What about your knight errant?'

'He took me to the parsonage. He thought she would help because she's a very old friend of his. Miss Stride took me back.'

'Home to Bishop's Rise?' suggested Julia.

'Home? Only till my father comes for me.' This was stated flatly in a manner that discouraged pursuit of the subject.

'Did you get into much trouble?'

The reply was nonchalant. 'I've had worse scolds, and I didn't get a whipping.'

Julia raised her eyebrows slightly, but the girl's confidences seemed to have dried up. She held out her hand. 'Come, my dear! There are some excellent refreshments indoors. Let's hurry and see if any strawberry tarts are left.' She waited seeing hesitation and distrust in her younger companion's face. 'I am no tattler. If you like, I will promise not to 'split' on you — cross my heart!'

'You promise?'

'Absolutely!'

With a happy smile the girl put her hand out to Julia, and they walked hand-in-hand back to the house. Each was conscious that in a certain measure friendship had been offered and accepted. Julia knew she could not yet pry into this strange child's secrets, but hoped that in due course opportunity would come for her to learn more. Yes, she might even like to learn more about the mysterious stranger who had come for the child. For some reason the incident had been much in her thoughts. Now, to find out that he was an old friend of Charlotte's! Sophie had not given him a name, and Julia was not sure she wished to put her future sister-in-law to the blush by asking her about some former beau.

The party broke up not long afterwards. The Countess was most affable on leaving. 'My dears, I do so look forward to greeting you at the Rise. Perhaps Miss Stride will bring you both to visit soon. We will arrange a date.'

With that her ladyship's barouche conducted the Selchurch party away with the twins and Sophie squeezed together on one seat facing Lady Selchurch and Arabelle.

★ ★ ★

Thus it was that ten days later Julia and Charlotte entered the portals of Bishop's

Rise. Sir Ivor had declined to accompany them, pleading press of business. It was a fine day with a few puffy clouds riding the sky. Knowing the ladies to be expected, the butler informed them that Lady Selchurch was receiving in the garden that day.

'Oh dear! I hope Lady Selchurch is not having one of her down days,' Charlotte whispered, as they were conducted through the house out into the grounds. She continued to talk sotto voce to Julia as they followed the butler. 'Lady Selchurch is a brave woman — so much to contend with — but she is subject to bouts of melancholy that quite cast her spirits into the depths.'

They were led at last through an elegant salon. On one wall a series of French doors led out to a balcony. The opposite wall was paneled with bas reliefs enclosing murals depicting mythic tales that Julia could not immediately identify. At the end of the room one dominating portrait hung in a place of honor over the fireplace of a woman seated, surrounded by her family, alfresco, with a partial view of Bishop's Rise in the background. Charlotte pointed it out.

'Alicia and her children,' hissed Charlotte. 'Painted eight years ago. Little Peter was still alive then.'

Julia scanned it with interest. It portrayed a

younger, more slender Alicia Selchurch, seated, holding an infant, angelic twin toddlers at her knee, a confident, bold-eyed lad posed with a hoop, and a young Arabelle leaning beside the chair. One single cherub was painted leaning in the bottom right corner of the canvas, suggesting the previous loss of a another child.

They were led out through one of the French doors onto a stone balcony with sweeping stairs to ground level. They entered a gracious walled garden, followed at a distance by footmen bearing chairs.

Like the neat surroundings of the parsonage, the walled garden at Bishop's Rise was laid out in formal style, with well-behaved flower beds edged by manicured grass verges. A number of curved stone benches were placed at intervals throughout the walks. The south-facing wall had espaliered peach trees and branches from a huge horse chestnut overhung the wall, shading a semicircular bench beneath. A tall copper beech tree stood apart near the entrance to the garden, saving the pleasance from too rigid a symmetry.

Beneath the beech, Lady Selchurch sat, rocking herself gently, on a swing suspended by long ropes from one of its branches. A few feet away from her, a striking young woman was lounging in a chair.

Lady Selchurch beckoned the two young ladies, and introduced them to Lady Cytherea FitzWarren, the daughter of an old friend she had known forever.

Lady Cytherea extended a hand and voiced a languid greeting. A fringed shawl draped from her arm, and indeed the air was cool enough in the shade to make it appropriate.

'How welcome you are, my dears,' Lady Selchurch was saying. 'I thought you'd enjoy sitting out in the fresh air — so beneficial as it is to the spirits. How kind of you to come and help drive away my blue mood. My poor Lady Cytherea has been the recipient of all my sad recollections.'

Julia perceived that Charlotte's foreboding proved justified. However, she decided, widows had a right to nurse feelings of despondency from time to time.

'As I was telling Lady Cytherea, my children are all my life now,' continued the Countess in a lugubrious tone. 'This swing, for instance, is not out of place in my little garden. I refuse to allow it to be so.'

'Certainly not,' agreed Julia. 'It gives a charming air of informality.'

'I allowed it for the children years ago, but no treehouse, you understand. That had to be beyond the wall. I thought it altogether inappropriate here. My poor little Peterkin was quite devastated, I remember.' The company was silent for the moment. She continued, 'If I'd known how short a time I would have him, I'd have let him have his way. It absolutely lacerates my memory of him that I denied him.'

Lady Cytherea twitched the shawl higher on her shoulders. 'You must not dwell on it, Alicia. You had a treehouse built — close enough. Do not reproach yourself. You were not a stern mother at all.'

'Yes, I did. Is that not so? And Peter could see his little sisters from it, though we could never see him, the naughty monkey. He would hide up there in the leaves like a little tree spirit, watching over his sisters.'

Julia was looking round curiously. Charlotte surreptitiously pointed to the horse chestnut whose branches over topped the wall near the curved bench. A wooden structure was almost completely masked by the leaves. Charlotte's eyes had thrown such a droll look that Julia could immediately envision a rather different scenario from the idealized one presented. Knowing the ways of youth, visions of peashooters and water bombs sprang to mind.

'If you would take my advice, you would have it taken down,' commented Lady Cytherea.

The Countess stared at the voluptuous creature beside her. 'How could I do such a thing?' Her voice rose in anguish. 'Pull down my little Peter's fortress? Not to be thought of!'

'But consider! Contemplation of it makes you mis — so dejected. By November, with all the leaves gone, you must see it quite plainly. How do you bear it in the winter?'

Charlotte broke in. 'You have a visitor, Lady Alicia.' She exchanged a speaking glance with the Dowager. 'He does not stand on ceremony, milord Vale.'

All eyes turned towards the far end of the garden. A gentleman in buckskins and topboots came through the gate. He strode towards them, confident albeit unannounced. Of no more than medium height, he was yet broad-shouldered. His coat was excellently cut, but worn with a casual air. His cravat was tied carelessly, and he wore his graying hair long in defiance of the current fashion for cropped heads. His face was blandly agreeable, with a smooth chin, and laughter lines at his narrow eyes, which suggested he saw life as an onlooker. By his vigorous step he was no dotard, however — possibly barely on the brink of middle age. He paused and bowed to the company, taking a quick comprehensive look, and his eye checking

116

momentarily on Lady Cytherea as he did so. 'A good day to you, Lady Selchurch. I see you have company. If I am de trop, I beg you will tell me.'

'Not at all, Sir Janus,' spoke the Countess. 'We no longer expect you to stand on ceremony with us.' She indicated a spare chair. 'You must know Lady Cytherea FitzWarren, and, of course, Miss Stride. Miss Valliant, this is Sir Janus Vale, a neighbor who comes to relieve our tedium frequently.'

His careless bow included Julia and Charlotte, but he paused by Lady Cytherea and brought a quizzing glass into play. 'Yes, indeed! The incomparable Lady Cytherea. It is quite some time since we have met, is it not?'

Julia noticed a sudden heat had crept into that lady's cheeks. Her eyes flashed and there was a slight flaring of the nostrils.

'Save your town manners for St. James. I am no miss in her first season to be on display for you, Sir Janus.'

'Will it mollify you that your looks are in even greater beauty than when you first set dance slipper in Almacks?' A peculiar smile played at one corner of his mouth. 'Worry more when I fail to look, dear lady.'

This visitor might put anyone to the blush, thought Julia. What strange manners, to single out one lady so obviously over the rest of the company, and in a manner so particular! She studied him surreptitiously. It struck her that he could have been the buck who passed her coming from the direction of Beesley's farm. The profile matched.

The man seated himself in compliance with an invitation from Lady Selchurch. 'Do not let me interrupt your conversation. I have no doubt it was amazingly interesting.'

Lady Cytherea regained her composure albeit with a waspish tinge. 'What if we told you we were discussing things only of interest to women?'

'Please carry on! I shall hold my own in any discussion you choose. I have deep interest in the fair sex.' His air of provocation matched hers.

Lady Selchurch dropped her fan.

'Children, we were discussing children,' said Charlotte hurriedly, and bent down to restore the fan to its owner.

'*Quel ennui!* A necessary evil, one supposes to ensure the survival of the species.'

Julia was intrigued. Here was a man apt to challenge convention. He would be willing to carry any conversation close to the mark. Such a man might be more at home in ton circles than in her own milieu, the lower gentry that was more conscious of respectability. She could not like him.

'La, Sir Janus,' answered the Countess peevishly. 'My mood is glum enough. If you aim to provoke us, you may take your leave now, sir.'

He laughed lazily. 'Acquit me, dear lady. I sensed your mood and hoped to provide a more lively direction to your thoughts. Ill-judged, I now acknowledge. I will engage to be morbidly respectable and not offend your company.'

'Ah, if your wedding had been similarly blessed with children, you would feel differently,' smiled the Countess dolefully.

'Then may my next wedding be more successful! But tell me how all your children do, Lady Selchurch?' He sat forward with an attitude of spurious interest.

The Countess rapped him lightly over the knuckles with her fan. 'You are a shocking rogue, and I will not let you annoy us. My children are all well, interesting and flourishing. I shall say no more about them.'

'A little bird told me — yes, I am sure I heard that they have a new, stimulating companion.'

Lady Selchurch stared at him. 'What can you mean?'

'A long lost cousin for the children?'

'We have Miss Kettle staying with us at the moment,' she replied cautiously.

'And when do you present this new child to your friends? I confess I am eager to meet one who has led so unusual a life so young — treading the boards, I'm told.'

'Stories you have heard are probably quite apocryphal,' said the Countess loftily. 'Unfortunately, the young lady in question romanticizes her past — and is sometimes too familiar with the servants. She will learn better. You really should not listen to ground floor gossip, my friend!'

'Hobnobs with the maids, does she? That's very bad.' His voice was grave, but there was a derisive gleam in his eye. 'Now where can she have acquired such a taste for . . . '

Lady Selchurch's complexion had suddenly become quite pasty. She cast a hand across her forehead. 'My dears, I am afraid I am unwell.' Charlotte sprang to her aid as she rose unsteadily from the swing.

Julia jumped up. 'Will you not sit in a proper chair, Lady Selchurch?' she urged. 'You will feel better directly.'

'No, no! I must go in. Charlotte, lend me your arm — no, no. Sir Janus, please give me your arm. Charlotte! Be so good as to fetch my woman.' She leant heavily on the accommodating male arm. 'Don't run, my dear, it's unnecessary! Please ladies, do not disturb yourselves! Refreshments are being brought out. Forgive my — my moment of weakness. It will be transitory, I promise you.'

She tottered off, clinging to Sir Janus in the wake of Charlotte's hastening steps.

'Well,' drawled Lady Cytherea. 'A touch of mal de balançoire, so far from the sea as we are.'

'In truth, I am sure Lady Selchurch would not have been so indisposed had she used the swing to the purpose instead of just sitting in it,' said Julia practically. 'No doubt the uncertainty of the movement caused her nausea.' Privately she considered rather that the tone of the conversation had upset her than the motion of the swing. Yet Lady Selchurch had called on her visitor for support.

Her companion smiled. 'The throne is vacant. The opportunity is yours, Miss Valliant. A rigorous heave ho would no doubt prove as beneficial as basking in the shade for your constitution.'

Julia laughed, more in politeness than amusement. 'Thank you, no! I cede the opportunity for such an exercise to you.'

'Riding is my form of recreation. Do you ride, Miss Valliant?'

'Quite regularly around my home. There must be some very pleasant rides around here.'

'I am not familiar with them, though I hope to get to know the area better.'

'Are you staying with Lady Selchurch, Lady Cytherea?'

Her companion explained that she had merely called on Lady Selchurch's hospitality to break a journey to her home in Berkshire, and would be leaving very soon. 'But it is so pleasant an estate — I vow I can't wait to return here.'

A desultory conversation ensued in which both ladies sought for some grounds of common interest, returning to the possible rides in the neighborhood, and sights to be seen. Suddenly, Lady Cytherea said, ''Streuth, it's chilly. I'm going in.' She rose abruptly and walked towards the mansion.

'Well!' exclaimed Julia, and then laughed. What a strange morning this was! In a spirit of caprice she seated herself on the swing and sawed herself backwards and forwards, enjoying the air rushing past her face. Up and up she soared, until she could get a fine view of the treehouse, perched amongst the branches of the horse chestnut beyond the wall. She caught a glimpse of something white moving in the tree.

'Julia, what are you doing?'

She eased her way down to a gentle swing.

Charlotte was gazing at her, arms akimbo,

though an amused glint lurked in her eyes. 'You are no longer seventeen.'

'And I might be seen from the house? I hardly care. Let us leave this place, Charlotte! These people are — difficult to admire.'

'Julia, don't say that! Why Lady Selchurch — '

'With the exception of Lady Selchurch, who, poor lady, has probably had to deal with the others all her life.'

Julia and Charlotte chose to walk back to the parsonage. Charlotte was concerned about Lady Selchurch, who had been in poor health all spring, and had not completely recuperated from the disasters that had befallen her.

'Sir Janus seems such a — such an earthy person. Did his conversation upset Lady Selchurch?'

Charlotte considered it. Sir Janus had been a frequent visitor, and had been a crony of the late earl. The Countess was familiar with his odd ways and provocative — sometimes salacious conversation. 'He's a widower — but don't, I beg you Julia, become interested in him.'

Her companion was amused. 'No, I promise not to. Besides, it sounds as if he is contemplating a new bride.'

'Not as far as I know. I hope he has not

been bothering Alicia.'

'Possibly she just could not stand him today.'

'Imagine,' Charlotte said thoughtfully, 'the strokes the poor woman has suffered over the last few years. The death of her husband. Her husband's brother and his family — drowned on the way to Greece — just swallowed up by the sea. Her own two sons — no, three sons dead. One died at nine days — you saw the cherub in the painting — I do wish she hadn't insisted on that. Peter, the apple of her eye, died at Eton of a brain fever — '

'Three sons?' prompted Julia.

'When they brought her husband home dead after his fall, she lost a baby. Less than three months, but they say it was a boy.'

'I would have gone mad, I believe. It would be too much to bear for me.'

Charlotte glanced sideways at her. 'You have had your own share of misfortune. Alicia Selchurch is a strong woman. Yet, the miscarriage of that last little babe was the greatest tragedy for her — he was the key by which she would have retained the Rise as her own home. That blessed entail! Why are things so set that a woman and her daughters can lose their home in such a fashion?'

'Do you think the new earl will expect her to leave?'

'I was with Alicia when he arrived. He seems quite an agreeable, even an altruistic person. I doubt he would expect Alicia to move. But that could all change if he took a wife, you know. Her wishes would have to be taken into consideration.'

'Is it in the cards that he should take a wife in the near future, do you think?'

'That I don't know, but I hear rumors. Soon, if Lady Cee has anything to do with it, I warrant.'

5

A few days later, Sir Ivor drove his sister to London, and dropped her off outside a pleasant, recently built residence just off Portman Square, before pursuing several errands in the City.

Julia was greeted at the door by Mrs. Farlaine. It was some eighteen months since they had last met, but they corresponded frequently, and Mrs. Farlaine was well versed on the news from Mallow. Events had brought the two women so much together over the last seven years that they had become close friends despite the difference in age between them.

Mrs. Farlaine drew Julia into the parlor for refreshments. She was a friendly, blunt, generous-hearted woman, not standing on ceremony, and in many ways the image of her late son. During his illness she had stayed more and more at home, no longer circulating in smart society. She had success-fully launched two attractive daughters, but that had been several years ago — before her eldest son's sad accident. Her inclinations for privacy had been shared by her husband. As a busy barrister closely connected with the King's Attorney General, he came much in contact with people of influence, but spent little time pursuing advancement in his career. Mrs. Farlaine worried over Julia's continued single status, but having distanced herself from her old society friends, she doubted that she was in any position to do anything about finding a husband for Julia in the brief span of a fortnight's visit, though there was one coup that she was eager to impart. Her husband had made the acquaintance of a gentleman from Julia's own district.

'The new Earl of Selchurch, no less! Ralph met him in the most unusual place. You would not believe! Of course, I acquit him of being one of those awful voyeurs who make a practice of visiting Bedlam and staring at the poor wretches there, but I am sure he had other reasons . . . but Newgate of all places!'

With the ease of long acquaintance, Julia laid aside her bonnet, and accepted a cup of tea handed to her. She looked quizzically at her friend. 'What's this, Moll? You have stolen a march on us by making such a grand acquaintance.' She took a sip. 'What did Ralph think of him — besides his penchant for prison visiting?'

'He must have taken a liking to him, for he

doesn't make friends easily, as you know. They got into conversation in the warden's office and found they had a friend in common — that poor Sir George Prevost who died this January.'

'Prevost? Should I know him?'

'Oh Julia! From the colonies. He was responsible for that absolute debacle at Sackett's Harbour, and got called home in disgrace. One can't help thinking his death was a Heavensend, for it saved him from a court martial, you know.'

'Oh, undoubtedly!' agreed Julia with amusement. 'But why was his lordship at Newgate?'

'I'm sure his motives were of the highest, though it doesn't sound as if he's Quakerish, or even like that odd Mr. Howard who made it his business to go round inspecting all the gaols. Ralph believes he was searching for someone. Of course, Ralph was there for professional reasons, though thank goodness he doesn't often have to go to that sort of place.' She gave an eloquent shudder. 'I make him take a bath immediately afterwards. I hope the other young man did. You have to be so careful. Oh! What is he like? A very personable young man, I am told, of pleasant countenance and not by any means high in the instep. I inquired particularly of Ralph, because I immediately thought of you, my love, he being so close a neighbor.'

'Thought of me?' cried Julia. 'Don't turn matchmaker on my account, I beg of you!'

Her hostess remained serious. 'So many years wasted, Julia! So many years being faithful to my poor son. You must not think I don't appreciate it and I honor you for it, but, as I've said many times, you should have freed yourself as soon as we realized that he would never come back to his full senses.'

'Oh, fiddlesticks! I'm no self-sacrificer. You should know me better, Moll! It was — to my advantage — as much as anything. Ivor has such terrible gudgeons among his friends, and was always trying to foist me off on one of them. He seemed to think it his brotherly duty. My engagement to Philip at least put a damper on his efforts. I am four and twenty — not quite at my last prayers!'

'But so many years . . . '

'Believe me, Moll, if I had met anyone I thought would suit me, it might have been a different story. I'm glad I didn't, because I would have had to make a terrible decision. Philip might have woken and there was no one I met who had half his sweetness of disposition or sense of adventure.'

'You can't be averse to meeting the new earl, anyway. We'll have him to dine.'

Julia threw up her hands as if to banish the thought. 'Don't invite him on my account! No doubt he's on the lookout for a fine lady with an even finer dowry. And in the extremely remote circumstance of his taking an interest in me, the idea of supervising a household with as many as fifty servants is quite stifling.'

'They have housekeepers to run large country homes, as you well know.'

'A more moderate gentleman for me, I thank you!'

'It so happens, Lord Selchurch is coming to dine tomorrow,' Mrs. Farlaine said triumphantly, 'and you can't blame me because Ralph invited him, quite by himself. He really surprised me this time!' She leaned forward confidentially. 'I really believe the old rogue had you in mind, my dear.'

Julia spoke lightly. 'Then I am wholly undone. Ivor and I are invited to Bishop's Rise to make his acquaintance, and I shall be perceived as setting my cap at him.'

'Beyond foolishness, Julia!' Then Moll Farlaine spotted a real stain of embarrassment on her friend's cheek. Abruptly she changed the subject.

The following day the two ladies embarked on a shopping trip, followed by a footman to carry the parcels. Julia had in mind to buy a wedding present for her brother. They first visited the showrooms of Mortlock's, the china dealer on Oxford Set. Here Julia found an attractive and unexceptional gold ornamented serving plate which so matched Moll's cups that she had to buy it for her as a hostess gift, much against that lady's protests. Proceeding to Rundell and Bridge, goldsmiths much patronized in the past by royalty, Julia purchased a pair of antique silver gilt serving dishes with domed lids, decorated with discreet honeysuckle foliage that she knew would please Ivor, an enthusiastic trencherman. From thence they returned to Oxford Street to stroll among the fashionable shops. Each lady treated herself to a new and modish bonnet. Julia put out of her mind an earlier intention to visit a modiste in view of the day's extravagances. Instead she planned on a visit later in the week to the Pantheon Bazaar to obtain a few ells of dress material to have on hand when necessity or the creative mood struck.

That evening, Julia dressed carefully for dinner in yellow twilled sarcenet. It was molded well to her tall elegant figure, with two rows of narrow ruffles at the wrists. The neckline was no lower than was fashionable, and she had put on a pretty string of cornelian agates. She frowned at her appearance in the cheval mirror. The dress was not in its first season, and the stones round her neck were of small value. She threw up her chin. Dining at the same table as a peer of the realm was no reason to wish herself anything else than who she was.

Although Mrs. Farlaine no longer employed a personal maid, she sent one of the parlor maids to see if she could be of any assistance to Julia. The girl was handy and enthusiastic. Julia emerged from her room, stylishly coiffed with curls artfully arranged over each ear, in good time to reach the drawing room before the guests arrived.

On short notice, Mrs. Farlaine had managed to bring in a distinguished colleague of her husband together with his wife, but was forced to call on the attendance of her cousins, the Barretts, who were first to arrive. They were well-known to Julia who had met them some half-dozen times over the years. They were full of enquiries about her brother's nuptials and whether the bride was well-favored, accomplished and well-dowered. Julia answered all their questions with good humor,

The Earl of Selchurch arrived promptly on the appointed hour, and was ushered into the drawing room. Julia noted he had a few inches above average height with a well-proportioned figure, and was dressed in a dark well-tailored coat. He wore his fair hair cropped quite short. It was the hair that misled Julia. A few days earlier, the fair, wavy locks had been unruly and much longer. Not until she looked directly into his face did she recognize him as the rider from Beesley's Dell.

For as long as a couple of heartbeats her face was frozen, lips parted trying to frame suitable words in response to the introduction. Before, his eyes had lit with amusement under the threat of her whip. Now they registered only polite interest. Regaining her composure, she uttered an acknowledgment, closed her mouth and dipped a curtsy, hoping her confusion had attracted no attention. How mortifying if anyone should think her so wanting in social graces that she was bowled over merely by meeting a peer of the realm! Apart from that one startled moment, no one would have faulted the cool grace with which she comported herself.

He murmured his pleasure at making her acquaintance, and she was relieved that he made no mention of their previous encounter. She wondered if he did not recognize her, or whether he was merely grateful for her similar reticence.

Conversation was general, until the call to the table. Much as Mrs. Farlaine would have liked to seat Julia adjacent to the Earl, the prior claims of an older married lady meant that Julia was conducted to the dining room by Mr. Barrett and seated next to him.

At the other end of the table, the distinguished colleague was soon making stringent inquiries regarding boundary disputes between the colonies and their neighbors to the south. Losing interest, Mr. Barrett favored Julia with his attention. He was marveling that she should be so calm about looking after an estate during her brother's proposed absence. 'So your brother relies on you without a qualm?'

'Indeed, it's nothing out of the way, sir. Women have always been used to looking after property when their menfolk have been away. If Ivor had gone off to war instead of a wedding trip there would be no question.'

'But you're just a younger sister. The wife of an owner would be an entirely different matter. A capable wife would and should shoulder more responsibility.'

'Do you think me incapable, Mr. Barrett?'

'What about the harvest, young lady?'

'Oh, I am really quite strong,' said Julia, straight-faced. 'You should see me in my sun-bonnet with my skirts hitched high, wielding a pitchfork.'

'I would not like to picture you in such a hoydenish stance, Miss Valliant,' commented Mr. Barrett. 'I believe you jest.'

'By no means! You would see freckles bloom on my nose, and calluses on my palms.' Julia suddenly was conscious that Lord Selchurch was looking at her from the corner of his eye, while he gave a measured response to a query from the distinguished gentleman. Was that flicker of an eyelid a wink? Surely that could not be.

'Don't try to pull a rig over us, Julia!' Mr. Farlaine was saying. 'There are laborers and to spare on your land. What you will have to endure is a lot of dull administrative stuff, if I don't miss my guess.'

'What's this about you planning to travel abroad?' Mr. Barrett shifted his ground of attack.

Refusing to be put out of countenance by talk of her future plans, she was nonetheless relieved when the subject veered to enquiries about the Earl's own travels abroad. It gave her the opportunity to observe him as he answered many questions on his impressions of the wilds of Canada and the aboriginal people he had encountered there. He was willing to enlarge on his adventures with a degree of affability, and drew such a picture of the beauties of lake and forest in every season of the year that Julia became quite rapt with attention. While he spoke, the Earl glanced around, including everyone in his discourse.

Suddenly, Julia realized that her eyes were locked with his. She was leaning forward, her chin resting on her hand, elbow on the table, totally immersed in visions of brilliant autumns and the pristine white of winter he was describing. Quickly, she removed her elbow from the table, and turned her attention to her plate of roast duckling. She felt her cheeks flame, and she dared not look at Moll who was sure to have noticed.

What must people think of her behavior? What must he think of her, goggling at him like some country bumpkin awed by the beasts at the Royal Exchange? The Earl's pleasant voice continued, and his eyes continued to include her, but he very quickly turned the conversation round to engage other people's contribution, and the talk ran readily, though without much contribution by Julia. However, despite the resentment she had harbored against the young man encountered in Beesley Dell, she admitted to herself that he displayed tact and address.

After dinner, the gentlemen joined the ladies in the drawing room, and were invited to inspect the blooms in the small conservatory at the back of the house. Roderick found a palm-shaded corner to speak to Julia privately.

'You are a lady of admirable discretion,' he murmured, 'and not in too militant a mood this evening.'

Julia lifted her chin. It was rather too late in the scheme of things for a show of hauteur. She cast aside her pique, unwanted. 'I scarce recognized you. How stupid I was not to have realized who you were!'

'Ah, you would not have flourished your whip at me, had you known I was not some vagabond fellow?'

'Rather than a person of utter gentility?' She challenged, then smiled ruefully. 'You startled me? I don't know how it was, I didn't know you were so near, though I had heard someone on the road earlier.'

'Shall we blame it on the sodden ground rather than a lady's bonnet that quite muffles her ears? That would be ungallant.'

She saw that he was looking at her speculatively, and realized that he must believe her knowledge of his identity might precipitate her discovery of the masquerade that had been run on her that day. She wanted to ask him about the incident, but that evening was not a suitable time. The mysterious circumstances might never be explained to her. She did not wish to push herself forward, despite the concern she felt for the forlorn young girl she had met at the parsonage. Obviously, he did not know that she had already made the connection. Let him wonder about it!

'You must know, sir, that Lady Selchurch — the Dowager Lady Selchurch that is — has invited my brother and me to visit when you are next in residence.'

He bowed — a little stiffly.

'You have reservations? I hope that this will not be an imposition.'

'Why should it be? And there is no other Lady Selchurch, by the way.'

'You will see much more company than the Valliants. The whole neighborhood is agog to meet you.'

'You scare me to death.'

With a blush, Julia recalled that she had accused him of being afraid of the burly man. Well, maybe she would apologize later. 'Tush, sir! I heard you were in public life. You must brace yourself for a long succession of carriages wheeling up to the Rise. Also, I'll have you know that any residual coolness between the Selchurches and the Valliants is now to become a thing of the past.'

'Quarreled with Cousin Basil, did you?'

'Not me. My brother. A jurisdictional disagreement between magistrates. It dragged on for years.'

'Ah, the old bare-knuckles thing,' called Mr. Farlaine who caught the end of their conversation. 'Ivor gets carried away with that, I vow.'

Julia interposed primly, 'My brother and the late earl had philosophical differences about prizefighting. My brother, Sir Ivor Valliant, is much opposed to such fights. He tells me these encounters are often placed where two or three counties come together to play on the leniency of some magistrates. I am sure Mr. Farlaine can explain the controversy better than I. Excuse me! Mrs. Barrett is trying to catch my attention.' She made good her escape, not wishing to go further into a bitter episode, mentally flagellating herself for having given opening to the subject. For all she knew, the new earl might be as great a sport-fancier as his predecessor.

As the guests took their departure, Julia heard the Earl asking permission to call in the very near future. She told herself that this was a conventional social gambit in which she need take no stock. However, the following morning, she decided to visit a modiste after all. It would be foolish to miss the chance while she was staying in London. She liked to be beforehand with the world, but there was no serious danger she would run out of her self-imposed allowance by the quarter.

When she returned to the house, she found that the Earl had paid a morning call. She berated herself for feeling cast down at having missed him. What have I to do with earls, she asked herself.

'But he is calling back this afternoon,' Moll was saying. 'He wished specifically to take you for a drive in the park, and I took it upon myself to accept on your behalf.'

Julia raised her eyebrows. 'Pretty cool, I would say, to send an invitation to one through another. He would have done better to have asked us both.'

'But no, my dear. Three in a curricle? Much too cozy! Besides, I must pay a call on an old friend — you don't know her, and would be bored to death. She is nigh on eighty and quite deaf, poor soul. No, you go out and be seen in the park with an eligible bachelor, my dear.'

Julia made a derisive response.

So, later that day, Lord Selchurch took up in his curricle a moderately acquiescent young lady, and drove smartly in the direction of Hyde Park and turned in at the gates. It was a gay scene, filled with a mélange of vehicles, riders and saunterers. Dainty parasols bloomed among the tall-crowned beavers. The sun shone more brightly there.

Julia complimented him on the mettlesome pair he was driving.

'We're making somewhat better pace today than another fine day I recall,' he responded in what Julia considered a brazen vein.

'Ungallant!' she protested. 'Somehow I thought that day would come up in conversation. Why precisely did you ask me out for a drive this day?'

'For the indisputable pleasure of your company!'

'Your sweetener does not move me. I think you wish to know whether I have made the acquaintance of Miss Sophie Kettle.'

He shot a sideways glance at her, and nodded his head as if confirming something he had previously thought. 'A capital shot! Is my young relative's exploit the talk of the countryside?'

'I thought you had concluded my discretion was admirable,' she countered dryly.

'Another hit! My apologies!'

'Accepted! I saw no need to betray her escapade.' She looked sideways at him. 'It is, of course, none of my business, but it seemed to me that Sophie Kettle is a profoundly unhappy young lady.' She hesitated, there being no response. 'Perhaps she does not get on well with her cousins? I sensed an antipathy there. Perhaps I'm presumptuous, but I feel I have something to offer her — a friendship, if you like. I hoped to renew our acquaintance when I recently visited Lady Selchurch. Unfortunately the visit was cut short, and I did not see Miss Kettle.'

'Why do you feel this keen interest in her?'

'I'm really not sure. She is unusual. Maybe there is so little happening in my own life that I must needs find someone else's life to bother about.'

'What has she told you about herself?'

'Absolutely nothing — especially about what she was doing in Farmer Beesley's field.'

He was silent for as long as ten seconds before he responded. 'You learned nothing more about Miss Kettle?'

'My knowledge about her is scanty. I gather that she is so recently from London that our country ways are a book yet to be unfolded. Lady Selchurch introduced her as her niece — I assume from your side of the family because of your interest in her, though maybe not. She described you as an old friend of Miss Stride, which completely threw me off the scent.'

'And Charlotte did not tell you more?'

'Heavens! I did not discuss it with her. I

could hardly quiz Charlotte about her old beaux. That's why I was flabbergasted to discover you were Selchurch.'

He grinned suddenly. 'A very old beau! Such an old beau that I scarce recognized her when I met her again at the Rise after nigh on two decades.'

'Oh, you were childhood friends!' exclaimed Julia, relieved to have this point cleared up. 'Charlotte has told me she met you as a child. Oh, I remember! Sophie did speak of her father. She looks forward anxiously for him to come for her. Is he perhaps in the army, stationed abroad?'

The grin vanished. 'Miss Kettle has become separated from her father, and wants efforts put in train to find him. That is all.'

She turned wide-set, gray eyes up into his and held them steady, unembarrassed by this challenging act. Another uncomfortable silence ensued.

Then he said, 'Your tactics are effective, Miss Valliant. You will not be satisfied until you learn more.' He narrated something of the history of Sophie's parentage, and how she had ended up on his hands.

Julia noted that he did not actually explain Mr. Kettle's absence. She fished for more information. 'But what took Sophie to the prizefight?'

'She was simply looking for a friend of her father, Mouche by name, who might have news of him. Why am I telling you all this? Miss Valliant, there has to be some alchemy about you that makes a gabbler out of the most tight-lipped envoy.'

At this point, the Earl was hailed by two gentlemen in the passing throng. He turned to see Joseph Rayne approaching, accompanied by a younger man in new scarlet regimentals whose likeness in features proclaimed his fraternal relationship.

'Pardon me, Miss Valliant. You must meet a good friend of mine, the Honourable Joseph Rayne. And this must be — Lieutenant Arthur Rayne, I see now!'

Joe Rayne was agreeably surprised to see his friend back in town so soon, and was loud in castigations that he had not got in touch. He accepted Roderick's apologies and plea of pressure of business, while casting interested glances at his companion.

After exchanging a few more words and engaging to dine with Rayne that evening, Roderick put his team in motion again.

'You were saying about Mr. Kettle's friend . . . ' prompted Julia.

'I have already told you more than I intended, Miss Valliant.'

'Rest assured I don't pass any of this on,

sir, unless to depress some of the more outrageous of the tattle-tales I hear.'

'Good of you!'

She felt a slap in his sarcasm, and tilted her chin up. By now they were heading back towards the entrance to the park.

'Draw away from Sophie Kettle! Her troubles are not for the faint of heart.'

'I most certainly will not. It seems to me that you are not doing a lot to help her. Have you thought of asking the dresser where this — Mouche, did you call him — might be found?'

There was a spark of anger in his eye. 'Thank you for your opinion! Actually I have been combing London for the man.' He cracked the whip sharply over the horses' heads. 'The fellow was early apprenticed in the building trade, though he never finished his time. With all the building going on in London, the streets, the houses, the bridges, somewhere he might have found work as a day laborer. I have been searching for him. Miss Valliant, you have no idea how many building sites there are in London at the moment. There is an explosion of structure. I am getting intimately familiar with brick dust, plaster dust, limecast and mud.'

Illogically gratified that she had dinted the armor of his composure, Julia gave a disarming smile. 'But why not seek more information from that theatrical dresser?'

In exasperation, he answered, 'Because, I have no way to get in touch with her. She was ejected from her lodgings and left no address. I have been there.'

'You told me she left in a hack. She must have had money for the jarvey, and you do not tell me she was carrying a valise. She may have returned to her lodgings for her belongings and sent them somewhere by carrier.'

'Sophie mentioned a carrier. Miss Valliant, you may be a help after all!'

His mood had warmed. She looked at him appraisingly. Well, if she gave more offence, she gave offence. 'Something else makes me extremely curious. Mr. Farlaine made your acquaintance in rather an unusual location. What were you doing at Newgate?'

'Viewing the unfortunate inmates?' His face was expressionless.

'And they charged you three shillings and sixpence for the privilege no doubt. No, I don't believe that — don't want to believe,' she amended, 'that you are the sort of fashionable fribble who would find amusement in gawking at the sufferings of others.'

'Gawking! Where did you learn that one, Miss Valliant?'

Julia cast this aside impatiently. 'I meant observing, of course. Tell me this! And I shall be bold as anything here. Was your visit to Newgate to do with Miss Kettle?'

He pulled the team abruptly to a halt and turned to face her.

'Do you consider prefacing intrusive questions with the statement that you are aware they are offensive sufficient justification for uttering them?'

'It seems I am pitchforked into Miss Kettle's affairs. I can add two and two, you know. If my arithmetic is faulty, you have only to deny there's any connection to put me off.'

There was time for little more conversation before the Earl handed her down at the Farlaine residence. Julia did not expect to see more of him. The whole episode had been a disaster. That she had gone beyond the bounds of civility, she was well aware. Yet, he had deserved it. He was rude, mocking and wholly wrapped up in his young relative. He had invited her out merely to ensure her discretion in the affair of his young cousin. Of that she was positive! In effect he had used her. She met Moll's interested inquiries in an evasive manner. She agreed he was most personable. Indeed, he was an excellent driver and a competent escort. What had they talked of? The large volume of building going on in the city. Dull stuff, really. They had met a friend of his in the park. No, she did not expect to see him again.

On the whole, she rather regretted that thought, for he had at times been an interesting and amusing companion. Not at all the kind of peer who was too full of his own consequence. She was astonished two days later when his card was brought up, just after the two ladies had returned from an airing. He apologized for short notice but he was there to beg Miss Valliant's company on an excursion not unrelated to their previous discussions, and he so quickly and smoothly begged Mrs. Farlaine's forgiveness for bearing away her guest in so familiar a fashion, that that lady quite missed the opportunity to inquire what was behind this cryptic invitation.

As Julia had not been forthcoming to Mrs. Farlaine about the precise nature of their previous relations, Julia could think of no ready excuse not to go. To refuse would cause unwelcome comment, and the thoughts of another drive in his company was not as loathsome as she would make herself believe.

'Where are we going?' asked Julia as they drove out along the New Road and heading east along the top of the city.

'The village of Islington.'

'Very well!' accepted Julia cautiously.

Roderick grinned. 'Are you afraid you're being kidnapped? Have no fear. I'll have you home long before dark.'

'No such fears beset me. I thought rather that we were on the trail of Mr. Mouche.'

'Ah! I have to apologize, Miss Valliant. Your guesses were getting too warm. There was no reason for me to distrust your discretion. Mrs. Farlaine looked quite puzzled when I mentioned our conversation of the other day.'

'I would not cause her the embarrassment.'

'You'll not meet me half-way. No matter. If you wish to be a friend to Sophie, I will have no secrets from you. I was looking for Mouche at Newgate. You guessed that, didn't you. He ran foul of creditors and landed in the debtor's side. Unfortunately — or fortunately for him — the gentleman in question was no longer there, someone having settled his debt.'

'And is gone without a trace?'

'Apparently! But I have found Mrs. Shackle, thanks to you.'

'Mrs. Shackle?'

'The dresser who had charge of Sophie.'

Julia was gratified. 'You found the carrier?'

'Just around the corner from her old address. I convinced him I was not a bill collector, so he gave me an address in Islington.'

'A bill collector! How could he believe that?'

'I didn't wear my best clothes,' replied Roderick meekly.

Julia laughed. 'Did the carrier give out client information so freely, then?'

He grinned. 'Freely? No. He got a yellow boy for the information.'

She laughed. 'Miss Kettle is costing you a fortune. Seriously, do you really think this Mrs. Shackle will have more information than you have got from Miss Kettle?'

'Getting information from Sophie is like pulling dandelions. It's hard to get all the roots out. Something is always left hidden.'

'You must be a gardener, Lord Selchurch.'

'My upbringing was modest enough. My father enjoyed it as a pastime, but found me an unwilling apprentice. But, I'll have you know I am familiar with many aspects of running a small estate.'

He was becoming more and more attractive to her. A vision of a small boy dutifully performing a designated task, perhaps slipping away to engage in nefarious small boy mischief crossed her mind. What a pity he was an earl!

'I'm glad you came with me today. Mrs.

Shackle might be hostile towards my interests. I'm counting on you to soften her stance.'

'You presume a lot. This lady will be amazed at your bringing a stranger to visit her.'

'Most people would be amazed at my bringing anyone to meet her.' He drew the curricle to a halt. 'If I am at fault, Miss Valliant. I shall take you home.'

Her guns spiked, Julia suddenly found persuasive reasons for them to carry on. For one thing, she wished to know more about Sophie Kettle, and, for another, she found she was reluctant to terminate their expedition so soon. 'I do not care to turn tail in so craven a fashion, sir. You have embroiled me in this affair. Let us continue!'

They found the address in Islington to be that of a tailoring establishment. Mr. Fells, tailor and brother-in-law of Mrs. Shackle, a thin man of punctiliously correct aspect, conducted his visitors upstairs to the back parlor where Mrs. Shackle was found hemming a shirt. Even indoors, she wore the same large bonnet with a goffered cap peeping out under the brim.

At the sight of Roderick, she rose with an alarmed squeak, dropping her work and losing the needle. Undismayed, the tailor's wife popped in from another room, bidding her sister make the swell company welcome.

The Earl introduced Julia to Mrs. Shackle as a new friend of Miss Kettle, and assured her that Sophie was well and thriving. He did not specify where Sophie could be found, but soon discovered that Mrs. Shackle had a greater anxiety that Sophie might be returned to her rather than for her to wish to hang on to Sophie's sleeve among her great relations.

'Well, I'm that glad she's back wiv 'er own kin where she belongs,' she croaked, as her equilibrium began to recover.

Deciding he would get more out of her by putting her at ease, Roderick complimented her on her fine stitch, and retrieved her fallen needle, which he poked into a pincushion on a table at her elbow.

'If we might interrupt you from your sewing for a few minutes, Mrs. Shackle, there are some concerns about Sophie. She is a young lady who keeps her own counsel. Yet, I know she is anxious to find her father. Can you tell me anything which will help her find him?'

After gathering her thoughts, she opened up a little. 'He was a chancy one, that Tommy Kettle. A fine, upstanding young fellow though, and I don't blame Soikey for wanting to meet up wiv 'er papa again, but I dunno if there's any chance.'

'What do you know about him?'

Mrs. Shackle shot him a wary glance. 'Begging your parding, me lord, what do you know about 'im?'

Deliberately, Roderick responded, 'I know that he got in trouble with the law. He was sentenced to hang, but mercy prevailed and he was transported to Botany Bay.' A sidelong glance at Julia revealed shock registered on her face. He carried on evenly. 'By now he has served his sentence. Sophie believes that he was released, and hourly expects his return, but she is afraid he won't find her. She seems to put her faith in a man named Mouche. What do you know of him?'

Mrs. Shackle flinched slightly. ' 'E's the fellow she's always off looking for. A no-good piece of rubbish, if you arst me. It 'appened when Lissie — that's Tom's sister what was my mistress — was still alive. 'E came to see 'er, and told 'er that 'er brother 'ad bin released. She was that elated for a while, expecting to see 'er brother come dancin' in the door any day. But it stands to reason, y'don't just come back like that from out there. Months at sea, they tell me, an' money needed for passage an' all. They don't want them cons to come back 'ere anyway. What she did do was to take all the money what

153

Mrs. Patience left 'er to look af'er Soikey an' sent it to Kettle.'

'How did she do that?'

'She found out about some boat due to ship out to Bot'ny Bay and got round the cap'in . . . put the boodle in 'is 'ands. Foolish, I call it, for it stands to reason you can't never be sure it got to 'er brother. But she said that sometimes you got to trust people. She was like that was Lissie.'

Roderick looked skeptical, but doubted that Mrs. Shackle had profited from any money Patience might have retained. More likely she had been put out of pocket and he would be obligated to do something about that. 'Do you know where I'd find this Mouche?'

'Hmmph! Soikey seemed to think she'd find 'im at a fair what 'ad some fights as a prime attraction. Sloped off there by 'erself, one day, she did. Scared out of me wits! I was, thinkin' somethink 'appened to 'er. No, I wouldn't know.'

Julia broke in, noticing the way the lady's fingers had been twisting at a scrap of the shirt fabric. 'Does talking of Mr. Mouche make you uneasy, Mrs. Shackle?'

She shook her head slightly. 'Not 'im! Just a titch of a fellow 'e is.'

Julia came forward and sat beside her. 'We

are not here to make this day uncomfortable for you. You must pardon me, but you seem frightened of something.' As Mrs. Shackle looked up hesitatingly, she captured her gaze and held it.

Mrs. Shackle smiled uneasily, showing yellowing, uneven teeth. 'Well, you don't seem as if you'll bring young Soikey back to me. She was a right burden, that's the truth, and none o' my kin either.' She stopped speaking. Under Julia's steady gaze, she continued, as if eager to get something off her chest. 'Well, as to that, it weren't that Mouche that bothered me. It was the other . . . the fancy dresser . . . not that 'e was flash, or anything . . . more in the old-fashioned style, I'd say. I know clouts, and plenty of flash fellows would visit Miss Lissie, so I know what to look for.'

'A gentleman?' interposed Roderick.

'Oh yes, I'd say a gentleman. 'E come around later, wantin' to know where Tom Kettle was. Soikey's pa was a friend 'e said. There was something about 'im. Soikey didn't take to 'im, though she didn't seem scared of 'im. But I was. The eyes — sent chills into me boots.'

'Did this gentleman have a name?' asked Roderick.

The old lady thought deeply. 'Short name

— Dell? No, it's gone. Arst Soikey — she'd remember!'

Afterwards as they drove back to the city, Lord Selchurch said to Julia, 'How do you do that? You were amazing. She would not have told me about her mysterious visitor.'

She laughed. 'I learned the trick — to my cost — from the local vicar. When I took my troubles to him, he would just chain my eyes, so that I found myself telling him much more than I had meant to. Unnerving, isn't it?' She looked him full in the eyes, feeling her color rise as she did so. 'He used silence. He just waited till I poured out my whole soul.'

He gazed back at her, amusement dancing in his eyes. 'Oppression by annihilating silence.' With one hand he turned her face to his so that their two pairs of eyes were enchained. 'You caught me once by that. I shall be prepared for it in future.'

So, there is to be a future, thought Julia. She pulled her chin away and broke the tie. 'Alas! Then you'd be better off watching the road.'

He laughed and turned his attention to his horses, as they came to overtake a slow-moving vehicle.

Over the next week, he claimed her company to view the Egyptian Hall, new since his absence from England, and entertained her and the Farlaines to supper and a play. Mrs. Farlaine was a keen observer of any little signs he made towards her guest. She had to admit that he was exceedingly charming and attentive. There was definitely a certain warmth in his manner towards Julia. Were his attentions serious? Early times, yet, she thought.

On the evening before Julia was due to return home, Selchurch waited on the family and Mrs. Farlaine contrived an opportunity for them to be alone, an act that afforded Julia embarrassment, and Roderick a sudden amusement.

Her eyes widened as he crossed the room to sit beside her on the settee. 'Oh, that is so blatant! I may commit murder.'

He touched the cheeks that had colored. 'What a bloodthirsty creature you are! I hope you don't, for I count Mrs. Farlaine very much my friend.' Taking her face gently in his hands, he gave her a gentle kiss. Finding she did not resist, he put his arms around her and kissed her in earnest. Feelings swept through her that intoxicated her senses, and she returned the pressure. They were lost for awhile to the passing of time.

Moll Farlaine was delighted when Sir Ivor's coach drew up to the door to collect his sister the next day. Wise in the ways of sexual politics, it would not do for Roderick to return to his landed estate before Julia's departure.

Sir Ivor was anxious to learn what the new earl was like. As they left the turnpike behind them, Julia told Sir Ivor about the Farlaine's dinner party and her embarrassment at finding the Earl of Selchurch and the stranger in the dell to be one and the same.

'Thought he might have been!' Sir Ivor said pensively. 'That gray sounded like Sir Basil's new hunter.'

'You thought . . . ' Julia gave her brother a withering look. 'And you would let me go on thinking it was some stranger.'

'Well, he would be a stranger — you'd never met him before.'

'It's not the same thing.'

'Find out who the lad was?'

'Some distant cousin of the new earl,' replied Julia airily, 'nowhere in line.'

'Lottie says there's expectation the new earl will be contracting an alliance soon. Lady Selchurch seems to be promoting some young lady — bit of an heiress, of course. It's someone he used to court years ago. His coming into the earldom made quite a change to his prospects.'

An uncertain quiver afflicted Julia's heart for a second. She forced herself to breathe naturally. That could hardly be true, she told herself. At no time in the five occasions when she had been in his company over the past two weeks had he made any intimation that he was about to become engaged to another female. If that were the case, the frequency of his attention might be described, if not exactly flirtatious, as definitely bordering on the dishonorable.

'That,' she said. 'An earl and a bachelor? Rumor will have him engaged to a dozen heiresses within a twelvemonth.'

6

As Lord Selchurch drove up the carriage sweep at the Rise, his thoughts dwelt on the refreshing Miss Valliant, and a pair of wide, challenging gray eyes and soft lips that had responded to his. He must remind Lady Selchurch of her intention to invite Miss Valliant and her brother to the house. He was speculating keenly on how many days it would be before they made a similar approach to his own. Maybe it was this pleasant anticipation that suggested to him that the well appointed equipage drawn up to one side of the entrance, might signal their visit, but the familiar maroon livery worn by its attendant servants disabused him of the fancy.

Giving his curricle over to the charge of a groom, he mounted the curving stone steps towards the main door, to come face to face with Lord FitzWarren who emerged from the main entrance, pulling on kid gloves as he did so.

'Ah, Selchurch,' he cried. 'What excellent timing! I'm sorry I missed you in town. How are you, my dear boy?' He then proceeded to give him laconic congratulations on his acceding to his kinsman's honors.

A little taken aback at being referred to as his 'dear boy' by his superior at the ministry, Roderick made a quick recovery and gave a conventional response. With sudden understanding, he recognized the ambivalence with which an officer of the crown might face a junior unexpectedly elevated to a social rank near his own. Roderick's mind slid uneasily to that embarrassing item in *the Morning Chronicle* a few weeks earlier. Did this jovial greeting suggest that Lord FitzWarren had not seen the item, or more appallingly, that he had?

'You're wondering what brings me to the Rise? You must know that Lady Selchurch is an old friend — a very old friend. It was time I paid my respects, besides dropping off my little Cytherea.'

'Lady Cytherea? Here?'

'She's staying with your Cousin Alicia for a few weeks. They've always had a fondness for each other, you know. Cytherea dropped in on her a few days ago, and the Countess just insisted that the minx stay with her to help chase away the megrims.'

Roderick managed an unexceptional remark.

'That brings to mind something Cytherea

mentioned. You've had no luck getting in touch with me since putting foot in England again. Come to Haldene soon and we'll have a chin wag about your future. We can't get into things here.' After a couple of common-places related neither to business nor the Colonial Office, he was gone, leaving a somewhat rattled earl uncertain whether the pending discussions would deal with future posting or his intentions towards Cytherea.

He found Lady Cytherea in close conversa-tion with Lady Selchurch in the morning room, and greeted her with the ease of an old acquaintance.

She pouted mischievously. 'Here I was, thinking to surprise you. What happens? No foot rooted to the floor! Not even one raised eyebrow! How abominable you are, Roddie! Truly, I cannot confound you.'

'Is that an object with you?' he smiled. 'Acquit me of stolidity. I collided with your father leaving the premises, and he told me you were here. I had time enough to greet you with proper comportment.' He accepted her extended hand, which he saluted with a light kiss to the fingers.

Lady Selchurch was an interested onlooker to their greeting. She said, 'This is all very comfortable. Welcome back, Roderick! Sit down my dears! We must hear all about

London, before we dress for dinner. Both of you will be weary after traveling. I've sent for refreshments.'

Over a glass of wine, Roderick gave a guarded account of his activities in the city. He sensed that the two ladies would neither appreciate his visit to Newgate nor his absorption with building sites. He mentioned having met a family by the name of Farlaine, casting a veil over the circumstances in which the acquaintance had originated, and that they had staying with them a young lady, with whom he understood Lady Selchurch was acquainted.

'Miss Valliant! Yes, indeed!' exclaimed Lady Selchurch. 'A recent acquaintance of mine, though she has lived not far away all her life.'

Cytherea added her approval dismissively. 'A prettily behaved young woman. I trust she enjoys her taste of city life?'

'As to that, she has made frequent visits to London,' said Roderick, suddenly irked by her condescension.

Cytherea leveled an amused glance at him. 'Obviously, I have jumped to a wrong conclusion. I have never met her in town. My mistake was to assume that she would move in our circles.'

'She is of a respectable local family, soon to be a connection of our parson,' interjected the Countess conclusively. 'We quite accept them now.'

Roderick's lips quirked at this, having received a trenchant history of the relations between the Selchurches and the Valliants from Miss Valliant herself.

'We will send cards to the Valliants for our soirée,' she continued. 'Indeed, we were discussing it when you arrived home. It is to be a reception for you, of course, Roderick — a gathering of the main families in the district. Your neighbors will wish to pay their respects.'

As Julia had warned him of some such eventuality, Roderick was able to face the prospect with fortitude. 'I must meet the local world sometime, I suppose.'

Cytherea laughed lazily. 'Too retiring by half. You are the Earl now, Roddie, and must make an appropriate impression. I hear you have scarce been here since May.'

'It will be just a small party. If the situation remains the same, you can have a ball or a grander what you will later on,' announced Lady Selchurch.

Cytherea gave her hostess a puzzled look. In what way might the situation change? Perhaps she was referring to the length of time she would remain in mourning, but that should not inhibit any arrangements the new

164

earl cared to make. She opened her mouth to frame a question, then abruptly changed to voicing her intention to make herself presentable for dinner.

As she left, Lady Selchurch gave Roderick a knowing glance. 'A most lively and amusing young lady. She is the reigning beauty of London, I hear. And of such a noble family . . . Apt to set the ton by the ears, though. 'Tis high time she was wed.'

Roderick felt as though he had been douched with cold water, but he managed a rallying reply. 'Matchmaking, cousin?'

She looked at him archly. 'Jealous, my dear? I seem to recall she is an old flirt of yours. Water under the bridge! I have in mind an old friend of Basil — a man much in need of a settling hand.'

Roderick suddenly grinned. He doubted Cytherea could be a settling influence on anyone. 'Do I know this gentleman?'

The Dowager smiled back amiably. 'Until my plans bear fruit, I must say no more.' She passed two fingers across her lips. 'Let us talk instead about your protégé. She has made an adequate start, cousin. I am told she learns quickly, but is abysmally lacking in discipline.'

'Miss Randall has not yet given her resignation, I hope.'

'Touch and go, Cousin! I expect it hourly.'

Roderick pulled a wry face. 'It was a woeful charge I put on you. The child seems a long time settling down.'

'She and the twins rag at each other rather much, but it is for them to change as much as her. I have spoken to them more than once. They see all too clearly that she was not brought up amongst people of quality, however much that gauche sister-in-law of mine might have tried to set her feet aright. They have to learn to accept her. Mind you, she can be a haughty little puss when she chooses. I am praying that things settle down, for I don't need more distress.'

Roderick purposefully ignored her criticism of Patience. 'What can be done? I may be posted away soon. Perhaps at the end of summer we can place her in some good private school where her manners can be polished.'

'Polished! Scouring is what's required, not schooling,' she laughed. 'No, I am too severe. I don't want to put you to the blush.'

Roderick looked thoughtful.

'Had you some academy in mind?' asked the Countess.

'My dear Alicia, I was hoping you would help me in this. Perhaps you know of some suitable school where she may learn the comportment of a gentlewoman in association with girls of her own class.'

'There's the rub,' replied Lady Selchurch dryly. 'What is her proper class? She has to learn more lady-like behavior. I'll make enquiries for some quiet, unpretentious establishment where she won't be made uncomfortable. Leave things to me! I will write some letters tomorrow.'

'I must rely on your judgment, Alicia. Much as she would like to find her father, he may never turn up. And if he does, our problems might well be doubled.'

'Heaven forfend!'

★ ★ ★

Having changed out of his traveling clothes, Roderick descended some time before the dinner hour. He heard music as he approached the drawing room. Lady Cytherea was seated at the piano, playing a country ballad. She turned as he entered.

'Don't stop! I remember that from Haldene Chase.'

'What else do you remember from Haldene Chase?'

He smiled ruefully. 'Maybe a little too much. Much better we put it out of our minds.'

167

She shot him a sideways glance, and fingered the keys again. 'You gave me no such impression aboard the frigate.'

He grinned. 'You took me by surprise.'

'Indeed! You jumped up and hit your head on the ceiling.'

'A deck beam.'

'What you will! Anyway, I took your concussion as proof of your welcome — and not the only proof, I might add.'

Idly, Roderick leafed through a pile of music on top of the piano. 'I saw an item in the paper — gossipy stuff about the frigate's arrival.'

'Pay no attention! The newspapers have naught to do but chatter about their betters.'

'You seem mighty cool about it.'

She spun round on the bench. 'Are you blaming me for that snippet of innuendo in *the Chronicle?*'

'No! No! Of course, not! What did your father think of it?'

She turned back to the piano. 'I have no idea if he saw it. I have told you, Roddie, that my father knows all I do. If he were upset by the item he would have no hesitation in calling you to answer for it.'

'How could he put it to my account?'

She spun round again to face him. 'I have a most liberal and understanding father. He made no attempt to withhold the letters you sent me from Montreal.'

A cold finger seemed to run down Roderick's spine. 'He knew I wrote to you? That was three years ago. You never answered. I thought you were not able to — or did not care enough to do so. It was over.'

'What makes you believe me so inconstant?'

Their tête-à-tête was interrupted as Lady Selchurch joined them prior to the evening meal.

In the absence of male company at dinner, Roderick did not linger over his port, but joined the domestic scene in the drawing room. Lady Cytherea was seated near the window and was engaged in sprightly conversation with Lady Arabelle. Miss Randall was presiding over a table where five fair heads were concentrating on picking up sticks. Lady Selchurch was playing with the youngest on her knee. Sophie sat close beside her, turning the pages of a rather dilapidated book.

Sophie looked up expectantly as he entered. He had no doubt that she was anxious to hear what he had been able to find out about her father. The opportunity to exchange a few words with her arose as the nursemaid came in to take away the toddler. Lady Selchurch, a fond parent, went with the maid to discuss her minor concern that the little one seemed to be throwing out a rash.

He pulled up a chair beside Sophie, and inquired what she was reading with such absorption.

'It is my mother's.' Sophie sounded defensive. 'Mrs. Bunting, who used to be her nursemaid, found it for me.'

'Mrs. Bunting? Ah! The gamekeeper's mother! I'm gradually getting to know my people.'

'She had kept it safe. She calls it a commonplace book. It has all sorts of verses and snippets, and see — my mother has drawn pictures, too.'

Roderick duly admired what she had shown him, surprised that she would bring so intimate a relic of her mother down to the drawing room. He suspected her overt perusal of such a personal object was an act of giving back identity to her mother whose name had so long been ignored in this house.

'How have you got on while I've been away?'

There was a little shrug. The eyes lifted from the page and looked at him full of expectancy. *Did you find my father? Did you find out anything?*

He responded to her unspoken entreaty. 'You want to hear what I have been doing.' There was a smile in his voice.

She nodded eagerly.

'I will tell you in short. We can talk more fully tomorrow. Firstly, I have discovered through official channels that your father was released some two years ago.'

'But is he back? In two years he must be back!'

'The official I spoke with thought it hardly likely he would have returned to England yet. You must not lose hope.'

'Mouche said — '

'Sh! Ah yes! Mouche! So far I have not found him. After a deal of talking to builders all over London, I found a laborer who knew a man called Mouche who'd been taken up for debt. I then started a trail around the prisons. In Newgate, I learned of a man logged in as Mason, stonecutter by trade. I believe that man to be your Mouche. However, to his good fortune and to our set back, he was no longer there. Some unknown benefactor paid his debts, and he was released. I spent time visiting more builders, hoping that he might have taken employment again, but so far I have been unsuccessful.'

'You did not find him. You gave up.' Her voice was flat.

He suppressed a feeling of irritation. 'He may be beyond finding. One laborer thought he might know of him. A worker he heard called Mouche by one of his mates was taken ill, and failed to return to work. He heard he died. However, when I examined the records, there was no Mason named as having died recently. The master builder who employed him took on a job out of the city and is not expected back till later in the summer. Why the grim face? I will make further enquiries, I promise. I mean to find out where he is now, alive or dead, and who paid his debts. I must spend some time here, but soon I shall go back again.'

'He'll never find me, my papa.'

Taking the book from her, Roderick closed it gently. They were receiving curious glances from the window direction. It was time to change the subject. The complaint was made that the children did not get on together. Sophie must learn to join with them in their activities. 'Come, Sophie! Have you never played at jackstraws? I am determined you will beat us all hollow. They are setting up for another round.' He drew her over to the games table, and, because it was him, she went, though reluctantly.

The following day, he sought out Sophie to tell her of his meeting with Julia Valliant. Miss

Randall had no idea where he might find Miss Kettle, but he quickly located her ensconced within the flimsy walls of the treehouse. He clambered up to join her.

Sophie jumped to her feet in excitement, and Roderick caught hold of her, as she seemed in danger of falling from her aerie. He had more to tell her about his visit to London.

'You met Miss Valliant? She is the lady who saved me — in the dell!' She bounced up and down in her excitement. 'You knew who she was?'

'Only when I met her! It was quite a surprise — especially to find that she had made your further acquaintance. I believe her a person we can trust, however.'

'So do I,' said Sophie warmly. 'Where did you meet her — at a ball?'

Roderick chuckled. 'No, Miss Quiz, somewhere rather tamer than that. In the house of an acquaintance. Miss Valliant seemed anxious on your behalf.' He looked at her searchingly. 'I took the liberty of telling her of your search for Mouche.'

Her quick frown made him wonder if he had caused her offence. However, she did not seem prepared to make an issue of his breach of her privacy. 'She is a right one. She didn't give me away before.'

'It was due to a good suggestion of Miss Valliant that we found Mrs. Shackle.'

'Mrs. Shackle! Will you send me back?' Her tones were devoid of fear. It was just a request for information.

'Would you be hurt if I pointed out that she does not exactly want you back?' He carried on after a pause, 'She is now living in Islington with her sister and brother-in-law.'

'What did she have to say?' Her tones were indifferent.

'She was telling me about a man who visited you in London — who scared her somewhat. Not Mouche, but another who was inquiring about your father.'

Eyelashes shrouded her eyes and she stared down at the ground.

'Who was he, Sophie? Mrs. Shackle thought you might remember his name.'

'I don't know.' A mulish look he'd seen before was back in her face and nothing was to be got out of her in the way of information.

Ruefully wondering why he had got involved with her problems, Roderick sighed and soon left her to her own devices.

Later that day, he rode out with Lady Cytherea who rallied him on his deep interest in a not particularly attractive child. 'It's not that I begrudge your time with her, Roddie. Obviously, you feel some responsibility towards her. But you are the Earl dearest. You have higher responsibilities.'

Her serious mien brought a grin to his face. 'No doubt I merit the lecture. The agent is coming tomorrow, and I'll be immersed in work if I'm to discover how to go on here. Believe me, I've already been up to my eyebrows in account books, much of which is Greek to me, not knowing the names of the tenants or many of the staff come to that. You'll be complaining when I'm least in sight for a few weeks.'

She tossed her head provocatively. 'As long as you spare some time from that tiresome chit for me!'

'You don't much care for her, do you? Have patience, Cytherea! Don't rate me over the attention paid to an unfortunate and needy child. Remember, you owe some company to Lady Selchurch, whose guest you are. You have no occasion to be jealous of my time, you know.'

'Jealous! Me? Are you inferring that I could be jealous of that common, awkward brat of a child? Rest assured life has other interests.'

The rest of the ride was conducted in frigid silence. Roderick was disappointed in her determined dislike of Sophie. He made no attempt to make peace. The discord would right itself, and it would not help his case to ingratiate himself with her.

Over the next few days, invitations to the reception went out to leading families in the district. Cytherea was recruited to assist Lady Selchurch in this tedious job. At Roderick's request, a card was sent to his friend Rayne including an invitation to stay for a few days.

Walking by the paddock beyond the stables one morning, Roderick watched a riding lesson in progress under the tutelage of the head groom. Mindful of Sophie's mortification at receiving riding lessons in the company of the younger children, Roderick was forced to admit that she had a point. Disparity in age of the pupils demanded that progress be governed by the needs of the youngest. On remembering the day when her drooping posture had recalled her mother's willowy form to him, he was pleased to note that Sophie was acquiring a decent seat on a horse.

At the end of the lesson, Roderick claimed the cousinly privilege of taking her beyond the confines of the paddock. They rode out together, but their outing was cut short by the rumble of thunder, and they arrived back at the stable as the first heavy drops began to fall. He promised to take her out the following day to make up for this disappointment.

Piqued by his continuing interest in his young cousin's progress, and anxious to restore herself in Roderick's good opinion, Cytherea appeared in the stables just as the groom was leading out the placid mount that Sophie was to ride. She had donned an olive green riding habit, with black frogs across the front and a black high crowned hat, saved from masculinity by a provocative gauze veil. Roderick was already mounted on the Basil's gray, which he had become used to riding.

He eyed her dashing apparel appreciatively, and grinned. 'Are you joining us this morning? It will be a tame ride for you, I'm afraid.'

She looked up at him challengingly. 'Then I must show you the way.'

'Saddle up the bay for Lady Cytherea, Oliver!' Roderick bade the groom. 'Is the mare spirited enough for you, Cy?'

She eyed the gray measuringly. 'I've a mind to try one of Sir Basil's other hunters.'

Roderick caught the message in the groom's eye. 'They're probably fresh, and I don't know the horses. I'll try out their paces later. The mare, Oliver!'

'My only choice, I perceive!'

He saw the gleam in her eye. That look had enraptured and alarmed him at the same time in the old days. Subjection to good sense did not always come easily to her. Whilst she might wish to smooth relations between them, she was nevertheless ripe for some way to assert her will.

Sophie Kettle arrived at the stables, decked out in a new dark blue habit faced with apple green, and a saucy little blue velvet hat with a self-colored plume. Previously, she had used a habit borrowed from one of the twins, to the content of neither party. She had preened in front of the mirror before coming out, and had been quite gratified by her appearance. Observing Lady Cytherea, her pleasure in the outing diminished. She hesitated for a second, then came forward and greeted them uneffusively. She went up to her mount, speaking quietly to the docile creature, offering a piece of apple, and stroking its nose. The groom came to help her mount.

Within two minutes the little troop was heading out along the driveway. The day was fresh after yesterday's storm, with little clouds scudding in the sky, resembling the sheep that were dotted over the green lawns sweeping down from the mansion. Roderick noticed a pair of sunbonneted ladies seated on a blanket sketching the huge pile. For a moment he wondered who they were, and then recalled that it was the practice to admit visitors to the grounds on certain days.

Lady Cytherea led the way, setting her mount to a brisk canter along the sweeping gravel drive. As the drive entered the wooded section, the road curved picturesquely among blooming rhododendrons. Gamely Sophie followed, urging her startled horse into a sudden movement that nearly unseated her, and she rode off, rather faster than she was used to, clinging on for dear life.

Muffling an oath, Roderick urged his horse forward, and caught up with Sophie as she reached a sharp curve. 'Rein in!' he ordered, as they rode neck and neck along the drive. Yet another startled visitor was forced to step quickly back into the bushes out of the way of the horses. Dimly Roderick was aware of a dark gray beaver hat being raised, but had no time to return the salutation as they dashed by. Finding his request to slow down unheeded, he repeated it louder. He wished to avoid seizing the horse's bridle. Resolutely, the neophyte rider attempted to gain mastery over her mount. Gradually the horse responded to tightening of the reins and reduced its pace.

The heightened color in his face frightened Sophie momentarily. She was canny enough to know this anger was aimed chiefly at Lady Cytherea, now out of sight round the bend, but, in the spheres in which she had been raised, she had often seen anger at one object translated into retribution taken out on the hide of a more lowly victim.

'I-I'm sorry!' she stammered out. The horses were now down to a walk.

After one look at her white face, he mastered his wrath. 'Quite a ride! You'll be leading the hunt in no time. Meanwhile, make sure you can see what's round the next corner when you're in full charge.'

She chuckled, relieved.

He looked back along the way they had come, mindful that some apology was due to the man they had so nearly overrun. However the man was no longer in sight.

Moving at a decorous trot, they found Lady Cytherea awaiting them where the drive opened into the country lane.

'Come along, you slow coaches,' she called gaily. 'We can avoid the road and cross the fields towards that interesting copse over yonder.'

He looked at the field of young wheat, and said, 'We should rather go along the road for a spell.'

They rode towards the village. Spotting a broad pasture, again the lady was anxious for a gallop. 'I cannot abide this pace,' she declared, and with that she set her horse at a rather solid-looking fence with a ditch before it, and was over into the field before galloping off over the daisy sprinkled turf.

'I wish I could ride like that,' sighed Sophie.

'I hope you never do,' said Roderick dryly, 'set your horse against an obstacle when you don't know what's on the other side, or trample a farmer's cornfield, come to that.' God, he thought to himself, I sound like a prosy schoolmaster. 'We will let Lady Cytherea enjoy her gallop, and we can ride as far as the village.' He glanced at her briefly, again reasonably impressed by the way she was turned out this morning. Her behavior had been satisfactory, even considering the risks she had taken by overreaching her riding abilities, and for that he laid the blame elsewhere. Maybe it was time to cement her in the good graces of Miss Stride. 'I had in mind to visit the parsonage, if that meets with your approval.'

At the parsonage gate, they came upon Miss Stride, basket on arm, returning from a shopping trip in the village. She welcomed them in, offering lemonade or 'something stronger if his lordship preferred it.'

Settled in the parlor, Roderick was giving a circumspect account of his visit to town, mentioning his new acquaintance with the Farlaines when a rap on the front door heralded the arrival of a visitor.

Charlotte nodded, half an ear on the murmur of voices in the hallway. 'I have met them.'

'It was my pleasure to meet your future sister-in-law at their house.'

'So I have heard,' declared Charlotte. 'Sir Ivor was quite disappointed to have missed the chance to make your acquaintance. He could not stay for the dinner party. Perhaps you will meet on Sunday. The second banns are to be read, so I depend upon him to be in church.'

'In fair weather or foul — and, God willing, on time!' came a voice from the doorway. Julia stepped into the room. 'Depend rather on me to get him there!'

Roderick sprang to his feet. There was a warm light in their eyes as they exchanged glances, but she looked away very quickly. He was conscious of an infinitesimal withdrawal. He had not thought her prone to shyness.

'Forgive me for not standing on ceremony, Charlotte,' Julia said coolly, 'but the door was open and your maid at some crucial stage in the kitchen.'

'Welcome, Julia! I need not introduce you to Lord Selchurch and his cousin Miss Kettle.'

'No, indeed.' She gave a polite hand to him

and both hands to the young girl beside him. 'How nice to see you again, Miss Kettle!'

'I collect Ivor is not on your heels?'

'Sadly no, Charlotte! He is caught up in local affairs. You see before you his emissary to discuss colors, wallpapers, textiles and swatches.'

'That is too bad of him,' declared Charlotte. 'This should not fall on you, Julia.'

'Wretch that he is! Details are not his strong point.'

The visitors chatted for ten minutes or so, and Roderick and Sophie rose to go.

Mindful of her friendly intentions toward the young girl, Julia said, 'I hope to entertain you at Mallow, some day. That is my home, you know. I would be so pleased if you would visit me there.' Her eyes lit with amusement at the sudden eagerness with which her invitation was received.

'Would you really? Cousin Roderick?' Sophie looked up at him half in delight, half fearfully.

'You must ask Lady Selchurch if she will let you visit.'

'How should I get there?'

He smiled. 'Would you like me to drive you there one day?' He looked at Julia. 'If I am allowed to visit, that is.'

Julia gave her acquiescence. She schooled

herself to show a friendly but impersonal face. She needed more than a few kisses to prove this man was serious in his intentions.

Roderick rode back silently. He had been conscious of the subtle change of attitude towards himself on Julia's part. She had been polite enough and sprightly in conversation, but a wall had sprung up between them. He would take the earliest opportunity to gain a better understanding.

Sophie watched him covertly. She had had little to say in the conversation at the parsonage, but had been conscious of restraint. She grew even more silent, and fell behind as they came together at the lodge gates with Lady Cytherea and a companion. Somewhere that lady had met up with Sir Janus Vale; they were riding slowly and talking in a friendly fashion.

As they came abreast, Lady Cytherea performed introductions, presenting Sir Janus as an old friend and neighbor of the Selchurch family.

'Charmed to meet you, Lord Selchurch, and please introduce me to your delightful young companion,' purred the gentleman.

Roderick answered civilly, performing the required service. He watched the piercing eyes, which engaged his momentarily and then seemed to slide with more intensity towards his young relative. He could sense her discomfort, and well understood her shyness before this rather disturbing stranger.

It turned out that Sir Janus had been bid to luncheon. As Lady Selchurch said, they had too little company to enliven them, and she was growing dull for lack of it.

Sophie left the group at the first opportunity, slipping back into the house and up to her room where she quickly changed out of her habit and into a plain muslin. The man who had ridden with Lady Cytherea was no stranger to her. She recognized in him the man who had so scared Mrs. Shackle. She wished to avoid him at all costs. The schoolroom seemed as good a refuge as any, and there she found Lady Arabelle and the twins sketching some wildflowers they had gathered on a ramble earlier in the day. Quietly, Sophie joined in the activity.

They had been quietly engaged in this occupation for over an hour, when Lady Cytherea's maid, Evans, scratched at the door, bearing a message for Lady Arabelle and Miss Randall to join her mistress in her chamber. 'My lady received a parcel from her modiste in London. Perhaps you would like to see her gowns. She is trying them on.'

The governess turned pink with pleasure at this mark of distinction. 'We would be charmed to do so — wouldn't we, my love?'

Lady Arabelle came to her feet with alacrity. 'Yes, Miss Randall,' she sighed. 'Lady Cytherea has such an elegant wardrobe. I wish I may have as much for my come out next year.'

The twins were envious of their sister's attention and immediately begged to be included in the treat.

Sophie looked up and smiled briefly at the lady's maid. She had made the acquaintance of Rosie Evans on one illicit visit below stairs. She longed to tease the maid about her new romance, which was being whispered round the servant's hall, and had as yet not reached the ears of the housekeeper. She would have said something but caught a slightly frozen look and tight shake of the head. Taking the hint, she concentrated on her sketching once more. She knew the maid was much afraid of getting into trouble, having learned of the scold she got from her mistress after they had been caught having a bantering conversation recently.

★ ★ ★

The following Sunday, Roderick remembered that banns were to be read for Sir Ivor Valliant and Charlotte Stride. He took a walk

186

in the direction of the village church, and slipped into the back, as the service had already started. He could see Charlotte Stride sitting beneath her father's eye at the front of the church, accompanied by Sir Ivor and Miss Valliant.

If he had planned on having a pleasant meeting with Miss Valliant at the end of the service, he was frustrated, for Lady Selchurch sailed down the aisle followed by her children, while the villagers politely yielded precedence to them. Spotting Roderick, she admonished him for not coming to the family pew, and insisted he be introduced to Mr. Stride on the instant, as that reverend gentleman had not yet made his visit in form. By the time he escaped there was no sign of the trio to be seen and he concluded that they had left the church by another door. There was nothing for it but to hand Lady Selchurch up into her waiting carriage, and, rather than overcrowd the vehicle, return to the Rise by foot as he had come.

7

Roderick spent time examining the estate records to find out if any moneys had been given to Lady Patience. The London solicitors had informed him that her money had been set up in such a way that she could not gain access to it if she married without her brother's permission. Lady Patience had not called upon the courts to appeal the situation apparently. Combing the estate records for the last fifteen years, Roderick made several requests of the bailiff to explain various expenditures. For the most part what he heard satisfied him, though a few entries in Basil's own writing were obscure and the agent either could not remember or had not been informed of their exact details. None of them were more than a few hundred guineas.

Joining the lunch table after one particularly frustrating session, Roderick found Lady Selchurch quite put out. She had omitted invitations to two families some miles to the west of Bishop's Rise, and she had found a note omitted from the Valliants' invitation inviting them to stay overnight in view of the distance they would have to travel.

'I would be mortified to omit any attention to them for Miss Stride's sake,' she was saying. 'If I didn't have enough to contend with!' She added this in a pettish manner that Roderick had never experienced in her.

'It is two weeks away. Adequate time to send out invitations,' pointed out Cytherea.

'Yes, but how irritating! We let go two of the grooms, after dear Basil's demise, and here we have Oliver complaining about there being so much to do. Now to have to send off two men in diametrically opposite directions, when we thought all had been done.'

'A practical way to exercise the hunters,' remarked Roderick. 'They are eating their heads off in their stalls.'

'Practical to you men! I find it inefficient.'

Roderick was wondering if some matter other than a want of economy was upsetting the Dowager. 'Give the Valliant's invitation to me,' he said calmly. 'I intend to drive Miss Kettle to visit Sir Ivor's sister, with your approval, of course, and that will provide a good occasion.'

Lady Cytherea rolled her eyes. 'Miss Kettle again!'

'Come with us, Cy!'

'Squeezed in the curricle? No, I thank you.' However, so congenially phrased were the regards she sent to Miss Valliant that

189

Roderick assumed she wished to repair any lingering strained relations with him.

Lady Selchurch had listened to this exchange with an intent expression. As soon as Cytherea left the room, she spoke with heavily portentous tones. 'You were so engaged that you missed a visit from Miss Stride this morning.'

'Oh yes? I trust all is well?'

'How could you have duped me so, Roderick?'

He stared at her bewildered.

'Don't look at me so innocent! She inquired if it was true to expect a significant announcement from Bishop's Rise in the near future. I asked her what in the world she meant — that I should hear it this way, Roderick — '

'Hear what?'

'That you and Lady Cytherea — '

Roderick was aghast. If Miss Stride thought he and Cytherea were involved, then no wonder there had been a cooling in Julia Valliant's demeanor.

'Your silence confirms it, Roderick.'

'No, no, Alicia. Assume no such thing!'

'Then you had best make it plain to Lady Cytherea, for when I sounded her out — scarce believing it could be true — she most certainly did not deny it, but remained so modest and unassuming about her expectations from you, that I feel I have been quite blinkered to what has been going on right under my nose. I feel so foolish when I consider the efforts I have been making on her behalf.'

He perceived he must tread carefully. Cytherea was obviously not prepared to relinquish him without a battle. As far as he was concerned, their kiss aboard ship had been no more than a greeting between old friends. Perhaps he should have made his position clearer when she had hinted of her father's change of heart. But how could she believe that a proposal of marriage that had been refused could be reinstated three years later without mutual consent? He had certainly not gone beyond simple friendliness while she had been staying with Lady Selchurch, and he had hoped that by this attitude she would have realized that their old romance would not be rekindled. Indeed, of late she had seemed so intimate with Sir Janus that he had assumed him to be the object of her hostess' scheme for her future.

'I hardly dare talk to my own guest — daughter of one of my oldest friends — for fear I might rip up at her.'

'Alicia! If ever I am about to be wed, I will tell you. Cytherea and I are just friends.

Nothing is about to happen that will take away your home. I promised you that.' He left the room hastily.

Later that afternoon Sophie accompanied Roderick to Mallow, and he carried in his pocket a note penned by Lady Selchurch inviting the Valliants to stay overnight, should they not care to drive home so late at night.

When the curricle arrived, Julia set aside the self-imposed task of sorting through the household linens to welcome them to Mallow and brought them into the house. Immediately, Sir Ivor came in and was gratified to meet the new earl at last. They very soon got on good terms. Charlotte had told him of the times they had played as children, including the pond interlude. Valliant demanded to be told the rights of it. Although Sophie had already heard the story, she sat forward and her face glowed at hearing praise for her mother whom she more often heard vilified than lauded.

'Well, I'm sure you'd've had a nasty wetting, but I doubt the pond was deep enough to drown you,' said the bluff squire.

'Don't try to water down my heroine,' protested Roderick. 'Not only did Patience save us then, but deflected the blame we should have borne when we came in late and muddy by talking back to her brother, who had me quaking like a pudding. What a domestic tyrant he was!'

Ignoring respect due to the departed, Sir Ivor categorized his late neighbor as a treacherous toad who put pride of rank over the comfort of his family. He warmed to Roderick even more upon the grounds that he did not argue with this judgment of the late peer.

They all wandered out through the garden, round to the stables and paddock, where Sophie was persuaded to give a piece of hay to the old nag she recognized from the day of the prize fight. It ambled up to poke its head over the fence to greet them. She was obviously delighted with everything she saw and did. Such unbridled pleasure made her the recipient of an invitation to visit for a few days while Sir Ivor and Charlotte were on their wedding trip. Much pleased, Sophie stammered out an awkward acceptance.

As the visitors were conducted back to the curricle, Roderick seized a moment to ensure that Julia had not been jockeyed into the invitation.

'Not a bit of it!' she declared. 'The reverse is true. With Ivor away I shall find it very dull. Believe me, I shall welcome her companionship. Together we will never be bored.'

'What will you do together?'

'Oh — ride, walk — even help with harvesting.' A roguish smile lit her eyes. She added, 'I shall turn your town mouse into a little country mouse.'

A glance at the others told Roderick that Sir Ivor was occupied showing Sophie the little dog cart that he and his sister had tooled around the property when they were children. Julia would let her drive it, he was saying.

Roderick paused, causing Julia to turn to face him questioningly. He took her hand. 'I thank you for the friendship you have for Miss Kettle. I want to tell you — but, you know — the mutual interest that you and I have in her is not what draws me to Mallow.'

The warmth of his voice and the ardor of the glance gave Julia a breathtaking feeling. Despite her brain warning her against falling in love with this engaging peer, her insides seemed to be fluttering in a most unusual fashion. He would have kissed her, but he glanced towards her brother, and instead brought her hand up to his lips.

'It seems a lifetime till you come up to Bishop's Rise. I will ride over before that.'

In a euphoric daze she watched while he handed Sophie up into the curricle and took his own seat. So much for the rumors that he was about to marry that FitzWarren woman!

'Fine fellow for one of the upper ten thou,'

remarked Sir Ivor, as the curricle rolled out of sight. 'You could do worse than fix his interest, Ju.'

'Don't be ridiculous, Ivor! Of all the downright vulgar notions — You drew Sophie away on purpose, didn't you?'

'Nay, I wouldn't do a thing like that,' he grinned.

'Besides, you are the one who told me he was to be married.'

He shrugged airily. 'Not sure I believe that now. Lottie's wrong about that. Got a notion he likes you. You can tell about the way another fellow looks at a female.'

'That's ridiculous. I've met him only five — perhaps six times.'

'Six times, eh? Then I'd say he's getting mighty interested.' He rubbed his chin thoughtfully. 'Time I was asking about his intentions.'

'Ivor, you fiend! You'll do no such thing — if you value your life!'

'He'd be an excellent parti, m'dear. You can't deny that.'

'Ivor Valliant! You must be desperate to keep me close to home.'

'No! Joking aside, it's been too long — enough about that — of course, I don't want to be raising your hopes. Selchurch would be a fine fellow, even if he weren't a peer of the realm. Now he's an earl he'll have all the matchmaking mothers on his tail. He's a plain man, though. Chances are a plain type of woman would suit him well enough — not one of your china dolls to simper and fawn over him.'

Julia thanked him dryly for the doubtful compliment. However, she admitted to herself that the Earl seemed to enjoy her company. They were already at the stage when they could talk together with ease, enjoying small jokes, and even knowing what each other was thinking some of the time. She sighed. The same might be said of her brother. Though not conceited, she was satisfied with her own looks, but had a moment of doubt. Her looks could not compare to the perfection of the features of Lady Cytherea. How could Selchurch stay in the same house with her and not be completely bowled over by that beauty?

She had never felt so attracted to any man as she did to the Earl of Selchurch — even her now dead, charming Philip, who some-times had shown an immature side of himself. Well, it was no use dwelling on it, though her mind tended to stray to agreeable daydreams of her new love.

In the interim before Sir Ivor's nuptials there was much work to be done. Julia threw herself into ensuring that the house would be at its very best when it came time for the bride to move in: drawers to be turned out, faded curtains to be replaced, and discarded linens torn up into polishing cloths. The whole household was set to painting walls, cleaning old paneling, buffing furniture and beating carpets out behind the house till the very rooks fled their rookery in alarm.

In the middle of this week of activity, Charlotte came in the gig, and again expressed her condemnation of Sir Ivor. 'How abominable he is! I thought the painting was to be done while you were in London.'

Shaking her head ruefully, her companion declared, 'Ivor is busy enough. There's much to plan, he tells me, if he's to be away for a couple of months. You should see his office — piles of leases and documents all set out neatly, packaged, with notes to me on what to do when. Lists of things that must be attended to by the week and by the day.'

Charlotte gave a cynical moue, and riposted by describing her own tribulations in finding a temporary replacement for the family cook still nursing her sister. Happily, she had found a woman in the village anxious to oblige, but unwilling to live in. 'Thank heavens Lady Selchurch has promised help from her kitchens for the wedding! I do not see why men must always be thinking their work is all important.'

Julia had often wondered at the strange relationship between her brother and Charlotte. They hardly seemed a devoted couple but they might deal well enough with each other for all that. Charlotte would rule the roost, no doubt, and maybe that was what Ivor needed. 'Believe me, Charlotte, I shall hang on your sleeve for years on the strength of accrued obligations.'

Charlotte gave a twisted smile at Julia's teasing rejoinder. She was not unaware that the marriage would cause problems in the family. Sir Ivor had told her of Julia's intentions to travel, and the likelihood that she would move out. Marriage for Julia would be the best plan, she had decided, and had been casting around in her mind for a suitable match. She shrugged slightly. After the wedding she would turn her mind to it. Looking up, she saw Julia eyeing her quizzically.

'Have you received your invitation to the affair for Lord Selchurch? Lady Selchurch seems quite poorly of late. I hope she will not be obliged to cancel.'

'Horrors! No! Let us hope not.'

Charlotte turned her attention to the

samples, pulling them out of her reticule. 'I've decided. The crimson brocade is handsome — and rich-looking, but I believe I really prefer the rose damask.'

One thing that resulted from the visit was a realization that Charlotte was expecting Ivor and Julia to stay over at the parsonage the night of the reception at the Rise. It was arranged that the Valliants were to pick her and her father up in their coach to bear them up to the Rise. Julia immediately saw a bone of contention rising.

On being applied to for his opinion on this, Sir Ivor was adamant in his refusal to stay at the Rise. Despite the peace made between the families, the specter of Lord Basil still loomed large in Sir Ivor's consciousness, and he vowed he wouldn't sleep a wink, even if, as he ominously declared, you could get him to go there in the first place. The new Selchurch might be a good enough fellow in his own way, but he'd met him now. Why go to a damned soirée to meet someone he'd already met?

Julia was ready to murder her brother. She recognized a bout of the stubborns that occasionally overcame him; but she held no fear that he would refuse to go to the event, for Charlotte would have had something to say about that. So it was with some slight feeling of disappointment that she penned a letter of acceptance to Lady Selchurch, but declined the thoughtful offer of beds overnight.

After their shared moment of intimacy during Sophie's visit, Julia had been sure that Roderick would visit her, but after three days of mixed expectation and despondence, she had her horse saddled and paid a visit to Nell to discover whether the family had weathered the measles satisfactorily.

On impulse she took the turn through Beesley Dell on her return trip, pausing at the spot where she had had her initial encounter with Lord Selchurch — and Sophie Kettle.

The snickering of horses up ahead alerted her to the presence of a vehicle. Urging Russet on, she came up beside a curricle drawn up against the brush, a familiar figure standing beside the fine pair of bays harnessed to it. She reined Russet in with an exclamation of surprise.

'Lord Selchurch!'

'The elusive Miss Valliant! I am forced to desperate measures to talk to you. Your brother told me whither you were bound.'

'But I never use this route.'

'You did once before. I was coxcomb

enough to think you might come this way again today.'

Julia felt her color rising. She had no doubt he had observed her pause at the spot where they had had their first encounter. How dared the creature spy on her in that fashion!

'It seems you have a vast amount of time on your hands, sir, that you needs lounge around in country lanes waylaying people.'

Roderick opened his eyes innocently. 'You make me sound like a malefactor. Whereas I, for my part, have strong views on young ladies venturing unescorted along deserted byways.'

'Beware telling me the nature of those views.'

He laughed. 'Will you not come down from your high horse. It is not comfortable to carry on a conversation so.'

'Is this for the purpose of dalliance?'

'Absolutely!' He grinned up at her.

'Then I must decline, sir, for rumor has you dallying in other directions.'

His face sobered. 'So I hear.' He held up one hand to her. 'Rumor lies. Come down, please! Just for a few moments.' Seeing her hesitate, he added, 'I am on my way to Surrey to visit my sister for a short while, and will not be back until my cousin's party.'

It seemed logical to allow him a brief interview, so she slipped off Russet's back, and allowed him to take her two hands in his own. He did not immediately relinquish them.

She said lightly, 'You must be anxious to see your sister. You have not been to her since your return, I gather.'

'True! There is an added reason. In London, I learned of a master builder who had employed Mouche, and I sought out his home. His wife could tell me only that he was in Surrey. She had no proper address, which gives me to think she does not write letters. I might be able to find him in that vicinity.'

Julia laughed. 'Sophie's business again, I see. I wish you success. Whether your sister will be flattered by a visit patched by frequent absences on a wild goose hunt, I cannot guess. May I have my hands back?'

With consummate grace, he lifted each hand in turn to his lips and let them go. He sensed her reticence in the face of rumor and realized that more time was needed for her to get to know him better and for the rumors to die away. That could only be after Lady Cytherea had left the Rise. He did not know whether he had sufficient patience to remain cool. He gave Julia a quick kiss, then cupping his hands, he provided a boost for her to remount Russet.

'I'm for Surrey now, Miss Valliant. But I look forward to welcoming you to Bishop's Rise at the end of next week.' He watched her as she trotted away towards the highway.

8

The reception at Bishop's Rise was graced with a fine summer evening. The party from the parsonage filed up the grand staircase to where the black lace-gowned Dowager Lady Selchurch stood at the front of the reception rooms introducing the new Earl of Selchurch to county families. Her Junoesque stature was erect, but she looked paler than usual, almost haggard under her rouge.

Roderick looked very much at his ease as he welcomed guests to the hall. Impeccably dressed in a black suit with a long-tailed coat, he had a few words of special welcome for every guest. Julia felt especially welcome by the warmth of his gaze.

It was months since Julia had been to any other than small neighborhood parties. She was exceedingly glad she had made that impulsive visit to the London modiste, feeling entirely confident in a simple bronze moiré silk gown, which emphasized her height and slenderness. Matching silk slippers peeped from beneath her gown.

The main salon was aglitter with a myriad of candles, although the late evening sun still slanted through the open balcony doors. Sir Ivor looked round in amazement. They had been in good time, but the room was filling up rapidly. 'Soirée they called it? That's town talk for a royal reception, more like.'

Entering behind him, Mr. Stride immediately saw Lady Cytherea who was standing making idle conversation with a local gentleman. She was dressed in a striking long-trained white figured silk with the low-cut bodice covered in little tiny pearls arranged in shell patterns. Her dark curls were pulled back and fashioned in a Grecian mode with satin ribbons.

'Charlotte, is that the Lady Cytherea you have mentioned to me? Maybe it is auspicious that I make her acquaintance. See, she is just breaking away. Present me, my dear!'

While Charlotte performed this office, Julia and her brother wandered around the salons provided for the entertainment of the company. At the end of the main salon, chairs had been set out and a string trio was discreetly tuning up instruments.

Sir Ivor sought out one particular salon, and viewed the several tables and decks of cards laid out there with approval. 'No dancing, thank goodness! Lady Selchurch will be in black gloves another nine months, I hear — but cards! Well, they know what's important.'

Julia's lips twitched. 'Tables, but no players yet.'

'Early hours!' Sir Ivor spotted a recent acquaintance. 'That is Tommy Stowe, a very good sort of chap who's a follower of the turf and races horses at Newmarket. That ginger-haired lady must be Mrs. Stowe. We'll find out, Ju.'

Julia obligingly followed to be introduced to the couple. It turned out the Stowes were marrying off a daughter that summer, and the lady was full of matrimonial flights. Bored with a somewhat feminine conversation, the gentlemen soon broke free and went in search of like spirits for a game of whist.

The arrival of guests having trickled to a halt, Roderick made his way around the rooms. Unobtrusive comments in his wake acknowledged him to be a proper lord, not high in the instep, well-traveled and interesting in conversation. He soon found Julia Valliant, still in conversation with Mrs. Stowe.

As she turned towards him, Julia sensed the pleasure he enjoyed in her company, although he extended cordiality to both ladies. The presence of Mrs. Stowe prevented her from inquiring whether his trip to Surrey had been fruitful, and she fell back on commonplaces. A feeling of euphoria gave her notice that her heart was in danger of betraying her. All her declared intentions were in danger of being cast aside — even her reluctance to become chatelaine of this vast pile in which she stood could be overcome by her attraction to this man.

He conducted them to that part of the salon where chairs had been set out. 'We are about to listen to a young lady — a soprano, a local celebrity possessed, I'm told, of perfect pitch and marvelous range, whom Lady Selchurch has found in the past to be quite an asset to her parties.'

At the other end of the room, Lady Cytherea detached herself from a circle of worshipful young bucks, and strolled towards the seating. A shadow fell between her and the sconce candles nearby, as an elegant, burgundy suited gentleman lounged out to intercept her. His long graying hair was caught back with a stiff black ribband, and his neck wear was tied with more care than was usual with him. She paused, recognizing Sir Janus Vale.

'Well met, FitzWarren!' He bowed slightly too ceremoniously.

With an expression somewhere between bemusement and vexation, she held out her hand to him. He suavely took it in his own and bestowed a not quite lingering kiss. 'Sir Janus!'

'You are about to take your seat for the music, I imagine.'

'That was my intention, sir.'

'Do not, I beg you, do so unescorted.'

'You know I don't care for such fustian!'

His eyes followed hers as she glanced towards the room where people were already congregating. Lord Selchurch was bending down to hear something Julia Valliant had to say.

'She does not hold a candle to you, my dear. You have no need to worry.'

Her eyebrows raised haughtily. 'Are you suggesting I should be jealous?'

'Did I not say you have no need to be?'

'Be damned to you, sir! Perhaps the green-eyed monster claws your back.'

She would have swept past him, but he extended his arm. To brush past would have created unwelcome attention, so she put her hand on his and accepted his squiring to the chairs. She stared at Julia. It was a measuring look.

Catching the stare direct, Julia held her gaze for a second, and inclined her head in acknowledgment of their acquaintance. Lady Cytherea smiled perfunctorily and made some comment to Sir Janus as she sat down. That smile made Julia a trifle uncomfortable. It seemed dismissive, as if the smile was not for her, but rather about her. She found the woman's manners hard to admire.

Roderick would have seated himself beside Julia, but there was a demand upon his attention.

'Ricky, old fellow!' Joseph Rayne stood beside him. 'You must have given me up! Trouble with one of my wheelers. I had to hire a new team.'

'No excuses will do, my friend. Let me make you known to Mrs. Stowe and to Miss Valliant whom you have already met.'

'Joseph Rayne,' preempted that gentleman. 'Profuse apologies for my interruption, ladies. Ricky, I came in at the same time as the bigwig. First time I'd met him. Thought you should know he's here.'

Comprehension dawned. 'Lord FitzWarren! I'd better go and welcome him. Why don't you sit here, Hon Joe, and entertain these ladies. Miss Delisle will be singing at any moment.'

'Planned timing!' grinned Rayne as he appropriated the seat beside Julia. Then his countenance turned lugubrious. 'Selchurch has to butter his bread, y'know. Looks as if the man's his future father-in-law.'

'Really!' exclaimed Mrs. Stowe in a 'tell us more' kind of voice.

'Oh, precisely! It's all over Whitehall. You

must know Lady Cytherea has been a reigning belle for . . . ' he frowned suddenly, 'three or four seasons now. That must be because Roderick Anhurst, as he was then, was away for so many years.'

Hollow-hearted, Julia castigated herself. So Ivor had been right in the first place! Charlotte too! Why was she being such a goose? She was harboring no expectations!

It suddenly occurred to Rayne that his conversation was receiving no encouragement from the seat nearest him, and he changed the subject, inquiring if either lady had heard this singer perform before.

'Miss Delisle is about to sing,' cautioned Julia.

When the music program was over, Julia could not have told anyone whether the soprano was sharp, flat or peerless. Her thoughts were too engaged. Her temples were starting to throb, and she would have gladly left to go home there and then.

She excused herself and moved out onto the balcony. It was refreshingly cool there. Strains from the ensemble that continued to play drifted out to her.

'Psst!'

The sound from above caught Julia's attention, and she was not greatly astonished to see Sophie perched in a tree from which she could overlook the gay scene within the house. She forced her voice into vitality. 'Are you the only party spy?'

'Ladies Caro and Kate were watching people arrive from the stairs,' said Sophie scornfully. 'You can't see anything from there.'

'There must not be much to see from there either, but I'm sure you can hear the music.'

Sophie slithered down to the balustrade and on to the balcony. Her old blue dress made her less visible in the twilight. The face she turned to Julia shone with pleasure. 'The music is so beautiful! I want to dance to it. Why is nobody dancing?'

'Because the house is in mourning for your uncle. The music is just for listening.'

'What should I care about that dead, old man?' Sophie stretched her arms out and moved in slow lithe circles, always to the end of the balcony, out of sight of the people within. Her appreciation of the music transformed her angular body into swooping movements until the music changed to a waltz. Smiling, Julia joined hands with the girl and guided her in the movements of the dance and they circled the area, Sophie quickly learning the twirling steps. Julia wondered why she was doing this. Was it a wish to control Sophie, to moderate the inhibition of her movements? Or was it to join her in a expression of rebellion against all things Selchurch?

'Caught red-handed!' A stern voice broke their trance.

They looked round guiltily. Roderick stood there watching them, his arms folded before him in an accusatory fashion. In a flash, Sophie was over the balustrade and had disappeared into the garden.

Julia faced him angrily. The turmoil she had been through put vinegar into her spirits. 'Lord Selchurch! That was not kindly done!'

Roderick grinned ruefully. 'I didn't realize I was such a figure of awe. The child is as nervous as a colt.'

Julia snapped. 'You are a peer, and as such must always be aware of the sway you exercise over your dependents.'

'You are right, Miss Valliant. I am sorry.' He came up very close to her, and she wondered what he intended. 'Call me Roderick, please! Let us finish the dance! Why waste the music, the first stars and a place to ourselves.' He met some stiffness, but he took her firmly in hand and began to move round in a fashion that melted her resistance. The music came to an end all too soon.

'Miss Delisle is to sing again. Perhaps you should go in, Julia, whilst I go and make sure that chit gets back into the house again.' He dropped a light kiss on her forehead and descended the stairs into the garden, leaving her with mixed feelings of outrage and uncertainty.

After a few moments, she followed his suggestion. She realized that tattle tale would result if they were to be seen coming in from the balcony together.

Immediately, Joe Rayne was at her side, finding her a seat to listen again to the entertainer. Afterwards he offered his escort to the salon where refreshments had been laid out. They rose and sauntered through the crowd heading in that direction.

Roderick, on re-entering the salon, was disappointed to see he was too late to take Miss Valliant in to supper, and did his duty by Mrs. Mumford, the elderly relict of a previous pastor at Selchurch, unwittingly finding himself sitting adjacent to Sir Janus and Lady Cytherea. He glanced across the room at Miss Valliant, but she was paying complete attention to her eating companion. He heard his name briefly as Rayne was talking to her.

'Miss Valliant, Ricky was telling me you are friends with the Farlaine family. I came down from Oxford with their son John.'

Not unaware of Roderick's presence seated close to Lady Cytherea, Julia murmured a suitable reply. She had thought she had met most of John's friends over the years. No doubt he was to some degree a fellow student of Philip's brother, but she recognized this as an opening conversational gambit. Perhaps Rayne was uneasy about the impression he had made on her that evening.

'Did you enjoy your visit in London, going to all the fine balls, I imagine?'

'Yes, I much enjoyed the visit, but no to the second part,' she replied, avoiding making this declaration sound in any way like a confession. 'The Farlaines have little taste for social activities. Neither can they afford the time.'

'And Lord Selchurch got you helping him with his poor little cousin, I hear. What a slowtop! Took you on a drive to Islington of all places! Next time you're in town, call on my escort. I'll do better by far. Vauxhall Gardens, Carlton House — anywhere!'

It was evident that Selchurch had given his friend only an abridged version of their outings in London. Possibly he had felt his attentions to her had been too particular in light of his lack of intentions in her direction. 'How kind of you, Mr. Rayne!' Julia's tones were off-hand. 'But my London days passed in such a whirl — I barely had time to do all that I had planned on.' He was, she thought to herself, too easy an acquaintance, but harmless. Their conversation did not seem to prosper, so she excused herself after supper to seek out her brother.

Sir Ivor, despite his earlier tepid reaction to the invitation, was enjoying himself well, hobnobbing with several cronies who had been vociferously surprised to see him entertained at the Rise. For that reason Julia was surprised to see him emerge hurriedly from the card room and to meet her.

'Time to go, Ju! The carriage is called for. I just stayed to finish a hand.'

Relieved of the need to plead an aching head, Julia was not unwilling to leave. Nevertheless she demurred. 'What is the panic?'

'The Reverend's feeling queer. Little Lottie's downstairs with him waiting. Too many lobster patties, I trow.'

They took their leave of the Earl who detached himself from a three-way conversation with Lady Selchurch and Lord FitzWarren, to ensure the carriage had been brought round and Mr. Stride made comfortable. Disappointed to see Julia leave so early, he would have offered his own carriage to take some of the party later, but knew that would be awkward. Charlotte would wish to go with her ailing father, and her fiancé would not stay without her. Even if Julia would remain without a chaperone, he, as host, could not devote all his time to her.

He would have escorted them out, but Lady Selchurch forestalled him. 'Stay here, Roderick, and keep Lord FitzWarren entertained. I wish to have a word with our departing guests.' She followed the Valliants and Strides down the stairs and caught them in the vestibule. 'I beg you will stay awhile, Miss Valliant. I have had no chance to talk to you and I am persuaded Mr. Stride would be more comfortable reclined in the carriage. I would offer my barouche but I see your own vehicle is as spacious.'

Charlotte immediately saw the convenience of this. 'An excellent idea, Lady Selchurch. Julia, my father feels guilty, I know, to drag you from the party so early.'

Julia protested that her convenience should not be a factor, and that she did not mind leaving early. It was obvious they thought she was being accommodating.

'Nonsense,' quoth Lady Selchurch. 'No need for self-sacrifice, Miss Valliant. When Sir Ivor has taken Mr. Stride to his home, he must return for you.'

There was no arguing with her, and Sir Ivor was willing enough, so while outside the coach wheeled away, Lady Selchurch called to a footman for lights and led Julia into a room not being used that evening, talking the while. 'I am so glad to bear you apart for a few moments. It has been on my mind to give Miss Stride a wedding gift of something from the Rise. I am sure she would much appreciate that as being a special reminder of the many happy hours she has passed here. When she is married, her time must be directed to the wishes of her husband. We acknowledge this and realize we cannot call on her company so frequently when she is Lady Valliant, especially in view of the extra distance from Mallow, though we hope she will come as often as she can.' She paused by side table. 'These silver candlesticks are exquisite, do you not think so?'

Julia nodded in mindless agreement.

'I brought them with me when I married, but they are just not in proportion to this room. I'm sure my dear Charlotte can find a place for them at Mallow. Or do you think the rose bowl would be a better gift? I had meant to ask Charlotte directly, but she was gone so fast — '

About that time, Joe Rayne sought out Roderick to quiz him on his coming engagement. 'Rot you, Ricky! Why am I the last to know?'

'To know what?' asked Roderick, thoroughly mystified.

'About the wedding! When is it to be? I expect to be best man, you know.'

Roderick laughed. 'You must be reading things into that snippet in *the Chronicle*. Obliging of you to draw my attention to it.'

'No, really! It's all over town. People know she's staying here — it got into the society snippets. Everyone reads them. Twice in the paper, Ricky! Your goose is cooked.'

His friend stared at him, humor draining from his face. 'If this is a joke, Joe . . . '

Joe nodded sagely. 'People are expecting an announcement, and what with Lord FitzWarren being here . . . Look, I was just rallying you, Rick. It's probably all just a hum.'

The company having begun to thin out, he was reminded that in any event he owed some attention to Lady Cytherea. Except for supper, their paths had hardly crossed that evening. If he were thought to be avoiding her it would cause as much gossip as if he clung to her side all evening. She was standing with her father and Sir Janus Vale. By the frown on his usually bland countenance, Lord FitzWarren was not entirely happy with his company.

Immediately, Cytherea was laughing, coquetting with Roderick, chiding him for spending time at her side when so many guests were vying for his attention as the man of the hour. Her tones were devoid of sarcasm, but she laid her hand on his wrist with a proprietary air.

'You are too unkind, Lady Cytherea. Most of my guests have already left. Here was I patting myself on the back. I thought I had done a competent job of speaking to all in the room. My guests are fading away. The rest of the evening is for the night owls.'

'Speaking of night owls, I'll see what company you have left in the card room, Selchurch.' FitzWarren turned to Sir Janus. 'Join me, Vale!' It was half invitation half directive, but Sir Janus demurred.

'Give me a few moments, sir. I will join you later with the utmost pleasure.' If it was to be understood that he wished a few more minutes to further his acquaintance with the Earl of Selchurch, he conveyed that possibility with the suavity of his reply.

FitzWarren gave his daughter a paternal pat on the shoulder, which seemed to carry the same message as a kiss good night and headed to the card room.

'Your guests keep country hours, I vow,' remarked Lady Cytherea. 'The Valliants left quite early, taking the Strides with them.'

'I fancy it was the other way round. The minister suffers much from dyspepsia, I believe, and they came as one party.'

'A charming lady, that Miss Valliant, and quite good looking . . . but no longer in her first season, I fear.' Then she laughed at her own presumption. 'An unkind person may say the same of me if they did not know how little I care for such Gothic notions. She is not without fortune, I hear. One does wonder why she was not snapped up this age.'

Roderick felt a strange need to vindicate Miss Valliant from any charge of lacking in attraction. 'There are reasons she was not wed long ago.'

'Well, all of us have reasons, Roddie dear.'

Irritated, he felt compelled to expand on his remarks. 'Mutual friends gave me her rather tragic story. She was engaged to their son. He got involved in a prizefight through a bet. A stubborn lad, who wouldn't give up easily, he received such blows to the head that he was knocked down and didn't get up again.'

'He died?'

'Eventually! He fell into a coma that lasted some three years.'

'Gracious! What did Miss Valliant do?'

'The Farlaines told me how frequently she visited, spending hours sitting with him, reading to him and generally relieving Mrs. Farlaine as much as she could by helping nurse him.'

'Why didn't she break the engagement? I mean, I can understand her offering to nurse, and giving comfort to the mother — but three years . . . '

'Quite the paragon!' murmured Vale.

'Incredible!' cried Lady Cytherea. 'Does she have ice-water in her veins? I could as well stay engaged to a log lying in a bed!'

Roderick subdued a moment of revulsion. 'What would you do in such circumstance?' he asked challengingly.

'What an underhanded question,' laughed Cytherea. 'What a sly fox you are, to try to put me out of countenance. You deserve that I should say I would immediately run off with . . . with Sir Janus here.' There was a slightly brittle pitch behind her laughter. 'Of course, I should nurse my lover, and sit with him, and engage all the best doctors in the world to treat him. And I would cherish him.' Her voice dropped to a seductive purr, and let her eyelids droop langorously. 'He would not stay long in that coma, I promise you.'

'I'll vow.' Vale's narrow glance slid from one to the other of them.

'Three years — can be a lifetime. Pardon me! I see Mrs. Mumford trying to catch my eye. Our carriage is to bear her home. I must make sure it is ready.'

Roderick breathed a sigh of relief as the last

221

of the conveyances bearing departing guests had pulled away from the door. Lady Selchurch, who had an eye for a rogue, had prevailed upon Sir Janus to stay, although his estate was at no great distance. Not finding him in the card room, Roderick went in search for him, feeling it would fall to him to see that gentleman had his candle and could find his way to his room.

The doors to the balcony that overlooked the garden were open and he stepped out. He could hear voices, one of them raised in annoyance. Hastening forward, he bumped into Lady Cytherea coming towards the salon, her hand fumbling at her neckline as she did so.

He stepped forward. 'Cytherea! Are you all right?'

She started and cast herself on him. 'Roddie! I'm so glad you're here. The idiot! Just keep him away from me!' She was shaking, possibly in anger, for he had never known her scared of anything.

'Who was bothering you, Cy? You're all right, I say. Calm down. Who upset you like this?'

He put a protective arm around her shoulder and looked around to see who had accosted her, but that person had disappeared into the darkness of the garden. Her clutch grew tighter, but she seemed to be getting a little calmer. 'Thank goodness you're here! No, everything's fine. Nothing happened.' Somehow her lips connected with his, and he found himself drawn down into her warm embrace. The scent of her filled his senses and his head swam. Mentally he cursed the champagne he had imbibed — just enough to make him lightheaded and to respond to her. He pulled his lips away and drew her to a stone bench. 'Now sit down, and tell me — has someone offered you some insult?'

She laughed shakily. 'Don't be so antediluvian, Roddie. It's nothing, really. No need for pistols at dawn, and I won't say who because you'll be wanting to draw his cork or whatever the expression is gentlemen use when they are about to create all sorts of mayhem. But please, don't tell anyone about this. I am perfectly fine now. Just hold me close, Roddie.'

'What has happened here?' Lady Selchurch was at the French doors. Except for a brief interlude of musical entertainment, she had been standing most of the evening. She leant heavily against the door jamb as she stared in surprise at the scene before her. Her eyes regarded the disarray of Cytherea's clothing as that young lady immediately pushed herself away from Roderick and stood up.

'Oh, Alicia. Nothing has happened. Nothing at all! A to-do about nothing! I vow it's time I took myself to bed.' She stifled an imaginary yawn.

'Of course, just as you will.' The dowager cast a look at Roderick, half questioning, half accusing. 'I will see you up, my dear.'

'No need, Alicia! You have your guests to attend to.' With great dignity, she gathered the train of her dress over one arm and, with the other hand, held the top of the bodice, which seemed to have suffered slight damage. Casually she walked forward through into the house where a curious Joe Rayne was approaching the French door. Behind him stood Julia, who had returned to the main salon with Lady Selchurch.

As Lady Cytherea strode into the light of the salon, the eyes of those nearest the door became riveted on her. The vivid blossoming of a love bite where the delicate swelling of her breast commenced betrayed a recent passionate encounter. Bidding the company a serene good night, she passed through the salon.

Roderick rose from the bench, somewhat surprised by the shocked faces arrayed in the doorway — Lady Selchurch, Joe Rayne and to his consternation, Julia Valliant.

He let one expressive word pass his lips. 'Damn!'

9

Roderick was abroad early after a restless night. Again and again Julia's shocked countenance registering hauteur and disgust had swum before his mind's eye. He had tossed and turned and hauled himself from his bed with relief at the first light of day.

His countenance betrayed none of the turmoil of his thoughts to the groom who saddled the gray. He mounted and rode briskly out of the park. His mind continued to turn over the compromising episode. It was unfortunate that Lady Selchurch had surprised that misguided embrace, which started merely as a friendly, comforting gesture. Her appearance had precipitated Cytherea's departure from the balcony, without waiting to amend her disheveled appearance. In the light of Cytherea's urgent plea for silence about whatever had transpired it was impossible for him to explain convincingly how slight his involvement had been.

By all that was honorable, he should have married Cytherea three years ago. He had been mad for her and the miracle was that she had all too enthusiastically returned his passion. The coincidence of a flattering posting abroad gave him cause for the conviction that his career was on the rise and that she could be his. But this was not to be. She had tearfully told him that by no means would her father accept his suit — begged him, in fact, not to broach the subject to Lord FitzWarren, lest she be betrayed into confessing her wickedness in succumbing to his passion. And so he had sailed away heartbroken, yet not entirely in despair.

Like any normal young man he had eventually recovered from his first love. On his return, it had come as a surprise to him to know that Cytherea assumed a continuation of their previous attachment. He had not committed himself on the journey from Deal to London, needing time to reassess his feelings. Strange that she had never questioned the cooler relations that now existed between them! He assumed she, like himself, had regretted an earlier loss of control during that halcyon summer three years before, and now at twenty-one had gained more wisdom. Before she had turned up at Bishop's Rise as a guest of Lady Selchurch, he had assumed her interest would die. He was beginning to realize how mistaken he had been. Cytherea wanted his courtship resumed. Now, again, there was fuel for the scandal broth. At bottom, he had no illusions. As an earl he was an infinitely better prospect than plain Mr. Anhurst, but was the ambition hers or her father's? Surely, he thought, the obligation to marry her that he had felt three years earlier must be negated by the intervention of time.

He rode a considerable distance, and on his return to the stable spent some time, rubbing his horse down. Oliver, the head groom, emerged to take over this job, but was waved away. Roderick enjoyed working with this fine horse and found the action a balm to his unsettled mood. Afterwards he walked back to the house, cutting through the walled garden.

Lady Cytherea was sitting on the bench against the wall, demurely attired in figured muslin. Her luxuriant dark locks escaped the spidery gauze shawl, which swathed her head and shoulders and was secured over her fine bosom by a large amethyst brooch. She looked exotic, like a denizen from a sultan's harem. Beside her stood Sir Janus Vale, one booted foot planted on the bench, carrying on what seemed to be an intense conversation. Cytherea was laughing wickedly at some sally. They turned and greeted Rod as he approached.

'I bid you good morning, Lady Cytherea,

Sir Janus!' he replied. 'My compliments on your being abroad so early, Cy. I thought you'd sleep till noon.'

'After my raking?' she finished for him, mockingly. 'You see before you a dutiful daughter, who saw her father into his carriage at eight o' clock this morning, I'll have you know.'

'While the delinquent host rides off, leaving his guests to their own devices. My apologies! I went further than I knew.'

She gave him an innocent glance from under her curling lashes. 'You could never go too far, your lordship.'

Ignoring her innuendo, Roderick directed a few pleasantries towards Sir Janus, and then said, 'Please excuse me! I must wash away the odor of the stables before breakfast.' So saying, he headed towards the house.

Evidently Lady Cytherea had no qualms at being in the company of Sir Janus. He had thought her assailant — was that too strong a word? — had been Vale. Moments before the incident, Vale had not been in the card room where he had expected to find him, but on the other hand FitzWarren was not there either and must have retired for the night. As host, did he have a personal responsibility to pursue the matter now that Lady Cytherea's father had departed? No! Cytherea obviously did not want that, and for his part he felt none of the jealousy, which should be the part of the suitor the world thought him to be.

The baronet watched Lady Cytherea, as her eyes followed Roderick's athletic figure mounting the balcony steps. He smiled, sardonically. 'Will you have him, FitzWarren? I'll take odds you won't.'

With the air of one not to be goaded, she replied languidly. 'You think not? What odds are you offering? I may be interested.'

'I dare not think so. You are not the gamester you pretend to be, my dear. But what ails you? Your rather clumsy sally fell on stony ground. Our all too respectable host will bore you to tears within six months, you know. His appetites are not large enough for you, my love.'

She looked at him levelly. 'And yours are? God, you're presumptuous, Janus!'

'Am I? But perhaps I have grounds for presumption.'

'Fie, Janus! That was another life. I was young and exceedingly foolish.'

'Ah! It would have been different had I been free.' His voice was bitter. 'But I am free now, FitzWarren.'

'Don't call me FitzWarren. I am neither one of your Etonian school mates nor a sporting crony. What is your wager?'

He smiled crookedly and gazed at his hands. They were long and slender. He drew a curious emerald ring from his little finger.

He handed it to her. 'You shall hold my pledge. It is of considerable value, I must point out.'

'Don't worry! I'll not lose it.' Her tones were contemptuous. 'And what pledge do you expect of me?' She placed the ring on her right hand. It fitted exquisitely over the knuckle of her third finger. She admired the play of the sun upon it, holding her hand up to the light.

'Only this. If by the end of the summer you do not have Selchurch's ring on your finger, you will move this ring from your right hand to your left.'

Her eyes met his, startled. Automatically she pulled on the ring to take it from her finger. 'That is unconscionable! You take advantage, sir.'

'Is that so? You stand to win both the ring and the grand position you crave. Your consolation prize is a baronet who is worth a hundred times the value of the young bachelor whose heart you tossed aside three years ago. For my part, I have prospered, my dear, and am, I venture to think, of a worth not to be despised by your father, who is, I understand, not unencumbered with financial cares himself.'

'I could just return the ring — now, or later.' She tried to screw the ring over her knuckle.

He smiled. 'You seem to be having difficulty returning it at this point. Go and soak it, if you wish! I venture to think that, if you keep it on, your own sense of honor — and I know you have a sense of honor of a kind — will be my pledge.'

Amusement seeped through her anger. 'My pledge, then, is my honor. Oh foolish man. I think you took that a long time ago. Lucky I was not to lose reputation to boot.'

'And Anhurst was your surety. You would have made use of him to avoid your — ahem, threatened embarrassment. Providentially, his ultimate sacrifice was not required.'

'You bastard,' she turned on him. 'You're the one who put me in jeopardy.'

'And I would have married you, in an instant,' he said soothingly, 'if I had been free. Don't forget my poor ailing Marietta was still alive at that time. How fortunate for us both that your — embarrassment came to naught.'

Cytherea gritted her teeth. Her thoughts went back to that time in her youth when she had been terrified that she had conceived. Roderick had been an ardent admirer, and providentially a guest at her father's country estate. It had been all too easy to inveigle him to her room at night. But it hadn't been necessary to carry through to the legitimization of the seduction. It had all been a false alarm. The denouement had been a tearful separation and laying all blame for the estrangement on her father.

'I know I am abominable. But we are right for each other, Cytherea. You think that he will put up with your nonsense, but he won't, my love. He wasn't brought up in our circle. He's too middle-class.'

She hunched a pettish shoulder. 'He's a peer of the realm.'

'It fell to him — after a series of unforeseen mishaps. He was not raised for the position. His father was a damned philanthropist, I hear — gave away much of his substance. Selchurch will spoil his tenants, and let his servants walk all over him. And he'd rather be poking around in some foreign midden than be here on the solid turf he inherited.'

An angry foot beat a tattoo on the stone base of the bench. 'You'll not talk about Roderick in those terms. He is a man with more honor in a lock of his hair than in your whole body. Don't you think I feel guilty about the way I used him?'

'Don't tell me you were really tempted to have him then.'

' 'Streuth, as to that . . . the wilds of America would not be for me. Now, however, as the Countess Selchurch . . . I have a mind to be a political hostess. I already plan my toilette for when he makes his maiden speech in the upper chamber. Maybe your ring is already forfeit.' She spread her right hand wide in mocking affectation.

'Having a title won't keep him on this sceptered isle.'

'You think not? When we're wed, he'll want to stay at home, I assure you — for a time, at least. Of course, I wouldn't want him in my pocket all the while.' She flitted a coquettish glance at her companion. 'He is talented, well-endowed in all those parts which appeal to a woman. He is clever. He is, above all, a gentleman.'

Vale laughed. 'A gentleman is the last thing you need.' Deliberately, he caught her right hand, and raised it to his lips.

'And he just may be — a better lover than you are.' She looked for a reaction.

For a second his smile disappeared. His tones were silky. 'But not lately. It's a Lenten lover, cherished Cytherea.' He caught her wrist before she struck him.

Angrily she flounced to her feet and strode

off towards the house.

Meanwhile, having changed out of his riding clothes, Roderick entered the breakfast room. Rayne, newspaper in hand, was pushing away an empty plate and accepting more coffee from a footman. Roderick helped himself to a small slice of ham with bread. Joe looked knowingly at the morsel his friend had taken and drew his own — erroneous — conclusions.

Oblivious to the servants' ears, he inquired coolly, 'So, when are the nuptials, Ricky?'

'Nuptials?' Rod threw his friend a look with a flick of the eyes to indicate the footman standing nearly. 'Ah, Miss Stride and her squire! Sometime next month, I understand.'

Rayne made a guilty 'Oh!' of comprehension, and then vaguely tried to sort out those individuals from amongst the company he had met the night before. 'Are they staying over?' he asked, searching for clues.

'No! Sir Ivor Valliant and his sister were to stay at the parsonage, Charlotte Stride's home.'

'Ah, Miss Valliant's brother! Of course! I didn't get a chance to meet him, Now, she is a peach of a female — the one you drove in Hyde Park. Do they live nearby? As I'm staying here a few days, I might decide to call.'

Seeing the footman otherwise engaged, Rayne lowered his voice and went back to the original and interesting topic. 'No game, old chap. London is all agog with expectations concerning la belle FitzWarren. You may not know too many in society, but they know Lady Cy, and they know you as the new earl, even if you haven't been much on the town.'

'How bad is it? I told you there's no real basis for all this.'

Rayne looked at him oddly. 'Well, it's not a matter of betting on you in the clubs, or anything. That happens all the time — or tattling — too many of those quizzes have nothing else to do. It goes deeper than that. It's an expectation — especially with Lady Cy staying here.' He tapped the newspaper in front of him. 'That's why I was checking the notices again — just in case.'

'When I contemplate marriage with the lady, I'll be sure to let you know,' said Roderick grimly.

'Don't poker up, old chap. You must admit you've been thick as thieves.'

Roderick scowled. 'Society has obviously added three and one and totaled a full dozen. Three years ago, I would have understood. There was something between us then. But now . . . this puts a damnable embarrassment upon Cytherea.'

'That's all well and good, but you're doing it too brown. I saw what . . . ' Rayne's voice trailed off.

A step sounded on the polished wood floor of the hallway. Lady Cytherea entered the breakfast room, looking invigorated by the fresh summer morning air. 'Such somber faces. Do I spoil some deep discussion? No, don't rise gentleman. What have we here today, Sidney?' She directed this to the footman as she surveyed the sideboard. 'Just some strawberries with cream and bread and butter, thank you.'

Joe Rayne's eyes were drawn like a magnet to the gauze scarf about her neck. He colored, hastily swallowed a gulp of coffee, and rose from the table, muttering something about letters to write.

Sitting down opposite Roderick, she wondered, 'Now what have I said to send him off at a high canter?'

'Joseph Rayne has his shy moments. He's somewhat in awe of you, Cy.'

She chuckled incredulously. 'We are hardly strangers, though our circles do not often come together. This will not do. I wish to stand on easy terms with all your friends, Roddie. He should have stayed.'

Roderick admitted to himself that she was looking and behaving charmingly this morning. She had the quality of a great lady about her. She could act, despite the occasional lapse into spicy repartee, with charm and consideration. Society would judge her quite suited by upbringing and connections to be the wife of an earl. He had loved her madly once. He would not denigrate that passion by passing it off as a mere infatuation.

Yet there was a different quality to the feelings that were growing in him towards Julia Valliant. He could not exactly articulate the attraction she held for him — almost a quiet sense of their belonging together.

He cast around for a neutral topic of conversation. 'Did your father enjoy last evening's entertainment?'

'Amazingly so. He found Delisle very much in voice.' She raised a strawberry to her lips and bit the tip off it. 'He much regretted having to leave so early, knowing that you particularly wished to talk to him.' Lush eyelashes swept up as she looked directly at him. 'It is unfortunate that you had no private time together.'

Roderick looked at her levelly. 'We chatted last night. But there was no opportunity for private talk.' Now was the time he should make the position plain to her.

'Oh, darling!' She laid the half strawberry

aside. 'I'm being too pushy, aren't I? I don't mean to be, of course. But our understanding has been of such long duration that I am guilty of taking you for granted.'

'Hardly an understanding!'

'What a hateful trick!' She laughed easily. 'Of course, you are free as the wind. You know that. But don't leave it too long, before you speak to my father. He is expecting your visit, you know.' She touched his hand with a light, possessive gesture. 'I think you'll get a amicable reception this time. He has been quite impressed by our constancy, and never at any time rebuked me for the letters you sent me.'

It was the second time she had cast those letters in his face. It was an implicit threat, he realized. Guiltily, he tried to recall exactly what he had penned in them. He had been at fault, he knew, but he had been so madly in love at one stage, that he could not bear being unable to contact her. He had entrusted two letters to individuals returning to England to deliver into her hands. He had been well aware that any parent would regard it as inappropriate for a young lady to receive letters from a young man to whom she was not affianced. He had received no answering correspondence from Lady Cytherea, and as his passions had faded, so had his urge to write letters. Free as the wind, she had said. He wished he felt that way.

What an impressionable dolt he had been in those days! His ambitions had been high, and he had dreamed of proven success in his career and the speedy advancement, which would, if not put him on an equal with her in status, at least make it possible that his suit could find favor. His family was of respectable lineage, at least. So busy had he been with the execution of this objective that he had failed to realize the primary cause of the objective had faded in importance. Now pressure was coming on all sides for him to align himself with the FitzWarrens. He could do worse, he admitted. It was a good match. They got on well enough together, and he certainly would have no problem in feeling lust for her, but that was not the same thing as love. He saw her faults, and as a friend could accept them, but for a lifetime? That was another matter.

She was so confident in her expectations. What a horrendous embarrassment it would be to her, if he turned his back on her! She had met him unchaperoned in the cabin of his ship, and if they had not been interrupted by a disembarkation summons, he did not know whether he would have stopped himself from throwing discretion to the winds. It had been a long voyage!

She gave a quick little look at his face. He was lost in thought. Instinctively, she knew when to leave well alone. She quickly rose. 'I must go. I promised to watch the children rehearse their play this morning.' Blowing a kiss to him, she was gone so suddenly that he had no chance to utter those words which needed to be said.

Ruefully, he left the table and headed through the main hall towards the stairs. As he stepped onto the parquet, a stocky, black-suited gentleman carrying a leather hold-all walked briskly past him. His eyebrows almost disappeared into his hair, giving him a strangely wondering expression. But for Piller, the butler, he would have dashed out the door without his hat.

Noting his lordship's look of enquiry, Piller turned to him as he closed the door. 'The apothecary from the village, my lord. He was called in to prescribe for Lady Selchurch this morning.'

'Nothing serious, I hope? He looked somewhat disordered.'

'I'm afraid I can't venture to say, sir. I understood it to be trifling, or my lady would have consulted her London physician.' He bowed his stately way back to the pantry.

Roderick went to look for Joseph Rayne.

He ran him to earth in his room, not writing letters as he had indicated but consulting with his valet whilst the man was arranging toilet articles on his dresser.

On seeing Roderick's gloomy face, Rayne dismissed his man and started in on his friend with no preliminaries. 'Making the decision to get married is not the easiest choice in life.' The unnaturally solemn look on his normally cheerful face brought a reluctant grin to Roderick's.

'Since when did you decide to advise me on marriage?'

'Experience, old chap. Nearly got to the point last spring, but luckily my great-aunt died and left me a legacy, before I popped the question. Point is, I didn't put myself in a position where expectations got squelched.'

'While I appear to be in that position?'

'Well, the more I think about it — after last night — you've got to take your medicine, my poor old friend.'

Roderick was nettled. 'Last night? What exactly did you hear about last night? I'd like to know more about last night myself.'

'I didn't need to hear. I saw! And so did several others, including Lady Selchurch. My man gave me a hint — the talk of the servants' hall! Sorry, old chap. You know how these things go.'

'Saw what, for goodness' sake? A kiss — meant to be a brotherly kiss, I swear.'

'Brotherly? Oh, come on Ricky! Of course I didn't see the kiss. You don't make those sort of advances where all the world can watch you.'

'You're making no sense, Hon Joe. One moment you saw it, then you didn't. It's too early in the day for you to be castaway.'

Rayne looked resentful. 'So you got a little carried away! I saw the mark you left. So stop trying to deny there's — '

'What are you talking about? What mark?'

'The red blotch — the love bite, gudgeon! Right there in all its glory on Lady Cy's . . . er . . . neck. And Lady Selchurch saw it too, though I'm not sure she'd know what it was. But she saw Cytherea holding up the lace on her dress — that's bad enough.'

'Oh, my God!'

'And Lady Cytherea walked across the room like a bloody princess. I must say I never saw anything like it! She's got style, I'll say that for her. But you have to marry her now, boyo.'

Roderick plumped himself down on the bed with a force that made the tester creak. His next couple of sentences expelled a force of language, which did little to release his feelings. There was nothing he could do to defend himself. Cytherea had enjoined him to silence. How like her to walk across a room, wearing the badge of passion, head completely unbowed! 'Maybe she was a little flushed. Easy enough thing to happen at a party!'

'It was on one side, dark red — no mistake what it was. To do her justice, she might not realize she had it — till she reached her looking glass.'

He met his friend's eyes. 'I can't talk about this thing.'

'Sounds as if you've said a mouthful already.' Rayne paced around the room. 'The thing is, it's not your style. Did she lead you into this? You know, when the women start scheming, it's a crafty man that can stay off the bridal path.'

Roderick shook his head. 'I'm getting notions that I don't like. Maybe I deserve all this, but I don't think so.' He waved an exasperated hand. 'Ah! I can't say any more.'

Rayne hesitated. If his friend did not want to discuss the matter, that was his privilege 'You obviously have a decision to make. I'll not interfere. But don't clam up yet. There's just one thing . . . '

Roderick got to his feet, patiently. 'One thing? Why do I feel you are about to interfere?'

'No, no, not at all. Something I didn't say to you three years ago. Oh, damn it to hell!' He spun on his heel and went to stare out of the window.

'Then don't say it! Listen, I know the stories going the rounds then. Cytherea told me all about them herself. She explained everything to me.'

Driven, Rayne turned back to face Roderick. His face was flushed. 'Cytherea is a fantastic creature. She has always been talked about. Maybe she always will be. Every man on the town is a little in love with her.' There was a painful silence between them. Joe eyed his friend's clenched fists warily. 'Don't draw my cork here, old chap. Blood on her ladyship's carpet — wouldn't do at all.'

'We can always go outside behind the stables,' Roderick managed quietly. He buffeted his friend on the shoulder, unnecessarily hard. 'I'm not angry at you, gudgeon. They're training a yearling in the paddock. Let's watch them try out its paces!'

Still Rayne had to have a say. 'I just want you to know. You're my friend, Rick. If you decide — one way or the other — I'll stand buff for you — no matter how hard the mud is slung.'

They exited by a corridor leading through the back of the house, passing the open gate to the walled garden. Rayne grinned and nudged his friend. They could see a pair of boots sticking in a horizontal position on a bench against the wall. 'Someone didn't make it home after the party.'

'No! Those feet belong to Vale. He was under the horse chestnut earlier. Maybe he was up too early. Let him have his sleep!'

Reclining on the bench, Sir Janus Vale was not unconscious. His hearing was acute. The conversation of two men passing the end of the garden did not go unnoticed. He raised himself to a sitting position. There was a tension in the air, an almost tangible feeling as if the very tree was breathing. It was peaceful, and he listened very intently.

He sighed heavily and got to his feet, kicking a leg of the bench clumsily as he did so. He walked away from the house through the open gate leading out of the walled garden that led to the stables. Out of sight of the garden, he strolled in the wooded area beyond for perhaps two minutes. Then he re-entered the garden. He crept back soundlessly on the grass verge to where the big old chestnut tree overhung the garden. A flash of white muslin flowered on top of the wall. Springing forward, he grasped a slender waist and found himself holding a twisting, clawing feline.

He deposited Sophie down on the bench in a hurry. 'Sit down, quietly! I'm not going to hurt you.' He smoothed himself down and breathed slowly. 'I was but helping you down. You might have missed your footing.'

Sophie answered angrily, 'I got up. I can get down again.'

'I have always found getting down the harder part.' His weary eyes took in the set of the tight little jaw, and two small fists clenched in her lap.

'You took away the ladder,' she accused him.

'Mea culpa! But that ladder was broken. A danger.' He gave a dismissive gesture. 'But at last, I find the elusive Miss Kettle. You have succeeded excellently in avoiding me these few weeks — even at the mill — the prizefight, my girl. Don't play innocent! I know you were there.'

'Who told you that?'

'You will find there are very few secrets in life.'

'What do you want with me?'

'Curiosity. Idle curiosity. I wondered if you had heard from your father.'

Sharp eyes flew up to his, then looked down at the ground.

'I perceive you are unprepared to trust me.' He sat down beside her, ignoring the way in which she drew away from him. 'You misjudge me, you know — and fail to give me credit. Your father would have died without my intercession. Is this the way you show your gratitude. To be blunt, he would have 'swung' as they say. It was magnanimous of me to help, for he cost me a lot of money.' He mused on this for a moment, faced with a child sitting mumchance on the bench beside him. 'Maybe an ill-judged act, for I doubt he remembers me fondly.'

A tigerish little glance met his. 'Are you afraid of my father?'

He laughed softly. 'Should I be? You almost persuade me. Kettle is capable of surprising one, that's true enough.' He noted the look almost of satisfaction that crossed her face.

'I have not heard from my father and I don't know where he is.'

'I believe that. It has been brought to my knowledge that your — sponsor, shall we say — has been making enquiries about a certain fellow of low esteem known familiarly as Mouche. He should desist.' He laughed again. 'Your face betrays you so easily. No. This is by no means a threat — merely a waste of time. The fellow in question is no longer with us. Deceased, kaput.'

'You are trying to scare me, and you won't do so.'

'My dear, then stop your teeth from chattering on this bright sunny day. We must talk
again, you and I. Go back to the schoolroom.'
He looked with some disgust at her frock.
'And change your dress. Climbing trees in
white muslin is not conducive to good relations
with governesses. But — before you go . . . '

She had risen to her feet, prepared to run,
but he detained her with a hand on her wrist.

'No word of this conversation to anyone
here at the hall, not to your cousin Roderick,
to any of your cousins, your governess
— anyone. Oh yes. Include in this interdiction anything you might have overheard from
your perch on high. No tattling-tales! Think
well! Maybe your father's good health
depends on it.'

She hunched one shoulder. It was an
awkward gesture, a gesture of defiance. 'I am
not a tattler. What was I supposed to hear,
anyway?'

He scrutinized her puzzled face, and was
satisfied. It was unlikely that a girl of her
years would have understood everything she
might have heard. Then, smiling, he released
his hold on her wrist. 'Wise girl! Do not
change your mind! You would not want your
escapade to be common knowledge. You
would be ruined. Her ladyship would not
want you here any longer and would send you

back where you came from. Go now! We might not deal badly together. Off with you!'

He watched her scamper off along the gravel path with a thoughtful expression on his face, and did not himself return to the house for some time.

10

The Valliants started back towards Mallow early that morning. Neither had breakfasted and both were in a quiet mood: Sir Ivor due to a sufficiency of Selchurch's excellent champagne and Julia from an unusual despondency. Indeed, she welcomed her brother's reticence, which relieved her of the obligation to uphold one side of a conversation.

It was, therefore, necessity rather than inclination which forced them to interrupt their journey at the White Boar Inn. One of the carriage horses had cast a shoe. A wait of some time was indicated while the animal was led to the nearby smithy.

Refreshed by the air, Sir Ivor decided to make up for the breakfast he had refused an hour earlier by ordering a meal of steak and eggs. Revolted, his sister accepted a glass of lemonade, which she preferred to take in the garden area behind the inn. Sensing her mood, he did not question her choice and betook himself inside.

Julia sipped her lemonade, and contemplated why an event that promised to be the highlight of her social season had turned into such a disaster. Not only had she seen little of her host, but she had received the unwelcome news that he was about to be affianced. That foolish dance had been but a whimsical interlude. What had possessed her, when her burgeoning hopes had already been dashed? Then as a climax she had had proof of his perfidy when the scarlet Lady Cytherea had emerged from an encounter with the man who had stolen her heart.

How could she have misread him? During their meetings in London, had she misconstrued their mutual interest in Sophie into signs of courtship? But invitations to the theater and later engagements in London had nothing to do with the child. Possibly those attentions were merely a gentlemanly expression of gratitude for her assistance. A mild flirtation as a reward? That did not explain their second meeting in the dell. Had she been so foolish as to fall in love on too brief an acquaintance? The worst part of it was that she would have been prepared to lay aside her disdain for his position and her plans for her own future! No matter how much she chastised herself for moping over a disappointment like a girl in her first season, her spirits failed to rise. She was blind to the sunshine dappling the small lawn and the soft breeze stirring the leaves of the oak trees.

How worthy of blame was Lord Selchurch, she wondered. Of course, a man of his rank was likely to look higher than a mere Miss Valliant, sister of a modest country squire, for his bride. Really, he had said nothing to awaken matrimonial expectations. Her eyes were open to the sort of romantic idiot she had been. She could not even blame her brother for encouraging her in those romantic dreams, for he had been the first to warn her that there were rumors of an alliance. What a fool she had been, ready to pick up a handkerchief before it had fairly been dropped! Yet the message in his eyes when he met her in the dell had been plain enough. He was nothing but an irresponsible libertine!

Enough! She forced her mind to think again of her plans for when Ivor had established his bride as mistress at Mallow. Maybe she could find a female of independent means who would enjoy acting as traveling companion — one whose family would be sufficiently liberal-minded to let her go — better still, no family at all. She sighed. Ivor would hoot at the possibility of her finding a respectable person of like mind to her own.

She heard her brother's voice in conversation with another man approaching round the corner of the inn. They seemed to be talking horseflesh; the fragment ' . . . believe I can find something to suit you . . . ' wafted to her ears.

Sir Ivor's bluff voice rang out as he ducked through the gate to the garden. 'Ju, here's Kestrel Barnard, whom you might remember.' She recognized the sculpted silver mane of the man who'd been at Mallow the day of the prizefight.

'I'm not so soon forgotten, I trust,' said Barnard and bowed with a mixture of old-fashioned courtliness and ego.

Forced out of her reverie, Julia smiled and extended a hand. 'Of course, Mr. Barnard. You are visiting this part of the country again . . . or still, maybe.'

'Oh, I'm here and there, Miss Valliant, and much pleased to be back in this part of the country.'

Sir Ivor interjected, 'Our friend is putting up here. We had a bite at the same board this morning.'

Any curiosity the Valliants might harbor as to why Barnard was in the area was satisfied without their being put to the trouble to ask. He was more than willing to talk volubly about himself. He was a gentleman of some means, and had varied interests. Most recently he had been fortunate in some

253

maritime ventures and was at the moment considering buying property in the neighborhood.

'A nice little estate — or a house to rent. That's what I'm on the look out for. Not as large as your place at Mallow, oh no, no. A fine old house that, but I'm looking for something neat — perhaps more up to the minute — with not a lot of land attached. I'm no farmer, you know. My interest has been in more diverse activities in the past, so I'm not looking at anything speculative. More of a place to settle.'

'Shipping,' explained Sir Ivor tersely to his sister. 'Mr. Barnard's been telling me all about trade in the South Seas. Interesting stuff.'

'I have an interest in a couple of merchant ships,' interposed Barnard modestly. 'But business talk is hardly what a pretty young lady wishes to hear on so gorgeous a morning. Her mind's full of other thoughts, the day after a grand occasion at an earl's residence, I'll make my guess.'

'Anything to do with other parts of the globe are of interest to me, Mr. Barnard. Was my brother boring on about the affair last evening? To me, life in the southern latitudes would beat a mere party quite hollow as a topic of conversation.'

'Now I cannot allow the other side of the world can be half as interesting as an important function at Bishop's Rise,' protested Barnard.

Julia persuaded him otherwise, and Kestrel Barnard was happy to describe many of the sights he had seen, to which Julia could only summon half an ear. Sir Ivor soon got into a discussion about whether 'those Dutchmen' were still trying to stick a spoon in Britain's interest there.

In due course, the carriage horse was brought back and the coach made ready for the Valliants to continue their journey. They said good-bye to their acquaintance of recent date, and continued their journey.

'By the by, Barnard is coming over some morning next week,' quoth Sir Ivor casually. 'I suppose we can provide a respectable luncheon.'

Julia merely raised her eyebrows slightly and acquiesced. She was used to her brother's starts and amenable to falling in with most of them. 'Not a problem in the world, dear Ivor, if he'll take potluck.'

'He's coming to look at Fieldfare.'

All was clear to Julia immediately. 'Ah, you need room in the stables. What a shame you have to part with him! Am I to guess what your present to your bride will be?'

Sir Ivor gave a small grin. 'I've got my eye on a neat little mare for Lottie. Someone I know, Tommy Stowe — you met him at the Rise — is gentling her, and I'll pick her up when I get back from the continent.'

'Charlotte will be thrilled. She's never had much chance to ride before.'

'Any road, this Barnard feller needs a horse, he tells me.'

'I thought you were getting rid of Gingerbread.'

'As to that, I get the impression Barnard's no bruising rider. Besides, he mightn't like the price I'll ask for Gingerbread.'

The conversation turned into an amicable wrangling about who needed what room in the stables, in which Julia carried her part only halfheartedly. She did not know why she was irritated at the prospect of having to entertain Kestrel Barnard. She put it down to her low spirits after the night before, and admitted to herself that Barnard was a pleasant enough man. If she had met him before she first encountered Lord Selchurch she might have raised considerably more enthusiasm at the opportunity of entertaining a personable, albeit somewhat older, gentleman. Rats! Was she still in a fit of the dismals? She gave herself a small shake.

The following day, Sir Ivor dutifully made

the return trip to join his fiancée in hearing the third reading of the banns. Julia declined to join him. The Earl of Selchurch was also in church, and Sir Ivor noted his disappointment at his sister's absence and drew his own conclusions. Both of them were love-bitten, he suggested to his beloved, who disagreed entirely on that particular topic.

A couple of days later, he nodded to himself knowingly when he overheard Julia telling the housekeeper she was not-at-home as his lordship's curricle was drawing up to the door at Mallow.

★   ★   ★

Lady Selchurch had not been at the service, suffering, by all accounts, from an indisposition that had started even before the night of the reception. It was said that a fashionable London doctor would be called in, it not being deemed advisable for Lady Selchurch to travel up to town.

It was becoming a strange house as the hostess kept to her room much of the day, appearing only at dinner, and then later not at all as she took all her meals in her own suite eschewing all her family. Lady Cytherea was the only one allowed in to visit her, and she coolly acted as a substitute hostess, declaring that it was the least she could do for dear Alicia, who was not feeling at all in trim. The children suffered a little by not seeing much of their mother, and tended to become unruly and bored; Miss Randall became harassed as responsibility for them sat more and more on her shoulders. However, assistance came to her in the form of Joseph Rayne, who persuaded her to let him take them on a few outings.

Having assured Joe that his hostess' indisposition in no way meant that he should depart the portals of Bishop's Rise, Roderick watched his friend's activities with interest. Rayne played the part of a doting uncle, organizing archery tournaments and croquet matches. Then, on finding stumps, bat and ball in the games cupboard, he engaged to teach the girls to play cricket. Miss Randall was scandalized at first, seeing how the girls hitched up their muslin skirts the better to run, but, on hearing that Lady Selchurch had no objection, joined in the exercise, and found herself to be a bowler with a competent underarm delivery.

One member of the younger set seemed unperturbed by Lady Selchurch's absence. Lady Arabelle, on the verge of being released from the schoolroom, was finding life could hold new and exciting possibilities, especially when Joseph Rayne took extra pains to make sure she held the bat in the approved position.

Even Lady Cytherea was willing to join the sport one day, much to Roderick's surprise. She proved a good hand at bat, but was chagrined when a deceptive ball from Sophie bounced under her bat and sent the bails flying. Fielding quickly bored her, so she sat out to watch. Waiting his turn at bat and doubling as an outfielder, Roderick came to sit beside her on a blanket spread out on the lawn.

'What a crafty little bowler your little protégé is,' she commented.

'Put spin on the ball, did she?' grinned Roderick.

'I don't suppose she ever played before, but some sneaky tricks come naturally, I believe. She's a fast runner, too, for a girl. What trained her in that?'

'What are you saying, Cy?'

Warned by the tone of his voice, she laughed self-consciously. 'Oh, don't mind me being so cross. The summer seems to drag, and that little girl demands so much of your attention.'

'I believe she needs it. She is not happy here. You could be more of a help to her, Cy.'

She shuddered. 'Enough that I am little

mother to the whole family! I hope to goodness Alicia makes it downstairs this evening.'

'Sophie is hoping to stay with Miss Valliant soon.'

'Ah, Miss Valliant shares your interest in the hapless wight.'

'She has been kind and sympathetic to the child, and a friend to one who has little gift for making friends.'

'What a paragon! I also take an interest in Sophie. Ask Alicia! We have had our heads together a score of times finding a school for her, and, yes, trying to correct her deportment.'

'There's little wrong with her stance. She is the image of her mother.' He had noticed that Sophie's bearing improved in proportion to the value accorded to her by others.

'That drooping attitude! Then her mother should have been trained to a backboard.'

Roderick said quietly, 'Patience was an old and true friend of mine.'

'Well, let us not quarrel. The day is too warm.'

He protested. 'The day is fine. Summer has scarce begun. Do you find it awkward with Alicia keeping her room, so much? Do you wish to return home?' He had said the wrong thing, he knew. The implication that he would be happy to get rid of her was there, and he had not yet found the words to clarify the situation between them. He cursed himself for letting it drift in this way, knowing that every day made it harder to change the situation.

He jumped to his feet to field a ball sent in their direction, and threw it to Sophie. Suddenly they were calling him to take his turn at bat. Caroline had misjudged her run and her wicket lay askew on the ground.

With a studied air of unconcern, Lady Cytherea left the playing field and strolled back to the house. Lord Selchurch was being as elusive as a housefly. On the ship she had sensed the hold she had previously had over him was not as strong. That was to be expected after a long absence, but she had had every confidence that she could reawaken feelings of passion in him and bring him to her feet again. To an extent she had been right, but her lackluster success had forced her into methods she would have preferred not to use. Reputation had never been her concern. Mealy-mouth notions of respectability were for the Miss Strides of this world. Not for a great lady! Feeding the rumor mill had been easy. A simple anonymous tip to a Grub Street hack about her trip to Deal had worked like a charm. A few well-chosen words to her maid and the interesting information that an engagement was soon in the wind circulated the ton. Her father's old acquaintance with Lady Selchurch had gained her entrance at the Rise. However, Roderick was no longer the easily manipulated boy she had held in her toils a few years ago. She would have to bring him to the point of a proposal in form as soon as possible, or he could slip through her fingers, and she would have allowed her reputation to be bandied about all to no purpose. She could end by looking ridiculous. In no good mood she went up to her chamber and rang the bell for her maid.

'Evans, I want a bath.' The young woman had been prompt in answering the summons. 'Ridiculous! My hair is like string. Whatever possessed me to caper around in the heat like some Mayday milkmaid!'

'If anyone could carry such a thing off, it would be you, my lady!' said Rose Evans in a placatory manner. 'I will see to your bath right away.'

'Wait! Have you talked to Lady Selchurch's woman lately?'

The maid paused. 'Mrs. Lovell is very close, my lady. She won't talk about her lady, not one little bit.'

'Is her health so very bad? She seemed well

enough yesterday.'

'She has sent for a London physician, I'm told. May I venture to ask — how did she appear, my lady, when you saw her?'

The mistress stared at her maid, but what she saw in her face made her answer carefully. 'In high bloom — though not a fever. She was in déshabillé again. Why?'

'It may be nothing, ma'am, but it's whispered that she sent for the practitioner who attended her last successful birthing.'

Lady Cytherea laughed. 'Fie, girl. What are you suggesting? Lady Selchurch — and who? Who has she seen? Of course, I don't know whom she has seen. Well, girl? Who do they think?'

Evans stammered, 'N-no-one, my lady. I don't know, really.'

'Whose name came up, ninny? Don't tell me nobody was mentioned in the servant's hall! Out with it, girl!'

'My lady, apart from the parson, the only man who comes over much is Sir Janus Vale.'

A vicious slap stained the girl's cheek. She jumped back, hand to cheek, tears starting to her eyes.

'That's for stupidity. Go and prepare my bath.'

The maid scurried from the room, and Lady Cytherea went to the window and stared out unseeingly. After a moment she left the room precipitously and made her way to the wing where Lady Selchurch had her suite.

By the time she was admitted to Lady Selchurch, she had regained only part of her composure, but was welcomed in complacently.

'Come in, dear Cytherea! So charming of you to give up part of this lovely afternoon to visit me. Sit down and tell me how all my little ones are.'

'At the moment they are playing cricket like perfect little hoydens.'

Lady Selchurch smiled. 'Don't try to bamboozle me, my dear. You were playing with my little hoydens, for I saw you from the corner window.'

Taking a firm grip on herself, Cytherea got to the matter that was consuming her thoughts. She disciplined herself into a friendly approach. 'Dear Lady Selchurch, I hope you count me your friend.'

'Why, of course, my dear.'

'It has come to my knowledge — how can I say this? There are disturbing stories abroad.'

'Stories abroad?' She moaned. 'What has that hell-born babe done now?'

'Not about Sophie Kettle! About you, Lady Selchurch. Tell me they are not true.'

Lady Selchurch fanned herself, feebly,

almost relieved. 'Tush! The tale is out. I would have kept my secret longer if I could.'

'You admit it?'

'That I am to be blessed with another olive branch? Yes, indeed, my dear. Isn't it a godsend?'

Her companion stared at her in bewilderment. 'A godsend? How can you say that? Aren't you concerned — about gossip?'

'It is unusual and might cause a deal of talk, I grant you.'

'Having a child? These things happen all the time. But so soon after your husband's death — You'll have to try to keep this secret. People will be scandalized that you did this — and you still in black gloves!'

Ponderously, the Dowager Countess rose from her couch, and as she stood between Lady Cytherea and the light streaming through the window, her thickening form could not wholly be obscured by the diaphanous draperies of her robe. Her face was illuminated with an expression almost of ecstasy.

'Be calm, my dear. It is hardly to be expected you would understand. It is a happening so wondrous, so unexpected. If I were a blasphemous person, which of course, I am not at all, I would compare it to the virgin birth.' She had a moment of serenity and then she tapped Cytherea lightly on the cheek with her fan. 'Your eyes give you away. You think I'm trying to run some rig.' She laughed almost girlishly.

Lady Cytherea began to fear for the lady's reason. To steady her, and to satisfy curiosity she fell in with the mood of her hostess. 'Indeed, my lady. You must have your joke. Will you have us all guessing as to who this happy babe's father might be. Shall divine intervention indeed be the tale?'

'Divine intervention! Indeed!' The rapt expression returned to her face.

Getting a little irritated by this echo of her words, Lady Cytherea nevertheless pinned a benign expression on her own visage. 'You must excuse me, dearest Alicia, but I don't understand this. Have you no idea of the father of this child?'

Lady Selchurch gave her a pitying smile. 'Oh ye of little faith. Do you think I would dishonor the memory of my own dear Basil, rest his soul, by playing him false? This is Basil's child. A nestling of my poor nameless mite whom I lost with their father last March.'

Cytherea rose to her feet, staring at her with disbelief and then in horror. She laughed uncertainly. 'That's not possible, Alicia.'

The other woman pressed her hands

protectively over her abdomen. Cytherea wondered why she had never really noticed it before, though Alicia's size and the flowing clothing she wore had disguised her condition.

The Countess looked at her companion archly. 'Impossible, my dear? When I am delivered of a full term child any time these next thirty days, we'll tell if 'tis impossible.'

A wave of faintness almost overcame Cytherea, but she pulled herself together. 'How incredible, and . . . and so marvelous a thing! Dear Lady Alicia, permit me to feel.' On receiving permission, she laid her hands on the taut abdomen where she discerned a vigorous thumping on its wall — by no means the fluttering of an early term embryo. 'How incredible,' she breathed again.

Lady Selchurch smiled fondly. 'I have felt all along — not daring to hope — I did not believe it possible at first. But twins run in my family, you know — both girls and boys. Arabelle was my lost Peter's twin.'

Cytherea thought fast. 'Identical twins? No, not identical twins.' She thought of Caroline and Kathleen, in many ways alike, but one could tell them apart easily. 'This child then could be a girl or a boy.'

'A boy, I am sure. Why else could such a thing happen to me?' She looked quizzically at her companion. 'You do not believe in the workings of Fate? Come, be happy for me Cytherea! This is a wonderful thing for me — for all my children.'

Cytherea could not force a smile. Pleading a bath awaiting her, she offered congratulations and turned to the door.

As she left, Lovell, Lady Selchurch's maid emerged from the dressing room. With a quick look she noted a certain distress on her mistress' countenance. When she spoke it was with a soft Scottish accent, and with the privilege of forty years of service. 'There's one who'll nae wish you a bonnie boy, my lady.'

'Probably not!' responded her mistress a trifle tartly. 'I believe she means to have Selchurch, and my boy will put a fine crimp in her ambition.'

'Don't you be worrying, mistress. I choose every wee bit of food and drink that comes into this chamber. Bide tranquil that I'll nae let anything noxious harm your bairn.'

Lady Selchurch regarded her old servant with amusement. 'Ah, Jeanie! Fie on your dire imaginings. You are giving me such Gothic ideas.'

Back in her chamber, Lady Cytherea dashed off a letter to her father, which she sealed and sent downstairs for mailing.

Soon after, the mail brought back a letter to Lord Selchurch, summoning him to a meeting with Lord FitzWarren two days hence at Haldene Chase, his country seat in Berkshire. His lordship had of late years found it convenient to conduct some of the ministry's business from his country home during summer. The tone of the letter was somewhat peremptory. That in itself was not unusual. As a junior colleague Roderick had oft-times been given pause by some curt missive only to find its brusqueness belied by a cordial reception. He supposed, wryly, that he had erred in thinking his elevation in rank would make a difference in FitzWarren's style of address. The timing was inconvenient; the distance was such that he could not reach Haldene and return in one day, so it would mean that he must miss Charlotte's wedding. He supposed he could try to postpone the interview, but as he had not resigned his post with the ministry, he owed a certain duty. He had no doubt his superior would want to inquire into his intentions on that very same account. It was a summons that could not be ignored.

11

A few days after the encounter at the White Boar, Mr. Barnard rode up to the Valliants' door on a hired hack. He spent some time in the stables with Sir Ivor, discussing the points of the horses available for his purchase. When the two men strolled up to the house shortly before noon, they announced that they had settled amicably on a horse, which might prove to be just what Barnard required.

'You must know,' he explained to Julia, 'I am not a fox hunting man. I just need a good-looking horse to get me around the countryside — maybe only for a limited time. That Gingerbread, now, is a fine bit o' blood — but he's not for me.'

Julia quite understood. He was town bred and no doubt had spent his life making his fortune in the city rather than putting horses over hurdles.

'I'll not take your guineas till you're positive.' insisted Valliant. 'My sister will show you around. Go out for a bit of a gallop! I've got to go over to a tenant this afternoon, but I can be back latish to settle the business. Hell of a thing, but it came up just this morning! I won't be more than an hour. You've got lots of time, eh Ju? It won't be any trouble?'

'No trouble at all,' assented Julia with composure. 'I must say, Mr. Barnard, you have made an excellent choice in Fieldfare, is it?' She did not elaborate, feeling that Gingerbread's propensity for shying at fast passing carriages would make him only suitable for accomplished riders, however fine his potential as a hunter.

So it was that after a simple lunch, Kestrel Barnard and Julia Valliant set out for a pleasant ride along the highways and byways near Mallow. Fieldfare was a well bred horse, just showy enough to appear a horse of spirit, a decent enough mount for anyone other than a hard rider.

Barnard seemed as much taken by the good appearance of the horse as its performance. He had a gentle joking style of conversation. 'The thing I insist on, is that the horse has a staying power that can equal my own.'

'And style to match,' added Julia wickedly.

He grinned. 'Not to add maturity! Miss Valliant, you'll be the death of me. All my self-esteem will be lying on the ground shredded at your feet.'

They paced the country lanes for a stretch,

and Barnard seemed at home with the animal in a short space of time. After taking a sedate canter across the meadows, Barnard proclaimed it to be just what he wanted. They slowed the horses to an amble, and enjoyed a pleasant conversation.

'The countryside and the horse are of themselves not sufficiently absorbing as conversational gambits,' said Julia after a while. 'Tell me more about yourself! You are a man of mystery, Mr. Barnard.'

'Mystery, I?' He gave a bland smile. 'What would you like to know, Miss Valliant? I engage to tell you anything with which I am at ease to narrate — and make up the rest.'

Julia was betrayed into a laugh. 'I suppose that is to say I am being impertinent.'

'Not at all. English misses are generally reserved. In other parts of the world the ladies are not so nice in their notions. They demand chapter and verse. It preconditions one to reticence.'

Julia's lips quirked. Reticence was not a quality she had noticed in Barnard. 'You have lived much abroad, I gather. Then answer me the questions those foreign ladies would ask!'

'My marital status? That is always the first question. I have a beautiful and long suffering wife, who is, unfortunately, not presently with me in England.'

'That is the sort of pertinent information that any society demands to know about its members. I suppose she will be joining you, when you have at last settled on a property, Mr. Barnard?'

'Possibly, possibly! It is somewhat in the air. That is why I would lease rather than buy. My wife's health, you understand, might not be able to support the damp weather in England.'

Julia murmured sympathy. 'I gather she is somewhere where the climate is kinder — though the summer here has been pleasant so far.'

'An indirect question.' He regarded her somewhat mockingly. 'My wife Phoebe is visiting in Ireland. She will not winter there. The Mediterranean would be better.'

'I still claim you are mysterious, Mr. Barnard. You would rent a house that you may not live in and you would buy a horse when you may go abroad.'

He laughed. 'Ah, you have found me out — a man of split mind.'

'Do you have family?'

'A little boy — and a girl. Little Adonis is my pride and joy. After all these years to have a son . . . '

'Adonis! How . . . unusual!'

'You laugh, Miss Valliant. But I have been

living in Greece, and have great interest in things classic.'

'I would not be so rude. And your daughter? You must be proud of her, too?'

'Psyche? Naturally, I am proud of her.' He seemed more anxious to talk of his son, but eventually brought the conversation round to the reception at Bishop's Rise. 'Tell me more about the soirée, did Sir Ivor call it? You must have met lots of interesting people.'

She hadn't. Maybe Ivor had. Although she was loath to talk about that evening, Julia told him something of the individuals she had encountered there as they rode back along the road towards Mallow. Her shrewd observations kept him amused, and she found him an appreciative listener. He seemed avid for information, and had a knack of placing the people she described into little categories. He summed up Joseph Rayne immediately as a complete rattle, so that she wondered if she had been too severe on the young man, for the Earl obviously valued his friendship.

'You don't mention too many young people. I hear Selchurch is a fairly young man . . . and the Countess has several daughters, I understand.'

'Quite a quiverful — if that can be said of girls?'

'I thought there was a boy.'

'Yes, but he died of a brain fever while at Eton some years ago. How did you hear of him, Mr. Barnard?'

He spoke casually. 'I must have heard it somewhere. Tell me, Miss Valliant, how many of the young ladies graced the ball?'

He seemed disappointed to learn there was no dancing, and that none of Lady Selchurch's children were present, but he did not seem disposed to relinquish the subject. He was particularly interested in the notables, such as Sir Janus Vale. Julia was somewhat amused, supposing him to be living the high life vicariously by his intense curiosity.

'And the new earl . . . what manner of a man is he?'

'Full of admirable qualities, I am sure.'

'That is all? Is there no more to be said?'

'When asked to describe a person of fairly short acquaintance, one can only sketch out a surface impression.'

He noted the stiffness in her voice. 'Yet you were doing so well with your new acquaintance of the evening. You obviously have reservations about Selchurch's character.'

'On the contrary,' declared Julia, too quickly. 'It is just that . . . '

'Just that?'

'His training as a diplomat brings forward

those traits, which must be designed to please.' Including raising expectations in women one week and branding the shoulders of others with passion the next, she thought to herself savagely. She mended her countenance and showed a smiling face. 'In fairness, he is a most amiable, even an unassuming peer. By common report, his accession to his position was unexpected, and he is taking things quietly. I believe his tenants approve of him.'

Barnard looked at her keenly. 'No doubt, with time, he will grow into his station and become as complacent and overbearing as the rest of his ilk.'

'Are you one of those who decry wealth and privilege, Mr. Barnard?'

'I shock you? No, not at all. I'm not one of your Jacobins, Miss Valliant. I merely make observations from life as it appears most typical. By accounts, however, I hear he is a very different man from the old earl — Sir Basilisk, as I have heard your brother refer to him.'

Julia's face lit with laughter. 'Unfortunately, he did have a reputation for inflexibility. Now he is dead — and beyond defending his good name. We should talk instead . . . ' She broke off, seeing a rider turning out of the gate of Mallow. 'If I do not miss my guess, I think you may be about to meet the new earl, Mr. Barnard.'

They paced their horses along the lane. Julia made no attempt to wave or attract Roderick's attention. It looked as if he was bound in the other direction, but he caught sight of them, and headed the gray towards them.

As they came together, Julia made the appropriate introductions. If, in the ensuing conversation, she implied a deeper acquaintance with Mr. Barnard than was actually the case, and failed to mention his married state, or that his business had been with Sir Ivor rather than herself, Kestrel Barnard made no sign of discomposure. After an amused glance at the elevation of Miss Valliant's chin he drew his own conclusions; and if he proceeded to display a greater degree of familiarity than was warranted by short acquaintance, Miss Valliant seemed not to object.

'I bear a note to you,' Selchurch was explaining. 'My little cousin was its author, and would not consign it to the post office. She particularly wishes to remind you of your promise to have her to Mallow to bear you company after the wedding.'

Julia could not hold back a smile. 'What a wretched child she is, to make you ride all this way with a letter she could have sent through the mail! I am sure you would have franked it, too.'

'There was an added reason. I am summoned into Berkshire on business at this singularly unfortunate time. As I will be unable to attend your brother's wedding, I wished to add my personal regrets. I have already written my apologies to Miss Stride.'

Berkshire! Lady Cytherea was from Berkshire, Julia recalled with an annoying tightness in her throat. On business, he had said. Surely an earl did not have to be 'summoned' on business? Without a doubt his mission was to seek the hand of the woman who by choice or necessity was to be his bride.

She swallowed. 'Sir Ivor will be disappointed. Your business in Berkshire is doubtless important. I trust it will prosper.'

Roderick looked at her with a wealth of sad comprehension in his eyes. He inclined his head in acknowledgment of her words and what lay behind them.

'Will you return to the house with us for some refreshment before you ride back?' Her tones bore little enticement. She was not surprised when he refused the tepid invitation and took his leave with a formality that equaled hers.

Julia and Barnard rode round to the stables where they chatted until the return of Sir Ivor from his appointment. Immediately talk centered on the question of satisfaction with the horse, and as soon as possible Julia left them to conclude their negotiations.

Leaden hearted, she made her way inside the house; she found the letter that Sophie had written to her, and took it to her room to read. The letter gave her some small pleasure. It was written in a school-girlish hand and was sufficiently brief, but surprisingly well construed. Sophie's education may not have been formal, but somewhere she had learnt her letters well. No doubt her mother had taught her early, hoping to win some advantage for her small daughter in a chancy world. She decided to put off replying until the wedding was behind her, and determinedly banished Lord Selchurch and all his romantic associations from her mind. Her time should be better employed on making plans to entertain Ralph and Mollie Farlaine who would be arriving on the morrow.

Roderick rode back to Bishop's Rise a prey to feelings of frustration. Circumstances were making things difficult for him to further his suit with Miss Valliant. He needed very much to come to an understanding with her, to explain the situation between Lady Cytherea and himself, and to reverse the misapprehension she must be under as to what happened on the balcony. He had not known she had remained at the Rise until he saw her frozen face. She had turned and left abruptly, and he had not learned the reason for her acute distress until his conversation with Rayne the following day. She had not accompanied her brother to church on the Sunday. He had likewise drawn a blank on riding over two days later only to find her unavailable. No doubt she had heard other rumors about himself and Lady Cytherea. She must consider him the sort of scoundrel who would become involved with two ladies at the same time. The situation would be hard to explain. Now, at last, when he did see her, he found her sauntering about the countryside with some self-assured fellow of ambiguous origin who seemed mighty at ease in her company. He was not sure whether the fellow should be considered as a rival, but Miss Valliant obviously preferred the stranger's company to his own.

Lady Cytherea's attitude had also undergone a subtle change, and he believed he had seriously offended her by hinting her stay should come to a close. She had been abstracted for a couple of days, even cool. Well and good! Maybe she was drawing away from him, and he could breathe a little easier. Joe Rayne noticed it and warned his friend against the possibly intriguing effects of blowing hot and cold on the male susceptibility. Roderick discounted it. She made no further suggestion that he apply to her father for her hand, but even Cytherea's changeability did little to alleviate the leaden feeling in his stomach.

On hearing that Roderick would be leaving for Haldene, Rayne announced, 'I'll be off the day you go, Ricky.'

'Sorry to desert you, but there's no need if you wanted to stay.'

'Lady Selchurch would think that pretty odd if you weren't here. I'll make a bolt to a friend of mine whose place is not too far from here. Courtney — I knew him at New College.'

Roderick remembered him vaguely from the reception. 'The Parliamentary hopeful! Yes! He seemed like a man who will make a name for himself.'

★ ★ ★

The day of his departure for Haldene he breakfasted quickly, and went to seek Lady Cytherea.

'I leave directly. Did you decide to avail yourself of my escort to your home? Joe

Rayne is heading off today — he has friends in the neighborhood — so you'll be quite dull here.'

She laughed teasingly. 'I vow you are anxious to be rid of me. Possibly I will go with you, and come back with you when you return. What do you say to that?'

'If that is what you want.'

'It will be boring here. But no. I simply cannot leave dearest Alicia while she is so out of sorts. But do not hurry back on my account, Roddy — though of course I shall miss you sorely.'

She always dealt him surprises. A few days ago she had been anxious for him to call on her father. Now she was treating it as a matter of no interest. He began to hope that she had given up on trying to engage him.

Roderick drove his curricle to Haldene, arriving late in the day. The house was not as large as Bishop's Rise, but more modern in style, and decorated in the latest mode, suggesting the infusion of considerable money.

My Lord FitzWarren was at his most affable. He welcomed Roderick at the door. He was carrying a gun and had an aged spaniel padding at his heels.

He ushered Roderick into his study, and called for refreshments before putting the gun away. After inquiring after his daughter's health, he opened the conversation with casual observations about sport in general, and inquired what sort of hunting Roderick had seen in Quebec. He poured Roderick a glass of wine and seemed in no great hurry to bring the subject round to why he had summoned him to the house.

'You'll see quite a few changes since you were here last,' commented the peer, as he settled himself more comfortably in his chair. 'We are in the midst of massive earthworks — getting a whole new outlook. You'll be interested in seeing how things are progressing. Any plans of that nature in line at the Rise?'

Roderick demurred. He was not planning, he told his superior, to make any imminent changes to his landscaping.

'Not in your line, is it. Well, as Earl of Selchurch you'll be paying some attention to the land. Best let that agent of yours advise you. He's got a good reputation. That's if you'll be staying on at the estate.'

'Clearly, I am obligated to spend some time there, and learn how to run a major estate. I can't pretend I was brought up to that.'

'You won't, of course, be resigning your place with the ministry at this time.'

'You know me well, sir. No, I do not wish

to relinquish my claim on your good offices. Though in the light of my new state, I would certainly hope that more responsibility would be coming my way.'

FitzWarren looked at him keenly; it seemed as if he would smile, but he did not do so. 'A clash of responsibilities! And life is too uncertain to make long term plans, eh? But you are ambitious. I approve.'

'Planning can be chancy at the best of times. True, my interests are not centered in landed estates. My instincts are more international. I am loath at this time to give up what I do.'

'Very wise!'

This last was said with such intensity, that Roderick's instinct for untoward contingency arose. Some of his superior's words were puzzling in the extreme. 'Pardon my obtuseness, sir. I'm losing scent of the fox here.'

FitzWarren leaned back in his chair thoughtfully. It was a full minute before he spoke. 'Is it possible you don't know?' Then as no light shone on the young countenance opposite him, ' . . . About Lady Selchurch?'

'What about Lady Selchurch?'

'That the lady is *enceinte*?'

Selchurch looked at him astounded. 'Is this some on dit you received from town? Frankly it's unbelievable.' He thought about his cousin's mysterious illness, but shook his head. 'It can't be.'

'You are wrong, my dear fellow. Little Cy writes me so. I know it's not general news, but Cy got a hint from her own maid and went straight to Lady Selchurch who confirmed it without any hedging. But I thought you must know, for it affects you most. You haven't engaged a valet yet, I gather.'

Roderick was distracted. 'A valet? Why a valet? No, I haven't had time — I've been coming and going too much.'

'Get yourself a man, then. The servants always know what's going on. Anyway, I can't tell you how sorry I am to hear this.'

'Yes. How unfortunate,' muttered Roderick, much disturbed, 'for the lady herself. It hardly affects me. Such things can happen in the best of families.'

'Not like this! You don't understand what has happened in this case — if it is to be believed. Lady Selchurch is not with child again — she is with child still!'

Seeing his companion was speechless, FitzWarren carried on with a hint of malice. 'You may not be the Earl of Selchurch at all, my boy. You see, apparently she was carrying twins. Only one of them was lost in the shock of her husband's accident — a boy, at that.

The other twin is still alive and kicking too, for little Cy wrote me that she felt it. If it's a boy . . . ' He gave a shrugging gesture.

For a long minute Roderick was silent. FitzWarren busied himself pouring a stiff drink of brandy from the sideboard and handed it to the young man. He took it with a lame grin.

'I'd better laugh about this, lest I disgrace myself. God, I will look such a fool!'

FitzWarren thought about this. 'I don't think so. It's not as if you puffed off your consequence. I'm glad you've kept a low profile since your accession. You have done nothing to give people a cause to laugh at your come-down — which may not happen at all, if Alicia pops out another girl.' He continued after a silence. 'Even if the babe's a boy, you'd still be the heir, and entitled to an allowance in that capacity probably. You'd likely be trustee, as closest male Selchurch.'

'An allowance from a babe? I'd hardly accept that. As for being trustee — that would not be a welcome responsibility, I can tell you.'

'I understand you, I think. Alicia has singular ill-luck with her male offspring.'

Roderick disclaimed quickly. 'You misapprehend. My wish for Alicia's child, boy or girl, is that it will be healthy and long-lived. I am saying, rather, that I shall not happily return to the Rise in such a case. I'd hope to be abroad in some overseas posting. I'd not be able to fulfil a trustee's duties.'

'Well, this has been a shock to you. I'll have you taken to your room. We dine in one hour. Take your glass up with you.' Deftly he replenished it. 'After dinner we will talk some more. You'll be feeling more the thing then.'

At dinner they were joined by a sister of Lord FitzWarren who directed the household during his daughter's absence, together with a companion, a cousin of sorts who added little to the conversation. The subject of Lady Selchurch hardly rose — only civil platitudes hoping that she was in good health and recovering her spirits after the death of her husband, to which Roderick gave polite conventional replies, while Lord FitzWarren stared into his claret. Thereafter the talk centered on Lady Cytherea and how they missed her and when could he spare her to return to them. He hardly knew how to answer this last, considering Cytherea was Lady Selchurch's guest rather than his own and gave a noncommittal answer.

Later the two gentlemen sat over their port and discussion became more particular about Roderick's career.

'The Secretary of State himself had warm words to say about your term over the Atlantic. How did you get on with the Shawnee? I hear you were in Tecumseh's old hunting grounds when the Plattsburg debacle took place. Too bad you were not with Provost. You might have steered him alight.'

'Hardly, sir! I doubt if I, as a civilian employee, could have had influence on the outcome. Sir George should receive recognition of the excellent terms he maintained with the French population, though. He kept them loyal.'

'Your loyalty does you credit. However, the man managed to turn victory into defeat — and then again at Sackett's Harbour.'

'My real regret is that I was so far in the backwoods that my recall reached me too late to get passage before the St. Lawrence iced over. I would fain have given Sir George my support.'

'Hum! Well, in the end it all made little difference. How would you feel about going back over there in a few weeks time? In fact, I need you there.'

Roderick was silent for a moment. He raised the glass to his lips, looking directly at his superior. This was almost déjà vu. He remembered the last time he was sent on a mission to Quebec. It had been a dismissal, a way of getting him away from Cytherea. Then he was not an earl, and now his position was in great doubt. He thought he understood.

'I need an advisor — eyes and ears — a moderate, level-headed man who will report directly to me. There isn't a faction over there that isn't at loggerheads with another — town against country, merchants against the farmers, the French habitants versus the Loyalists, the Church and the non-conformists — you name it.'

'Is it a Selchurch you need, or an Anhurst?'

A smile teased the corners of FitzWarren's lips. 'A Roderick! You understand the situation over there. You've the knack of dealing with people on many levels. Do not flatter yourself you are the only one that can do it, but you'd be an asset. And do not presume to attribute my motives!'

Roderick met his gaze levelly. 'Three years ago, I left England's shores . . . reluctantly . . . but in pursuit of the call of duty. Obedient, if you will. I am not that same person.'

FitzWarren pursed his lips thoughtfully. 'You could have refused that particular posting, you know. It would not have hurt your career had you done so.'

Roderick pensively stared at the play of the

candles on his wineglass and drained it abruptly.

'There was nothing personal in it,' continued FitzWarren.

'I completely understood that posting.'

'No, you didn't understand. No reason why you should.' He refilled Roderick's glass and then his own. 'I am not a Roman father, you know. I have never believed that parents own their children.'

Roderick regard him levelly and waited for him to continue.

'Truth to tell, I was surprised you accepted the position with so little question. I had my suspicions. But I don't interfere.' He turned his chair slightly, stretching his legs before him, and regarding the tips of his shoes. 'I had been anticipating a request for an interview from you. No, no my boy! Permit me to digress here! Three years after the fact it need no longer be a sensitive issue. You and Cytherea were going at it pretty hot and heavy. I'm not a complete idiot, you know. A normal father would have been flexing the horsewhip. However, that's not me. I would have been more than grateful to see Cytherea settle down with a steady young man, with good prospects and fine family background. But I didn't think it would work. Ambition, you see!'

'Ambition?' Earlier, Lord FitzWarren had uttered praise for that trait.

'Cytherea's ambition! She'll not be satisfied with a small life. Her wish is to be a star in the firmament. No little patch of blue for her. I believed her affections to be engaged, but I did not believe they were strong enough to conquer her aspirations.'

'But why Quebec?'

He shrugged. 'A training ground! You enjoyed the years there, didn't you? A young man's country! You liked the adventure of the wilds, the mystery of the primeval forests, the ripple of the streams, the romance of the river?'

'There was much to enjoy, yes — but Cytherea would not have. It was a test?'

'It was a test,' he conceded. 'But not for you. The test was for my daughter. For you it was a favor. If she had no wish to go abroad . . . if she would not wait a few years — but then, you couldn't expect Cytherea to stay pining at home for you.'

Roderick's lips twitched. 'The picture does not leap to the imagination, sir.'

'Then you ruined the whole thing. You became an earl.'

'An earl for a season, only, I begin to fear.'

This amused FitzWarren immensely. His shoulders shook. 'So you are confounded by a miracle. I have always believed miracles to be good things.'

'To be honest, this miracle is in the nature of an embarrassment to me.'

'Understood! But the child could be a girl, in which case your position will be unchanged.'

Roderick shrugged. 'I can't pretend such a situation is even tolerable. I dread to think of the on dits raging in town when this gets out.'

'Would such a thing affect your decision whether to go back to Montreal?'

'There are things to be thought of: trustees, if the child should be a boy, arrangements for looking after the estate. I should still be the heir, and it is to be thought I would have some responsibility in it.'

'Hum! I wonder if you wouldn't be better off at arm's length in such a situation. There are cousins on Basil's mother's side who could take a share of responsibility. Take a few days to think over this situation. I must know soon.'

'Is this in the nature of a further test, sir?'

'You have not been pounding at my door to demand my daughter's hand, sir. I regard it more in the nature of a reprieve. Yes, I have been aware of the rumors engrossing the town like wildfire. Perhaps I recognize the fell hand at work, and have done my best to dampen such wildfire. Rumors only last a while. All the more reason to head back to the wilds, and leave them to die out. Tell me, how is my daughter treating the situation at Bishop's Rise?'

'With equanimity, sir.'

Lord FitzWarren raised his eyebrows. 'Really! Tell me, do you see much of that rakehell Vale around there?'

'Rather a fixture, sir.'

'Hum! Not the son-in-law I'd choose, I fear. Yet I don't feel justified in going against my own principles. However, he is not the question at the moment.'

He leaned forward over the table, and tapped his forefinger deliberately on the wood. 'But hark ye, young Selchurch! I won't have Cytherea hurt. See that you keep her reputation high. I'm relying on you to keep any more scandal away from her name. Don't jilt my daughter! If she gives you up, which would not surprise me, if you're no longer a peer — see, I know my own darling's little faults — that's her prerogative. She's a woman, and society will understand that. But if you put shame on her, forget the whip — it's my shotgun I'll be oiling.'

Was it worth it, Roderick thought, to point out that he and Cytherea were not actually engaged, nor had he after that first rejection renewed his suit of marriage?

But Lord FitzWarren was all smiles again. He laughed uproariously. 'Here I am, making myself out an ogre again. I rely on you, Roderick my boy, to make all well. I depend on you.'

12

The day following, Sir Ivor Valliant led Miss Charlotte Stride to the altar at the old Norman parish church beside the parsonage. Mr. Stride conducted the ceremony with a beaming face. His daughter's alliance with a prosperous squire of good family within ten miles of the parsonage was cause for rejoicing, especially after so long and uncertain a courtship. The wedding was not a substantial affair, but it was attended by such notables as the Dowager Lady Selchurch and Lady Cytherea FitzWarren. It was generally accounted a pity that the Earl was not in attendance. From further afield came Mr. and Mrs. Ralph Farlaine who seized the opportunity for a brief stay with Julia. The sun smiled on the occasion, the bells pealed merrily, and the wedding breakfast was held on the lawns at the parsonage. A few scenes from The Tempest were presented by the Selchurch children as a compliment to the occasion, and Sir Ivor and Charlotte Valliant set off on their trip to the continent in a brand new coach purchased by Sir Ivor in honor to his new bride in a moment of extravagance.

Briefly emerging from seclusion, Lady Selchurch had temporarily relieved her mourning in consideration of the festive nature of the occasion by donning a voluminous overdress of mauve over gray silk with a loose black lace pelisse. In view of her recent lack of health, Charlotte led her to a seat in a shady place. No hitches arose to disturb the enjoyment of the day. The roasts were well dressed, varied and plentiful, and the excellent champagne was provided from the cellars at Bishop's Rise. The event was declared to be a success.

Before the couple left, Charlotte seized a few moments to talk to her new sister, promising to write every week; she had already provided a detailed itinerary where letters could be sent to the bridal couple. 'How long do the Farlaines stay?'

'I lose them Saturday. Mr. Farlaine cannot be absent any longer, and he does not care to travel on a Sunday.'

Charlotte nodded in solemn approval. 'But cannot Mrs. Farlaine be persuaded to stay? I do not like the idea of you being alone so many weeks.'

'She has some midweek engagement, so she will wish to travel back with Mr. Farlaine.

Don't fuss, my dear! Sophie Kettle comes to bear me company soon.'

'So I hear.' A frown crossed Charlotte's face. 'I hope you won't regret your generosity. That girl is too young, too troublesome and definitely not my idea of a suitable companion. Why don't you send a letter putting her off till we return?'

'Worry about making my brother happy!' was Julia's sole reply. So it begins, she thought to herself wryly. Charlotte, however well meaning, will always want to guide my behavior.

Mrs. Farlaine, of course, missed Selchurch, and made pointed enquiries as to whether Julia had seen much of him, as they headed to Mallow aboard the Farlaine traveling coach. Ralph Farlaine was enjoying a doze in one corner.

Julia replied that she had seen him on a few occasions, but begged her friend to put no significance on that fact, their meetings having no more import than the normal course of visiting between neighbors.

Mollie Farlaine sounded vexed. 'I made sure a romance was in the air.' Something in the expression on her friend's face silenced a playful accusation of feigning coy. 'I am sorry, my dear. I shouldn't be prying in this vulgar fashion.'

Julia feigned interest in the passing scene, as she answered casually, 'Don't be a ninny! There was never anything between us. He was just starved for company in London. It was a pleasant interlude.'

'The wretch didn't pursue his interest, then?'

'Believe me, there was nothing to pursue. In fact, we are expecting a match to be announced — one more suited to his status and fortune.'

'Oh?'

'You met her today. Lady Cytherea FitzWarren. Rumor tells it, anyway.'

'That glorious creature! All beauty and radiance! Oh, my poor friend! And with a considerable fortune and expectations, I have no doubt. Why can't life be fair?'

No more was said on the subject and two days later the Farlaines departed. That day was marked by two other visitors to Mallow.

The first was Mrs. Beesley. Disappointed to find that Sir Ivor Valliant would be absent for some weeks, she asked to speak to Miss Valliant. 'I'm that disappointed,' quoth the farmer's wife.

'Is it a legal matter? Perhaps I could direct you to another magistrate.'

'No, no, Miss Valliant. It's just that I wanted to talk to Sir Ivor hisself. I must thank him for letting off my son, young Charlie. He dropped charges against 'im. He didn't charge my Beesley neither. That's a relief off my mind, Miss, as I'm sure you'd guess.'

'Oh, I see,' answered Julia. A noble gesture in celebration of his marriage, she conjectured. More likely it was because he expected to be absent next quarter sessions. She led the woman out, inquiring about the health of her family, accepting thanks again on behalf of her brother, and declaring it was quite unnecessary for Mrs. Beesley to bring in a fine young goose from the cart, as there was no company at Mallow to give proper justice to such a feast. She conducted Mrs. Beesley to the door, and was relieved to find the bird had not yet gone to its reward, judging by the hissing from the crate in the back of the farmer's cart. She waved good-bye, relieved that her first action on behalf of her brother was no more onerous. Therefore, when later that day the manservant asked if she would see Mr. Barnard, she assented, without questioning whether it was proper to receive him.

He entered cordially. 'How kind you are not to deny me, Miss Valliant.'

She greeted him civilly, and said, 'You know, then, that Sir Ivor is still on his wedding trip.'

He spread his hands wide, palms upwards in a dramatic gesture. 'My dear Miss Valliant. My visit is to you.'

'Then I am intrigued. This is not a business visit, I collect.' She invited him to sit and sent for refreshments, the while reminding herself that as he had declared his marriage, his visit was not likely to be an act of gallantry.

'Now I have two extra pairs of legs, my horizons are somewhat enlarged, Miss Valliant. You may count on me as a neighbor.' He seated himself, hands on knees, in a relaxed attitude. There was a mischievous glint in his eye that betrayed some knowledge of what was going on in her mind.

They conversed for a while on bland topics, until Julia decided that all this was pure hedging. 'Mr. Barnard! Why are you here?' The eyes that met his were full of clear challenge.

'A neighborly visit?' A smile lit up his whole face, but Julia did not relax her ruthless gaze. His eyebrows shot up. 'My dear Miss Valliant. Am I to understand that you are on to me?'

One eyebrow elevated slightly. 'May I point out, sir, that if I am not 'on' to you, you will have burned your bridges.'

His lips twitched. 'We fence still, I see. What gave me away?'

'Your thumbs.'

He looked down at his spread hands. The two thumb tips came together to form almost a perfect Roman arch. 'Ah, my daughter's thumbs!'

'Sophie has the curliest thumbs I've ever seen. They almost look double-jointed.'

'Little enough to go on.'

'It was later that I realized the truth. You named your daughter Psyche. There was a woman — Mrs. Shackle, you may know her — she called Sophie by that name, but I thought she was saying Sukey.'

Tom Kettle nodded. 'As soon as I first mentioned my daughter's name, I knew I had made a mistake.'

'Most people would not know. She is now always called Sophie. It is not unknown for young people to prefer one given name over another.'

He nodded. 'Her mother always preferred Sophie. It was a less exceptional name, she said. My first wife had a simplicity about her that had nothing to do with naivete. A pureness of character.'

'Then Sophie is not like her mother — more complex — like you, perhaps.'

'I do not know my daughter,' he acknowledged sadly. 'Oh, I have seen her. I have strolled the park at the Rise a time or two to catch a glimpse of her. She is growing into the image of my Patience.'

Julia hesitated. 'Have you made yourself known to her?'

He scowled down at the carpet. 'What would she want with me? She is where she ought to be — in the home of the Earl of Selchurch. She is the granddaughter of a peer of the realm.'

'Your quest for a property — was that all a take in?'

'Regrettably yes! I could not settle here, but I needed some excuse for being in the vicinity.'

'Why do you come to me?'

'Miss Valliant, for a very good reason! She is to visit you. My Lord Selchurch let it drop, if you remember. I had hoped she might be here — that I could talk to her — meet her without her knowing who I am.'

She was astonished. 'How could you treat your daughter so — fail to reveal yourself to her, when it is the most important thing of all to her to find you?'

He sighed. 'Believe me, I have thought about this. I can do nothing to enhance her position in life. I would be an encumbrance. I have seen her, dressed fine as you please, in the company of quality folks. Here am I. I have associated with the dregs of society. A father like me would be a source of shame to her.'

'Yet, by appearance, you seem to be prospering.'

'Come to that, I fared better than most. When I got my ticket of leave, I wanted to hurry back to my sister to reclaim my daughter as soon as could be. I knew by then that Patience had died — had been dead some three years. Yet, it was necessary for me to make something of myself — to get money — to buy clothes. There are few opportunities for city folk out there in New South Wales. I tried to get a group of players together.'

'You were an actor?'

'I was always an actor, before ever I took service in Selchurch's ménage. That little band of actors with which I was temporarily associated had so little to go on with — no money, no theater.' Pensively, he added, 'And blessed few audiences.'

'Was your — second wife one of those players?'

'Not an actress — nor a convict — oh, my goodness, no! She was the Irish wife of the Greek captain of a Dutch merchantman. Her husband's ship went down in a hurricane. The crew managed to launch a boat. She along with some of the crew were picked up by a ship bound for New South Wales, after drifting around on the Pacific for five days.

Others including her husband didn't survive. She was stranded without funds, and without friends. Most of the crew managed to find berths in other ships. The troupe came to her rescue, and she spent time with us, starving with us, helping any way she could for what keep there was. She and I found we dealt well together and married. About then I was fortunate enough to get funds from my sister, praise be, so we took passage in a small vessel heading for Sumatra where her first husband's company had a trading post, and were able to take ship for Europe. Much to my amazement, I learned that I had married a woman of substance, for her husband had an interest in other vessels trading in the Indies.

'I sent a letter to my sister. Receiving no answer, I came to England only to learn that she, like my dearest Patience, had shuffled off this mortal coil. I cannot describe the anguish I felt in losing both wife and sister. Worst of all, I could not learn what had happened to my daughter, my little Psyche. Eventually, I came back to Bishop's Rise, hoping that somehow I could learn something of her. Then I saw a young girl riding one day, and I knew she was living there! I knew my own daughter!'

'What relief you must have felt!'

'So, Miss Valliant, does my daughter come to you soon?'

Julia felt some indignation. 'Mr. Kettle, Mr. Barnard, I urge you to go to Bishop's Rise to meet your daughter. Declare yourself to her!'

'I might be turned away from the door. I'll not put that humiliation on her. My dependence is on your good nature. Let me visit my daughter while she stays with you.'

Thoughtfully, Julia weighed this. 'I cannot comply with your request. Your daughter is not here, and I must think seriously about this. I do not wish to go behind the back of Lady Selchurch if she entrusts Miss Kettle to me. Go to the Earl himself. He is more likely to be sympathetic towards you than anyone.'

He took his leave rather abruptly after this. He was adamant that his daughter must not know him. However, he could not pin Julia to a promise that she would not tell his daughter that he was in the neighborhood. She could appreciate his scruples. Was the right thing to do necessarily the best thing to do? It caused her such indecision that it would be a few days before she would follow through on her promise to invite Sophie to stay with her.

★　★　★

About this time Lord Selchurch, or Roderick Anhurst as he was more apt to think of himself these days, arrived back at Bishop's Rise. Several quiet days at Haldene had done much to reconcile him to the situation.

If indeed Alicia was pregnant with Basil's child, and a healthy male heir was born, he must lose his rank. Three months ago he had neither expected nor desired to be Earl of Selchurch. His sole ambition had been to pursue a successful career in the service of his government. Loss of the earldom would enable him to concentrate on his career, which providentially would be of no interest to Cytherea, as he now realized. She had no ambition to be the wife of a minor colonial official beginning his rise through the ranks. Not only was she, as she would admit, a poor sailor, but the limited social circle in some semi-civilized outpost would not attract her in the slightest. Marriage with Lady Cytherea had long since ceased to be an intoxicating prospect. It had never figured in his mind as a stepping stone to promotion.

On the other hand, what if the baby was a girl? He would keep rank, house and estate, and retain the mantle of consequence he had been beginning to assume these past weeks. Life would have significant doors opening to him. He would take his seat in the Upper

Chamber and have an influence in the running of the country. Important posts abroad might come to him, which he would accept. Unfortunately, he would have Cytherea blandly assuming that the engagement proposed three years ago, but never really entered into, was still alive. With the knowledge that originally she had lied to him about her father's disapproval of a match, he realized the extent of the manipulation she had exercised. A certain diminution of her eagerness that he approach her father, which he had marked a few days earlier he now recognized as coinciding with her knowledge of Lady Selchurch's interesting condition. He reflected cynically that she had swiftly told her father of this cataclysmic news, but had not thought it expedient to drop a word in his own ear. What other prevarications had she been responsible for? How naive had he been three years ago when as a green youth he had first become involved with her?

Suddenly it struck him as hilariously funny. In truth his affairs were in a state of paradox. If he lost his rank, his friends would commiserate with him, but he would be relieved of his most pressing problem. On the other hand, if confirmed in his rank by the birth of another girlchild, he would still be faced with the choice, which threatened his honor. As the second footman came to take his gloves, he wondered what was causing his lordship to be grinning like Punchinello.

After changing his raiment, he went to the Dowager's suite. The elderly Scottish maid admitted him reluctantly on her mistress' bidding.

The condition of Lady Selchurch was growing obvious. That stoutness that had enabled her to mask the situation no longer kept her secret. She was sitting near the window, rather defiantly embroidering a baby cap.

Lady Selchurch had not been looking forward to this interview. Under the circumstances, she had expected outrage and disbelief. Instead, Roderick was standing in the doorway in a relaxed attitude, though his arms were folded. An ironic gleam lurked in his eye. Prepared for battle, she was now reduced to querulousness. 'Sit down, cousin! Please, do sit down. Don't stand there like a hanging judge. I know we have something to talk about.'

She did not call him the familiar 'Selchurch,' he noted, and remembered, surprised, that she had never done so, even from the start. He had put it down to resentment. Why had she ever been party to his presentation to the neighborhood? He had noticed a certain volatility in spirits just prior to the reception. He could only conclude that she had not been convinced of her continued pregnancy until after the invitations had gone out, though she may have suspected it long before by hints she had given. How stupid of him not to have paid attention!

He approached and picked up her handiwork, a charming confection of cambric and lace, which he turned this way and that. 'Is this for a boy or a girl?' He returned it to the table beside her. 'Accept my congratulations on your happy news!'

She eyed him, suspicious of the sincerity in his voice. 'Can you say that? Can you say that, Roderick, truly?'

'I mean it.' Then he drew in a breath. 'But I must be blunt — at some risk of offending you. This child you carry — is it Basil's child?'

Her ladyship bridled. 'That is hardly a question a gentleman would ask.'

''Tis a question that this nobleman needs to ask.'

'Yes, the child is Basil's. I did not play him false, even in death.' She directed a deliberate regard at him. 'I'm sure you wish I had.'

'Hardly!' replied Roderick impatiently. 'You must admit it puts me in an awkward position. However, I can't blame you for the trick Dame Nature has played on both of us, Alicia.'

Picking up her handiwork, she put in a couple of stitches, but they were not straight, so she put her work aside rather than betray any ripple in her self-control.

'I was not afraid of your anger — but I dreaded your anguish.'

He shook his head and gave a rueful smile at this disarming remark. 'It was a facer. You should have told me, Alicia. It was FitzWarren gave me the news a few days ago.'

Her face lengthened in indignation. 'Lord FitzWarren knows?'

'His daughter told him. Did you think she wouldn't? He's a good friend of yours. Maybe he kept me there these five days to get over my first shock.' He took a seat beside her. 'Neither of us knows what the outcome of this all will be, so I'll not rail against Fate, but wish you every blessing in the anticipation and conclusion of the birth.'

'Cousin Roderick — you are a true nobleman.'

'I'm more like to be a laughing stock.'

A wary peace was established between them. There should be no immediate announcement of the situation. Though the news must eventually emerge, both agreed it was preferable to avoid advertising this extraordinary situation for public titillation. It would be a nine day's wonder soon enough. Lady Selchurch had been formulating plans, she told him. Shortly she intended to repair to London where she would be under the direct care of her *accoucheur*. She intended to take no risks with her precious burden.

The situation seemed an ideal time to clarify his relations with Cytherea, but, when he tried to bring up the subject, she shied away. He understood. All further talk on the subject would be in abeyance until Lady Selchurch was delivered of her child.

After riding one morning, he returned to the Rise to find Joe Rayne waiting for him. He had driven over from the Courtenays where he had been staying after leaving the Rise. He had a tale to tell.

His friends had received a visitor fresh from town, who on learning that he had recently been staying with Roderick, put him through what he regarded as an indecent catechism about his visit. 'Fella's an awful quiz! Anyway, he was plaguily keen to know all about any understanding you have with Lady Cytherea. It turns out that there's betting in all the clubs now. Will you and Cy make a match of it!'

'Good God! It's not as if I know that many people in town.'

'Needless to say, I pokered up a bit, but he had a shell like a tortoise. According to this chap the odds are lengthening and he's wondering whether to lay off a bet.' He leaned towards his friend conspiratorially. 'I could have cut him off, but it struck me I should try and find out how the tales wag.'

'What utterly disgusting details are about to emerge now?'

'Well, up to about a week ago, odds were pretty well on — general knowledge that Lady Cy was staying here, and you'd been here too, most of the time. Then the odds changed somewhat dramatically for some reason. Must be something I don't know. Did you have it out with her? Not that I'd tell that prying shuffler anything.'

Roderick drew his brows together sharply. Had rumors of a possible new heir reached London?

'Funny thing! I was wondering if Vale had anything to do with it.'

'Vale?' Roderick spoke the name sharply.

'The chap mentioned that he saw him in the city one day last week — dropped a hint that he knows Vale quite well. The tale is Vale's betting.'

'I wonder which way Vale is betting!' muttered Roderick, tight-lipped.

Joe Rayne stayed for lunch, and it was well

into the afternoon before Roderick could speak privately with Lady Cytherea. He found her seated on her favorite bench skimming over a novel. She looked up and smiled lazily.

'I have something I am duty bound to tell you, Cytherea.'

'You make that sound quite dire. No arguments, I hope. The day is too warm.'

'Cytherea, we have been skating round this topic for too long. We need to come to an understanding.'

'I thought we had, my dear.'

He ignored this. 'Are you aware that our names are being bandied around in the London clubs?'

She yawned ostentatiously. 'They always bandy names around the clubs. It seems their purpose for existence?'

'They are making bet as to whether we will eventually marry.'

She laughed. 'Is that all? Ignore it.'

'It does not please me to ignore it. We must find some way to set it about that there is no foundation for such rumors.'

'Well, perhaps it would not be wise to do that. Let us cool down a little and use our heads! To make a big fuss might create exactly the sort of attention we would wish to avoid. It is no great matter, after all, if they guess which way the wind is blowing.'

'Cytherea! The point is the wind is not blowing in that direction.'

She looked at him archly. 'Do you say so? Do you intend to jilt me? The consequences to you would be severe.'

'Our engagement never was. You — not your father, but you — ended it before it was fairly begun — before I left for British North America.'

She shrugged with wide-eyed innocence. 'I fail to see how that makes a difference. Everybody believes an understanding exists. It is the same thing. Would you have me to be an object of pity and derision to the ton? You could not be so cruel, Roderick. Besides, you owe it to me, who surrendered herself to you in that act that puts formidable obligations on the male party.'

He sighed. She could always arouse feelings of guilt in him reminding him of that one fateful occasion. 'Will you still wish the connection if Lady Selchurch brings a boy into this world?'

Cytherea sighed. 'Life is full of uncertainties. Of course, I understand, my dear. You do not wish to hold me to our engagement in the light of an uncertain situation, and I respect you for it. But you do not get rid of me so easily.'

Roderick had a mental vision of a mound of dough which, no matter how many times pounded down, would rise again. He looked at her baffled. Men and women played by different rules. A woman could change her mind on an engagement. If he were no longer the Earl of Selchurch, the world would hardly be surprised if the connection were severed. Rather they would expect it. However, a man was honor bound to go through with an engagement or become a figure of contempt and be liable for legal consequences. It hardly mattered that his one proposal had been refused; the whole world believed them to be engaged. For the moment, she would cling to her position like a limpet to a ship's bottom.

Lady Cytherea rose serenely and walked back towards the house. Concealing her disquietude, she made her way to her chamber. Her erstwhile lover was trying to wriggle off the hook, and if she was not careful he might succeed. The uncertainty about the succession was no time for weakness. She would feel on much firmer ground once Roderick was confirmed to be the Earl of Selchurch.

As Lady Cytherea entered her chamber, Rosie Evans was laying out clothes for her mistress to wear to dinner. An expression of annoyance escaped her lips. 'Do that later,

Evans! Go and fetch my book! I left it on a bench in the walled garden. It's overclouding. Now before it rains!'

After the maid departed on this commission, Lady Cytherea strode back and forth in her chamber. On impulse she headed to Lady Selchurch's suite, not quite knowing why she was going, other than a need to monitor the progression of her hostess' pregnancy. Her hostess had not appeared anxious to see her of late. In fact, she harbored the unpalatable suspicion that Lady Selchurch was trying to drive her away through sheer boredom. There had been so little company at the house in recent days. Her excuse for remaining was to supervise the children, with Miss Randall's help, of course, a role which even she considered ludicrous. Now that Roderick had returned, he might be persuaded to invite a few new faces to dine. She would proffer herself as hostess.

After seemingly earnest enquiries into the Dowager's health and spirits, she told her how much her children missed her presence daily.

'How is all my little family doing?'

'Why will you not see your children? They think it very strange that they have not seen you for days. La! The questions they ask! And Arabelle is much concerned in her quiet way.'

'Did you have some specific reason for your visit, other than to nag me about seeing my children? Don't you know I miss them? But I could not keep my secret if they knew.'

Your secret is already out, thought the other to herself, but she said, 'You should not be shut up all day with none but your woman to talk to. It is not healthy. You have missed another fine day.'

Lady Cytherea stood at the window that overlooked the walled garden. Evans had found her book, but was not immediately returning. She was looking up at the tree, which overhung the wall, and by the movements of her hands and head she appeared to be talking. Was she reciting poetry to herself, she wondered. How odd of Evans! No! She was talking to someone in the treehouse.

The following morning before breakfast, Piller brought Roderick a tersely worded request to wait on Lady Selchurch without delay. Surprised, he did so. He found Lady Selchurch pacing back and forward in some perturbation. He had never seen her angry before, and after a moment's admiration of her majestic figure striding up and down, hampered by her girth, he begged her to cease lest she cause a premature event.

'Calm down, you say. That woman! What

lengths will she rise to next. She is not Lady Selchurch yet, however much she may anticipate that state. She does not give orders at Bishop's Rise. If she is ever Countess of Selchurch, I shall be gone from here, Roderick, be assured of that!'

'Are you talking about Cytherea? What has she done?' he asked in some amazement.

'Lovell, my woman, tells me — informs me, if you please — that the head gardener has been given orders by your Lady Cytherea.'

'Your guest, cousin, but continue.'

'She has told him — and she knew just whom to tell, because he's been wanting to get at it this many a year — to dismantle little Peter's treehouse. How dare she! And the thing is, it could easily happen, because I can't see the house in summer because of the leaves. Sometimes I see something white moving about in there, so I know someone is in it, but the house could be pulled down and I wouldn't miss it till winter.'

Roderick frowned. 'What would make her do such a thing? That is a mighty cool piece of intrusion.'

'She must be in a pet at Sophie. The girl climbs up there. I have seen her come down over the wall. Please give the child a hint not to be invisible when people are talking below!'

'I'm glad you sent for me. The treehouse stays as far as I am concerned. Does it bother you that Sophie climbs up there?'

'Why should it? She is not happy here, Roderick. If she finds solace in her refuge, I'd not deny her that. I was somewhat of a tomboy myself when I was that age.'

'You have a kind heart, Alicia. I should have mentioned before, Miss Valliant has invited her to stay for a few weeks. Does Sophie have your permission to go?'

A little taken aback by the warmth of his compliment, Lady Selchurch sought refuge in tartness. 'Oh really? I wonder what Miss Valliant can have in common with our tiresome little kinswoman. Certainly she may, if she won't be a sad burden to her.' Her face brightened. 'The more I think of it, that is an excellent idea. If she keeps Miss Valliant company while her brother is away, then the summer will be nearly over, and a suitable school might be found for her in the meantime.'

Roderick found Sophie in that very treehouse. Grinning to himself he scaled the tree and joined an astonished scholar, reading a history book in the cool, damp privacy of the leafy fortress. Her mother's commonplace book lay by her side.

When the groundskeeper put a ladder to

the bole of the old horse chestnut, he nearly fell off the fifth rung, to find the object of his demolition occupied by the Earl himself.

'Ah, good man!' remarked Roderick. 'You've brought a ladder. The old steps are unaccountably missing. If you should come across the missing steps, be so good as to get them repaired and reinstalled.'

The man scratched his head in a bemused fashion. 'Why am I to repair the steps if the tree fort is to come down, me lord?'

'This excellent treehouse has had a reprieve from the wrecker's mallet. Let it be known that no one lays so much as a crow on this structure if he wishes to keep his position.'

The man inched down the ladder. 'But, sir, what am I to tell the lady? I made sure that if she was to be mistress here, she'd want it down.'

There were full ten seconds before Roderick could control his voice on an even keel. 'Lady Alicia Selchurch is mistress here, until such time as I marry.'

Later that morning he spoke to Lady Cytherea. 'I fear you were under a sad misapprehension. Lady Selchurch has no wish for the treehouse to be removed. But all is well. It is saved, and no one will do it damage. Lady Selchurch would have been distraught if anything happened to it.'

Cytherea reddened. 'Tush! She refines too much on it. It is unhealthy to be so doting on a child who is long gone. Better she had no reminder.'

'Our hostess is planning to have another boy to put in that treehouse.'

Lady Cytherea lost her temper. 'You are quite impossible, Roddie. If you think that she will have a boy, then you are tempting Fate. She will have a girl, and you will still be the Earl of Selchurch.'

Roderick snapped, 'Try not to be ridiculous about this, Lady Cytherea! The gender of the child is already set. 'Tempting fate' as you term it cannot alter that fact.'

Two days later, Sophie received a letter through the mail. Her feelings of importance at this singular event in her life were diminished by Miss Randall's insistence on opening the missive. It was part of her duty to do so, she pointed out warily. Sophie forbore making an issue of it, but waited possession with a baleful glare. When eventually the sheet was handed over, she read that Julia was asking her to come the following day. Deaf to Miss Randall's bleated protests, she rushed impetuously from the schoolroom in search of Roderick. The most likely place was the smaller library, which Roderick had been using as his study. The door was slightly ajar, and she knocked on it, pushing it open when a voice called to enter.

She was right into the room before she realized the figure seated at the desk was Sir Janus Vale.

13

Sir Janus was the first to recover from their surprise. 'Your protector is not here, Miss Kettle. Stay! Don't go! I have long wanted more talk with you after our delightful chat in the garden.' He made no move to rise. 'Come — there's no reason to be afraid. Won't you sit down?' He indicated a chair beside the door.

She mistrusted his coaxing tones but remained in the room. Her words sounded gauche even to her own ears. 'What are you doing here?'

He raised his eyebrows. 'In Selchurch's sanctum? Don't fear! I am not trying to usurp Lord Selchurch's private place. Just a book I needed. He was so gracious as to allow me to look for it in here.' He clapped the covers of an old book together, a faint cloud of dust erupting. 'A matter to do with old surveys. Come, sit down! I don't bite.'

Sophie sat gingerly on the edge of the chair, and then settled herself back, assuming a poised attitude. 'What do you want with me, sir?'

'Nothing, my dear! Nothing at all! My

needs are with your father.'

'Then I cannot help you. I have not seen him lately.' She nonchalantly picked a piece of lint from her sleeve.

He gave an appreciative chuckle. 'So casual! Yet not so knowing!'

She regarded him warily.

'He is not far away. No, no! I cannot tell you where. He's gone to earth, it seems.'

She leaned forward, her sangfroid broken. 'He is here? I do not believe you.'

The humor left his face. 'Any child of mine would be whipped for that.' Then, remembering that it was not his design to frighten her, he modified his tones. 'However, I see I do not put you to the blush. Suffice it to say that I am not in the habit of lying. He has been seen — by old staffmates. You know that he once enjoyed a — a position of trust on these very premises.'

'That he was a footman here? People have made sure I was aware of it.'

'Don't be bitter, Miss Kettle! I would be the first to admit that he was worthy of better things.'

'Who has seen him?' She did not need to ask the source of his information; his servant frequently awaited his master's convenience below stairs, and was on amicable terms with several of the staff.

He shrugged. 'You cannot expect me to display all my cards. It is enough that you know that Tom Kettle has no wish to be found. Enquiries I have initiated have revealed that much. Perhaps he is using a stage name. However, a possibility occurs to me. Perchance the two of us, if we allied our forces, could find him!'

She lowered her gaze to the entwining rose pattern of the carpet.

He gave an indulgent smile. 'You distrust me. Who can say you are wrong to do so? Some might say I did grave wrong to your father in the past. Yet his own fault to me was great. Now he may be in a position to hurt me even more severely.'

She raised her head. 'How?'

'Report says he has come into possession of a piece of paper. It is of no value to him, except perhaps revenge. I want it. I would even be willing to pay a modest sum for it.'

'Why are you telling me this? I cannot help you. If my father has proof of . . . '

'Merely a statement, made on a death-bed.'

Perception lit her face. 'Mouche!'

'Ah! You are somewhat aware. Death-bed accusations cast an undue influence on public opinion, however illusory they might be. Therefore I am prepared to go a little out of my way to put my hands on it.'

'Why are you afraid of his accusations? Are they true?' she asked shrewdly.

'I will only know when I see the document. A gray area, you understand. Howsomever, I have it on firm authority that your father will not reveal himself to you.' He noted her expression of dismay. 'He believes his — re-emergence into your life would be to your disadvantage. However much I may agree with him, I am prepared to sacrifice principle on that point to enlist your cooperation.'

There was a long silence. Sir Janus waited, idly buffing his nails on the superfine of his coat and examining their luster. The ticking of a clock on the mantelpiece dinned loud into Sophie's ears.

Eventually Sophie uttered, 'I don't see what can be done.'

'Oh come, my dear, I expected more of you. I see in you a person of considerable resource, if all I hear of you is true. I propose we put our heads together to make a plan.'

'Why should I help you to hurt my father?' Her voice was scornful.

'No hurt is intended. Once I had that piece of paper in my possession, I would not have to fear your father.'

She hesitated. 'If you are thinking of some type of exchange — the paper for me — ' She drew in her breath sharply, realizing he had been waiting for her to make such a suggestion. 'Something like an abduction?'

'What an adventurous little hussy you are, and how propitious the suggestion came from you!' He looked at her benevolently. 'I concede that such a procedure could have merit. There would be no crime if the victim were willing.'

'But you don't have me to exchange, have you?' Her eyes glinted maliciously. 'I am perfectly safe here under the protection of the Earl of Selchurch.'

'But missing your father, I must point out. Come to that, you may not long have Lord Selchurch to champion you.' A quick look at her face told him that this thought had struck home. Sophie, too, had been listening to household gossip.

It was not with any real intention of getting involved that she pointed out, 'I can't help you. According to you, my father does not want me any more.'

'No. You have misinterpreted my words. His regard for your well-being is so profound that he sees himself as beneath your exalted condition. He believes that his return would blight your prospects in society. Such proof of affection speaks of an interesting vulnerability.'

'Then my father is wrong! Society means little to me. I am not at all cut out to suit society. Even I know that. I would rather be with my father in poverty than be cooped up with the Prince Regent himself in a mansion.' She looked conscience stricken. 'Though Cousin Roderick has been everything that is kind and fair to me.' An astute Sophie decided it was safe enough to play along with him, trusting on her own good sense to keep her out of danger. 'I might consider helping you.'

'Everybody gains. You gain a father. Your father gains his daughter.'

'Can I rely on your good faith?'

He sighed. What an odd child this was. A changeling from the back alleys of the city. 'You can. We will arrange it for tonight sennight.'

'How unfortunate! I will not be here. I am to stay with Miss Valliant.'

For some moments there were proposals and counter proposals. At last Vale said, 'All right! We will do it at the Valliant's house. That will be considerably easier. I will arrange for two men — two quite pleasant fellows, I assure you — to collect you from that house — Mallow is it? — next Friday evening. I will arrange to be bidden here for cards on that night. You must come out to meet them as soon as it is dusk. We must be sure of the time, so that the coach is not hanging around where it might be discovered by some late caller. And it must be known that you are abducted. Can you scream?' Sophie looked a little dubious. 'Scream you must. And the coach must leave with a good deal of noise. There must be no doubt that an abduction has taken place. It must be noised abroad. What will Miss Valliant do, do you think?'

Sophie's glance darted left and right as if seeking inspiration. 'Where would she go for help? Her brother is away from home. Here to the Rise?'

'We must hope so. Somehow you must predispose her to do so. Then the servants would know. Those who are protecting Kettle would get hold of him. How would he then know how to retrieve you? Leave that to me to think on!'

He rose to his feet to conduct her discreetly from the room. 'A week today, Miss Kettle. I'll get word to you if there are any changes to our plan.'

*　*　*

Roderick conveyed Sophie to Mallow. Despite Julia's warm welcome to Sophie, he again

329

underwent her attitude of indifferent civility. Frustration seized him that he could not pay proper court to her while he was still perceived to be involved with Lady Cytherea. Yet he must do something to crack that shell that chilled her heart.

In reply to her carefully uttered offer of refreshment, he said, 'I'll not stay, but I beg a few moments of your time, Miss Valliant.'

To refuse his request under Sophie's interested eye would present an uncalled for humiliation to him, so Julia assented. 'Firstly, I will see to the comfort of my guest.'

'I wait for you in the garden.'

After she had conducted Sophie up to a small sun-filled bedroom at the side of the house, she descended, prey to apprehension of the embarrassment that must surely face her.

Roderick was pacing the drive, blind to the border of riotous sweet-william beside him. He turned eagerly and came to meet her as she approached. He would have taken her hands, but her arms were firmly folded in front of her.

'Miss Valliant. Thank you for giving me this chance to talk to you!'

'You have something to discuss about Sophie, perhaps?'

He said explosively, 'No! Let us not talk of

Sophie!' He realized she would not make it easy for him, and spoke gently. 'There is so much I wish to say to you but I cannot do so. Your attitude speaks to me with ringing tones. You believe me to be a double-dealing scoundrel. If I am guilty, I am certainly not guilty to the extent that you believe.'

'It is not necessary that you explain yourself to me.'

'It is, Julia, as I value your friendship!'

'The friendship you desire is too warm, sir. You have taken advantage of me. To pay court to me, while engaged to another is not the part of an honorable man.'

'I would agree with you whole heartedly, if I were engaged.'

'What are you saying? It is well-known you are engaged. What I observed at your assembly requires it.'

He controlled an impulse to shake her. 'What did you observe, that night? Lady Cytherea leaving the balcony! You saw nothing of what occurred outside. Yet you have made a grave judgment.'

The confidence in his voice had its effect on her. 'What did happen? The lady looked — had experienced some violent encounter. It was not you who kissed her?' She looked at him searchingly. 'You are not answering.'

'When I found Lady Cytherea, she was

trembling and in some distress. Yes, I kissed her. Do not turn away! The kiss was meant as a comfort, while she regained her composure. We were old friends.'

'You are telling me that you were not responsible for the disarray . . . '

'Yes! She would wish me to say no more.'

'Convenient! I understand the qualms. However, once you are wed the scandalmongers will turn their attention elsewhere.' She turned away.

He moved round to face her 'Listen to me! It is true that years ago I would have married her . . . '

Stone-faced, Julia listened as he gave a delicate account of his past dealings with Cytherea, omitting all details prejudicial to her reputation, and described how he found himself in his present predicament.

'In effect, what you are telling me is that Lady Cytherea is clinging to you over an old declaration, which she did not accept at the time.'

'Basically! She maintains we are engaged. I do not.'

'Yet you kissed her.'

'Idiot that I was!' He ran his hand through his hair. 'If I had never met you, I might have been content to drift back into an understanding with her. But I did meet you. And I swear to you that I have said nothing to her that justifies her continued expectations. I'm in the devil of a fix!'

'Then you must get yourself out of your fix!'

'Easily said!' Yet there was something in her face that gave him hope, though her arms were still tightly crossed. 'I love you, Julia. There . . . I have said it! I have said what I have no right to say, while I am mired in this situation.'

Her hand went up to cover her eyes, lest her face betrayed the depth of her feelings.

'I am sorry.'

'Do not be sorry! But go away! To be friends is too hard.' She could not look at him. 'I — I thank you for all you told me. But do not come back!' She ran inside the house, as the threatened tears began to spill.

The days that followed for Julia and Sophie were packed with a succession of drives in the neighborhood, visiting the village or walking Sir Ivor's dogs and visiting the nearby farm to see the calves and watch the milking. Sophie learned to drive the dog cart. They went riding a couple of times accompanied by March. Sophie was put up on Julia's well-mannered mare, Russet, while Julia rode one or other of her brother's horses.

Much of the time the conversation ran

merrily. Sophie told Julia of her hideaway in the old treehouse. Julia talked of her plans to see something of the world, finding a kindred spirit in her young companion.

Yet, it occurred to Julia that the other was brooding on some secret matter. Conscious of her own duplicity in failing to tell Sophie her father was in the area, Julia nevertheless felt that the girl should be encouraged to talk about her problems. She remembered how tremendously important some problems had seemed to her when she was about Sophie's age.

In the evenings they sometimes enjoyed a game of cards, cassino being a favorite. One evening, Sophie commented suddenly, 'When I played cards with my Aunt Lissie and Mrs. Shackle, we didn't just keep score. We used to gamble. My aunt would say it was never too early to learn how to make a shrewd bet. I used to bet whopping amounts, and I often won.'

Julia cast an amused glance at her as she strategically brought her ten of diamonds into play. 'Indeed. You must have got vastly rich.'

'Well, as to that, it wasn't real money. We gambled with the buttons in Mrs. Shackle's button tin. Little buttons were farthings, bigger ones were pennies, and the really big buttons were sovereigns.'

'Poor Mrs. Shackle! To lose all her buttons.'

Sophie grinned. 'We always gave them back in the end.'

'Alas that I have no button tin! We could have turned the parlor into a gambling den. Dried peas would be too tame, I suppose.' It gave her an idea through which she might be able to encourage Sophie's confidences by a more subtle form of enquiry. 'We can make our own stakes. We can play for forfeits, rather than gold.'

Sophie giggled. 'I once saw a group of players — in the green room, you know — playing a gambling game. They didn't have any money, and they were playing for each other's clothes. It was very funny. I think the man who suggested it was in costume — not his own clothes at all. And one man was ver-rry unlucky!'

'Say no more,' begged Julia. 'The vision appalls my mind.' For the hundredth time, she wondered at the strange upbringing the child must have had after the death of her mother. 'No, these forfeits would not be material possessions, but — secrets! The loser has to tell a dread secret to the winner.'

Sophie eyed her, her head cocked a little sideways. Her mouth gave a mischievous little smile. 'That sounds corky. Starting from this game?'

'Certainly starting from this game.' The game had been pretty even, but she managed to allow Sophie to win first time.

'I get to ask a question,' said Sophie, rubbing her hands.

'Do your worst!'

'Why aren't you married?'

Julia grimaced. She should have expected such a question from a twelve-year-old girl. If ever a game would be prone to cheating, thought Julia, this would be it. 'I almost was once.' She quickly related the story of Philip and the disaster that thrust him into that long twilight state between life and death. 'Since then, no gentleman has come up to scratch,' she ended. 'Your deal!'

Sophie took the cards and shuffled competently. 'Hm. How awful! I didn't know people might get killed while boxing.'

'It was not the sparring gentlemen do. It was the bare knuckles fighting that goes on till someone either goes down for the count or his second throws in the towel. Philip did it all for a bet.' Her tones were bitter, but then lightened. 'So be warned. Bets can be dangerous things.'

They played a second game, and this time Julia won handily.

'Now it's my turn. Let me see — something to strip your soul bare.'

336

Over the course of the evening, Julia learned much about the other's life at Bishop's Rise. The treehouse and the tiresome proclivities of the other children figured largely in the accounts. It sounded as if Miss Randall's life was full of strife. Sophie's lack of reticence, however, convinced Julia that whatever was bothering her was something deeper.

Julia called a halt.

'Can we play again tomorrow? I have to catch up.'

'There speaks the true gambler,' laughed Julia.

The next day brought a letter from Charlotte. At the time of writing the couple was putting up at the Clarendon in London, on the eve of departing for Dover. All had been such a whirl that she had not even had time to write to her father.

That evening, play continued. An intimation that the game had got out of hand came to Julia when Sophie asked her, innocently, 'Are you in love with my Cousin Roderick?'

She felt her cheeks reddening, but tried to keep her answer off hand. 'What sort of question is that? He's a very likable person, of course, but — '

'The easy answer would be 'no,'' observed

the wise child sitting across the little card table.

Julia threw her a glance of acute disfavor, only to be answered by a sphinx-like smile. 'I scarce know.'

'I saw you dance with him.'

'What good would it do for me to be in love with him? He is — involved, with Lady Cytherea.'

Sophie let this equivocation slide. A thoughtful frown settled across her brow, and she cried out when Julia suggested they have an early night. Childlike, Sophie begged for one more game. Julia agree reluctantly, with an embargo against any more enquiries as to her private emotions.

Luck favored Julia with a winning hand.

'Well, young lady! What leading question shall I ask? I have not sufficiently delved below the surface. I know! I require you to tell me a secret.'

'What sort of secret?'

'Any secret! I've run out of inspiration.'

Her young friend eyed her in impish thought, and with the air of one delivering a coup de grâce, announced, 'The Countess of Selchurch is increasing.'

Julia stared at her blankly. 'I meant a secret about you. Forfeits have to be truth, you know. I don't like your joke.'

'It is true.' Sophie leaned forward, her face suddenly absurdly anxious. 'I would not lie about Aunt Alicia who has been nice to me. Everyone knows about it below stairs.'

Abruptly, Julia gathered the cards into a neat pile and fitted them into their leather bound box. 'This game was not a good idea. I am at fault for having started it. Would you care for a glass of milk before bedtime?'

'You don't believe me?' Sophie studied her face, not quite understanding her sharp reaction.

'I have to accept it. Her ladyship's servants would never invent such a tale. The idea is just distasteful — a lady of her position — so soon after her husband's death.' Julia rose from the table. 'I don't care to listen to gossip.'

Mortified, Sophie refused any milk and went upstairs to bed.

Half an hour later, a white-robed little figure drifted into Julia's room. Julia was sitting in bed, a book open before her.

Sophie sat next to her on the bed. 'Lady Cytherea doesn't really love Cousin Roderick, Julia. She just means to be a countess. And — and Cousin Roderick does not pay much attention to her.'

Despite herself, Julia could not ignore this. 'What makes you say that?'

'He never holds hands with her, or anything. Besides, I've heard things.'

'You'd best keep them to yourself.'

Sophie looked as if she would say more, but snuggled up to her friend instead. 'I just don't like it when I see you're not quite happy.'

Julia was touched. It was the first overt gesture of warmth that the young girl had made towards her. 'Silly! I'm not in despair. Neither have I useless expectations. Marriages among the cream of society are seldom based on love, you know. Money marries money; blue blood marries blue. It's the way of the world.'

Sophie hunched her shoulders. 'That was the sin of my parents. They went against the rules, and they suffered for it.'

Consolingly, Julia put an arm round the child. For a moment she was tempted to break faith with Kestrel Barnard and tell Sophie that her father was no more than seven miles away. She had made no promise not to tell. 'Maybe we won't play forfeits any more. I'll see if Mrs. March keeps a button tin.'

The girl's mood changed. 'Yes, if you like. I will win vast fortunes from you. But there is one thing I have to add — about the Countess.' She peeped at Julia tentatively, wondering if she would get another snub. 'It will astonish you. Besides, it will restore her good name in your sight, Julia. Truly!'

Julia sighed. 'Don't tell me Alicia has contracted a secret marriage only four month's after her husband's death. That would not recommend her to me.'

'Do you know when she is expecting? Within the month.'

'What month?'

'This month.'

Julia was shocked into silence.

Triumphantly, Sophie chattered on. 'You see why I had to tell you it all? Lady Selchurch could be expecting an heir.' She clambered off the bed, and walked to the door. 'And now, I'll leave you to read your verse.' She presented a mischievously smiling face, which was the last part of her to disappear round the closing door.

Half angry at the child, Julia tried to get back to the book, but she found the Byron's lines no longer claimed her attention. Her brain started to whirl in contemplating what Sophie had said. Preposterous! It could not be. If Alicia had lost one baby in March, how could she have another in the middle of summer? Could such a thing be? Could it? What if it was a boy? What a disaster for Roderick!

What a disaster for Lady Cytherea! What a tantalizing situation! No, she didn't believe a word of it!

It was too dark to read. She gave up on her book and settled herself for sleep, only to toss and turn into the early hours before sleep overcame her.

The following day was a quiet one. After lunch, Sophie threaded some beads, and Julia sat down to catch up with her correspondence. She was in the middle of describing her misadventures with gambling games to Mrs. Farlaine when she heard a commotion outside. The stamping of horses' hooves and the creaking of doors opening brought her to the window. With surprise she saw the Valliant coach.

Her brother's personal servant got down from the box. There was a muffled burst of swearing in which Julia recognized the rhythms and intonations of her brother's favorite oaths. Next she saw Charlotte directing the unloading of baggage.

Abandoning the letter, Julia was out in the driveway in a flash to greet her sister-in-law. 'Charlotte! What has happened to bring you home so soon? Where is Ivor?'

'Good day to you, Julia! He's still in the coach.'

Julia found Sir Ivor stretched out on the

cushions, one leg encased in wool and bound in splints.

He summoned a sheepish grin when he saw his sister. 'Hello, Ju! I had a nasty fall going below aboard ship yesterday. There didn't seem much point in carrying on, so we came home.'

Julia's eyes were fixed on the immobilized member. 'Is it broken?'

'Like kindling! They took me to a butcher in Dover who set the bone.'

'A butcher!'

'Well, he called himself a surgeon. There was no staying there. The inn — not to be thought of. We nighted at Farlaine's. I'd have slept on the sofa, but no — they had to call every servant including the boot boy to heft me up two flights of stairs. I'd have fain not come down again, this morning, I can tell you.'

'I can't think how you would be so afraid they would drop you,' said his bride crisply. 'They bore you down with exquisite care, besides Mrs. Farlaine summoning her own doctor to have another look at you.'

'But, all the way from Dover? What must you be thinking of? All that jolting! It must have been agony for poor Ivor.'

'Do you think I don't know?' snapped Charlotte. 'He would have it so. I dosed him as much as I dared with laudanum. We're here!'

14

Until crutches could be made for him, Sir Ivor could not hope to negotiate the stairs, so temporary quarters were set up in his ground floor office. It was not in his nature to cosset himself, and if he was not to be enjoying his honeymoon, he declared himself fit to receive visitors, and attend to any magisterial duties that might come up.

After making him as comfortable as she could in the small bed squeezed in beside his desk, Charlotte saw to unpacking the luggage in the large main bedroom at the front of the house, and then marched down to the kitchen. There she got on good terms with Mrs. March who proudly showed off the store cupboards, and conducted her on a tour of the premises. The cook left her at last to make the necessary preparations to prepare a dinner that would do justice to the new mistress' first meal at her own board, though she considered it a crying shame that the master would be forced to eat from a tray in his study.

Finding that Julia was deep in a conversation with Sir Ivor in which the name Beesley seemed to occur quite frequently, Charlotte fetched a sunbonnet from her room and walked outside to see what improvements she, as the new chatelaine, would like put in train. The entrance was plain and lacking in importance, she decided. A new brass knocker should be a priority. The ivy should go, but she knew better than to antagonize her sister-in-law. Next year, perhaps! It was dry enough to explore the spinney and she entered it to see if it had pleasant walks. She found a path that followed the course of the driveway, so that there was no fear of getting lost.

She was somewhat surprised to see a man in topboots and sporting a patterned waistcoat dismount from his horse, and leave it tethered beyond the gate. There was something clandestine about the way he walked up the rather overgrown driveway, keeping to one side as if anxious not to be seen from the house. As she stepped out of the spinney he seemed startled to meet her short, slight figure in a muslin dress and sun bonnet, but he quickly recovered his composure. He touched his hat. 'Good day, miss!'

Charlotte returned his greeting calmly. Maybe the man had good reason for being where he was, though his discreet manner made her suspect he might have an assignation with one of the maids. How she handled this situation might be the keynote to how she planned to go on in this house.

'Would you be the new young lady as is staying here?'

Charlotte thought quickly. Was this something to do with Sophie? She knew that the young girl had a tendency to get mixed up with strange people. Papa's daughter would not lie, but was not above prevarication. 'Such a description might apply to me.'

'Then this is a lucky stroke, miss.'

Her mouth curved into a feigned smile. 'And why is this?'

'I've a note to deliver to you — on the quiet. You're expecting it, I'm told.'

She gave him to understand that she certainly did understand. Taking the note he handed her, she glanced at it quickly to see that it was not actually addressed to anyone in particular. The man had doubtless been directed to deliver into the hands of one person only, and relief at the apparent success of his mission showed in the manner he was already edging away towards his horse.

Outrage filled her spirit. Young ladies did not receive letters from gentlemen without the knowledge and permission of their natural guardians — whoever those guardians might be.

Hastening to the house, she went up to her bedroom. She threw off her bonnet, and looked at the note. It was sealed. Ought she to open it? What had experience taught her? She remembered an incident from her own youth, when a young acquaintance from the village had had the temerity to write to her, and the severity with which her father had reacted to the situation. He had insisted on opening the letter himself. She had deeply resented her father's action, knowing that her own judgment and the propriety of her actions had not deserved to be called into question. Ah yes! But could she say the same of the propriety of the actions of little Sophie Kettle? Should she consult with Julia? Yet Julia was all too indulgent of Sophie's actions, and might not exercise the severity that the situation demanded. She, Lady Charlotte Valliant, was now the mistress of this house, and on her devolved judgment of what was fitting here. She reached for a small nail file from her dressing table and pried open the seal. Her eyes rounded as she read the words:

My adventurous Sophie,
   Our plans go forward, but we must act a day earlier. Come to the front gate at ten this evening. Wear something warm.
   V

She gasped. What was this? An elopement? Impossible! Sophie was too young. Could her correspondent be one of those degenerates whose taste ran to extremely young girls? But no. She saw nothing about Sophie that would arouse passion in a man other than the freshness of youth. Who could 'V' be? Vale? Hardly! How would he come in contact with a girl in the schoolroom? She would think about what to do.

After dinner, Sir Ivor was in a great deal of pain with a slight fever. He blamed it on the sultriness of the weather. It was out of the question for Charlotte to bring up the subject of Sophie with him, and she administered a dose of laudanum hoping it would help him to sleep. When she left his study, Julia and Sophie were no longer in the drawing room. She eventually found Sophie in her bedroom, watching lightning flashes, which were answered by the distant growl of thunder. Sophie disclaimed all knowledge of Julia's whereabouts.

Charlotte decided. She must be the one to confront this mysterious perverted being. He would discover that he had a determined, virtuous woman to confound his wicked plans!

She threw on a hooded cloak, which she had bought for the sea voyage. This villain would be taken by surprise, lest he melt away into the copse in the twilight.

The first few heavy drops of rain came down, as she left the house. As she approached the spinney, a flash of lightning illuminated a coach waiting in the drive. How could it have approached the house so silently?

'Halloa!' she called softly. 'Is anybody there?'

'Of course we are, sweet thing!'

Another voice interposed, 'Quick now! You do your part! You're supposed to scream.' Hands seized her arms, and started to pull her towards the coach.'

Charlotte became alarmed. Her voice rose. 'Stop it. Let me alone. Let me go!'

'Louder, miss. Louder!'

'No. We don't need the screamin.' Here, Charlie! Put this sack over her head.'

Charlotte struggled madly. Her foot kicked out and caught one of her assailants on his knee, and he muttered a curse. Then she started to scream, though not through any wish to cooperate with the confusing messages from her captors. She was bundled into the chaise and felt it pull away, hearing much clatter and commotion despite the enveloping sack.

From her room Sophie glimpsed Charlotte

scurrying down towards the copse. Intrigued, she could not imagine where she was going. She ran to the main bedchamber to get a better view of the drive, and opened the casement, careless of the rain. She heard Charlotte's screams and the rattle of the coach. As she turned away with alarm, she noticed a letter lying on the bed. After a moment's inward struggle, she read it in the waning light. Any feelings of guilt were washed away. That was her letter!

With amused comprehension, she returned to her own bedroom, to consider what must be done. Surely the abductors would speedily realize their error and a furious but unharmed Charlotte would come stamping up the driveway. Yet as the minutes passed, and the night sky darkened, this did not happen. It occurred to her that all this might be turned to good account, if her father could be persuaded that it was she who had been taken rather than some stranger her father neither knew nor cared about. But she must reach Sir Janus without delay, before it became bruited around the countryside that Lady Valliant was missing.

Impulsively, she donned her riding habit, and descended the stairs in stockinged feet. It could not be too difficult, she told herself, to put a saddle on Russet, that most good-natured mare, and ride to Bishop's Rise. The rain was tailing off and with any luck the moon would come out from the clouds soon.

Sophie crept past Sir Ivor's study. He was snoring jerkily. She pulled her riding boots on in the flagged back hallway, seized a convenient umbrella and let herself out into the wet night.

Making as little noise as possible, she pulled open the stable door and slipped inside, pleased to find it dimly lit by a lantern hanging on the wall. Too late she realized her plans were overset, as Julia emerged from the shadows.

'Oh, it's you, Sophie.' Julia's eyes took in the riding costume. Her tones were ironic. 'Going for an evening ride, I see! Such a fine night! What start are you up to now?' Then, taking in the stiff little back and look of frozen dismay on the girl's countenance, she said, 'If you are so anxious to go home, I will drive you back to Bishop's Rise in the morning. There's no reason to dash away just because my brother and his wife came home, you know.'

'What are you doing here?'

'I was just bringing a treat to Gingerbread. He is such a nervous nag.' She went back to the far stall where the large horse stood, shifting restlessly, and rubbed his nose some more. 'He's not called Gingerbread because of his color, but because of his treat of choice. Maybe I shouldn't give it to him. Maybe the spice makes him excitable. Gingerbread hates even the slightest thunderstorm, you know, and Ivor would normally come out and talk to him on a night like this.'

Sophie came closer to her, and put her hand out to the horse as well. She said in a small voice, 'I have to go to the Rise, dear Julia. Now. Tonight. It's really, really urgent!'

'What were you planning on doing? Saddling up a horse and riding out? I am sorry, but you can't do that. I would not for the world be disobliging, but you've never ridden in the dark. Were you thinking of taking Russet? I have the greatest dislike of people borrowing my horse without permission, you know.'

'I can find my way. Please lend me your horse, or one of the others.'

'You think you can find your way. Forget that plan! I'll not have him putting his foot in some rabbit hole in the dark and ending up in my brother's state.'

Her little jaw was set obdurately. 'I didn't want to tell you this. It will make you hate me.' She spoke with all the intensity of a twelve-year old. So she told Julia about her interview with Sir Janus and the proposed mock abduction.

'But I was not going forward with it, Julia. I never really meant to.'

Julia was inclined to blame herself because she had it in her power to reunite this child with her father, yet had hesitated to do so. Now Sophie had embroiled herself in a desperate scheme to smoke him out. Her mind flashed to a discrepancy in the tale. 'Then, if you are not going forward with the scheme, why the riding clothes — the creeping around in the dark?'

'I told you the truth, Miss Valliant. On my word! Truly, I am not going forward with the plan at all — only, something worse has happened.'

'My heart is in my boots. Tell me fast!'

Sophie licked her lips. 'Didn't you hear?'

'Hear what?'

'The coach! The shrieks from the front of the house!'

'You can save your ghost stories.'

'No story! There was screaming. Maybe the servants . . .'

'The servants are all at the back. Charlotte is at the front, though. Did she hear anything?'

Sophie was betrayed into a nervous giggle. She nodded.

Turning her attention away from the horse, Julia looked down at the child sternly. 'What mischief have you been up to, Sophie. Out with it. Now!'

Sophie had never heard those tones from Miss Valliant before. The laughter was wiped from her face. 'It's not as terrible as it could be. They won't hurt her. Sir Janus said they'd be gentle men.'

Julia gripped her arms. 'What! What has happened?'

'They took Charlotte. She was the one screaming.'

'Some men have taken Lady Valliant?' Gingerbread threw his head up violently, and Julia brought her tones down an octave. 'No, no, you're all right, Ginger, darling. Be still now! Some gentlemen have taken Lady Valliant?'

'No, not gentry, I don't think. Two just plain men pulled her into a coach and drove. I saw it.'

Belief needed confirmation. 'How do you know it was her — and why would they do such a thing?'

'They thought it was me.'

Conviction propelled Julia into action. Seizing the lantern in one hand, and Sophie's hand by the other, she pulled the anxious girl out of the stable and towards the house.

Pulled along behind her at full tilt, Sophie gasped out, 'If you don't . . . mind my saying so . . . it was her own fault.'

Julia stopped abruptly. 'You'd better explain that.'

'Sir Janus — he said he'd send a note if the plans were changed. Charlotte got hold of it. But I don't know why she went out to the coach instead of me.'

'Where is this note?'

'It's — it's lying on her bed.'

Still holding the lantern Julia hurried upstairs. She put aside as irrelevant the question of how Sophie knew a note might be lying on Charlotte's bed. In fact, Julia imitated Sophie's presumption, opening the door and entering without knocking. Immediately finding the creased white sheet of paper lying on the bed, she picked it up and took in the brief message.

'Oh, Charlotte! You idiot!' she exclaimed.

Sophie was inclined to giggle again.

Julia rounded on her. 'It is not funny! Far rather it was you they took. You were a conspirator. It would have been a prank, a folly. But now! My god! Don't you realize how serious this is?'

Sophie's eyes widened. 'They won't hurt her. They'll bring her back. Really! She's of no use to them.'

'Don't you see? It's an abduction! It may be a capital offence — I'd have to ask my brother — but the men who took her are in a slew of trouble.'

'Well, then, they'll bring her back all the quicker — won't they?'

'You don't understand. She is the wife of a magistrate, a person of stature. That gives her immense credibility. If she sees their faces, she will be able to bring them to book for their criminal actions. It could be transportation or worse for them. Now are you so sure they'll bring her back?'

Sophie's lip trembled.

Julia cast around in her mind for what to do. She guessed that Charlotte had given Sir Ivor a dose of laudanum by the snoring from his den. There would be no help there. She had a poor opinion of the village constable.

'Sophie, we must go straight to Selchurch.' She thought for a moment. 'No, we cannot go to Bishop's Rise and arrive in the middle of the night. Even if we spring the horses — not to be recommended in the dark — no one would answer the door to us. Yet we must try.'

'They will stay up late at the Rise,' put in Sophie cheerfully. 'Sir Janus will be there — he particularly said. I was to predispose you to go there.'

Julia comprehended fully. 'Ha! What Ivor

would call an alibi!' She thought furiously for a few moments. She did not know if Selchurch would be at home, and she did sense that Sir Janus was probably one person who could be relied on to make sure Charlotte was safe. Moreover, he might be able to arrange that the scandal of the abduction did not get out. 'Yes! We must do it. This cannot wait till morning.' Without more ado she ran to the kitchen where Eli March lounged, enjoying an evening pipe. His wife and the maids had already gone to their beds.

Much aggrieved at being called upon to bring out a coach at that hour of the night, he shrugged on his coat, reminding her the while of unreasonable demands she had made to him over the years. To hear him say it, one would have thought she had a history of making fits and starts in a random fashion. He had served the family for some thirty-five years, so she bore his scold meekly enough, merely agreeing with him and thrusting him out the door.

'I'll explain all to you later. Will Mrs. March still be awake? While you're harnessing the team, I'll run up and have a word with her lest she thinks you've slipped out to the alehouse.'

With his contemptuous 'Humph!' sounding

in her ears, she climbed the stairs to the attic, and found the housekeeper in a dressing gown, brushing out her long gray hair. She made the excuse that Lady Valliant had been called home on a minor crisis, and adjured her to make sure Sir Ivor suffered no alarm. Her mind was spinning in an effort to know how to keep the real situation quiet. She thought perhaps the only member of the household who need learn that Charlotte was missing was Eli March. He would be with them and must be pledged to secrecy.

The sky cleared after a while, and the moon gave enough light for the travelers to make good time. Approaching the Rise, they found the gate cottage well lit, which confirmed that there was company at the Rise. The gatekeeper admitted them without query, volunteering that his lordship himself had driven in only a few minutes earlier.

★ ★ ★

Roderick, in fact, had just passed his hat and driving gloves to Piller. A burst of laughter and a clamor of conversation drew him into one of the smaller salons, where he found Joseph Rayne and Sir Janus Vale engaged in a game of piquet. By the piles of guineas in front of each man it appeared that luck was running evenly. Interested spectators were Lady Cytherea and Lady Arabelle. Miss Randall was hovering in the background, no doubt wondering how to usher her eldest charge out of grown-up company at a reasonable hour.

'Can't stay away, I see, Hon Joe!' he greeted his friend. 'Good evening, Vale! I looked to see you tomorrow.'

'No, surely it was the Thursday you said,' quoth Vale smoothly. 'No doubt you are in the right of it. My memory plays tricks on me.'

'Ricky! Glad you're back early!' remarked Rayne. 'I didn't realize you were to be out tonight. Not to undervalue present company though. We've played some pleasant games that everyone knew.' One droll eyebrow arched. 'Then the ladies got fatigued and Vale was looking for something meatier — thus the scene of mild depravity.'

One of the younger footmen entered to deliver a few murmured words in Sir Janus' ear. The baronet's mouth tightened, and he gave a brief instruction to the man. In a second his expression was bland again, and at the end of the hand he picked up his money and excused himself from the game for a while.

'Selchurch, will you sit in?' He inquired

casually. 'There seems a matter which calls for my attention. Such a bore!'

Roderick declined, but Cytherea was more than happy to challenge Joseph to a rubber of piquet. Her reputation as a gamester must perish by lack of practice, she declared, as she took her seat. A new game commenced, and Roderick amused himself by watching the play for a few minutes.

The game was briefly interrupted when Sir Janus returned to say his curricle was called for. With a million apologies, he took his leave.

Lady Cytherea looked up from her cards. 'La, we are all so dull tonight! Thank goodness you have come back, Roddie. We actually played spillikins earlier!'

'Don't let me distract you. Your dangerous opponent could skin your hide.'

'Oh, I can both play and listen with all due diligence, my dear sir.' She made a play of fluttering her eyelashes at Rayne, rattling him into making a hasty discard.

A few minutes later, the footman re-entered the room and murmured low-voiced to the Earl. Startled, Roderick glanced at the clock, which showed almost midnight. He glanced at Joseph and Cytherea, quite immersed in their game, and slipped out.

In the rose salon near the main entrance,

he found Julia pacing up and down in an impatient manner. She paused as he came in. 'Your lordship! I had hoped to speak to Sir Janus Vale.'

'He has just recently left us.' He took her restless hands with concern and led her to a sofa. 'Come sit down! You seem quite distraught, Miss Valliant. What disaster brings you here at such an hour?' He looked round. 'And where is Sophie. I was told she was here?'

She looked round vaguely. 'She was here a moment ago. It is important that I speak with Sir Janus.'

'Am I not even second choice, my love?'

For a second, she looked directly into his eyes, and then disengaged her hands from his grasp. This man chose the most inappropriate times for his flirtations, but she must enlist his help. In her confusion she stated the case baldly. 'Charlotte has been abducted. Sir Janus is responsible.'

'Sir Janus has abducted Lady Valliant?'

'Don't look at me as if I'm an imbecile! I may be on the verge, but I am still sane, I assure you. Oh, where is that child? Explanations would be better coming from her.'

'I'd as soon explanations came from you. I thought your brother and his wife to be on the continent.'

'They returned early.' Julia gave a confused explanation of all that had occurred as Sophie had related it to her, and as Roderick listened his brow darkened.

'That hell-raised chit. I'm mortified that she has put you to this distress.'

'It was about her father. She would never have gone through with the plan, she tells me.'

'It's always about her father.' He put his finger on a crucial point. 'Why would Kettle be presumed — lurking in the shadows?'

For a moment Julia was silent. Then she said, 'He could have made himself known to someone at the Rise. He — he — he might be remembered by some of the older staff.'

Her brief hesitation was not lost on Roderick. 'How could Charlotte have done such an ill-judged thing?'

'She would see it as her Christian duty, you see,' she explained. 'By the note, she might well have suspected some kind of elopement. Quite shocking when you consider that Sophie is so young!' She heaved a sigh. 'My brother was in no case to help. And tomorrow morning Ivor will wake up and his bride will be missing, and — and — he'll try to get out of bed, and do worst damage to his leg — and now Sir Janus is not where we expected . . . ' Running out of words, she sat back on the sofa and plumped her hands in her lap in frustration.

Roderick thought rapidly. He could see the possible repercussions as easily as Julia. What had set out to be a harmless, if unsavory, strategy, had the potential to turn out adversely should the abductors panic. 'We will see that nothing bad happens. We shall get Charlotte back safely.'

'How will we do that? Sophie said that Vale did not tell her where he planned to take her. I believe that that fact alone had put her off going along with his plan.'

He rose from the settee. 'I will find young Miss Kettle. Maybe she knows more than she has told you.'

The footman was hovering outside the door, his instincts warning him that his services might be called upon.

'Did Miss Kettle go upstairs?'

He replied that he rather thought not. The bedroom candles could be accounted for, as only Lady Arabelle and Miss Randall had gone up recently. After a hesitation he offered diffidently. 'I just found the main door ajar, my lord. Be sure, I closed it after admitting Miss Valliant and Miss Kettle.'

Julia had come to the salon door and overheard this. 'It's a cool, pleasant starry night, at that. But it's high time the child was abed.'

Roderick looked at her appreciatively. 'We'll wander out to retrieve the wanderer. Don't lock us out, Sidney!'

The footman allowed himself a slight grin. That he would do such a thing! Roderick had instructions for him before escorting Julia down to the drive.

'My attempts at trivializing this search are vain,' said Julia. 'No young girl should be outside the house at this time of night. Where do you think she might have gone?'

'Looking for someone who would know where her father is.'

'But why outside?'

'Who knows? Most of the household staff have gone to bed. We could walk round to the stables.'

Suddenly they were aware of March standing nearby, anxious to speak. He excused himself for interrupting. 'Miss Julia, I have been wondering whether to go up and knock on the door for you,' he continued.

'I am sorry, March,' said Julia distractedly. 'I left you without giving you any idea of how long I should be. Soon I shall let you know what I am going to do.'

'Nay, I don't wish to hurry you, miss. 'Tis something else.' He paused dramatically. 'It's what I thought I seen. And what I don't see now is Miss Kettle with you.'

The attention of his audience was engaged.

'There were a vehicle came round from the stables. I seen a young lady run out in front of it just nigh here. Very dangerous, I thought it. Anyway, it stopped and took her up. The moonlight plays tricks, but I did think it might ha' been Miss Kettle. Bless me, I ain't sure. I've been shifting from one foot to the other, not wanting to start a wild goose chase. It could ha' been anyone.'

Julia turned quickly to Roderick. 'Who . . . ?'

'You missed Sir Janus only by five minutes or so. He had sent for his coach, but, if it were not ready, he might well have gone round to the stables. It looks as if it were him.'

Roderick thought for a moment, and turned to the coachman. 'Thank you, March,' said Roderick. 'Miss Valliant will be returning home. Take the coach round to the stables. You'll find fresh horses awaiting you.'

Julia looked as if she would argue the point.

'Normally at this time of night I would have you stay rather than be jauntering around the countryside. But you must go home, in case Lady Valliant returns there.'

She sighed. 'You probably have the right of it. But I hate to play so tame a part.'

'There is your brother to think of,' he reminded her. 'What will you tell him?'

'I shall make up some story.'

'Miss Valliant, you shock me. I had always believed you a woman of integrity. But will he believe you? It's pretty hard to account for the absence of a new bride.'

She made an attempt at lightness. 'Of course he'll believe me. I never lie to him.'

He was looking at her rather ironically. 'You must learn not to stutter.'

Julia blushed. She was conscious of the fact that she had not been candid about meeting Kestrel Barnard.

'I must go to Sir Janus' home,' Roderick was saying. 'The devil of it is that we can't be positive that that is where he was headed. I've also to find who of the household staff is in touch with Kettle. I'll question Piller. He's been here an age and might know something.'

'Wait! What a bustle that would cause! There may be another way. There is a small coaching inn on the road to Mallow, called the White Boar Inn.'

'I know it.'

'Mr. Kettle is there — using a different name.'

Roderick's eyes narrowed. 'Now why am I

learning this at such a late date, I wonder. Miss Valliant you suffer from being too much in the company of my cousin.'

'Oh, Sophie does not know. The thing is, he most particularly charged me that I should not tell her about his presence. Yet, he wanted to meet her. I — I had not made my mind up what to do.'

His eyes narrowed. 'Have I by any chance met this man?'

She nodded. 'Mr. Barnard! He made my brother's acquaintance and later bought a horse from him.'

'The smart you were riding with, when I was so grievously in the way?'

'You were not in the way. That's childish!'

'I most certainly appeared to be de trop. That's beside the point. You have known about his whereabouts for several days. It did not occur to you to tell me?'

'It was not convenient to tell you. Besides, I am telling you now.'

'You skirted the whole thing when you told me about the abduction. Have you any other surprises for me?' His tones were clipped and cold, and he did not wait for an answer. 'Your carriage will be at the door soon. You must go home, Miss Valliant. You can do nothing more here, and I must waste no time. Leave Barnard to me. I'll find him at the inn, God willing.'

'But what about Sophie?'

'Sophie Kettle is my responsibility — and that of her father. Go home, Miss Valliant! Get some sleep and be ready to cope with your brother tomorrow.'

15

Sir Janus Vale squinted along the long barrel of a pistol, which glinted in the moonlight. He rested the nozzle on the edge of the window in the door of the traveling coach, which stood at the bottom of a sandstone quarry. From somewhere up above the sound of pebbles chattering down the track above drew his attention. He made as if to cock the pistol, but thought better of it.

Suddenly, a hand twisted the pistol from his grasp, and he let out a surprised oath.

'Is this for protection or elimination?' The calm, cultured tones speaking from the darkness were familiar.

'Anhurst — Selchurch!'

'Whichever you chose.'

Sir Janus regained some of his suavity. 'My compliments! I had no idea of your presence.'

'I learned a lot from the Shawnee.'

'But I hope not violence.'

'If necessary! Where are Sophie Kettle and Lady Valliant?'

'Hey, dey! I would have expected more finesse from Lord FitzWarren's protégé. But you must not worry about them. They are perfectly safe, I assure you. Am I to understand you have linked up with the slippery Tom Kettle?'

'Do you really think you are in any danger from Tom Kettle?'

'Ah! Might I be? Prison can be such a brutalizing thing, they say. He has quite a reputation with his fists. He might feel a little justification in, er, milling me down. I could not allow that.'

'Don't you have your henchmen within call?'

Sir Janus shook his head, smiling slightly. 'My *henchmen* are busy complicating the situation, I fear. Their continuation in my employ will be short-lived.'

'A strange place for a meeting, this! Are you alone? You seem bottled up here.'

'Ergo the pistol. But I have other resources.'

'Another way out, no doubt!'

'Tell me, how did you find me here?'

'You obviously wanted Tom Kettle to find you. The trail was plainly marked.'

'And you found Tom Kettle. How interesting! You must tell me how. I am consumed with curiosity.'

Roderick ignored this. 'I now understand your surprise visit to my house this evening. Kettle upset your plans.'

'Damn him! He would have vanished into London before I had my chance at him.'

'It upset your timing, and forced your valet into the open. When I found Kettle an hour ago, he was about to go to the hedge tavern past the village where your man had baited the hook. He went there, driving my curricle. The landlord duly directed him to this quarry, and your valet followed him out, not realizing I was behind on Kettle's mount.'

'And where might my man be now?'

'He met an accident at the top of the causeway. Finding his quarry lying on the ground, apparently having fallen from the curricle, he went close enough to discover exactly how hard Kettle's head might be. Kettle was too fly for him.'

'I'll warrant!' Kestrel Barnard came round the side of the coach. His shoulders were hunched forward in a belligerent attitude. 'He's still there, tied up with strips of his neckcloth.'

'A familiar voice! Kettle by the sound of those trenchant tones — and in a threatening posture!'

'He was carrying a pistol,' interposed Roderick.

'Which is in my pocket!' added Barnard.

'No matter! The Earl of Selchurch will be

my protection against mayhem and blood-shed.'

'Don't count on it!' snarled Roderick. 'Abducting females is sufficiently frowned on to excuse any violence that might accrue to the perpetrator.'

'Have I merited your hostility?' complained Vale. 'Well, perhaps. But that is another matter. Sophie Kettle — such a resourceful young lady — came with me quite willingly. It was all a ruse to flush out my old colleague Kettle, here, and it has worked quite admirably.'

'What of Charlotte Valliant?'

'An unfortunate error. But all can be put right. A spirited lady, but not unreasonable, I hope.'

'Where are they now?'

'Safe — in bed sleeping. Sleep is something we are all short of, gentlemen. I suggest we get to business.'

'What makes you think we can do business?' demanded Barnard, pugnaciously.

'The situation, my dear fellow. The situation. It needs to be resolved. But why do you not come in and make yourselves more comfortable.'

Deftly, Roderick unloaded the pistol and returned it to its owner, before climbing into the coach. He was followed by Kettle.

'I hope you pointed it away from me when you executed your disarming act.' Vale's voice was mocking. 'But a good thought! Now we can be more civilized.'

'If you think this is civilized,' said Barnard. 'Three blind men in conference sitting in a coach going nowhere at the bottom of a quarry, then thank God I'm no member of the quality.'

Vale slid his hand into a pocket, pulled out a flask and offered it round. 'Then let us all meet on common ground.'

'And get on with things,' declared Roderick. 'You both want something. What? You go first, Vale!'

'You must be looking a little red-eyed, Selchurch — I know I am. Yet I'm sure late night sessions are not new to you — Red Indian powwows with smoke getting in your eyes. Yes, I am sure you have had smoke in your eyes.' He looked at Kettle. 'Tom! You sound healthy. I'm told you look even prosperous — distinguished, in fact. The air of the antipodes seems to have been kind.'

'No thanks to you!' Barnard's voice rasped. 'Imprisonment, brutality, heat, disease. Place them on your table for a start. The prison ship — three months on a scurvy plagued bucket, chains, starvation and noisome water and fighting for a share of what there was of

373

it. These are all to be placed at your feet. The break up of my family, the despair of my loving wife, the abandonment of my innocent daughter. What of these?'

'You crossed me. You came to me for help. I gave you a chance. Oh, don't play the innocent. You were anxious enough to get a dig at Selchurch — your wife's brother.' His head turned towards Roderick for an instant as if trying to gauge his reaction. 'You got it wrong, and now you complain about the price you paid. You cost me a small fortune, including this quarry which property I had to deed to Selchurch.'

The idea popped into Roderick's head that he was the sole audience to a melodrama played out by two overacting thespians. Their faces were pale ghosts in the gloom. He could only listen for clues in their voices.

'You put up the purse and I fought to win. 'Twas you thought I'd lose, so you bet against me. You thought I'd happily go down when I learnt the Basilisk stood to win twenty thousand guineas off me. You even promised me a share o' your winnings. No, you didn't bribe me. You just thought it would be enough to take the edge off me — off my will to win. But I fought to win, damn you! I fought for the purse. You can't fault me for that.'

'Just a minute,' interrupted Roderick. 'Am I to understand that Selchurch put a wager on you, the brother-in-law he would not acknowledge?'

'He didn't know it was me. I was the Thrasher — a coming man — in those days. Selchurch watched me twice, and didn't even recognize me. You think he looked at his own footmen? Those seedy louse traps we wore on our skulls were disfiguring, no mistake.'

'And you arranged this bout, Vale, with all the little ironies involved?' challenged Roderick.

'Selchurch needed a setdown. He was getting quite strange. I could barely talk to Alicia without his pulling a Friday face. Did you know she's a relative somewhere back along the line? A second cousin or maybe a third, I was never sure about those relationships. He was so damned jealous. I couldn't wait to see his face when I told him he lost money on Kettle — except that he didn't, damn your eyes, Tom.'

Barnard addressed Vale again. 'Then you made the excuse the pug was doped and denied me the prize money. It was a true blow that felled my opponent.'

'Ah, you should have let well alone. You oughtn't to have stolen the prize. But all water under the bridge now! Our present

Lord Selchurch has no wish to hear ancient history.'

'On the contrary, I find it singularly illuminating,' remarked Roderick. 'Lord Basil's involvement is new to me, though I knew he was a follower of the Fancy. Carry on, gentlemen, I beg you!'

'They wanted me to say the pug had been tampered with, but I wouldn't do that.'

'Who suggested that?' asked Roderick.

Barnard shrugged. 'The magistrates. They just asked me about it. But they got nothing out of me, for I thought it wasn't so — at the time.'

'It would hardly be to my advantage,' said Vale. 'More to yours, Kettle.'

'Are you trying to suggest . . . Damn your eyes, Vale! I'd not do such a thing. I could win without resorting to slipping some drug to my opponent.'

Roderick interrupted their rising voices.

'Gentlemen, let us move on! Vale, you point out that it would not have been to your advantage to harm the man you had bet money on. You, Kettle, claim it would be beneath your dignity to do such a thing. Consider this! Many other people who had made side bets might have an interest in Kettle winning. Keep to the point! What is it you want of Kettle, Vale?'

'His assurances. Oh, you will think me naive, if you like, Selchurch, but I believe that a promise from Tom Kettle will suffice to give me a guarantee that my life will not be turned back to front because he has returned to these blessed isles — and the surrender of a certain piece of paper.'

'A deathbed statement by Mouche Mason?'

'You know about Mason?' Vale did not sound surprised. 'I have been guilty of no wrongdoing, you understand, but certain, ahem, disclosures might be embarrassing. Youthful indiscretions he might remember. Idle rumors can always be denied. People have damned me down to the ground for years with no effect. But deathbed confessions — they have a way of sticking.'

'Like slime!' agree Roderick cheerfully. 'They can have the odor of credibility. You must tell me more about this Mason. I spent many hours looking for this man without a great deal of luck. Call it curiosity. How long was he in your service?'

'Not long. He disappeared from sight very suddenly after the fight.'

'How did he become involved?'

'Mouche was the son of a French maidservant, serving the chère amie of some marquis who got hung by his peasants

— didn't even make it to embrace Mme. Guillotine, I was told. The lady fled the country. Her maid must have been with child already, or she'd hardly have bothered bringing both servant and baby. The mistress gained respectability by wedding a builder. In the course of time, Mouche apprenticed with that same builder. He was working as a stonecutter when he first sought my employ.'

''Mason' does not sound a French name.'

'Ah, but he was not Mason in those days. He changed it later to suit his calling, and, I think, to evade creditors.'

'A betting man, I have no doubt. How was he originally listed among your staff?'

'I really don't recall,' drawled Vale. 'You can't expect me to remember such details. I have an agent for that.'

'Perhaps it will come back to you. Your memory seems keen on the other particulars.' Roderick looked toward Barnard. 'Well, a piece of paper seems not too great a request, always on the understanding that no major transgressions are recounted.'

'And what is it that you want, Kettle?'

'I'm not asking for reparation,' quoth Barnard. 'What's past is past, and I've come out of it better than you would think. I have enough money. The accumulation of more money for the sake of it is not an ambition of mine. The death of my poor Patience can't be laid at his door. She had the beginnings of the lung sickness before I took up prizefighting. It was money I did it for, after all. Money to make things comfortable for her. Money for lawyers. Selchurch was dragging his feet on releasing money that was rightly hers, even though he knew she was ill, the bastard, for I made sure he knew about that. That's all passed, and I can only hope he burns in hell.

'All I want now is to see my daughter brought up in the station enjoyed by her mother. The death of Basil Selchurch made that possible. She's now living where she belongs. That's why I was set hereabouts for those few days. I just wanted to make sure she had a proper place in things. I was pretty pleased about it all, until I saw you, Vale. I didn't like that at all. I'm wondering what you are doing at Bishop's Rise, and whether you mean to try to harm me through my little Psyche. I want to know what are you doing at the Rise?'

'Hm! Why do we do anything, I wonder,' remarked Vale thoughtfully. 'You know, I can always come up with half a dozen reasons at least for most of the things I do. Why was I at the Rise?' He stretched both legs out as well as he could in the cramped space. 'You must see the attractions there are great.

Dear Alicia — an old friend — the Rise has been a second home. The incomparable Lady Cytherea, too, a delightful conversationalist, and of exquisite beauty!' His head turned towards Roderick.

'Cut line, Vale,' said that gentleman. 'It's been a long night.'

'Ah, yes, and Miss Kettle. A most intriguing and challenging young lady. One needs all one's wits when dealing with her. Unfortunately, I did not see much of her. She was usually among the schoolroom set. However, when it came to my attention that your daughter was in residence at Bishop's Rise, it struck me that she might lead me to you, Kettle. I thought she would be the magnet to draw you forth to reclaim your child.'

'You decided to kidnap her and use her as bait. You used her, you . . . '

'Tut! You misinterpret what has happened here. Mea culpa, but not entirely! The brain that planned the scheme was not mine, dear Tom. The mastermind was that of your daughter. She was the author of the plot.'

Barnard spluttered angrily. 'Preposterous! Why should she do that?' But something in his voice made Roderick suspect that he appreciated the adventurous spirit displayed by his daughter, and was more than willing to believe that this was a true account of what had occurred. 'Why on earth would she do that,' he repeated.

'Did it not occur to you that she is anxious to meet her father?' cut in Roderick.

'To meet me? But she wouldn't even remember me — she was just a babe. And what sort of father do I make for her — a released prisoner — a ticket of leave man.'

'Well, I can't imagine why she would wish that either,' drawled Vale, 'but that is the way the hand played and I was willing to be partner in the enterprise.'

Silence fell on the little group.

Roderick spoke first. 'Vale! Do you have the two young ladies in question, and can you aver that neither are the worse for their experience?'

Vale shrugged. 'In each dull life a little adventure should intrude. Yes, they are none the worse for their experience. Do I have them? No.'

'But you know where they are?'

He nodded. 'Possibly! They are in no immediate danger.'

'What about you, Barnard?' Roderick looked round at the man beside him, who still seemed deep in thought. 'I don't know if you hold any real threat over the head of Sir Janus here. Certainly, if you have evidence of any serious crime on his part, I would not be a party to withholding it. As far as scandal is concerned — Sir Janus himself has admitted, his reputation is not spotless. To add fuel to that scandal might or might not cause him actual harm, and from what you have said, to do so is not an object with you. What is your position now?'

It seemed as if Barnard came to a sudden decision. 'I'm agreed,' he said. 'You shall have the paper I got from Mouche. It seems I must see my daughter. She's my child, all right. She won't let it go, if she's set on a course. We have things to talk over. It is agreed. I am no threat to you. You will be no threat to me and we'll shake on it.' He took off his hat, and pulled out from under the band a piece of paper that had been many times folded and gave it to Roderick. 'You hold it, Lord Selchurch. Give it over when we get back Sophie.'

16

Lady Valliant found herself sitting on damp sward in the dark. She had been unceremoniously dumped from the chaise. She had no idea where she was — somewhere in the woods. A grove of trees surrounded her, and starlight muted her surroundings into a collage of dark grays. As the sound of hoofbeats and creaking of the carriage faded into the distance, other nocturnal noises crept into her consciousness — wind soughing in the treetops, the hoot of an owl some distance away and indeterminate rustling in the undergrowth. Her heart was thumping, and she chided herself for foolishness; being afraid of the dark was for children! In fact, she told herself sternly, she should be vastly relieved to be free of the two thugs who had manhandled her so grossly. Loosening the confining embrace of her cloak, she stood up, and peered around. Her attention was riveted by something that sent hope gushing through her, followed by trepidation. More disturbing than the solitude was the suggestion of light slanting from door marking the situation of some dark dwelling. The top of a chimney was outlined against the sky. She stood up, scarcely knowing whether it was safe to approach it. Obviously she had been set down here because her abductors knew of the location of this house. She was meant to enter it.

Somewhere in the night a loud report cracked the peace of the forest. There was a sudden flurry of wings, followed by silence. Her heart was in her mouth. Be calm, she told herself. It's probably just a poacher. Gathering her courage, she carefully felt one foot in front of another, and soon found she was on a fairly level path. Reaching the door, which was slightly ajar, she raised her hand to knock, then changed her mind, nervous of some trap. Unable to see much through the aperture, she inched the door open until the interior was revealed. A low ceilinged room, neatly appointed, with a sturdy homemade rag rug upon the floor met her gaze. An open fireplace, ready made up with kindling but unlit was on the chimney wall, with a door on the far wall, suggesting a further room. As she slipped a foot across the threshold, she could see a table in the center of the room over which hung the oil lamp, which was the source of light.

She gasped. Quietly seated at the table, her hands placed in front of her in a composed fashion, was Sophie Kettle.

For a few seconds nobody spoke. Then, lips tightened, Charlotte approached the table and glared down at the young girl. 'Are y-you responsible for the ord-ordeal I've been through this night?' She was angry, as much by the fact that her voice was betraying her as by finding Sophie involved at this stage of development.

Sophie looked at her critically. 'You don't seem to have taken great harm. Your hair requires some . . . '

'Not much harm! I have been seized by uncouth ruffians who laid their d-dirty hands on me. They put a horrid sack over my head. I have been driven in the dark all over the county — five counties for all I know, for I've no idea where I am, for hours and hours. Now I am abandoned in positively stygian darkness in the middle of a forest.'

'How can you say aban — '

'As a climax, I find you at the bottom of this whole degrading episode.' Charlotte paused for breath. 'Perhaps you would have the goodness to inform me where we are.'

'Miles from anywhere, I should think,' quoth Sophie cheerfully. 'But take comfort! There is a soft feather bed in the room above this. We're here till morning, anyway.'

'Thank you. I would prefer my own bed.'

Sophie shrugged. 'Do as you like! Personally, I don't want to grope about in the dark woods.'

'I'll find a lantern. And you must come with me.'

Sophie followed her eyes up towards the oil lamp hanging from the ceiling. 'It appears to be attached by a metal hasp. It won't easily come down. We can't move till daylight.'

Charlotte's voice was firm. 'We cannot remain here alone. It is too dangerous. Believe me, the discomfort out there in the darkness cannot be worse than the danger that can await unprotected women here.'

'I know all about dangers. More than you, I warrant. Forget that sort of danger!' Sophie rose and moved to a small dresser against a side wall. Beside it could be seen the first few steps curving up to a closed in staircase. She picked up a stubby candle holder with a half-burned candle and came back to the table to reach up to light it from the oil wick. 'Go up to the bed, Charlotte — Lady Valliant, I should say. When it is light, we can talk about what we should do.'

'No, no. We must leave here. We can take the candle.'

'And I'll lay you a shilling to a shirt button that it will be out before you've gone a hundred yards. Listen to the wind!'

Patiently Sophie watched as Charlotte went to the door and hesitated on the threshold, obviously weighting the danger of being benighted in the woods. Thoughts of a comfortable bed brought her back. She had not yet had all her say.

'What is this all about, Sophie? You have not told me how you came here. You must know where we are, or were you also brought here with a sack over your head? I don't think so. You're far too calm.'

'No one played blind man's buff with me. But I cannot tell you where we are . . . yet. All right, I do know what it's all about, but I cannot tell you that either. And — and it's not all my fault what happened, either.'

'Oho! So you admit to some fault, then.'

'Not so much as you! Why did you pretend to be me?'

'Pretend to be you! I did no such thing.'

'I saw the note addressed to me. You read it.'

'Of course! Young girls do not receive letters from gentlemen. I am the lady of the house and had every right to read the letter to a young girl under the protection of Mallow. Certainly I have the authority to send any person making an assignation to the right about!'

'What makes you think I would have gone?'

'Your reputation!' hissed Charlotte. 'Your little habits of disappearing.'

'I'll not stay to quarrel with you.' Sophie picked up the candle holder and made towards the stairs. 'I'm for bed! You do as you wish!'

Charlotte was still torn. However, no advantage was to be gained either by sitting up or by getting lost in the woods. A few hours of sleep snatched from this dreadful night would be better armor against whatever the day ahead might bring. 'Wait!' she commanded. 'I am coming up also.' She followed the guttering candle up the staircase to an attic bedroom, which boasted a decent quilt-covered bed set in an alcove. A stand with a wash basin and a small mirror stood against one wall. The elusive scent of old lavender hung about the room, reassuring in its wholesome fragrance.

'Whose cottage is this?' Charlotte asked, looking round the room with an air of grudging approval.

'The old lady who sleeps in this bed has been called to a sick relative. Ask me no more,' was the gruff response.

'Well, I'll sleep in my clothes,' declared Charlotte, 'and lie on top of the covers — though I doubt I'll sleep a wink.' So saying she climbed onto the bed and turned her face to the wall.

Several hours later, as the sun was beginning to filter through the trees outside the little dormer window, Charlotte was awakened by the sound of a chaise. Her sleeping companion had already arisen and left the room, she discovered. Hurriedly she pulled herself across the bed. She pushed her feet into her shoes and peered out the window. As she watched, she saw Sophie rushing forward and then stopping as if with shyness before a silver-haired gentleman Charlotte did not recognize. Sir Janus Vale watched somewhat benignly. Frowning, she went back to sit on the bed, and think what this might mean.

Sir Janus Vale! What had he to do with Sophie? Yet she had wondered about that 'V' inscribed on the note sent to Sophie. She had not wanted to believe a man of his years would send out lures to a child. Her heart was filled with disgust. Was he acting as a procurer for that silver-haired fellow? She'd heard of such evil.

The sound of another equipage brought her back to the window, to see a curricle draw in behind the chaise and Roderick dismount. Strange goings on, but maybe not as dire as she had suspected if he were on the scene!

She breathed a grateful prayer that she would not have to divulge the worst to Lady Selchurch! A few hours of sleep had mended her state of mind. Her alarm was now a thing of the past to be replaced by an urge to have her grievances heard, and to wreak vengeance on all guilty parties, whoever they might be. Hastily, she did what she could to repair her appearance in front of the mirror and descended.

The people from outside had crowded into the ground floor. A tousled young fellow was crouched at the fireplace, alternately scratching his head and plying the bellows at a reluctant flame. Roderick, Sir Janus and the silver-haired stranger were standing somewhat apart at the table. Sophie was now clinging to the arm of the stranger as if afraid he would run away.

At the sight of her, Roderick stepped toward her reassuringly. 'Lady Valliant! Are you hurt at all? Don't be alarmed. You are quite safe.'

Blinking back responsive tears, Charlotte allowed herself a brief moment of frailty, as she submitted to the comforting embrace of an old friend. Another second and her old militant self was regained. Freeing herself, she looked around at the group.

'Now will someone explain to me what is

happening?' Her hot gaze skewered Vale as the most likely guilty party. 'Why have I been the victim of a most brutal and petrifying abduction?'

Momentarily put out of countenance by such a sudden onslaught, Vale made a swift recovery. He pulled out a chair. 'Please, Lady Valliant, allow me.' He waited as she stiffly accepted his invitation to seat herself at the table. 'Tell me if you are hurt! If you have suffered any hurt, I will personally flay the perpetrators alive. I'll horsewhip them. I'll make sure that their filthy carcasses are fed to the dogs.'

'Rodomontade!' snapped Charlotte. 'I want the men arrested and charged.'

'But your hurts, madam? We should find out if you are injured.'

'I am much bruised. No doubt I shall be finding more bruises for days.'

'How did those men bruise you? Did they beat you?'

'For goodness sake, why go on about the bruises?' She showed a little perverse pride. 'I put up a good fight. I would expect to get bruises. They seized my person. They kept me prisoner, until I was scared for my life because I had seen them and they knew I could tell them again if I saw them. They nigh suffocated me with the filthiest sack that ever saw a turnip. I want those men arrested, and I want them to tell who paid them to abduct — not me, but her.' She pointed at Sophie dramatically. 'Who would want to kidnap a young, innocent girl — and probably trepan her away to some Turkish harem?'

The three men looked quite startled, and Charlotte felt a mild satisfaction that she had voiced the most extreme of her fears.

The silver-haired man leaned forward. 'Lady Valliant, we have not been introduced. Kestrel Barnard! I beg leave to say something. Certain events have been in train over this night — for which, I haste to say — I had no agency. There are several matters here that are the cause of distress to various persons present, and I would suggest that I lay out to you a brief outline of what has occurred. These events demand concessions from every person in order that they be ironed out with the least amount of discord to all present.'

'Finally, someone who will inform me! Let it be a round tale, sir, with no prevarication, which I promise you I will be swift to detect.'

Kettle drew in a breath and leaned forward a little. 'I place myself as spokesman for the parties involved on the firm ground that I was not one of said parties, and can, therefore, be said to be — if not neutral — possibly the last person to — ahem — take up cudgels on behalf of the abductors. What we have here, Lady, is no capital crime . . . no attempt to do harm or violence to any innocent child or woman. It is no more than a silly prank that went awry. You were purely mistaken to be Miss Kettle. Put no blame on her! Her motives were born of love rather than mischief. No doubt she has already expressed her dismay that you were taken up in the carriage rather than her. If you have suffered bruises, I venture to suggest it was because of this dreadful — no, let us not be overly dramatic — unfortunate mistake of identification that was made — and, if I may be as bold as to say, an understandable mistake for yours is a most youthful figure, my lady, and my daughter tall for her age.'

'Dreadful is a word I would — your daughter!' Charlotte had been sitting impatiently, her hand not resting on the table top, fingers poised to drum her exasperation at these lengthy periods. At these words she stood up, flushed, breast puffed out like an angry pullet. 'Kettle! You are Tom Kettle! You have given yourself away. And you sought to fool us by giving a false name! You are the cause of all the disruption in the Selchurch family.'

Barnard recoiled slightly, a flush suffusing his face. 'I — I, the truth is, Lady Valliant, I have used Barnard as a name for a few years now, an 'tis like second nature. Kettle ever lacked dignity.'

Roderick intervened. 'Lady Valliant, we are old friends. This may not be in the best tradition of British diplomacy, but more in the words of old playmates — take a damper! You are a little bruised and your feelings are outraged by what has happened. We all understand that, and are sorry that this has happened to you. But you have taken no great hurt, and there is more at stake here — how to resolve a serious quarrel between two men — how to settle the future of a young girl and above all — how to do this without arousing the devil's own scandal.' Gently he induced Charlotte to seat herself again, though the brimstone in her eye made no promise that she was much mollified.

Sir Janus took one of the chairs at the table wearily. 'Be brief, my friend. We have all lost a deal of sleep between us.'

Roderick described how Kettle had found his daughter and made his self-sacrificing decision not to make himself known to her, resulting in the plot hatched with Sir Janus. 'Then you stepped in, hoping to save Sophie from what you perceived as danger.'

'Thereby making yourself quite a heroine,' interposed Barnard with a small bow.

'Or, marplot belike,' muttered Sophie.

'How did you know Kettle was in the vicinity, Sir Janus?' Roderick hurriedly asked.

'One of the nursemaids at the Rise had spotted him hanging around the grounds, and thought she saw in him the old Kettle who had once lived there and married Lady Patience. In due course my man — ahem, learned of it.'

Roderick continued, 'Although Sir Janus and Mr. Kettle have had their differences, each is willing, I believe, to make peace. I should emphasize that in acting so speedily to help us find you, Sir Janus put himself at a disadvantage in negotiations. You owe him some gratitude for your prompt deliverance.'

'Delicately put!' murmured that person.

Charlotte looked briefly at Sir Janus and nodded her head with a bare modicum of grace. If anyone other than Roderick had made such a suggestion, she would have scouted it, and it was almost too much to be put in the wrong on top of everything. 'Then I thank you, and I'm sorry if my remarks put you out of countenance, Mr. Barnard.' Then she closed her lips tightly.

'As for the miscreants who assailed you, Lady Valliant,' continued Roderick, 'I can't help thinking it would be better for all concerned if you would forgive those hapless buffoons. No doubt they will receive short shrift from the hand that sent them. If they were taken to court, their very heads might be at risk — or be faced with transportation, despite the fact their intentions were never truly criminal. Do you desire so harsh a revenge?'

'As to that, my husband might have something to say. He is a magistrate, you know, and would be the proper person to handle the matter. Can you imagine how angry he will be at the insult endured by my person?'

'Your husband need know nothing about it, if you don't tell him.'

'How could he not know!'

'Miss Valliant will tell her brother that you went to see your father. You were anxious about his health. The convenient truth is that he has been troubled by some trifling stomach disorder these past few days. We can easily concoct some story as to how you learned this after Sir Ivor had been put to bed early with a dose of laudanum.'

'I see no reason to lie to my husband,' said Charlotte stiffly.

'Don't you? Miss Valliant does not know you are safe. What would happen if she told him you were abducted?'

'He would be so angry he would . . . ' She

paused, comprehension dawning. 'He might get up and do damage to his leg.'

Sophie thought it was time to put in her mite. 'And he'd want to quarrel with Sir Janus. They would fight a duel, and it would end by one of them lying dead at dawn in Beesley's Dell.'

Charlotte blanched.

'A bloodthirsty prediction!' drawled Sir Janus. 'My only hope is that Sir Ivor, as a magistrate, will not be so indifferent to the law as to pursue such a violent course.'

'Of course, it's up to you, Charlotte,' said Roderick, taking the reins again. 'If you must tell Sir Ivor, so be it. However, it might be better to escape the scandal that would ensue if knowledge of this episode were bruited about. Surely you don't want wild conjectures of the treatment you received during the time you were unaccounted for. Oh, don't be offended. I know nothing truly bad happened. Those men would not have dared go beyond the line. But rumor cannot be controlled. Avoid it in the first place, Lady Valliant. Let it go!'

All joined in trying to persuade her of the good sense of this course. Though not at all satisfied, she could see the wisdom of their position. When Barnard put in the clinching argument that a large portion of forgiveness must be expected of a daughter of a clergyman, her own conscience became ranged against her and she grudgingly assented.

'May I make a suggestion?' interposed Sir Janus. 'The morning is still young. Perhaps Lady Valliant could reach her father's house before the servants are awake. Does your father bar the door, Lady Valliant? I am persuaded that the parson in a small village does not feel the need to lock his door at night.'

'Sometimes not,' conceded Charlotte. 'He likes to think the best of his flock and would be loath to think any of them would break in at night.'

'That is what I have heard of him. I offer you my traveling coach, which is just outside — and the escort of one rather jaded manservant. It can take you very swiftly to your father's house, and with any luck no one will question that you were there all night.'

She looked round at the company. All seemed to be in agreement.

'Lose no time!' added Roderick. 'The servants will soon be stirring. Perhaps you will take Miss Kettle with you.'

However, here his suggestion met disagreement. Sophie was adamant in her refusal to go. Emboldened by finding her father, her instincts told her to give him no chance to disappear. By the time Charlotte was ensconced in the coach, she had lost patience. 'Well, we cannot continue to argue this, if I am to reach the parsonage before the housekeeper arrives. The maid is a little deaf, and I can slip into the house while she is still in the kitchen. How far must we go?'

'No more than three miles.'

'Three miles? I could have walked home? Where is this house?'

Roderick smiled. 'You don't recognize my gamekeeper? Not a regular churchgoer, I fear.'

She looked at the young man, just struggling into the cottage with a full bucket of water from the well. 'Ben Bunting! Of course he is! Now I recognize him.'

'An innocent bystander in all this, I assure you. An excellent fellow who did not panic when he learned two strange females had slept in his mother's house. We will have some explaining to do to him, I am much afraid.'

'We're in the home wood! And Sophie must have known.'

Charlotte swallowed hard, and seemed to come to grips with the better part of her nature. Before the door was closed, she said brusquely, 'Bring the little demon to me in a couple of hours. It will seem as if she was making an early morning visit, and it will not be known whence she arrived.'

At this point, Vale delivered his instructions to his manservant, who, rather pale from his rough handling, was doubling this day as coachman. 'Get going man, to the village parsonage. Quiet about it as you go! Don't wake the village. And your mouth stays shut if you value your position.'

The two men re-entered the gamekeeper's cottage. Neither the luxury of tea nor chocolate was to be found, so the water heating over the fire became destined for ablutions. Sophie declared a glass of water was all she required to slake her thirst, and Bunting was able to come up with some spruce ale to refresh the gentlemen.

'Ain't nothing else to offer, sirs. A couple of buns is all that's in the house, and they're so mortal stale. I couldn't offer them.'

'Let's hope your mother gets back soon,' replied Roderick in a friendly manner. 'We don't want you fading away from lack of a square meal. Look man! We'll not be intruding on you much longer. Go up to the servants' hall and get yourself something to eat — and I rely on your discretion.'

'Rest your mind, me lord. They won't question it. It's more than one meal I've had there over the last couple of weeks. They know about me ma being away. It's just her sister's bin really poorly. She'll be back soon.'

'Good man!' Roderick pressed a couple of guineas into his hand. 'Did you have any more trouble with poachers, last night!'

'Well, one was out, sir, but I had no luck nabbing 'im. I let off a round of buckshot at him, but I doubt I peppered 'im.'

Back inside, Roderick said, 'One problem seems resolved. The matter of the abduction of Lady Valliant — with any luck — may die a natural death without scandal. I've squared the only servant at the Rise who knew anything strange went forward. The Valliants' man has their family's interests at heart and won't chatter — Miss Valliant seemed convinced of that. You, Vale? Somehow I am sure you will control your people.'

'Mr. Bunting wouldn't dare say a word,' put in Sophie.

The others looked at her inquiringly.

She smiled mischievously. 'I might tell all about his assignations.'

'We don't need to resort to threats,' put in Roderick hastily. Glancing briefly at Barnard, he observed a frowning query ruffle his composed brow. 'That young man merits our thanks and apologies rather than our prying into his life.'

Sophie blushed, surprised by this mild

rebuke, and pressed her lips together. She had thought she was quite clever for having found a safe haven for the kidnappers to leave Lady Valliant. She suspected Bunting would be out courting before going about his nocturnal pursuits. He had made the acquaintance of Miss Rosie Evans, and quite a romance had ensued. Cytherea was a careless mistress, and, though she was apt to stay up late, her maid still managed to slip out of the house to tryst down beyond the garden wall, not far from the treehouse.

As Sophie met her father's eye, she realized that he was regarding her with a searching, even a troubled gaze. With a sense of humiliation she realized she had been found wanting in his eyes.

Then he said, 'We must assume the incident will hold without scandal. We should get beyond it. The escapade had its desired effect. It flushed me out. Now what?'

'The paper, I believe!' drawled Sir Janus. 'How bald a request! Put it down to the earliness of the hour.'

Roderick walked to the fireplace and regarded the steaming kettle. 'No doubt Miss Kettle feels in need of refreshing — as do we all, though our needs can wait. Sophie! Does our good Mrs. Bunting have a wash basin above stairs? Yes, I'm sure she does.' He tipped some of the heated water into a jug.

Quick to take the hint, Sophie took it from him and bore it up the stairs. She understood that there were things to be said that she would not be privy to.

'Let us go on from there.' Roderick seated himself at the table with the other two men and regaled himself from a mug of ale. 'We have reached the stage where neither regards the other as a threat. Agreed?'

Barnard nodded.

'When that paper is mine, I shall let you know,' was Vale's contribution.

As the scrap of paper was passed across the table, he said, 'I'm no threat to your peace, Sir Janus. Read it. It's all I have.'

Sir Janus looked at him searchingly as he took the paper. Then he read the contents, his brow darkening. 'This is it? There was no 'deathbed confession?' Just a letter from a physician, saying Mouche died of a typhus fever?'

'The doctor had no idea where to send it,' supplied Barnard. 'I offered a better chance of finding his family.' He glanced at Roderick. 'Yes, sad to say, whatever he might have known went to the grave with him. He went all of a sudden, I'm told. I wasn't even there.'

'You cheated me!' snarled Vale.

'Well, isn't the pot calling the kettle black!'

'You led me to believe . . . '

'What matters what you believed? That's what I had to offer. Uncurl your lip, man! Be glad it's nothing damning.' Barnard leaned back in his chair. 'Despite what he did or did not do, Mouche always stood my friend. He found ways to get a couple of messages smuggled to me in New South Wales through new fellows. That suspicion of drugging gnawed my mind for years. By the time I was free I had worked it out. It made no sense for you to drug my opponent. You were the secret person who had put up the purse, but you stood to gain twofold on the bet you had with Selchurch. I heard about Mouche dropping out of sight so quickly after my arrest, and the finger of suspicion was pointed at him. Now what I never told at the time was that I'd seen Mouche talking to Basil's man on the quiet. It struck me that if Mouche let on to Selchurch that you were my sponsor, he might feel justified in taking steps to protect his own interest.'

'What are you saying?' Roderick looked at him narrowly. 'Are you accusing Selchurch of drugging the other prizefighter?'

'There's no proof such a thing happened. All I know was that I was questioned on it. They must have believed I knew nothing, for they didn't pursue it.'

Roderick glanced at Vale, who was staring into his mug pensively. 'If Selchurch found out Sir Janus was betting against his own man, why would he not just repudiate the bet? He would have sufficient grounds.'

Barnard shrugged. 'Selchurch played to win. Maybe he chose to turn the tables on Sir Janus here.'

Vale lifted his head. He spoke contemptuously, 'Selchurch wouldn't do that. He was a gentleman, if you understand what that means.'

'If he's your idea of a gentleman, I'd like your definition of a weasel.'

'Lucky you were that he didn't cry foul!' A bitter expression sat upon Roderick's face. 'Would that he had! Don't quarrel, gentlemen! The facts are not all in yet.' He rose to his feet. 'Kettle! You say this Mouche was in some way a friend of yours.'

'He wouldn't drug a pug for my benefit, if that's what you mean.'

'I'm not implying anything of that nature. Do you know his real name?'

'He was ever Mouche. My stars, I'm stupid. It must be on the cover.'

'Which I have not read — but I'll wager a monkey that it was Légere.'

Sir Janus Vale found his eyeglass and stared at Roderick in feigned admiration. 'Demme, you're right! That was the fellow's name. Now I'm sure this has some great significance. Here's the letter. It is directed to his mother, Mrs. Légere — a courtesy title I have no doubt.'

'Mouche told his real name, in the end.'

'Where did you hear the name, my lord?' queried Barnard, his attention caught.

Roderick was quiet for the longest time. He strode up and down, deep in thought. Then he said, 'Gentleman, now we all have things that shall remain between the three of us. I did not hear the name — I read it in a small record Selchurch kept of private disbursements. I was endeavoring to find out exactly what monies went to Patience out of what was her private fortune. I did find a modest amount paid out to her about the time of the whole incident. It was so small as to be an insult. But just before I came to her name, there were two amounts recorded against a Maurice Légere, the first for 50 guineas and a second for 200 guineas.'

Vale swore. 'It was Basil then. The Devil's own scoundrel!'

Barnard nodded approvingly. 'That's the piece that was missing. Good work, your lordship. How did you make the connection?'

'The French name, perhaps. I was puzzled by the entries in the ledger book, for they seemed to have no connection with anything before or after. I had been led off the track by the name Mouche. It is given to a police agent in France. Of course the word also means 'fly.' Together with the man's description as being quite small gave me to think it was a nickname. I have observed how frequently family names have some connection with the physical characteristics of the family in general. You might compare it with the way Mouche, a stonecutter, chose to call himself Mason. Légere suggests someone of slight build. It had meant nothing to me until I found out Basil Selchurch was deeply involved with the whole prizefighting fiasco. Suddenly it becomes a horrible possibility that he bribed this Mouche to make sure the Thrasher won. We can assume he had not yet discovered that the Thrasher was his brother-in-law.'

'Selchurch has a lot to answer for,' growled Barnard.

'He's already been called to his reckoning. For that reason, I would be happy if this fact does not emerge from our discussions. The truth can't hurt him anymore. It can hurt his widow, a fair and good-hearted person for all that she was married to Basil. It would also cause me some embarrassment insomuch as I have stepped into his shoes.'

'Enough has been said,' snapped the

407

baronet. 'Where is my confounded carriage?'
He rose and left the cottage abruptly, and
went to pace up and down the gravelly track.

'What will you do now?' asked Roderick of
his remaining companion.

'Spend a little more time with my
daughter. Go back to London. My time is
finished here.'

'What of Sophie?'

His eyes widened. 'The best place for her is
here. I can't offer her what's hers by right.
But I'll tell you this. She's been allowed all
too much licence, and needs a tighter rein.
She needs schooling in true gentle manners,
among people of integrity to offer a good
example.'

'You waive your parental rights, in effect?'

'No, no. I will agree to meet the costs of
her schooling, aye, and provide a dowry for
her in due time. I'm a warm man these days.
Would you tell me she has no future here?'

Roderick was thinking that he did not
know if he had a future there himself. He was
about to explain his strange situation when a
smothered gasp drew their attention to
Sophie who was standing at the bottom of the
stairs. It was obvious that she had overheard
the end of the conversation at the table. She
said not a word, but both men could read the
anguish in her face.

17

Julia descended the stairs the following morning to the sound of her brother's voice calling grumpily for his hot chocolate. She fetched the cup from Mrs. March and took it through to him, declaring with an assumption of cheerfulness how rare was a chance to wait on him these days and how was he.

He moved himself carefully to sit up, while she hastily put aside the cup to arrange the pillows to support him. 'Oh, fine! I'm fine.' He bent a sagacious eye on her. 'Lottie not up yet, eh? I'll roast her for being a lazy puss.'

'Well, that's where you'd be at fault, Sir Grouch. While you were peacefully snoring, Charlotte was forced to attend to her father, who has not been at all well.'

Sir Ivor grunted, then frowned. 'That's odd.'

'What's odd?'

'How would my father-in-law know we were back here instead of jaunting about the continent?'

Julia found something not quite to her satisfaction about the way the pillows were arranged and plumped them vigorously for a few seconds. She was a terrible liar, she admitted to herself. How remiss of her it was not to have made a practice of fibbing, so that it came naturally when needed. She giggled at the thought.

'That's all right! It's perfect. Don't fuss!' He settled back, as her slightly flushed face came into focus again. 'What's funny?'

'Nothing — just thoughts.' She picked up his chocolate and handed it to him, saying vaguely, 'Someone must have passed the word along.'

'Hmph! What ails the old man — stomach acting up again?'

Gratefully, Julia seized on this. She needed to invent a condition sufficiently serious for the parson's daughter to rush to his side, yet not so dire that the parson might experience a miracle recovery by the time Sir Ivor next saw him. Knowing Stride was of a dyspeptic habit, she vaguely described a condition of severe discomfort much due to his daughter's absence, and dwelt on Charlotte's concern that the new housekeeper understand exactly how to feed him. She waxed a trifle imaginative about how much of the actual food preparation had previously fallen on Charlotte's hands and the attention needed to safeguard the parson's delicate health.

Beyond complaining bitterly of the parsimony of a household that would turn his wife into a cook general, he merely remarked that far be it for him to act the martyr over it. He fondled the wool casing on his leg gloomily.

'There's no reason to fear she'll make a habit of it, once she has the housekeeper cooking dishes just as Mr. Stride can enjoy them,' said Julia with a creditable appearance of composure.

'Tush!' exclaimed her brother, putting a brave face on it. 'I trust her judgment. My little Lottie will be back as soon as may be.'

Julia's eyes twinkled. Marriage had had a most mollifying effect on his usual morning persona. 'I'll get Mrs. March to bring you your favorite breakfast.' Escaping, she sought the housekeeper, to make sure their stories were not contradictory.

By mid-morning, Sophie was restored to her, driven by a man employed by Mr. Stride. There were dark circles round her eyes, and she seemed subdued as if not quite sure of her welcome. She bore a note from Lord Selchurch, which Julia untwisted and scanned quickly.

My dear Miss Valliant,
All is well! I am writing from the parsonage. Lady Valliant is now here, safe

though severely put out. I have arranged for a coach to restore her to Mallow this afternoon.

Relying on your good offices, I am sending Sophie back to you. I would wish to cause as little remark as possible at the Rise. People assume her still to be staying with you.

My apologies that I cannot bring her in person, but I am departing for London within the hour. Lady Selchurch has called on my escort and she will be residing in the townhouse for some weeks. Expect me back within a few days, at which time I hope to furnish some explanation of everything that has been going on.

Yrs. etc.
R.A.

Julia heaved a sigh of relief. Charlotte was safe. Anxiety to learn more had to be put aside. Sophie was in no case for interrogation. Julia took her inside, murmuring, 'Slip up to your room, little one. Your eyelids won't stay open under their own power. I'll pass the word that you are indisposed today.'

Once alone, Julia reread the letter. Couched as it was in polite language, she searched for hints of more than ordinary warmth. My dearest Miss Valliant! Was that any more than the merest politeness? He had been angry with her when they last parted, yet earlier there had been a look in his eye that she could not mistake. No, the tone of the letter was too cold, too conventional. Yet he had declared his love for her. Well, she had sent him away, and what could he do about the situation he found himself in?

Angrily, she changed into her riding habit and went to the stable. While March saddled Russet for her, she found herself in the tack room. Deciding against taking her riding crop, she found herself fingering the handle of the whip that had formed part of the accoutrements of their first meeting. Her hand gripped it for an instant, then relinquished it. Her eyes blinked tears, and then she laughed at herself. No man was worth turning herself into some wild harpy. Mounting Russet, she would relieve her feelings by a brisk gallop over the fields.

Hunger drove Sophie downstairs by noon. Sir Ivor, hearing her voice in the hall, chided her for being a 'slug-a-bed,' and showed no suspicion she had not passed the night under his roof.

Later, after Sophie had done moderate justice to some cold meat and a wedge of gooseberry pie, she told Julia that she had become reacquainted with her father. 'He is a most handsome man of very graceful parts. Now that I have a father, I can feel a complete person. But, he had to go to London. He will visit me here soon. I assured him that he could come. Is that all right, Julia?' Her voice sounded curiously offhand.

Julia assented without hesitation 'Now I am all agog to hear what happened from the moment you stepped into that villain's carriage. I missed all the adventure by being sent tamely home.'

Sophie looked all innocence.

'You were seen, so don't try to pull a rig. We both know Sir Janus was at the bottom of this. He deserves to be pilloried.'

Soberly, Sophie considered this. 'It is all to be hushed up. Charlotte has been persuaded not to lodge a complaint. Besides, she would not want to look so foolish as to be mistaken for one less that half her age.'

'Your claws are showing, Miss Mew. Will there be hissing and spitting when Lady Valliant returns this afternoon? I'd better be prepared now.'

Guardedly, Sophie picked out a tale of finding the abduction vehicle close to the estate of Sir Janus; the kidnappers, having nowhere else to go, had accepted her own diffident suggestion that a safe haven for Lady Valliant might be the gamekeeper's cottage on the Selchurch estate.

'Why there?'

'You see, Mrs. Bunting, who is the gamekeeper's mother, remembered my father from the old days and was kind to me. She would feed me cake and talk about my father — she remembered him. I felt she would not mind. She is away from home.'

'Wasn't the gamekeeper there?'

'He leaves his lamp on when he comes in late. How Mrs. Bunting would scold him for wasting oil! He didn't even realize anyone was there till morning.'

'Was there no better place?'

'Not one I could think of,' responded Sophie simply. 'Would you suggest the home of Sir Janus?' Her eyes glinted. 'What a screech there would have been — in front of the servants!'

A tight-lipped Charlotte arrived home sufficiently before the dinner hour to retire to her room, refresh herself and change. Luckily, Sir Ivor was enjoying a nap, so she could be at his bedside when he awoke, and, primed by Julia, be ready to give him an encouraging account of her father's condition that was not far from the truth. If upon waking Sir Ivor found his wife's attitude a little tense, he must have put it down to the tedium of the drive over from the parsonage, for he said nothing, merely being satisfied to have her at his side again.

Although Charlotte could not yet bring herself to say a word to Sophie, she poured out all the horrors of her nightmare to Julia later in the evening. The narrative lost nothing in the telling.

'When they found out I was not their intended victim, I thought they would let me go, but they were scared to do that, especially when I told them I was the wife of Sir Ivor Valliant. The younger one insisted they change plans — something about not wanting to get his parents involved. Immediately, I realized I was in peril.' Her thin breast heaved at the remembrance. 'I had nothing to lose, so I told them to their faces what they were — debauchers and procurers.'

'You didn't!' Julia was awed by a sudden image of Charlotte at her moral prime.

'Oh yes! I scratched the face of the younger one, the hobbledehoy who first pulled the sack off my head, Charlie he was called. I'll know him again — What are you grinning about, Julia? This is not funny.'

'Nothing. I was wondering how Charlie would explain a scratched face to his mother.'

Charlotte stared at her.

Pulling her face straight, Julia said, 'All

criminals have mothers — especially young ones.'

'Are you mad, Julia? What have mothers to do with the case? I must say that I expected a little more sympathy.'

The following day, Kestrel Barnard came calling on his daughter. She had been awaiting his arrival without animation. Julia and Sophie were in the stables when his horse was brought round, and they returned to the house to find him enjoying a bantering conversation with Sir Ivor in the squire's office cum infirmary. Sir Ivor had only the haziest idea of who this little Sophie Kettle was who was staying in his house, and when Barnard and his daughter went out to stroll in the gardens, Julia stayed behind to try to explain the relationship. It was a ticklish matter to persuade him that a man who chose to be called Barnard rather than his proper name of Kettle was a fit person to be entertained under his roof.

'Dashed havey-cavey! Always thought there was something shifty about the feller.'

'And that's why you sold him Fieldfare!' murmured Julia. She got up from where she had been sitting on the side of his cot. 'Here comes March who's going to shave you this morning.'

'Shave me? God in heaven, surely I can do

my own shaving. I'm not ill — just have a cracked bone.'

'Indeed not!' came Lady Valliant's brisk voice from the doorway. 'No one shall shave you if you wish to do it yourself. I will fetch towels and hold the mirror myself.'

Wishing her sister-in-law good morning, Julia was relieved to find a full night's sleep had done much to repair that lady's temper. Harmony was evidently to be restored. She left the newly wedded couple to their own devices, and went to the drawing room to complete the letter she had started when they returned so unexpectedly to Mallow. Barnard and his daughter had been gone for a long time, understandably for they had years of absence to catch up with, but eventually they were to be seen slowly pacing along the drive. Of late, Sophie's posture had been much improved, but there was again a suggestion of dejection in the droop of her shoulders that dismayed Julia.

Kestrel Barnard stayed only to take his leave. His face was untypically grave, and Sophie had lapsed back into her inward-looking self. Lady Valliant came through to the hall and exchanged a few stiff words before he departed, and Julia and Sophie walked him through the house to the stables.

'So why the long face?' asked Julia of

Sophie when they were alone, and was alarmed to see slow tears coursing down her cheeks.

'He doesn't want me. Nobody really wants me.'

Not knowing what to say, Julia offered her a handkerchief.

'He has a wife — and a baby boy!' Sophie's words came out in snatches. 'He lives in a foreign land . . . While I was waiting for him to come home . . . he was . . . looking for a new wife.'

'Don't judge him harshly, Sophie. I don't know much about it, but you don't often hear of men coming back from New South Wales. It would be difficult. Without his new wife, he might never have come back at all.' Julia linked arms with Sophie as they moved back towards the house. 'Learning you have a stepmother is a dreadful shock, to be sure. But he knew that your mother was dead, after all. He must have missed her very much. Think of a second marriage as a compliment to the first.'

Sophie stared at her. 'How do you know that?'

'Know what?' Julia saw the chasm yawning at her feet. 'Ah, your father knowing about your mother's death. I have to confess . . . My brother and I met your father as Kestrel

Barnard. I guessed his secret, and charged him with it.' She stopped at the stable door and collected her thoughts. 'Now, don't get angry, Sophie! Just listen! Just listen to me! Your father loves you. You should have heard the pride with which he spoke of you — and the baby — your brother, Sophie — and I have no doubt that your father really does want you. Why else would he have come to find you?'

'He is not anxious to take me away from here.'

'But he sees you living in a grand mansion with grand relations. He believes that taking you away from that will ruin your future. Why else would he have me keep his secret? Half of me believes he is in the rights of it.'

Angrily, Sophie disengaged her arm away from Julia's. 'Think about this then! If you had told me, none of this abduction business would have been needed at all.'

★ ★ ★

Once Charlotte realized that living at outs with a guest in the house was hardly a dignified course, she took in hand Sophie's musical improvement. Her low-pitched voice and good ear for music gave Charlotte hopes that she would make a fine contralto with some practice in breath control. This put Charlotte in mind of her intention to have her harp conveyed to Mallow — a step that was to be taken on her return from the continent. Immediately, she sent a letter to her father requesting that he have his manservant crate it up carefully ready for transportation.

One day, Joseph Rayne dropped in at Mallow while returning to London. Sophie was having a lesson at the time, and was persuaded to sing a simple song for the duly appreciative young gentleman. When Charlotte folded away the sheet of music, they could turn their attention to all the interesting news from Bishop's Rise.

'Do any of the Selchurch girls go to London with their mother?' inquired Julia.

'Not one. Lady Cytherea is still bearing them company. Good natured of her, I suppose,' reported Rayne.

'It is generally expected that she will become one of the family in due course,' explained Charlotte.

'What do you ladies think of such a match? — Lord Selchurch and Lady Cytherea, I mean.' Rayne seemed to wish to dwell on the subject, not knowing how unwelcome this topic was to one of those present.

'Has a marriage actually been arranged between them?' asked Charlotte.

'As to that, the situation is not at all clear. I'm not sure — Ah, well, least said soonest mended they say. He did propose, you know. Three years ago, but that was before he went off to the colonies. I thought nothing had come of it, and then suddenly it was on again when he got back. Now the rumor mongers have really got him boxed in. You must have seen the sly innuendoes in the papers. If he wanted to get out, the poor chap couldn't. He can't offer an insult to the lady by walking away. His reputation would be mired in the gooey stuff, I can tell you.'

'But she could walk away,' observed Julia, finding her voice.

'Can't think why she'd walk away from such a top-bough connection.' He sounded disconsolate at the thought. 'Well, ten to one, she'd make a rare countess — bred to it, y'know, but I think she'd lead Ricky too wild a dance, if you ask me.'

After he had gone on his way, Sophie seemed bothered by a perceived injustice. 'Cousin Roderick cares not a tiny bit about Lady Cytherea. Why may she change her mind but not him? Why can't he just walk away? It's an unfair shame!'

By the following day, Sir Ivor was no longer confining himself to his study. While he was in no shape to tackle the stairs to the bridal chamber, he could, with the aid of a newly acquired crutch and the strong arms of March, gain the drawing room, where he sat in a comfortable chair, his leg supported on the piano bench. During the afternoon and evening he could chat with occasional callers and play at cards with his wife, sister and guest. He was teaching Sophie to play piquet subject to his sister's interdiction against gambling — no loser's secrets. She was an apt pupil; in fact, under the aegis of three intelligent and cultured people she was gaining more experience of civil behavior than she had with the Selchurch children, her sojourn there having been fraught with quarrels and frustrations.

One sunny morning, after an energetic ride, Julia and Sophie found Sir Ivor and his wife sitting out on the lawn. Charlotte had just finished reading aloud a letter she had that day received from her father. She reported the highlights to the latecomers.

'Your harp is crated and ready for transport, but Papa is hoping that our coachman will collect it — indeed, when the carriage goes, I shall be in it to see how he goes on, you can imagine — I am much better in health now. His bilious habit is under control, and he has managed to walk as far as the Rise for news of Lady Selchurch

. . . quite appalled to hear she is increasing — can you credit that? She kept it secret from her children up to the point of leaving to go to London. What a shock that will be for the little ones! Papa has faith in the report that the child is Selchurch issue . . . will be consulting the bishop. Oh, dear! Maybe I should not have been telling this in front of Sophie, but she would have to know.' She was so amazed at this very interesting news from the Rise that she did not notice that neither Julia nor Sophie evinced any surprise.

'Bless me, I don't see what the bishop can do about it,' said Sir Ivor critically. 'Especially if it's a nine-month child. I should think you could tell about a thing like that.'

'I'm sure the bishop would advise him to support Lady Selchurch to the best of his ability,' put in Julia tactfully. 'Go on, Charlotte!'

The sound of hoofbeats in the driveway interrupted the reading. A messenger dismounted, and approached the group to ascertain who Miss Valliant might be. Julia frowned over the note he handed her for a few moments, before calling Sophie's attention. 'It's a message from your father, Sophie. He requests — no, the tone is a little stronger — requires you to meet him at Bishop's Rise tomorrow morning. Oh dear, I hope we are not in for more strange doings. He wishes me there, too.'

'Let me see.' Unabashedly, Charlotte took the letter and scanned it. 'How demanding! You'll not go — after all that has happened?'

'Very little has happened,' Julia reminded her, meaningfully.

'Sophie's papa? That Barnard fellow?' said Sir Ivor sleepily. 'Why can't he come here?'

Julia ignored this. 'Give the note to Sophie! It concerns her most.'

Reluctantly, Charlotte handed it over.

'What do you say, Sophie? Am I to pack your boxes? I am not sure what this portends.' Seeing that the girl was confused, Julia added, 'We can always bring your things back again.'

'You're going, aren't you?' accused Charlotte, fuming a little. 'Then we'll have the carriage out, for I shall come, too. Make no mistake!' She added grudgingly. 'At the very least I shall pick up my harp.'

'The return trip might be overladen,' muttered Sophie darkly.

18

Lady Selchurch's reasons for removing to the London house were twofold. Firstly, her *accoucheur* had strongly advised that she settle herself where he could attend her personally in good time before the arrival of the baby. Secondly, prey to whimsical dreams about the safety of the newborn, she believed her present situation demanded extraordinary care. If she was being irrational, she considered that the prerogative of the last months of pregnancy, and there was no need for her to broadcast her alarms. Newborns were always at risk. A significant betterment in her fortune hinged on the survival of her child. It would be a boy. Why else would Fate have presented so unusual a circumstance?

She apologized to Lady Cytherea for leaving abruptly, and abandoning one who had been a valuable companion to her. She could not feel that Cytherea's dear papa would approve of his daughter remaining at the Rise without benefit of chaperone.

'Please don't give it a thought, my dear Alicia,' replied Lady Cytherea gaily. 'My father is le duc de Laissez-Faire. He will not be perturbed that I should stay to support the family. Much the contrary . . . he would want me here to stand by your daughters, and be among the first to hear your good news rather than while the summer away at Haldene.'

Lady Selchurch could find no words to argue with these benevolent sentiments.

The carriage set off for London soon after eleven. Lady Selchurch, who had called on Roderick's escort, was adamant that he travel within the carriage with her; she felt like talking. He humored her wishes, and arranged for a groom to bring the curricle to London by easy stages. Jeanie Lovell followed closely behind in another, baggage-laden vehicle.

'And that goes to show,' Lady Selchurch bewailed to Roderick, as they bowled down the drive, 'how hard it is to get rid of company when they are entrenched in one's home. How does one order the daughter of an old friend to leave, even when it might be thought she had overreached the point of acceptable hospitality?'

'Indeed, I don't know!' agreed Roderick, smiling.

'But, you must forgive me, Roderick dear. I was forgetting your intentions towards her.'

'The intentions are all on her part, I assure you.'

Lady Selchurch stared at him. 'There is nothing in it? Roderick, really?'

'There is no betrothal, cousin. I proposed marriage once and was refused. Then I found her staying here — your guest.'

'My guest! Well, I had other plans. But recently I was told there was a firm understanding between you. She told me that!'

Roderick stared at her. 'Oh, Lord!' he groaned. 'She bams the two of us!'

'You foolish boy! You should have made your position plain at the outset of your return. And not let her pull you back in.'

He knew she was thinking of the episode at the reception. 'I did not immediately see the danger. You are right. The moment I got into her carriage at Deal, she suggested her father might be more amenable to receiving me as a son-in-law. I should have said something then. In my surprise at seeing her, I did not realize how far my own feelings had changed. God grant you have a boy, Alicia!'

Instructions had been sent ahead to prepare the town house, so they arrived to find dust covers taken off the furniture and a warm aroma of baking in the house. Lady Selchurch had begged that Roderick stay a few days, and he was willing to fall in with her plans. The following day he ventured out on a round of visits, both social and business, including calls on the Farlaines, the Sel-church solicitors and his office at the ministry. On returning the third day he found that Joseph Rayne had left a card whilst he was out.

Sallying forth the next morning, he was suddenly conscious of someone at his elbow. He turned swiftly.

'A fine morning to you, my lord!' It was Kestrel Barnard.

'Kettle! How are you?' They stopped and gripped hands. 'Why didn't you come to the house? No need to lay in wait for me outside, you know.'

The man's eyes twinkled. 'Barnard might. I worked one winter in this house. There might be a few within that could resurrect Kettle.'

'Much I care for that!' Roderick clapped him on the shoulder. 'Walk with me!' They strode side-by-side along the street. 'I'm glad to run into you, for something has been bothering me about the late Mr. Légere. Was it you who bailed him out of Newgate and paid his debts?'

Barnard nodded. 'He was very ill — nigh on to death.'

'I am curious. He was partly responsible for your troubles. Why did you do that?'

'Because I owed him much. He made sure

Patience and Psyche had money to live on. I didn't know why he was so flush with money, I admit. I thought he'd won his pelf on me. It was always money in, money out with Mouche. Now I realize what he gave them was conscience money. I bear him no grudge.'

'Anyway, what brings you to town? I thought you busy getting to know your daughter.'

'Well, I can't be forever in the country, you know.'

Roderick perceived his companion to be hedging. He merely responded, 'No, of course!' and walked on in silence.

'What do you see in my Sophie's future?'

'God, man! I can't even see my own future. What's on your mind?'

'As I see it, Sophie's sitting pretty. Her family has accepted her. She'll have a chance at education, clothes, meeting people of good background — maybe marrying someone of high degree. She seems caught up in the enticements of the high life. Lord knows why I should be despondent about it. It's her destiny, after all.'

Roderick cocked an eye at him. 'Then I have been much mistaken in Sophie.'

Barnard gave a wry smile, which carried no humor. 'I do not blame her. Who would want an old prison inmate for a father.'

'Have you discussed this with her?'

'A little. I told her about my life as it is now. She is totally in agreement with me.'

Roderick frowned. 'You surprise me. I thought Sophie mad to be with you. Make sure she is not saying what she thinks you want to hear. Think on this! I have been instrumental in getting Sophie accepted by the family. It is temporary. Lady Selchurch engaged to look after her until proper school could be found for her. It was not a permanent arrangement, and it has only been partially successful. Sophie does not always get on with the other children at the Rise. Eventually, I hope they will come to accept each other. To a large extent that's why she is staying with Miss Valliant, a most generous and sympathetic lady.'

'Miss Valliant, yes! I am in warm appreciation of her thousand estimable qualities. But you, as the head of the family, took Sophie in charge. Your influence could change things for the better.'

Roderick gave a wry laugh. 'Perhaps you have not heard. My status as head of the family is much in question. Tomorrow — or next week, I may again be plain Mr. Anhurst, junior attaché expecting to be sent to the ends of the earth at short notice.'

Barnard stared. 'I'd heard rumors. It is true

then? The unbelievable? There may be a babe to push you out?'

'At which stage my influence to ensure Sophie's social success becomes moot. I cannot guarantee that Lady Selchurch will continue to sponsor her, though I have every faith in her good nature. If I remain Earl of Selchurch, I can ensure Sophie has a home at Bishop's Rise, and that her mother's fortune will become available to her at the proper time. However, if I am no longer Earl, I will be powerless in both those respects. If you failed her then, Barnard, be sure I would step in. My interest in her happiness remains keen.'

Barnard frowned. 'Hold there, my lord! Money was never a great object to me, 'cepting when I downright needed it. The thing is that it's Psyche who presents the cold shoulder. Look! I turn off at the next corner. I'm at the Bath Hotel. May I beg fifteen minutes of your time, my lord?'

What ailed Sophie? Roderick mused as they made their way towards the Bath Hotel. She had been so anxious to meet her father, and by her demeanor last time she saw him she was filled with pride in the man he had turned out to be, despite his desperate life. What could have happened to change her mind? He was not sure whether he should suspect Barnard of trying to evade his proper role, despite the man's claims to the contrary.

'Come up, my lord!' Barnard was saying. 'There is someone I would like you to meet.' Two minutes later he opened the door of his chamber with a flourish and ushered him in. 'Mrs. Barnard, my love, come forward to meet the Earl of Selchurch.'

Roderick recovered from his surprise to see a woman past the bloom of youth, bending over a cradle. She stood up immediately, and he took in pale blue eyes, and fading red-blonde hair tinged with fine strands of silver at the temples. Her light-complexioned face was comely, with a calm, sweet expression, but there was enough of a chin to show she had a will of her own. She dropped a shallow curtsy.

'Mrs. Barnard!' Roderick bowed. 'So this was your surprise in store. An excellent one, on my life!'

She had a soft Irish brogue. 'Thank you! I have been looking forward to meeting you, Lord Selchurch. I am just recently here, from County Cork where I have been visiting family for a few weeks.'

'And showing off her new son,' put in Barnard. 'And a fine strapping boy they all thought him, you can warrant.'

Roderick gave his congratulations. He was

surprised to hear that Barnard had a small son. He wondered what Sophie would think of that. She was a girl who put tremendous importance on her own concerns. Her little dream world had contained two people — her father and herself. Suddenly that little world was four. He thought he might understand Sophie's change of attitude.

After the exchange of a few commonplaces, Barnard said, 'It is our intention to be traveling to see Psyche again. Mrs. Barnard is all eagerness to meet her new daughter.'

'Indeed I am!'

'I hope the sun shines on your meeting, Mrs. Barnard. You will find Miss Kettle a most interesting child.'

Barnard beamed. 'We return tomorrow. No doubt Miss Valliant will allow us to call, though I'm not sure she's my ally in this.'

Roderick nodded absently. Was that what this meeting was about? For Barnard to obtain his sanction to introduce Mrs. Barnard to her stepdaughter? Hardly necessary, he thought, but he could not deny his support. 'Do not allow your daughter to push you out of her life, Barnard. Look, I plan on going back to the Rise tomorrow. Count on me if you want further discussion about this.'

After duly admiring the small baby, he left the premises and made his way to his friend's rooms in the Albany. As good timing would have it, he found Joe Rayne delivered from the ministrations of his man, freshly shaved and cravatted, and ready to venture forth. Airily dismissing claims of other friends to his company, he welcomed Roderick, and called for claret on the instant.

'What happened to you the other night?' was the first question out of Rayne's mouth. 'I dropped in to visit and found myself dragged into a social evening, and you not there till the early hours.'

'I'm sure you made the best of it,' grinned Roderick.

'I was busy doling out all my coin to your Lady Cy, who's a devil of a lucky player, and the next moment you'd disappeared.'

'Separated you from your roll, did she?'

'She got the cards, though she's not much of a gambler, for all that.'

'You don't think so?'

'Not a bit of it! When she doesn't get the cards, she plays a very close game. You might call her a canny player.'

'True enough! Maybe that makes her a successful gambler!'

'Any way, one moment I was doling out cash, the next moment you'd disappeared. Made off into the night? Shabby treatment to your guests.'

'You weren't my guest,' replied his friend brutally. 'Frankly, I was taken aback at seeing you. I hoped you'd come to cut me out.'

'With Cytherea? I'm not even in the running, old fellow.'

'What happened to your promise to support me?'

'No hope! You're doomed, my boy,' said Rayne lugubriously. He brightened. 'Unless — is there any truth to that rumor that brought me to town? I couldn't even ask Lady Arabelle about it.'

Roderick whistled. 'Has Alicia kept it from her own children? God knows what garbled story they might hear. Out with it! What's the story?'

'That she's increasing? It really rocked me back. You never can tell, can you?'

'Don't be commonplace, Joe!'

'Ah, but the second cock and bull doing the rounds is the child is Selchurch's — Basil that is.'

'As long as they don't mix us up. There are enough on dits about me.'

'It's true then? Phew! No wonder the odds are upset in the clubs! Well, it's as I was about to say. If the brat's a good healthy boy — you'll be out of the title. You'll be out of your sweet inheritance. But you'll be out of the woods, Ricky my boy.'

'Believe me, I'm praying for a boy.'

Joe Rayne stared at him, open-mouthed. 'You really mean that! You'd wish away a title to get rid of a woman? You know, you're quite crazy, Ricky. Just call off! I told you I'd stand by you.'

Roderick shook his head. 'You know I can't. She could end it, if she wanted to. I'd look an idiot, but that's the way of the world. If I am seen to be jilting her, they'll call me all kinds of scoundrel.' He thought for a moment. 'Not only that! Cy won't call it off, either. She'll hang on till after the baby is born.'

'And make her decision then.' Rayne drained his glass. 'What does she call it?'

'What do you mean, what does she call it?'

'What does Lady Selchurch call her . . . sprig?' Joe cleared his throat modestly. 'My father had a theory about babies — what they'd turn out to be. You know the way women sometimes give call their unborn infants a pet name — I'm told I was called Wolfgang, like that Mozart fellow — can't think why. Maybe my mother thought I'd be musical.'

'She was misguided. I've heard you play the piano.'

'Gammon! You haven't heard me on the flute.'

'Thank god!'

'Anyway. My father said he knew I'd be a boy, because she gave me a man's name. He said it worked every time, sisters and brothers alike, and I'm the eldest of eleven. One of me sisters was Flossie, I remember distinctly.'

'I don't remember meeting a Flossie. I thought I knew all your sisters.'

'But, don't you see, when she was born she had another name altogether. That's the whole point. The principle is you go by what the mother calls the baby before it's born. So, did you ever hear her call the brat anything?'

'Can't think I did,' drawled Roderick. 'So your father's interesting theory won't help.'

'Could be a girl, then.'

'And Lady Cytherea will stand by her claims. My honor will still be on the line. I'm not sure how expensive I count my honor.'

Suddenly serious, Rayne looked at him, his wide eyes narrowed. 'You really mean that, don't you? You're that anxious to get rid of the most sought after . . . woman in the whole country.'

'It's funny. I thought you were about to say the most sought after prize on the marriage mart?'

'No, she ain't. Not by a long step. Wasn't snapped up while you were away, though there were a welter of chaps running after her. Then it's settled. We've got to get you out of that damned entanglement.'

'Is this a change of tune or just a variation?'

'Look, I didn't like to tell you this before. I've hinted enough and now I'll say it straight out. The woman is a by-word! Don't glare at me. I know you have some feelings for her, but you need more than that. She gets herself talked about. Don't get any ideas she was wearing the willow for you when you were away.'

'I wasn't exactly a saint, myself.'

'Did you tell her about it?'

Roderick grinned bitterly. 'Yes. There was a liaison in Montreal I was honest about. I thought it would give her second thoughts. Unfortunately, she forgave me with exquisite grace and — good humor. You never saw anything to equal the charm of it.'

'Ha! Charm she is capable of — when she chooses. So how are we to get you out of this?'

'Don't think I haven't been racking my brains.'

When he returned to the house, he found the place abustle due to the arrival of Lady Selchurch's sister, Mrs. Leslie. She had already taken in charge the ordering of the household, and intended to be there until after the birth of the infant. He soon learned with some amusement that the lady was much put out that the impending blessed event had been a complete surprise to her. She was a talkative lady, and certainly no secrets were safe with her. All the household was aware that she had received a letter in which she learned only that her sister had need of her in a medical emergency. On learning the truth a whirlwind of activity had transpired with the engagement of nurses and laying in supplies to be brought in and enquiries put in train as to a suitable wet nurse, should Lady Selchurch be persuaded the fashionable way was best for her child.

That evening before dinner, Roderick joined Lady Selchurch in the drawing room and declared his intention of returning to Bishop's Rise the following day.

She rallied him, 'Do you turn tail at the thought of the advent of my little one — such a commotion as there will be in the house?'

Roderick was taken aback. 'No cousin. Do you truly need me here?'

She smiled at him, archly. 'No, you silly boy. But don't you wish to make sure no counterfeit baby is smuggled in?'

He laughed. 'By all means do so, if it pleases you! No! How can you think me of so suspicious a nature? Besides, would your so respected physician lend himself to anything other than the most proper proceedings?'

She laid her hand on his cheek for a moment. 'You are so excellent a young man. I shall be sorry when my little Basil puts you out of the succession.' She wondered why he was suddenly grinning. 'You prevaricator. Confess, you really would like it to be a girl. That's only natural.'

He demurred, but became serious. 'Alicia, I have to caution you! You are so sure it's a boy. You cannot tailor events to fit your fondest hopes by an effort of will. Your disappointment could be overwhelming if the babe is a girl. Whereas Cytherea . . . ' He stopped for a moment, much struck by an idea. 'Whereas Cytherea is not much of a gambler! Alicia, I begin to perceive there is much value in the mystery . . . ' He sprang to his feet. 'Yes! Tomorrow I shall go back to the Rise.'

Lady Selchurch watched him, astonished, as he took a turn up and down the room. 'What bee is in your bonnet? No matter. My own head has been completely out of curl. It occurs to me that I left the Rise like a mad woman. Whatever must my children think of me? I did not explain why I was leaving for London. I did not even see them. They must be devastated at so unnatural a mother.' She wrung her hands for a few seconds. 'I will write a letter — no, that won't do. Roderick! You must speak to them for me. I shall rely on you.'

The vision of imparting such bizarre news to a bevy of damsels ranging in age from infant to eighteen sprang to his mind. Something of this must have shown in his face, for the Countess hurriedly carried on. 'Speak to Arabelle! She's a sensible girl, and will tell the other children that they are to have a new brother.'

He nodded. 'I will engage to do so, if Lady Cytherea has not already performed that office.'

'Ah, yes! Lady Cytherea! That brings us to another thing. Cousin Roderick! If you are to marry that woman, that is your affair. I could hardly then refuse her the house. In the meantime, I shall be returning to the Rise in a few days with my new baby. Do not let me find her there when I return!'

He was rendered speechless. The calm assumption that she would produce a male heir gave her the twin assumption that she was absolute mistress at Bishop's Rise. Well, she always had been in truth, he mused.

The following morning he received a letter from Lord FitzWarren, which fortified his decision. He drove immediately to the Colonial Office on Downing Street to receive instructions. He then had one other particular private errand to perform before returning to the house.

Some time after noon, he went to take his leave of Lady Selchurch. Lovell was not anxious to admit him to her boudoir, but on his sending a message that he was about to depart, she let him in. Lady Selchurch was resting on a sofa, with her sister fussing about, urging her to take a little wine. He was somewhat unnerved to learn that her ladyship was expecting the child within a few hours. She was in labor and a footman had been dispatched with a message to the physician's residence.

'Do you want me to stay, Alicia? I had no idea it was so close.'

'No, you must go.' Lady Selchurch sounded a little short-tempered. 'This child might not be here for hours yet. Do what I asked of you last night! Only then can I feel safe to return with my child. Haven't I made myself clear? I want that woman nowhere near my little Basil. Go now!'

Roderick was much relieved that she did not require his attendance, for his plans would have been quite upset. His eyes met those of Mrs. Leslie, who gave him an encouraging nod.

'Then I am gone, cousin. Heaven grant you a safe delivery.'

443

19

Roderick came to Bishop's Rise early the following morning accompanied by Mr. Stride. The parson joined Lady Cytherea who was entertaining company in one of the smaller salons while Roderick sought a quick interview with Lady Arabelle, attended by a curious Miss Randall. He was relieved to learn that their mother's condition was no longer news to the children, Lady Cytherea having made no bones about discussing the situation once Lady Selchurch had left for London. Still innocent in the ways of the world, any doubts about the paternity of the child did not exist for Lady Arabelle, and the peculiarity of the situation had not occurred to her. However, much struck to hear of the imminence of the blessed event, she stationed herself in one of the salons overlooking the drive to watch for a messenger.

A little before ten o'clock, Roderick joined Lady Cytherea, Mr. Stride and the morning callers, Mrs. Stowe and her daughter. He caught Lady Cytherea muffling a yawn, which she adroitly turned into a welcoming exclamation.

Mrs. Stowe was all curiosity about his recent journey, squiring her ladyship to London. 'And how is the dear dowager lady? We heard she is in — delicate health.'

'Much better, Mrs. Stowe. Quite blooming, in fact.' A demon of mischief made him say, 'Now you must tell me how Mr. Stowe fares. He was complaining of a touch of gravel, I seem to recall.' A side glance at Lady Cytherea surprised a look of exasperation. He maintained a straight face, knowing his deflection of the inquiry did him little service in the minds of the ladies, all avid for the latest news of Lady Selchurch.

The visit by Mrs. Stowe and her daughter lasted the socially acceptable half hour. If they nurtured feelings of frustration that the arrival of the Earl had stemmed confirmation of the rumors swirling about Lady Selchurch's sudden absence from home, it did not show on their polite faces. They took leave of the company and made further bows to Lady Valliant, Miss Valliant and Miss Kettle as their paths crossed in the entrance hall.

Consternation crossed Roderick's face as the latter three entered the salon. Following close on their heels came Sir Janus Vale, who had slipped in by way of the French doors and through the grand salon.

'Egad!' quoth Lady Cytherea. 'I declare Lady Selchurch has not this many visitors in a twelvemonth.'

Mr. Stride gave a half-smile to Roderick. 'Well, my lord. By the nature of your business, you will have need of witnesses.'

Roderick looked at him for a long moment and seemed to come to a decision. 'So be it! Welcome, ladies — and Sir Janus. I beg you will all sit down. Your arrival is opportune. You are about to be witnesses to a proposal.'

Most astonished, the newcomers found themselves seats, exchanging small bows, nods of recognition and words of greeting.

Roderick took a deep breath. 'As you are probably aware, over the past few months there have been some expectations of an announcement from this house with regard to the future plans of Lady Cytherea FitzWarren and myself. London society has paired us off in a tide of absolute assumption. The most glittering event of the Season! The wedding of the Earl of Selchurch to Lady Cytherea FitzWarren, reigning belle of all London and neighboring counties.'

Lady Cytherea half-rose from the sofa, then subsided and disposed herself gracefully, thereafter giving him her keen attention. Charlotte quickly looked at Julia, catching a fleeting anguish in her face before self-control was re-established. Sophie's mouth formed silent 'Oh.' Sir Janus moved closer to Cytherea, one corner of his mouth lifting in something between a sneer and a snarl.

Roderick continued, 'However, circumstances can emerge to throw confusion on the expectations of the populace at large. Intervention has come in the form of an unexpected child — a child who could deny me my status as Earl of Selchurch and the possession of my lands and wealth.'

All eyes were trained on him.

'She has the baby?' Cytherea's compelling interruption was a statement as much as a question.

Roderick turned to her, and replied soberly, 'Doubtless she has. Lady Selchurch was going into labor when I left the town house.'

'You left — at such a time!' Hers was not the only voice raised in protest.

Vale laid a cautioning hand on Cytherea's shoulder.

'I could stay no longer if I was to reach Selchurch by nightfall. As it was, I saw lights on at the parsonage and Mr. Stride was good enough to put me up.'

Further ado was to be heard outside, and Roderick forbore continuing until a newcomer was announced.

'Lord FitzWarren!'

That bland peer strode into the room, and paused with amazement to see so many intent faces focused on the young man standing in the center of the room.

'I see I interrupt something. A thousand apologies!' He looked round with an assumption of haste and sat on a chair next the door. 'Don't let me impede whatever is going forward.'

Despite the tensions that gripped him, Roderick could not repress an inward ripple of hilarity. Surely the gods were playing with him once again! He bowed in his superior's direction, half defiantly. 'You are most timely, sir. You find me in the throes of a proposal to your daughter.'

'A decent one, I trust.' This off-hand remark concealed Lord FitzWarren's surprise.

'I understood I had your permission. I was also about to announce that you are sending me back to British North America. I shall go, whether I be Earl or no.'

FitzWarren nodded in confirmation.

Roderick turned back to the company at large, and carried on. 'As I am on the verge of making a proposal of marriage, I should make the point that my wife will accompany on that mission. Does anyone here dispute my right to make such a stipulation?'

No one voiced any objection. Cytherea's brow contracted slightly. Sir Janus merely looked sardonic. Lord FitzWarren calmly crossed his legs, and gave Roderick a long enigmatic scrutiny.

Piller entered the room quietly, bringing a card on a salver, which he presented with a low bow. 'A gentleman and his wife to see you, my lord.'

Roderick glanced at the card. 'Show them into the library, Piller! I will be able to give them a few moments directly. Perhaps Miss Kettle would care to join them.' This last was low-voiced.

Hastily, Sophie jumped up. 'My father is back from London?' There was a rustle of muslin as she hurried from the room.

Roderick continued, 'Madam, you must wonder why I am proposing to you in so public a fashion. It is simple. There have been too many misunderstandings between us, and too many public interpretations. It is time to put them to rest.

'If I am the Earl of Selchurch, so do you have the status and breeding to make a countess. You bring with you, I am told, a respectable dowry of twenty thousand pounds.' He paused for effect. 'Of course, if I am not the Earl of Selchurch, that will be considered a stroke of fortune for me. As plain Roderick Anhurst, my estate is somewhat below your fortune. I do not lead you into high expectations, Lady Cytherea. I do not know if I can promise you happiness or contentment. I do not know whether I can make you a countess or the wife of a minor attaché in a distant colony. What I do demand from a wife is that she take me for what I am.'

Julia could not see his whole face, for he was in profile. So, he had given in! Yet, she was mystified by this cold, public declaration. Arranged marriages were customary among the aristocracy. Even so, a bride might expect some rudiments of romance attached to a proposal. Was he counting on an angry refusal due to its inappropriate circumstances?

'This new posting gives no time for banns. I must sail within the fortnight. Therefore, I obtained a special licence while I was in London.' He drew the document from his pocket and held it up for all to see. 'The Reverend Mr. Stride is here to perform a wedding ceremony before these witnesses. Lady Cytherea, I ask you to marry me — this day — this hour.'

Triumph and hauteur warred with each other on Cytherea's face. However gratified she might be by his offer, she felt its lack of ardor and recognized food for lampoon in its subsequent public report. She must ensure that the on dits of this day's doings would resound in her favor. She must be all dignity.

She began by smiling graciously. 'Lord Selchurch, I am quite overwhelmed by this sudden offer. Indeed, it will be my earnest wish to be your bride with all possible dispatch. However, I protest this sudden flight. I need a few months to prepare for a wedding.' She shrugged delightfully, and looked round at the company. 'Everyone will agree. Yet I will not be difficult about this. If you do not care to wait until you can get leave, then I will engage to wed in two weeks before you go. And I hope — indeed, I invite all our witnesses to be present on that happy date, Lord Selchurch.'

There was no mirrored smile on Roderick's face. 'I repeat my offer, Lady Cytherea. The wedding shall be here, by special licence — this day — this hour. Your father is here to give or withhold consent. My only stipulation is that it be done now.' He pulled out his pocket watch and glanced at it. 'At the time the clock strikes eleven.'

'I didn't credit him with being such a blackguard,' exclaimed Vale admiringly.

Lady Cytherea sprang to her feet, her face going red and white by turns. 'That is abhorrent! You insult me by this proposal.'

Roderick's hands made an expansive gesture of protest. 'An offer of marriage cannot be called an insult. Consider, Cytherea! Once before you accepted my offer of marriage, albeit without parental consent, only to change your mind within the week. This time you may have no change of mind. I await your decision.'

'Why such haste? I need more time — time for bridal clothing, wedding arrangements — What about settlements? My father — ' Cytherea looked around. 'Parson Stride — surely you must see how improper this is?'

The minister had been of mixed feelings about the propriety of the situation when Roderick had explained it to him the previous evening. However, his vocation forced an honest reply. 'If there is no impediment, I will perform the ceremony. Look to your father, Lady Cytherea!'

'Papa! Will you allow this?'

'Are you asking me to grant my permission or withhold it, my dear?' FitzWarren smiled at her rather ironically. 'Or is it advice you would rather have?'

'Do you know . . . '

'Did you think I knew when I entered this room? The answer is 'no.' I have no intelligence that can be of assistance to you.

My intent in coming here was merely to make enquiries as to how Lady Selchurch goes on. I expected to find Roderick in London whither I am bound today,' he turned to Roderick, 'about the business.'

'Papa! An American wilderness!'

'It should be a most interesting time for you,' put in Roderick. 'The sea voyage would be over before you knew it. The scenery is magnificent.'

'There is no hurry, Roderick darling. We could be wed when you come back to England — if you are but going for a year.'

'Who knows how long I shall be gone?'

She shuddered. 'Give me time to think.'

The room fell silent. Cytherea made as if to go to her father, but instead paced up and down the room, pausing every now and then near Sir Janus, whose presence seemed to have a steadying effect on her. He moved to the window, and at one stage she paused for a low-voiced conversation with him. The rest of the company sat in silence.

Roderick moved to the fireplace and leaned one arm on the mantelpiece close to a magnificent ormolu timepiece. He followed Cytherea's movements with an interested eye. 'You have lots of time, my dear. Forty minutes now.'

She would have said something, but Sophie

bounced back into the room, full of enthusiasm and quite ignoring the atmosphere of tension and disquiet. 'Cousin Roderick! I have two parents now!' She stood on tiptoe and placed a peck on his cheek. 'It was all a misunderstanding with my father. They came from London to fetch me, as you won't be able to look after me any more.' She ran out again, quite excited.

Sir Janus crooked a smile. 'Now what's the significance of that? I suspect they are playing you like a salmon, my dear.' This quietly to Cytherea.

Her mind was in a whirl. So the little brat was going with her father — and he was just in London! What did that mean? Did they believe that Roderick's support was no longer of value to the girl? Roderick would no longer be Selchurch, therefore no longer responsible for her? That he was going abroad? But wait! Could it mean that Sophie believed once he was married to herself, she would discourage his interest in Sophie? How true! She spoke quietly to Sir Janus. 'Maybe the Kettles want me to think he is no longer the Earl. Or the very opposite! Does Roddie know about the baby all the time? That it's a boy? Is he trying to trap me into wedding him? No doubt he has his eye on my dowry — and

Papa! Papa's influence would be vital if he weren't the Earl anymore.'

'What, upright Rod? If he's acquisitive he hides it well. But that little minx? She may well poke her finger in your pie.'

'You are right. She's no friend to me.' Suddenly, Cytherea swept away from the window, and strode into the center of the room. 'I am decided. It shall be today as you wish. And which lady will act as my maid of honor?' Her eyes traveled past Charlotte's compressed lips. 'Perhaps you would be so kind, Miss Valliant.'

Taken aback, Julia almost rejected that dubious honor, but pride came to her aid. If she was a witness to this horrific charade, she would play her part in it. All the easier to forget Selchurch afterwards! And no one must think it bothered her in the slightest. She looked haughtily at Roderick's impassive face, as she rose to her feet, and wordlessly followed Lady Cytherea to her chamber.

The prospective bride called for Rosie. 'Pull out my gold dress, the one with the gauze spangles. You have half an hour to make me look better than ever in my life. Thank goodness my hair was well-dressed today. Get the robe — no, come here, Evans!' She pulled the harried girl to one side. 'What are they saying? Have you heard any news?'

The maid cringed. 'I know you don't want me speaking to — well, Miss Sophie came right up to me and told me it's a boy for sure, but it's all rumors, my lady. Some saying it's a boy, but some are saying it's a girl. It seems they heard the couple arguing the topic.'

'What couple?'

'Miss Kettle's father that was a footman years ago — and his wife. They are just up from London. But some say that anything he tells them, they'll believe the opposite. Oh, my lady, I wish I could tell you for sure.'

'Get the dress! God grant it may not be crushed.' She turned to her attendant. 'Miss Valliant, if I wear this gauze shawl, with my diamond circlet, shouldn't this make a headdress quite out of the ordinary? 'Streuth! There is so little time to plan. What a serpent the man is! Why is he doing this to me?'

Julia's throat was still too constricted for her to utter a word, though, truth to tell, she could feel some sympathy for the challenged bride.

Cytherea paused in the act of rummaging through the compartments of her jewel box to answer her own question. 'Why? I think it is because he is afraid. Yes — you noticed he mentioned my dowry. Rather crass to do that in quite those circumstances, don't you think? He wants to secure me in case he loses his estate.'

Julia managed an answer. 'I don't believe that. But you were right when you denounced so abhorrent a proposal.'

She nodded. 'It is hateful! He will be sorry for it!'

'It is not my business but — is this a proper basis for a marriage? You must needs have fond feelings for one another, surely?'

Cytherea laughed scornfully. 'Love you mean? Don't be so provincial, Miss Valliant! What have love and marriage to do with one another? Did you hear him offer me love?'

'No, I didn't. He thought you would make a suitable countess. That's sad!'

'Not really!' She was stepping into the rustling gown, as Rosie helped her arrange the folds gracefully. She preened herself in the mirror, and allowed Rosie to help her with her headdress.

Julia could not resist saying, 'Can you be sure you'll be countess? You must be prepared to wed Lord Selchurch only to find he is just plain Roderick Anhurst.'

'Of course I'm sure! You don't think that chit Sophie had me fooled? In her own way she was trying to make me think Alicia has a boy. Too subtle by half! They are trying to confuse the whole issue, she and her father, by spreading counter stories.'

'How could her father know one way or the other?'

'Well, if he has just come up from London —'

'He came yesterday. Early in the afternoon he sent a note to me from the White Boar Inn, just nigh here. It is hardly likely for him to know more than Lord Selchurch, or tell Sophie.'

A hissing noise left Lady Cytherea's lips. 'That gutter brat! Her nature has more twists and turns than the thieves' hatchery she grew up in. Damn you, Miss Valliant! You've put me full of doubt again.'

Not used to being damned, Julia replied frostily. 'If I give you doubts, I am being of sterling service to you.'

At this juncture, Miss Randall slipped into the room. 'Oh, Lady Cytherea, I heard about your wedding, and came to see if there was aught I can do. Can the children watch?'

The bride spun round and shook Miss Randall by the arms. 'Is there anything new?'

Miss Randall blinked at this treatment. 'My goodness! The whole house abounds with gossip.'

Lady Cytherea turned away and stared at her reflection in the mirror. 'And so the stories go! Will I be a countess or prey to a fortune hunter? Wait!' She started at herself so long that it seemed as if she had forgotten the presence of the other ladies. 'If I guess wrongly, I can get an annulment afterwards.' Suddenly she beamed at her reflection in triumph. 'Annulment! That is the answer! There will be no consummation! After the ceremony, I shall go straight back to my father's house — especially if the plan is to leave the country — which I do not intend to do. Three months aboard a squalid bucket of a ship!' She shuddered. 'I will have so many things to arrange that I can easily . . .'

Julia's gasp caused Cytherea to turn abruptly.

'Well, admit he deserves I treat him so!'

Julia's voice was calm but determined. 'Enough! I cannot support you in such an odious plan. I'll not lend my countenance to this travesty of a wedding.' So saying, she abandoned the bride.

Julia hurried through the house, if not in high dudgeon at least in high disgust. She had barely enough command of her feelings to leave a message for Lady Valliant that she would walk back to Mallow before passing through the main door.

As her foot touched the bottom stair she heard her name. She froze for a moment and looked back. Sophie was poised at the top of the flight, her hand on the stone balustrade.

'Julia! Don't leave! Don't give up on him!'

Wasting no time, Lady Cytherea fell back on the services of Miss Randall who felt much distinguished to fill the role of her bridesmaid. Deeming it part of her duties, she filled the ears of the bride with roseate visions of how great a countess she would prove to be.

After bearing such fulsome compliments for several minutes, Cytherea said, 'Thank you for your good wishes, Miss Randall. Now find the children if you want them at the ceremony! Rosie can finish here.'

When a glowing Miss Randall entered the schoolroom, she found Lady Arabelle with her younger sisters. Jubilation reigned paramount. The twins were bubbling with elation. The younger ones were vociferous and jumping up and down, though not entirely comprehending their own excitement. Miss Randall was aghast. If Lady Cytherea took one look at these children, the wedding would be off. Abandoning the task of restoring order, she took herself down to Lady Cytherea's room . . .

'Come along, Miss Randall! It is time.' Lady Cytherea was already heading towards the grand staircase.

'Just a minute, Lady Cytherea!'

'It is time! We do the thing now. Oh, I see!

The children! Well, they'll just have to miss the ceremony.' She swept down the staircase. Miss Randall followed her, bothered by her conscience, but consoling herself that whatever came later, she, little Hetty Randall, would have had the great honor to be bridal attendant to the famous Lady Cytherea FitzWarren. How proud her parents would be when they read about this in her next letter!

The library door opened, and Roderick emerged. Mr. and Mrs. Barnard and Sophie were on his heels. He turned at a sudden commotion. Joseph Rayne entered the hall without ceremony, finessing Piller's efforts to announce him. Ignoring the company also, he rushed up to Roderick and clapped him on the shoulder. 'There you are, old chum! I've been searching for you all over. Lady Arabelle gave me a hint where to find you.'

'Joe! I thought you were stuck in London.'

'No. I came up — sprung 'em, in fact, as soon as I heard the news. Congratu — '

Roderick held up his hand. 'Stop!'

'But, I'm the bearer of the tidings you wanted to hear.' All eyes were suddenly on the new arrival. There was a clamor for news.

Roderick had to raise his voice authoritatively.

'Quiet! Not another word, Hon Joe.'

'What's the . . . '

'Allow my intervention!' Mr. Stride stepped forward. 'I will take Mr. Rayne aside and explain what has transpired, with your permission, Lord Selchurch.'

Roderick nodded. 'Your lips are sealed, Joe! It is a matter of honor. Mr. Stride can explain all.'

'He must tell!' cried Cytherea. 'He comes from London? He must tell!'

Her father stepped forward. 'No, he must not, Cytherea. I will not let you do this. If you wish to forgo this engagement offered under the terms that you do so in ignorance, do it with dignity! The proposal that has been put to you has been audacious, but I believe it an honest one on Roderick Anhurst's part. I will not have my daughter run shy. Gamble, if you must, but don't bet on certainties. You'll lose.' He looked at his daughter very steadily.

His daughter hunched a shoulder. It certainly seemed that the news was propitious for Roderick. Rayne was trying to congratulate him, was he not? Rayne was too transparent for deceit, she believed. Yet her father had called Roddie 'Anhurst.'

In the meantime, Roderick ushered the Barnards and Sophie back into the salon and they ranged themselves among the small group of witnesses. His eyes searched rather anxiously for Julia, realizing she had balked against the role assigned her. He closed the door firmly and prepared himself fatalistically for the next ten minutes.

There was nothing bridal in the spirit of the little group of people that came together. Stoically, Joe placed himself beside his friend, a hang dog expression on his face. The parson came to stand ready for the wedding party to be assembled, prayerbook in hand. 'Lord FitzWarren! Will you please come forward to stand with your daughter.'

20

'Miss Valliant has returned to the house, sir. She wishes to be readmitted. May I show her in?' Piller stood at the door.

Roderick nodded. 'We will wait for her.'

Lord FitzWarren was standing to one side, leaning against the wall, in disregard of Mr. Stride's request to stand by his daughter. He watched the butler carefully. Piller had used the plain 'sir' rather than 'my lord,' and his bow was shallow. There was a subtle change in the man's demeanor. Did Piller know something? Servants often knew the ins and outs of things before their masters in his experience. He gave his daughter a long steady look and made a little shake of the head. There was something mesmerizing in his regard.

Julia's entrance caused a momentary distraction. Her back was straight, her look determined and her face flushed with exertion. Her breath came a little too fast.

Lady Cytherea lost a fraction of her self-possession. Julia Valliant was scornfully returning her own disdainful glance with an intensity that was also a threat. The spiteful cat meant to challenge the wedding. How foolish she had been to voice her thoughts in front of her! She would report her plan to withhold consummation, and Miss Randall could be called upon for corroboration. Her eyes flicked to Sophie as she crossed the room and ranged herself at Julia's side. That eavesdropping little brat might know something to her disadvantage, too. She looked again at her father. There was that warning in his eye that she could not ignore.

'Mr. Stride, are you ready to begin?' Roderick's voice was cold. 'Time has run out.'

Suddenly, Cytherea threw aside her gloves. 'No! A thousand times no! It is insupportable that I should submit to proceedings so — so prejudicial to my own interests. I will not have it be said that Lady Cytherea FitzWarren threw herself away on a — a speculation.'

Her father declared, 'Pride wins the day! Bravo Cytherea!'

'Phew!' Afterwards, Roderick had no idea whether he made that sound outwardly or inside his head. He immediately looked round at Julia, but she, chin high, refused to meet his eye. Possibly he had lost a promising career and earldom both. Had he also ruined his future?

He bowed his head to Cytherea. 'Your

465

choice, my lady. May your future contain a better prospect than me.'

'May you languish in a log cabin, decorated with flaming arrows!' She responded pleasantly.

Roderick was surprised to see her tugging at a dull gold circlet with a flashing green stone on her finger. Never having given her a ring, he wondered if this were a symbolic gesture — to cast a ring — any ring — in his face. In her impatience, she put her finger to her mouth to moisten the knuckle and pulled it off with a gesture of triumph, and placed it on the other hand.

Sir Janus gave a cynical laugh. 'My trick, I gather.' As he led the angry beauty to the door, he spoke to Lord FitzWarren. 'I have an urgent need to speak with you, sir. Yet I feel a few moments grace may be permitted.' As they left, his voice was still audible from the hallway. 'You shall have all the display you want, my beauty. We will wed in an abbey, and I promise never, never to put you aboard anything bigger than a punt.'

They were beyond earshot when she murmured, 'I was lying when I said Roddie was a better lover than you.'

Most of the people remaining in the room breathed a collective sigh of relief, and looked round at each other, unsure what to say. Lord FitzWarren, however, had a distinctly unpleasant expression on his face.

Then Mr. Stride turned to Roderick. 'Am I to offer you sympathy at your blighted hopes, or congratulate you that you did not get enmeshed in your own trap?'

'No hearts are broken beyond repair!' replied Roderick. He offered up a silent prayer that he spoke the truth.

After a few words with Mr. and Mrs. Barnard, he saw Mr. Stride and his daughter going out to the Valliant carriage. He walked with them, thanking the parson for his attendance, although his services had not been required in the end.

To Charlotte he said, 'Do you wait for Miss Valliant?'

'It was her vowed intention to walk, sir.'

He looked surprised. 'Then I will try to persuade her otherwise. It is too far.'

'It was her determination. Foolish of her! She insists that there is not room in the carriage for two ladies and my little crated harp. What nonsense! I won't put it on the top for her or anyone.'

He grinned. 'Certainly not! Depend on me to see your sister-in-law home safe, Lady Valliant.'

As he returned to the house, Lord FitzWarren's coach was brought round. Two industrious footmen were bearing out Lady Cytherea's trunk. He had to give her maid credit for a high degree of proficiency in packing.

He found FitzWarren restively pacing the floor of the salon. He regarded him ruefully. It had been unfortunate that he had witnessed his daughter's undoing.

FitzWarren was muttering to himself, 'Vale! Vale!' It almost sounded like a swearword. Then he stopped in front of Roderick. 'You deserve that I hang you by the heels. Damn you for your prudence and damn you for your honor! Never in my life have I witnessed a more cold-blooded disentanglement.'

'She will be happier with Vale.'

FitzWarren snorted. 'I can't blame Vale on you, can I?'

'You have the power to forbid the banns!'

He shook his head moodily. 'Not my style. I always gave her freedom. She has made her choice.' He set a hand on Roderick's shoulder. 'You played her fair — I believe. But you owe me, my boy. You're in my debt, you know.'

Roderick looked at him suspiciously. 'How is that?'

'Your man Piller gave you away. A little thing like his deportment. Little Cy missed it, and I had to give her a hint. Otherwise you'd have ended up in the soup, the pair of you.'

'Which reminds me — Rayne! It's time I got the true state of affairs.'

FitzWarren laughed softly. 'You still don't know. You don't care either.'

Five minutes later, Roderick found Julia deep in conversation with Mr. and Mrs. Barnard. He knew that Sophie had come to terms with her enlarged family, for she had recognized real warmth in the love willingly extended by her new stepmother. She was looking forward to meeting her small brother, and would be leaving the shades of Bishop's Rise behind her. As Sophie's future seemed plotted in a sanguine direction, he had no scruples at detaching Julia somewhat abruptly from her companions.

The Barnards let them go with an exchange of knowing glances. He pulled Julia into the rose salon.

'What are you doing? Are you out of your mind?'

He grinned guiltily, and released his hold on her. 'I've little time for manners when my career threatens to whisk me out of your life.' He sobered. 'What I have to say to you is of the utmost importance to me. There is so much to explain!'

'I find it hard to accept any explanation of so strange a day.'

'It was all for you, Julia.'

'That's — that's humbug!'

He hurried on under her incredulous eye. 'No, it's not humbug! Now I can say to you all the things I wanted so much to say before.'

'Now that Lady Cytherea has found the fortitude to refuse so amiable a proposal?'

'Lady Cytherea acted as I hoped she would. She prides herself that she is a gambler, but she likes an edge. I presented her with a fifty-fifty choice. Even odds dismay her. It was Earl or nothing for her.'

Julia's eyes blazed fire at him. 'You imbecile! You were prepared to gamble my — your happiness on the slender chance that she would back out at the last moment. I assure you, sir, Lady Cytherea is well out of this engagement — arrangement — whatever it was.'

Roderick was silent for a long moment as he met her glare and absorbed it. Then he shook his head. 'There was never a formal engagement. I told you that before. Some day I will tell you all of the story, but I cannot — not at this time. I have caused the lady sufficient offence.'

'I would call it a grievous humiliation. You proposed to her in a very public manner.'

'So that she could refuse me — in a very public manner. In truth, it was not intended

470

to be so public, but my time was short. News of Lady Selchurch's delivery could be expected hourly. I had to act. When I saw you come in, my resolution was almost shattered, for to play the part of such a cur in your sight was a wretched prospect to me.' She made as if to turn away, and he seized her shoulders. 'More people were present than I had counted on. The Barnards I expected, but not so early in the day. I believe their meddling convinced Cytherea that I was acting the part of a fortune-hunter.

'Rayne's arrival nearly dished me. He came in all congratulations. To Cytherea it meant I was still earl. To me it suggested the opposite — that I was free of the whole business. It was the hardest thing in the world for me to do to ask him to shut up.'

'And believing the Selchurch baby to be a boy, you would still have married her?'

He took her face firmly in his hands and made her look up at him. 'When it came to the point? That is asking too much of integrity. Indeed, Cytherea would not have honored me for it.'

'You would have broken your own conditions?'

'God help me, I would have in the end, yes! But for the sake of her pride, Lady Cytherea had to be the one. She had to make the rejection.'

'And if she had stood firm, and followed through with the wedding?'

'Then I would have proved myself a thorough going cheat. Any marriage between us would have been a disaster. Dissatisfaction for her, despite her ambition! Misery for me! Honor would prove too dear. Even if it damned me forever in your eyes and in the eyes of the world, I could not have gone through with it.'

In that declaration of dishonor he melted her resistance. She moved closer to him, and their lips met awkwardly, for she was crying, then laughing.

'You left. When you came back into the room, it gave me back hope that I had not alienated you entirely. My dearest love, what made you come back?'

'Oh that!' she said offhandedly. 'I was about to cross the stream — south of here, about to take the short cut past the village — when I remembered my reason for visiting here in the first place. Mr. Barnard! I could not leave Sophie's rapport with her father to chance. I had to return.'

'And you ran all the way back for Sophie's sake?'

'Not entirely,' conceded Julia. She dropped

her eyes demurely. 'I could not let you embark on so ruinous a marriage without making some push to save you.'

'And how did you plan on doing that?'

'Had the wedding proceeded, it would have been interesting. I was keyed up to jump in at the 'just cause' part.'

Roderick lifted an eyebrow. 'Oh, on what grounds?'

'On the day that you will tell all, so then will I.'

'Prevaricator!' He kissed her again, this time with a good deal of passion. The tension of the day and the weeks before were washed away in that kiss, which held all the promise of a remarkably happy future.

He let her go, eventually. 'I cannot tell you how much I have longed to express my feelings for you in that way — or what I have borne needing to stifle those feelings I have held in my heart for you.' The look that she gave him was not completely forgiving. 'For heaven's sake, help me, Julia! It's not often a man proposes to two women within the course of a morning.'

'Am I required to wed within an hour? It seems unjust to Lady Cytherea for the terms to undergo change.'

He mistrusted the satirical light in her eye. 'I am being punished still, I believe. Truth to tell, I have to leave England soon, as I am taking the post that Lord FitzWarren is still offering me. Generous of him — part of him must want to throw me in the stocks.' He brought her two hands up to his lips. 'Come with me, Julia! Come as my wife! I can't give you much time to make wedding arrangements, but we will manage it if you will say yes. You want to travel. You told me once. There is a whole world for us to see.'

'Is it a travel companion you are seeking?'

'It's you, Julia. Yes, a travel companion for my soul, but much more than that — my heart's delight — whatever makes life complete, a love for always, wherever in the world we go.' He gave an anxious grin. 'Oh, one more thing. You must also be my friend!'

Julia was in no doubt about her decision. She happily agreed. There was one concern, less than a reservation in her eyes, but needing confirmation.

'But are you sure about the baby? Is it really to be a little Basil?'

There was a discreet cough, and they became aware of Piller's presence. He stood at the door bearing a silver tray bearing a bottle of champagne and glasses. Without waiting for permission, he trod forward and placed the tray on a table.

'Here is your answer,' quoth Roderick. 'Let us all of us now drink a toast in celebration of the birth of a new Earl of Selchurch. May he have a full and fruitful life!'

THE END

We do hope that you have enjoyed reading
this large print book.

Did you know that all of our titles
are available for purchase?

We publish a wide range of high quality
large print books including:
Romances, Mysteries, Classics
General Fiction
Non Fiction and Westerns

Special interest titles available in
large print are:
The Little Oxford Dictionary
Music Book
Song Book
Hymn Book
Service Book

Also available from us courtesy of Oxford
University Press:
Young Readers' Dictionary
(large print edition)
Young Readers' Thesaurus
(large print edition)

For further information or a free
brochure, please contact us at:
Ulverscroft Large Print Books Ltd.,
The Green, Bradgate Road, Anstey,
Leicester, LE7 7FU, England.
Tel: (00 44) 0116 236 4325
Fax: (00 44) 0116 234 0205

ANGELINA

Janet Woods

Angelina's arrival is a catalyst for many changes at Wrey House. Her mother, the countess, is forced to come to terms with a daughter she didn't even know existed, but her sister, the exotic Rosabelle, is not so accommodating. But are they really sisters? Certainly the countess cannot recall having given birth to twins, and it takes a dramatic confrontation with her husband's mistress before the truth is revealed. Soon the young women become involved in intrigue. Who is the highwayman? Angelina knows, but refuses to betray the felon.

THE SIX-MONTH MARRIAGE

Amanda Grange

Unless Philip, Lord Pemberton, could arrange a six-month marriage he would lose his inheritance. But how could he find a respectable young lady to go along with such a scheme? Coincidentally, Madeline Delaware was desperate to escape from her dissolute uncle, so what better solution could there be? But the six-month marriage turned out to be far from the peaceful interlude that she had envisaged. And why, when the marriage was simply a convenient arrangement, did Madeline find it so difficult to think of its end?

THE CHASTE WIFE

Delia Ellis

Obedient to the wishes of her father, sixteen-year-old Barbara Cornford allows herself to be married to Marcus, Viscount Reyne, the son of her father's childhood friend. However, her mother stipulates that the marriage should not be consummated until Barbara is at least eighteeen. But, by then, her husband, finding marriage unattractive, has joined forces against Napoleon. Returning to England only after eight years have passed, he writes to inform his father-in-law that he intends to claim his bride. But Barbara is not sure that she wants to be claimed by her errant husband!

THE MAJOR'S MINION

Linden Salter

Determined to prove her brother innocent of murder, Katherine sets out in male disguise to find the real criminal. The most likely suspect is Major Lancaster, a hero of the Peninsular War. After she saves the Major's life, he offers her a place in his household. He finds in this intelligent and sympathetic youth (as he believes) a person to whom he can unburden his soul, while she finds in him something very close to her ideal man. But as her love grows, so does her belief in his guilt, and she faces the agonizing choice of sending either him or her brother to the gallows.

THE LADY AND THE LUDDITE

Linden Salter

A heroine from Bronte country, and a Robin Hood of the Industrial Revolution: two people powerfully attracted to each other, on opposite sides of a little-known class war that saw the ruin of England's green and pleasant land . . . Shirley Keeldar is a 'brave, true, beautiful lady' in the eyes of Tom Mellor, the leader of a band of strong men in their doomed fight against the machines that are destroying their lives. But in the class-ridden, war-torn Regency world of 1812, she's also his enemy.

EDWINA PARKHURST, SPINSTER

Patricia lucas White

Talented writer Edwina Parkhurst begins an adventurous, real-life journey when she accompanies her sister, Olivia, and her nieces to visit Olivia's abusive husband in Oregon. To provide a 'proper' escort for them, Edwina disguises herself as a boy. When outlaws abduct Olivia and the girls, gunfighter Tal Jones is wounded trying to prevent it. Nearly blinded, he is rescued by Edwina. Alone together in the wilderness, Tal teaches 'Ed' the art of survival, and Edwina begins to recognise in Tal the kind of hero she has been searching for and writing about in her 'sinful' dime novels . . .